T0267609

LEO MARTINO STEALS BACK HIS HEART

ALSO BY ERIC GERON

A Tale of Two Princes

LEO MARTINO
STEALS
BACK
HIS
Heart

ERIC GERON

HARPER
An Imprint of HarperCollinsPublishers

FOR THOSE WHO KEEP
AN OPEN HEART

I, LEONARDO ANTHONY MARTINO, LOVE LOVE.

I just don't love how I haven't found it yet.

I take my chunky, blue scrapbook bedazzled in diamond rhinestones from the center drawer of my desk. Every time I've got a crush, like today, I document it here. It's bursting with taped-in tidbits. The bookmark from the book signing with Lincoln? Check. The wristband from the hayride with Vincent? Check. The smiley-face sticker from Travis? Check.

Don't worry. No locks of hair. That's where I draw the line.

Grandma Gina used to say I was sentimental, like her. She used to scrapbook. It's been three years since she passed, and I've kept the tradition going into high school, comforted by the snip of scissors and the tear of tape. Of course, I'd never tell anyone besides Dillon and Varsha. They get me—from my sentimental scrapbooking to the checklists that I make for practically everything, like my Back to School Checklist and the one for how to have the best summer ever, which included reading ten books (check!) and getting muscles (still a "work in progress," sadly).

As I flip through my scrapbook to avoid folding my laundry, I grimace at a photo of my first-ever crush, Lincoln Chan—Eastfield High's Most Popular—and quickly skip his section.

There's Julien, Vincent, Travis, and Enzi. Each one of them made my heart soar, sing, patter, and plummet. I relive the emotional roller coasters by simply turning to any of their sections: weeks, months, and—in Lincoln's case—*years* later.

Pages boast ticket stubs and delicately pressed flowers. Restaurant business cards and photo-booth printouts, with silly poses involving plastic bowler hats and wood mustaches on Popsicle sticks. I had a genuine connection with each crush. In every instance, I saw a glimmer of something extraordinary taking shape. Each crush showed me the promise of my First Great Love Story. The hint of something real. Reciprocal. *Ours*. The scrapbook stands as proof it wasn't all in my head. That *we* and *us* and *ours* were well within reach until, well, they weren't.

Each love story stopped at almost.

One by one, my crushes vanished in a *poof* before anything could materialize into more than fading mementos stuck to scrapbook pages. Walked away. As if I'd never meant a thing.

But I love love too much to give up searching for it.

I land on a fresh blank spread at the back, and glue in a picture of Sergio Rodriguez, Crush Number Six. He's standing on Jenkinson's Boardwalk—with his dark features, cute big ears, and neon Speedo—shielding his eyes from the sun with his hand. Even though he's been a classmate since forever, we talked for the first time this summer while vacationing down the shore. Two weeks later, I can still smell his banana sunscreen and coconut deodorant body spray.

In my scrapbook, I scribble the sharp crests of waves, embellishing them with silver glitter. I add beach tags from our days in the sand. The brochure to the stinky aquarium we visited. Photos of the ocean. Order tickets from the bakery. And the IHOP logo torn from the corner of a kid's menu from when we shared a hot stack of pancakes before trekking to the beach and lying side by side in the sand.

I remember the way Sergio fixed me with a smile, letting his sights linger.

"Hey, Leo?"

I froze. "Yeah?"

"I like hanging with you."

My stomach felt like it did when I was on the Pirate Plunge. I was happy.

Along the top of the page, I doodle hearts, dabbing them with pink glitter. Now, thinking about seeing Sergio on the first day of senior year tomorrow sends my stomach into knots. True, my other crushes haven't worked out. But I'm hoping things with Sergio *will*, finally leading to my First Great Love Story—without the part where he vanishes in a *poof*. Each time that happens, Mom tells me I'm a rare bird. That it's not easy for someone as *special* as me to find just *anyone*. That it's going to take a person just as special—and just as *rare*—to be able to recognize those qualities.

I close my bloated scrapbook with a sigh and run my fingers

across the diamond rhinestones adhered to its cover. The constellation of diamond rhinestones makes me wonder if I really *am* a diamond in the rough. But I end up concluding that I may be more like the rough.

Because the sticky thing about loving love?

It usually doesn't love me back.

"FOR THE HUNDREDTH TIME: IT'S NOT YOU! IT'S THEM!
All of them," Dillon insists.

"You *have* to say that. You're my best friend," I protest. When it comes to my love life, I'm really starting to believe I'm the problem. Otherwise, the math just . . . isn't mathing.

We finish a lap through the crowded school halls, which are abuzz with that raucous first-day-of-school energy, and start another lap, holding our iced coffees. The before-class coffee laps are a new tradition, thanks to my Back to School Checklist, which also included taking a full hour to get ready, arriving to school twenty minutes early, and personalizing our lockers. Check, check, check.

Dillon offers a sympathetic smile. "I mean, some of those guys have been terrible."

I wince. "*Terrible* is such a strong word."

Dillon challenges me with a deadpan stare.

"Seriously, I'm convinced my problem is *me*."

His deadpan stare persists, even as he takes a slow slip of his iced coffee. "It's your inner saboteur talking. Again."

"Ugh. Maybe." I glance around the hall, but there's no Sergio in sight. "Do I look okay? Be honest."

"When am I ever *not* honest?"

Now it's my turn to give the deadpan stare.

"Yes. You look nice," he relents.

"*Nice? Just . . . nice?*" I press.

"What's wrong with nice? It's better than *okay*," he says. "If you told me I looked nice, I'd think that was . . . well . . . nice."

With his glossy brown hair, white collared shirt, and beige khakis, Dillon *does* look nice.

Mom's consistently described Dillon as nice, ever since we became friends in ninth grade, when we discovered our shared love of putting fried eggs on everything. Pizzas. Burgers. Salads. You name it. And as a Nice Guy—one of the few left, apparently—Dillon's the best sounding board a friend could ask for. And with no drama of his own, he has plenty of room for mine.

I beam. "You always look nice."

"Why, thank you kindly."

We're halfway down the hall when I stop short at the trophy display case, which boasts a framed photo of Sergio with a swim team medal hanging from his neck.

Dillon knocks into me with a yelp, his plastic cup nearly flying from his hand.

I let out a wistful sigh. "He's so dreamy." I catch my reflection in the backboard mirror and gasp. I look *far* from nice. The skin under my eyes is purple from not sleeping a wink. How did I not notice that in the bathroom mirror at home? The humidity alone has given my hair a next-level poofy factor. I pull at a wayward coil, only to forlornly watch it spring back into place. And my buttercup-yellow T-shirt has way too many wrinkles. Taking the full hour to get ready was all for naught.

"Dillon, you are a filthy liar." I pull my hair into an apple-size bun. "No *wonder* I send all the boys running."

Dillon rolls his eyes. "Hopeless."

"Hey! Check this out!" Our third best friend, Varsha, appears beside us, phone thrust in front of her. I realize too late that she's showing us a video of a ten-foot alligator lunging at an unsuspecting old woman strolling on a marshy embankment.

"Varsha, no!" I cover the screen with my hand. My insides are already churning enough as it is.

"But you love my animal attack videos."

Varsha is obsessed with anything animal-related. Especially attacks on humans. Apparently, it's fine if it's justified. She especially enjoys scenarios like elephants trampling their whip-cracking ringleaders.

She clocks my blue mood. "Oh. Still no word from Speedo?"

"Still no word."

Two weeks ago, when I saw Sergio tanning in a lawn chair on the beach—yes, in his Speedo—I nearly tripped face-first into some kids' sandcastle moat. After Sergio bolted up in alarm, I took his concerned thumbs-up as an invitation to stroll over and say hi. He ended up inviting me to hang out that night—and every day after, too. Sure, I mostly watched him play hours on hours of *Diablo IV* in the dim den of his family's vacation rental, but there were so many bright moments too. Like when he convinced me to ride in the back of his two-seater bike to the bakery. Or when we met at the beach to hang and he'd packed a picnic basket for us. And one night, he let me pick which movie we were going to watch (*Lord of the Rings*). We ended up watching all three films and then went to IHOP and the boardwalk, where we shared a vanilla-orange-cream soft-serve swirl before slipping into the air-conditioned aquarium.

It was only two weeks, but they were two glorious weeks.

"I wish I could've gone down the shore with you. I still really want to learn how to surf," Dillon says. While I spent half my summer down the shore, he was at an art camp in Maine.

Varsha gives a reproachful look. "You know my theory on sharks and surfing, right?"

"That a person is more likely to get struck by lightning?" Dillon asks.

"Are we talking about my odds of Speedo wanting to be my boyfriend?" I chime in.

"Hopeless," Varsha says before taking a sip of her iced coffee.

"So hopeless," Dillon adds.

"He's the one!" I insist.

Varsha gives me the side-eye. "You say that for *every* crush."

"No, but it's *different* this time."

"He also says *that* for every crush," Dillon asserts.

4

"You guys!" I whine. "I can't graduate from high school being that person who's never had a relationship," I say, despite knowing my friends are in the same boat. "People will judge me!"

Varsha cocks her head. "Honestly, who cares?"

"Clearly not you two."

"Fine. Check to see if he got back to your many, many texts," Dillon says.

"Leo, no! I told you not to keep texting him!" Varsha cries, swatting me.

I give a sheepish smile. "Well, he wasn't replying! What was I *supposed* to do?"

As I slide my phone out of my pocket to check if Sergio has replied to my question posed yesterday at 5:34 p.m. asking how he's doing, I feel the paper-thin PS5 skin decal of Lilith, one of the demons from the game *Diablo IV*, come up with it and flutter down to the floor.

We all stop to look at it.

"Your gift fell," Dillon points out.

"Thank you, Captain Obvious." I scramble to get it, but Varsha beats me to it.

"*Gift?*" she asks.

"What? You know I'm a gift giver." I take back the sticker I've been holding on to all weekend, wondering when I should give it to Sergio. It's not like I *meant* to get him something. Mom surprised me with a trip to Paper Source, and I ended up wandering into Game World, where I just so happened to find a sticker from Sergio's favorite game. Talk about fate! Obviously, I had to get it. Plus, it was only a few bucks. Still, I'm chock-full of nerves thinking about giving it to him today.

A small gesture for me always seems like a big deal for someone else, and never in a good way.

I slip the sticker back into my pocket, thinking of the scrapbook tucked in my desk drawer. My stomach clenches as I imagine yet another chapter closing, another door shut.

"Oh, come on." Dillon smiles at me, and I know he knows exactly what's on my mind. "It'll happen for you. Trust the process, remember?"

Trust the process.

Dillon adopted the catchphrase from our art teacher, Mr. Yokoi. I can't see how it applies to painting a still life, let alone my love life.

Dillon hitches up his backpack. "Besides, there's so much more to life than romance."

"Oh yeah? Like what? Robotics?" I tease. Truth be told, I've always admired how he and Varsha have a whole lot more going for them than purely chasing after romantic pursuits. In fact, Varsha doesn't care about romantic pursuits at all, since she's aromantic. Varsha prefers posting knitting videos on her TikTok and raising money for wildlife conservation. Meanwhile, Dillon spends his free time programming robots and fine-tuning his tenor voice in hope of joining the all-state chorus.

Dillon grins. "Actually, yes. Did you hear about the Clean-Bot? It can fold laundry!"

I groan. "If my first boyfriend is a robot, so help me god."

Varsha fixes me with a withering gaze. "Just be thankful you weren't eaten by a gator." She shoves her phone back at me, where something—or some*one*—frantically splashes around. Good thing we're in Jersey.

Senior girls from pom squad stop in front of us to record a TikTok, using the packed hallway as their backdrop. Sakura Nakamura lifts a LAST FIRST DAY OF SCHOOL poster while her friends hem in around her, all of them looking like they might burst into nostalgia-induced tears.

As the pom squad records themselves talking about how devastated they are to be one step closer to the end of high school, Dillon leans close to us. "Happy last first day of school, friends."

Varsha shudders. "High school can't end soon enough."

"For real," I add, catching Sakura eye Dillon with a flirtatious smile. It's so obvious she likes him, but he can be pretty oblivious to that kind of stuff, unlike me—the Hypervigilante.

"Forget Speedo," Varsha says. "We're not even going to know him this time next year. I'll be studying bio at Princeton. Dillon will be engineering robots, and you'll be, well . . . You really should at least start by figuring out which teachers you want to ask for letters of rec."

I sigh. "Why does the thought of that make me incredibly sad?"

"The fact that we'll all be on different journeys, or the fact that you don't have a dream college to apply to and are behind in even *thinking* about the application process?" Varsha asks.

Unfortunately, she's right—I have no idea what's next for me, post-graduation. I have no idea what's next for me this morning with Sergio. "No," I reply. "The fact that Speedo could be just a long-lost memory by then."

7

Varsha squints. "I'm not sure, but I'm concerned." She says it with love. Varsha and I became close friends the day she affectionately made fun of how I sliced an avocado crosswise versus lengthwise in ninth-grade Home Economics, which was followed by her offering to let me put all my textbooks in her locker so that I could make my own locker into a bona fide "snack locker," which is what you'd get if a hotel minibar and a theater concession stand had a baby.

"You don't actually know where things stand with him yet," Dillon reminds me.

Varsha gives a reassuring smile. "I mean, he could just be a really poor communicator, and if things don't work out for whatever reason, you're going to find someone better."

"Yeah. Totally," Dillon agrees. "I mean, you're total boyfriend material. Who *wouldn't* want to date you?"

"Hmm. Let me consult my scrapbook," I joke. But deep down, I'm serious. And I don't *want* to find "someone better." I *want* Sergio. He's not *like* anybody else. He can do the most spot-on Gollum impression, packs the best picnic spreads, and the sound of towels rubbing together sets his teeth on edge. Plus, he lets out this adorable squeal when a demon attack leads to a game over.

"Fierce Five sighted." Varsha nods as Sakura joins Lincoln Chan, Travis Matthews, Katie Cooper, and Eamon Troy, aka the Fierce Five—our school's trademark flock of hot, rich seniors, which includes not one, but *two* former crushes. Crush Number One and Crush Number Four.

My friends and I shrink back and share a collective shudder.

While the three of us spend most weekends rating ice cream flavors and watching Disney movies, the Fierce Five—and a majority of the school, TBH—spends their time partying and living in their own R-Rated Realm.

Apparently, that makes everyone way cooler than us. To add insult to injury, Eamon pantsed Dillon sophomore year and accidentally grabbed his underwear, showing his butt off to half the grade . . . and Sakura told Varsha the gum she chewed really brought out the yellow of her teeth. While I haven't been personally attacked—though Travis did say I looked "goofy" once and used me to do his Spanish homework—Lincoln and Travis are the It Couple, which *feels* like a personal attack. Even three years after Lincoln ditched me, seeing them together still stings, whether they're posing in coordinated (and steamy) Halloween costumes or simply holding hands in the hall.

Is it my imagination, or does Lincoln shoot us a mocking smirk when he spots us? This place is a haunted house of past crushes.

See earlier: High school can't end soon enough.

At least Sakura doesn't seem to hate our guts—evidenced by how she's eyeing Dillon up and down again. Not that he sees.

"Jerks," Dillon whispers once they're out of earshot.

Varsha smooths her hair. "I still haven't forgiven Katie for spreading that rumor about how I bring my own toilet paper to school because the cheap toilet paper here gives me a rash."

"Isn't that true?" I ask.

"Yeah, but still!" Then Varsha lowers her voice: "I'd love to see any one of them get chased down by a grizzly." The imagined scenario is starting to appeal.

"But then Sakura wouldn't be able to give Dillon elevator eyes," I whisper.

A blush creeps into Dillon's cheeks, and he grins in good fun. "No, she didn't!"

"I agree with Leo on this one. She totally did. Either that, or she was scrutinizing your outfit to make fun of it later." Varsha appraises him. "Not that it's a bad outfit. You look nice."

"There's that word again."

Dillon shrugs. "Well, whatever that was, I'm not interested. I have better—"

"'—things to do with my time,'" Varsha and I conclude in mock unison.

"Exactly!" Dillon throws an arm around each of us. "You guys know me so well."

Sakura's association with the Fierce Five aside, it baffles me why Dillon wouldn't spring at the chance to pursue her when I'm out here in a love desert. He isn't aromantic like Varsha, yet he's never liked anyone, at least that I know of. Last year, after Varsha came out, he told us that he's "straight but maybe not," but that it was irrelevant because he's not going to date until college. Unlike me, he thinks it's irrational to date in high school because you're not going to end up with that person anyway. Personally, I think it wouldn't hurt for him to just let go and let love in.

When Dillon and I first started hanging out, Mom asked me if I had a crush on Dillon. I almost did a spit take. I'd insisted that we were just friends, and that the only time he'd given me a heart palpitation was when he volunteered me to be the speaker for a group project in tenth-grade Language Arts. On the other hand, Sakura is *definitely* experiencing those heart palpitations on the reg. I wonder if she hasn't admitted it for fear of her so-called friends finding out she has the hots for a Mere Peasant.

We pass through another long white hall with glaring fluorescent lights, and I give a cursory scan to the students continuing to stream in from the entrance. Still no Sergio in sight.

"Ugh! Where *is* he?" I mutter, finding I *actually* miss him. I can feel it in my bones. I shared a real connection with him, more real than with anyone else before him. He opened up to me, sharing he likes ASMR—something he hadn't told anyone. And the next day, I came over with a junky old keyboard I found in the garage of my vacation rental and told him to close his eyes while I clacked the keys. The smile washing over him. The dreamy way he looked at me after opening his eyes. Not to mention the many sweet gestures. We watched all three *Lord of the Rings* together—the *extended* editions, for crying out loud!

There's no *way* I could have misread the situation this time.

I fidget with the faded paper wristband that he gave me to join him at Jenkinson's Boardwalk—hard evidence that it wasn't all a dream, which only makes me feel more sick to my stomach, like when we spun way too fast on the Tilt-a-Whirl.

Then the troubling—but familiar—radio silence after returning to Eastfield.

Did I text him one too many times?

Then—

I stop and squeeze Dillon's arm. "OMG, there he is!"

Leaving the cafeteria with a Taylor egg-and-ham sandwich is none other than my six-foot-tall crush. He's wearing a *My Hero Academia* T-shirt and Converse high-tops, and he's got a stylus and tablet under one arm—no doubt sketching Marvel superheroes whenever he gets the chance.

Our eyes lock as our paths cross in slow motion. My heart races as I search for that familiar playful way he'd looked at me the past two weeks.

It's so different from how he's looking at me now.

Suddenly, his handsome face breaks into a huge smile. He waves, and I wave back. My stomach clenches, and then does it again at the idea of pushing myself to give him the sticker. But seeing his radiant smile gives me the permission I've so desperately needed to proceed with my plan.

But then time speeds back up and he passes by without missing a beat.

"Mary Allison!" Sergio wraps Mary Allison Pointer in a giant hug and spins her around as she squeals and asks about his summer.

He wasn't waving to me at all.

Dillon wriggles in my grip. "You're cutting off my circulation."

"Oh. Sorry." I release his arm. "What should I do? Maybe he didn't see me? Should I go over there?"

"No!" Dillon hisses.

"Yes!" Varsha urges me with a nudge. "Go! Go! Go!"

I approach Sergio, grinning even though my throat has gone bone-dry. "Hi, Sergio!"

Mary Allison stares at us with a confused look on her freckled face. The stretch of silence lasts an eternity. Finally, she takes the hint and waves goodbye before ducking into the rush.

"How are you?" I ask—after I remember how to use my mouth to form sound.

Sergio blinks, bold black eyebrows climbing, his whole sinewy body tensing up. "Good, good." His eyes dart around like he's checking out who's watching us.

"Oh, good!" My voice climbs an octave. I reach for the sticker in my pocket. My heart feels like it's going to hammer right out of my chest. "I—I got you something. I saw it and thought you might like it, you know . . . you mentioned wanting one and . . . yeah." My hand snags.

"I'm good. Thanks, though." He gives a thumbs-up.

The kind you'd give to a stranger on the street—not to the person who watched you play *Diablo IV* in a big fluffy towel in the den of a vacation rental for two full weeks.

"See ya." Sergio vanishes around the corner before he can even see the sticker I finally remove from my pocket.

Cheeks burning white-hot, I spin to face my friends.

Varsha winces. "Oof. That was rough."

"Seriously." Dillon massages his arm as we continue down the hall.

"Maybe he's just having a day," I try, optimistic even though it feels like my heart just plummeted to the fiery depths of the Burning Hells.

Varsha sighs. "We love you, Leo, but you're hopeless."

"And Speedo's another terrible guy," Dillon adds. "Sorry."

Something inside me crumples. I wouldn't say Sergio is

terrible, but I get the sense now that the feelings are *far* from mutual.

Dillon pats my shoulder. "Like I was saying, it's not you. It's all of them."

I've always wanted nothing more than for one of my crushes to crush on me back—and to have my first real boyfriend. Or at least a Valentine's date. Yes, my crushes have let me down—and my friends can't be *totally* wrong about me being boyfriend material. Right?

Or am I fooling myself? Wouldn't be the first time.

The rest of the morning flies by, helped along by my thoughts racing a mile a minute.

By the time Calc starts, with Lincoln Chan ignoring me as per usual from across the aisle, I'm more convinced than ever that my problem is me. No matter what my friends say, there must be *something* wrong with me. Am I an ugly, awkward troll and just don't see it? Maybe I'm not as self-aware as I thought.

Like some sort of Rubik's Cube, I twist and turn, desperate to unlock what I might have done to scare off Sergio. How else could things have gone from one hundred to zero? Again? In the notes app, I form a checklist of questions to ask him: 1. Do I have bad breath? 2. Is my body too pale and stringy? 3. Am I too chicken for refusing to wade in the waves when you wanted to go surfing? That last one comes with all the morbid ocean-related fatalities Varsha's planted in my mind over the years.

Before I know it, I'm in eighth-period Lit with Sergio, who's playing some game on his phone under his desk, glancing up every now and then so he doesn't get caught. I try to ignore the daydream playing out in my mind of running my hand against the prickly short hair of his fresh fade cut and tracing the spiral of his ear.

Look at me. Please look at me.

I fidget with the sticky end of my wristband, which reminds me of the boardwalk, which reminds me of biking to the bakery and nibbling our crumb cakes while watching the ducks from a bench by the pond. The sun growing warmer, spurring us to pedal his two-seater to the beach. Chaining it to the rack and walking up the sagging, splintered stairs, past the tall green reeds, through the fence, and onto the sun-warmed dunes, flip-flops in hand. Spreading our towels out and lying with our eyes closed and sunglasses on as we soaked up the rays, despite every part of me internally shuddering at thoughts of sun damage and melanoma.

Even then, I couldn't stop thinking how wonderfully surreal it felt to be lying beside him. We never interacted during the school year. He was a swimmer, a gamer playing D&D with his tight-knit group of friends, and I was off in my own world. I'm the one nobody takes seriously, known as the kid who a bird pooped on during laps in Phys Ed. Or the kid who farted during a moment of silence for a fallen crossing guard during a Halloween assembly in fifth grade. I was suspended for three days because the principal thought I did it as a joke, making the sound with my mouth to get some laughs, and I didn't have the guts to tell her otherwise. Sergio and I would have never come together if not for the uncanny twist of fate of both our families renting neighboring beach homes. It was like magic.

From my spot in the front row, I sit up straight and answer Mrs. Welsch's question on our summer reading. Perhaps Sergio would fall in love with a perfect student.

I stare hard, once more willing him to look at me. Still no dice.

After he refuses to look my way, I tune out Mrs. Welsch going over the syllabus and doodle hearts in my notebook. The smell of his coconut deodorant body spray brings me back to looking into his eyes on the beach as we laughed. The memory reminds me that we *did* have something special, and that I should go for it. Take one last shot.

Push yourself, Leo.

When all fifty-seven agonizing minutes of class are over and the bell rings, I pack up with the speed of a cheetah and step around his desk to face him. I swat back the nerves and force a big smile.

"Hey . . . uh . . . Long time no talk," I say, my heartbeat drowning out my voice. *Is* two days a long time?

"What's up?" he says.

"Everything okay?" I finally ask, fighting the urge to turn tail and run.

"Yeah, why?" He trains his attention on his backpack zipper, which is refusing to close, like how I'm refusing to shut up.

"I was wondering . . ." My face flushes and I give a cartoonish audible gulp. "I had a lot of fun hanging out with you and . . . I just get the sense that . . . Did . . ." My throat feels like it's literally closing up. "I was wondering what happened. Why we stopped talking and you seem like you're not into it anymore?" I grip the edge of his desk to keep the classroom from spinning.

Sergio succeeds in zipping his bag and shoulders it, its anime-themed key chains jingling.

"Oh, and I got this for you." I offer the Lilith decal.

Zubin George, one of his D&D friends, appears by his side. "Hey, man, ready for our *Mario Kart* marathon? Alex says we can play at his place. His dad got a sixty-five-inch TV!"

I keep my sights on Sergio, my eyebrows climbing higher, hand outstretched.

Sergio looks at the sticker, then laughs. "Dude, you're such a try-hard."

"A . . . *what*?" I utter.

"A try-hard. You really need to chill, man. You're not exactly cool as a cucumber."

Although the rejection is familiar, the bite feels fresh like the first time. Any last bit of hope I'd been clinging to is officially dashed.

"No hard feelings." Sergio grins and Zubin looks askance at me before they exit.

I let out a deep, shuddering breath, in a state of shock and hurt. Just like with all my other failed crushes, my heart physically aches. Like someone lodged a knife in it. Like another piece has been chiseled out.

Sometimes, I wish I didn't feel things so deeply.

LATER THAT NIGHT, I'M SINGING ALONG TO *NSYNC'S CLASSIC
hit "Thinking of You" in my room as I scroll through Sergio's
Instagram photos. The song ends, and I let out a mournful sigh.
It starts over again. I scroll ever onward.

"Uh . . ." says Varsha over FaceTime, looking up from whatever she's knitting in her room with its jungle-print wallpaper.
"You've gotta change the song. I can't keep hearing it."

"Oh. Sorry." I pause it and return my attention to the homework sprawled out on my bed. "Guys, I can't focus," I confess.

"Let it go, Leo." Dillon offers his sweet, lopsided smile over
FaceTime, the one that always makes everything seem at peace
in the world. Behind him, his paint-splotched bedroom wall
boasts framed reproductions of his favorite artists from Warhol
to Bosch, and his ultimate favorite, Graffix. Some of Dillon's

own pieces are up there too: vibrant, splotchy still lifes and landscapes.

With its string lights, slanted ceiling, and window overlooking the turnpike, my attic room is usually cozy, but on hot days like today, the top floor traps the heat, making the place stuffy. Perhaps my room would look a little nicer if I wasn't always so focused on guys. Which may explain the mountain of stuffed animals I'm half buried in, who are *always* down to cuddle.

"I *wish* I could just let it go," I mumble, tapping a highlighter against my opened AP Bio textbook. I don't think Dillon or Varsha really understand just how much these kinds of things affect me, and I don't *want* them to know or ever have to go through it themselves. I'm already trying to tone back the muchness I've been feeling so I'm not just trauma dumping on them. I don't want to scare them off, either. Their company is helping to comfort me more than they know, and I'm grateful for that.

"Maybe, just maybe, you should take a break from crushing?" Dillon suggests.

"Is that even possible?" Varsha asks. "I mean, it's *Leo* we're talking about. The same guy who wrote his number on a receipt at the Cheesecake Factory because the waiter smiled at him."

I groan. "I can never show my face there again. Goodbye, Adam's Peanut Butter Cup Fudge Ripple." I take nice to mean interested, or interested to mean nice. I can never get it right. And no one's ever interested.

"I *told you* leaving your number was creepy."

"Varsha, not exactly helping the whole 'it's not you, it's them, Leo' pep talk." I glance at a paragraph in my textbook about single-stranded RNA. Single-stranded, like me.

"A little constructive feedback never hurt anybody."

"Why don't you join a club this year?" Dillon asks. "You can *try hard* at, like, Robotics Club."

I suppress a groan. I shouldn't have told them about Sergio's "feedback."

"Yes!" Varsha agrees. "That could be a *great* distraction."

I brighten. "Like the GSA! Oh, wait. Aren't all its members straight?"

Varsha ignores me. "Join Speech and Debate! Or Paw Club! You love cats!"

"I do." I pet Miss Tiramisu, my black-and-white cat curled up on the bed.

"I've heard you sing," Dillon says. "Join the A Cappella Club with me!"

"Speaking of cats," I begin, "I've been told my singing voice sounds like a cat. A *dying* cat. Remember?" Thanks for that one, Enzi Aguta. Just another crush who crushed me.

"Come on. Join *something*," Varsha says. "I mean, even if it's Knitting Club."

I regard the handmade purple knit headband she's got on. "Ha! Says the girl who has a TikTok account dedicated to her knitting." I pause. "Think any cute boys are in Knitting Club?"

Dillon sighs, then shakes his fists. "Hopeless. Hopeless, I say!"

Varsha leans into the camera. "I'll have you know there are plenty of cute boys in Knitting Club."

I tap my highlighter against my textbook, thoughts slipping back to Sergio.

"Remember," Varsha says, "it's not too late to join Paw Club." She shows off a pet-size knit frog hat that she's 90 percent done making for Miss Tiramisu. "Think she'll like it?" she asks.

Miss Tiramisu glares at me as if to say: *Don't even think about it.*

"She'll love it," I reply. "So, either of you in need of an awesome demon decal?"

Dillon looks up from his tablet. "Either of you want to write my supplemental essay?"

"No thanks." Varsha pulls up the hood of her tiger onesie. "On both counts."

"Sergio really does love games, doesn't he?" I muse. "Like playing games with hearts. I've decided I hate him." Of course, I don't really mean it. In fact, just an hour ago, I liked one of his Instagram beach posts, in some convoluted effort to remind him of how he maybe once felt for me, in some desperate ploy to make him reconsider wanting me. As if by liking the post, I could jog a precious memory of us soaking up the sun side by side. Mind you, it wasn't *our* beach. Scouring his socials, it's as if our two weeks of hanging out together never even occurred. All twelve hours of *Lord of the Rings*—for what?!

But I have to remind myself that it's over, and any attachments I had to him need to be severed. For my own sake. I feel silly missing someone who essentially wants nothing to do with me, yet again.

"You can't get mad at someone just because they're not attracted to you," Varsha says.

"Watch me!" I shake the Lilith decal in my fist and let out a pained roar.

Dillon's crooked grin returns as he points his stylus at me. "Leo, how many of those have you had?"

Beside where I'm bundled up, atop the wide saddle of my unicorn plushie named Meep, sits an opened box of powdered donuts that Mom left for me as a first-day-of-school treat.

"Six," I say, popping another in my mouth. "Seven," I amend through a dry, powdery mouthful. I grab the box that the Play-Station came in and finish taping it shut. "Well, at least I get four hundred dollars back from Game World and can cancel that subscription to Crunchyroll."

"I can't believe you actually bought a PlayStation just to relate to him," Dillon says.

"*I* can." Varsha's back to her knitting. "There's the Cupcake Club. You could join that."

"Think there's a Documenting All the Things You Did to Scare Off Your Crushes Club?" There's a distraction . . . kind of. I traipse over to my desk. On it sits a framed photo of Gran, and beside it, her big old box of arts-and-crafts supplies, including stickers, scissors, tape, and scraps of paper in every shade, color, and texture.

After propping my phone up against my desk lamp, I open my scrapbook to the glued-in photo of Sergio from the beach. Another person gone from my life for good.

"You could start a scrapbooking club," Varsha chimes in.

"Can clubs exist with only one member?" I snip off my wrist-band from the boardwalk and tape it in beside game tickets I never cashed in on. Then I snip the Lilith decal into a heart shape, peel off the backing paper, and place it with tweezers.

I smooth it out, eradicating any bubbles, then pluck a Sharpie from the box and draw a lightning bolt down the center of it.

Capturing the feeling of love was always the intention of my scrapbook. It all started when I had gone over to Gran's one sunny afternoon to help put up her Easter decorations. It was our tradition. We always set up her holiday decorations together. As we did, I found myself telling her about my crush on Lincoln. I had all these strong love feelings and didn't know how to let them out. "I have just the solution," she said with a twinkle in her eye, and sat me down to show me how to scrapbook.

She started by sharing a scrapbook she'd kept of Grandpa before we'd lost him to lung cancer. In it, there were torn old photos of them taped over doilies and yellowed newspaper clippings. I thought it was so romantic, how she'd kept a book full of memories of the two of them with ribbons and stickers, glitter and glue. Before I knew it, she was handing me a new scrapbook. My very own.

Over that summer, she watched me insert memories of Lincoln, smooth out stickers and tape. Over time, I got better with designing each page, trying to capture how Lincoln made me feel. Next to me, Gran would crinkle away at her latest work. I remember how she brushed her bony fingers over a picture of me and told me I was the best grandson. And not just because I helped her put up and take down decorations every holiday, or patiently walked with her to and from restaurants, since she took forever using her cane and refused to get a wheelchair.

Although Gran's gone, her scrapbooks remain. She's in their pages. There's something comforting in that, just like she said.

None of my crushes are gone, but any chance at romance with them sure is. Just like Gran, I capture every detail, so that when I look back, the memory is so potent, I can return to that warm, glowing moment in time, like some sort of mental time-travel trick. Gran knew I was a hopeless romantic. Or as she put it, "a sensitive young man who feels things extremely deeply." She wasn't wrong. I'm the type of sensitive that feels the sting when one of his best friends lovingly says: "I hate you."

She thought it was my greatest strength, but I'm beginning to realize it might be my biggest weakness. Especially given how today's page speaks less of love and more of loss.

At least with Sergio, I know what went wrong, as much as it hurts. Knowing it was one small thing is better than assuming it was everything about me he didn't like. I take a deep breath, trying to put together the pieces of why each crush hasn't worked out. I wish I *did* know, I realize—for closure purposes. To sleep easier. Why did they walk?

Maybe seeing it spelled out will make it easier to let him go. I jot down the reason Sergio slammed the door shut on my First Great Love Story: TRY-HARD. Then, next to TRY-HARD, I write No THOUGHTFUL GIFTS! Seeing it spelled out like this may make it easier to move on.

"Come on, Leo. Join a club. Look into colleges. Take things seriously," Varsha pleads.

Keeping up the hunt for love *is* serious . . . to me.

But I don't say that to Varsha.

"Hey, I wasn't kidding about needing help with my supplemental essay," Dillon says.

"How do you guys keep all this college application stuff straight, anyway?" I ask.

Varsha waves. "Hello? Remember we got that checklist end of junior year?"

"Just because I love checklists doesn't mean I love *that* checklist. Speaking of which . . ." I lift my Back to School Checklist off my desk, with its glued-on paper-cut pencil and backpack. "Let's see, looks like I did everything except for"—I start the satisfying check marks in boxes and pause at the last two action items—"give Sergio his gift. And have a good day."

"Maybe you need a Have a Good Day Checklist," Varsha suggests.

I sigh, dropping my Back to School Checklist in a desk drawer and thumbing through my scrapbook. And I'm back to thinking about what I could have done to repel Sergio—and every crush, for that matter, like I'm some Human Stink Bomb.

"I'm never going to find my one true love," I mumble.

"*One true love?*" Varsha cuts through my thoughts, and I realize I must have said that aloud. "Maybe start with something more practical, like, I don't know, finding a boyfriend?"

"I'm shocked you don't have a checklist for *that*," Dillon jokes.

But wait . . . Just like that, as I reach the blank white pages of a new spread, something clicks.

"A CHECKLIST!"

Both Dillon and Varsha stare wide-eyed at me. Even Miss Tiramisu peeks over.

"What now?" Varsha inquires.

"A BOYFRIEND!" My heart is beating fast. The answer has been in front of me this whole time. Sure, it's no magic spell, but a checklist could be the next best thing. I use checklists for everything else. Why not for love? If I could change things that my crushes didn't like . . .

Varsha brushes her bangs aside. "Leo, why are you smiling like that?"

"You said take things seriously. Well, what about taking *getting a boyfriend* seriously?" I say, ignoring their mollified expressions. "I could follow a checklist to find one."

"A checklist? I'm all for formulas, but what ever happened to trusting the process?" Dillon asks.

"Umm! I think Leo's problem is that he's *too* trusting. Remember the time he got that email saying he won a trip to Barbados and clicked the link that ended up being a virus?"

I hold up a guilty hand. "RIP that laptop."

"Tell us more about the checklist idea," Varsha says.

I hold my phone close to my face. "Okay. Hear me out. The checklist would be a work in progress. But I could use it to become *actual* boyfriend material!" I say, breathless. "You know, change things up. Work on the things that made my crushes walk away in order for me to attract a boyfriend."

Dillon winces. "Oh, I don't like it."

"This is a great idea!" Varsha says at the exact same moment. "As long as you're not considering going after Speedo again," she adds. "Please find a boyfriend who *isn't* him."

Hearing his code name only reaffirms my decision to change every part of myself in order to become the perfect boyfriend—before I give up on love forever.

"Not only do I think this is a bad idea, but we don't even know why most of your crushes walked out on you."

Dillon, being a scientist, is *always* into experiments, so I'm slightly taken aback by his response, but I know Varsha, practical and ambitious as ever, is down to help me conceptualize.

"Well, Sergio did give him a data point," Varsha says. "One word. *Try-hard*."

I flinch.

"Oops. Too soon?" she asks.

"Yes. But also, yes." I'm once more hunched over the blank spread of my scrapbook, smoothing my hands over the possibilities. I don't know why I never thought about changing myself to yield different results all this time. Isn't that the definition of unwise? Being the same Leo over and over again, and somehow thinking I'm going to find a boyfriend?

I want people to take *me* seriously. Not some joke with dried bird poop on his head.

I place a hand over my heart. "I, Leo Martino, vow to create a checklist to get a boyfriend by the end of senior year."

Dillon squints. "I'm not sure that's something you can control."

"I think it's something you *can* control," Varsha counters. "I mean, this checklist could actually work to get you your first real boyfriend. Think about it. You've attracted Abe before. Who's to say you couldn't do something like that again with someone else? You know . . . with a little fine-tuning?"

Abe. Our old code name for Lincoln "Fierce Five" Chan.

"Just a reminder, we still hate the Fierce Five for making our lives hell," Dillon adds.

I give a cheeky grin. "Y'all, if Abe can change, why can't I have a little glow-up of my own?" I think about how by becoming the best version of myself, I can attract a guy who wants to stick around. Maybe after years of unanswered questions, *this* is the final answer. Maybe my First Great Love Story won't only exist in my head for much longer.

"It may be important to note that Abe didn't change for the better," Dillon adds.

I brush the air aside. "That's not the point."

Varsha rattles her knitting needles. "I love a project! Yay. Okay. We need to extrapolate any feedback, like the 'try-hard' thing, to find the starting point for our first checklist item . . ."

"What's the point of getting a boyfriend senior year?" Dillon cuts in.

"Just because that doesn't appeal to *your* rational senses," Varsha says, "doesn't mean it's not something Leo's been dreaming about ever since he saw that scene in *Thumbelina* when the fairy prince . . ."

Actually, it was the "It Only Takes a Moment" number in *Hello, Dolly!*

While my friends bicker, I begin riffling through the box of stationery on my desk, looking for the perfect color to paste into my scrapbook to create the base of my checklist. The more I think about the checklist idea, the more excited I am. I've always been a lowly caterpillar caught in a torrential downpour. But this checklist could transform me into a beautiful butterfly.

I pluck a sheet of seafoam-green paper from the box, then glue it onto the blank page of my scrapbook and smooth it down.

"By semiformal come January, could I really have a date to twirl me on the dance floor? By Valentine's Day, could I really have a boyfriend to take me out to dinner and bring me red roses? And beyond, a happily ever after?"

"I still think this is a bad idea." Dillon sighs. "But we support whatever you want to do."

"You guys are the best." It's nice to have friends who I can talk to about anything.

Well, maybe not anything. Keys jingle from downstairs, and a pit forms in my stomach.

"Ugh. I should go," I say with a casual air. "Dinner."

Sometimes, it's just easier to pretend that things at home are fine.

After we say goodbye and hang up, I get to work at my desk. I uncap the black permanent marker and write the phrase BOY-FRIEND MATERIAL CHECKLIST at the top, and realize I'm sweating. Out of habit, I get up to turn the plug-in fan on high. It used to drown out the sound of fighting. But home has been quiet ever since Dad left.

I don't know how Mom's managed not to die of a broken heart after what happened. But that's the thing about Mom: she has a resilient heart. And so do I. That's why after every heart-break, I've managed to pick up the pieces.

Even after a day like today, when I feel like I've given away the last piece of my heart and now there's nothing left but a black hole that threatens to pull me in forever, deep down I know that's not my fate. Being jaded and broken is not who I am. It's not who I want to be.

I take a good look at myself in the bathroom mirror, at my frizzy hair and mouth that sags at one corner in contemplation.

You're not exactly cool as a cucumber . . .

I return to my room and carry my scrapbook into bed. I may have been tempted to write off love for good, but I refuse.

In careful, neat lettering, I write down the first item on my checklist:

1. BE COOL AS A CUCUMBER.

I pull out a leftover print of my last yearbook photo and tape it onto the page opposite the checklist. I have a mouth full of braces, eyeglasses that are too small for my large eyes, and so much gel in my hair that it looks like gasoline.

As much as it hurts, I place a glittery butterfly sticker right over my face, hiding my big goofy smile, one that is surely True Love Repellent.

Goodbye, Leo.

Hello, Boyfriend.

"WE'LL BE TALKING EVERYTHING FROM ADAPTATION TO
evolution this year," says Mr. Garcia.

Two days later, I've opted to sit in the Devil-May-Care Back
Row as opposed to my usual Teacher's Pet Front Row, struggling
to focus as Mr. Garcia rattles off topics he'll be covering this
semester—struggling to focus because I can't help turning my
attention to my singular checklist item, *Be Cool as a Cucumber*.
Which means I've been trying hard to not try hard.

Which is like not thinking about thinking.

I glance down at my black T-shirt and jeans that I typically
wear to work. With today being school picture day, I tried not
looking like I tried too hard to pull an outfit together. I embraced
the windswept look after the breezy drive in Varsha's car, but
after catching my reflection in my phone, I'm afraid I look disheveled. And like somebody stapled a tumbleweed to my head.

Did I choose the right shirt? Is my hair looking *too* windswept? What does it mean to be cool as a cucumber, anyway? Certainly not second-guessing myself like I did throughout the SATs.

On top of all that, I've been struggling to exorcise my lingering ache for Sergio, but the attraction and the anger are fighting inside me like fire and ice dragons. It's awkward enough that I've brushed elbows with him in Lit the past few days, but he hasn't acknowledged me once since our so-called talk on Monday.

Luckily, not thinking about thinking eats up a lot of my time, and before I know it, I'm seated in the auditorium with a few others, waiting for our senior portraits to be taken. The best I can hope for is that I look "nice."

Onstage, a photographer snaps away, waving students up one by one.

My phone buzzes in my pocket.

Dillon: Hope your pic goes well. Remember—you have a great smile! 😁

I give the text a heart.

I can hear Mom now: "You suffered years of braces for that smile. So smile!"

And Gran, too: "You've got a face that belongs on the silver screen."

In my phone, I stare at my teeth. Were my canines always so pointy-looking?

"Martino, Leonardo," calls the photographer, making my stomach lurch. How can I be so confident one minute and so insecure the next? I try clinging to the words of support.

Ignoring the feeling that other students are watching and scrutinizing me, I hand him the packet detailing which type of picture and background I selected. As he scans it, I sit on the stool and make a last desperate attempt to relax my limbs, then do my best to level a cool gaze at the photographer.

From the audience, I see a few students sneaking a peek. I shift uncomfortably and feel red-hot heat creep into my cheeks. This is nerve-racking. I smile, like Mom and Dillon wanted me to do—until I see none other than Travis Matthews skateboarding into the auditorium.

"Hey, bros!" Travis kicks his board up under his arm and, ignoring Mr. Potesky's bark of admonishment, dives into a seat in the front row, where he fist-bumps his punk rock skater bud.

It's rare to see Travis Matthews without his other half, Lincoln Chan. Travis looks just as good as he did in Spanish class last year, with his thick, shoulder-length coils, ratty black T-shirt with guitar pick hanging from a chain around his neck, silver nose stud, and spiky cuff bracelets.

Varsha and Dillon blacklisted him when they found out that he was using me to do his Spanish homework and allegedly told everyone about how I had a big old crush on him. And then, at junior prom, when my friends and I struck our happy poses in the photo booth, Travis told me not to smile so wide because it made me look goofy.

Seeing him definitely makes my smile falter. *Is* it too wide? Why is that bad? The more I think about it, I'm not sure how else one *should* arrange their smile. Tight-lipped looks irritated. No smile looks sad or constipated. And only a little bit of teeth looks like I just sucked a sour lemon. In fact, Travis is giving the widest, goofiest smile right now, and I think he looks great.

We lock eyes, and I purposefully look away, resisting the urge to grin like the happy-go-lucky fellow I usually am. I need to get with the program—the Boyfriend Material Checklist.

Which means I need to tack a Non-Smile addendum onto my first checklist item about being cool. Narrowing my eyes at the camera, I dim down my smile. Sorry, Mom and Dillon.

Snap!

I catch a slight nod from the photographer as he eyes the screen—what does *that* mean?

"Matthews, Travis!"

My mind is still reeling when I almost crash into Travis after he forgoes the steps and leaps onto the stage from the side, like some sort of practitioner of parkour.

"Good going, bro." Travis offers a fist bump and a puppy-dog smile.

Seriously, how come his Big Goofy Grin makes me want to kiss it?

Maybe those smiles only work on certain faces—

Hold up. Did he just give me a compliment? And a fist bump?!

I fight breaking out from ear to ear into an enormous toothy grin. It takes every bit of energy to keep the corners of my mouth from twisting upward as I will myself to look bored.

His sights linger on me for another second before he bolts past me for his photo.

Good going, bro, indeed!

It's only lunchtime and I'm already marking off that first line on my checklist like a pro.

After avoiding a table of marines outside the cafeteria who are trying to sign up recruits and challenging students to do chin-ups on a bar, I enter the zoo that is the high school cafeteria.

The cafeteria puts me on edge, especially since Dillon and Varsha sometimes have club meetups during our lunch period, like today. But I've come somewhat prepared. To avoid the nausea-inducing game of where to sit when they're not free, I made a checklist for how to survive a lunch period without them.

First up was researching my peers' class schedules on Instagram to figure out where to sit, but I don't know anyone well enough to coordinate anything. Next up was trying to connect with a classmate from last period to sit with. Both of which also require trying too hard, so I didn't bother with either today. Instead, I try winging it and finding the first available spot. If *that* fails, I'll just eat lunch in the library while I read the latest Whiskered Warriors novel, *Mice of Flame and Paw.*

It takes extreme restraint to not swivel my head 360 degrees like an owl in order to survey every face. Very subtly, I note the tables. I've never been nerdy enough for the nerds or geeky enough for the geeks. They know things. They're in fandoms. Like the athletes in their fantasy football brackets. The books I like aren't great literary classics. They're mostly vampire manga and graphic novels about pastel ponies or mice bent on saving their sacred woodland.

Fortunately, I find a spot at a relatively empty table before other seniors start filling in around me. They talk to each other as they unpack their lunches, not seeming to notice that I'm here. I catch snippets about the batting averages of baseball players. Yeah. Can't relate.

Besides, anything baseball-related reminds me of Dad.

After I set my backpack down on my chair to hold my spot, I stand in line for a Sprite and a bag of Doritos. Normally, I buy lunch from the teacher's line. The food's better there—you just have to pay more. (Thank you, part-time job.) It's worth not having to suffer the sandwich line snaking out into the hall. If I'd really been on my Lunch Checklist A game, I would've packed a meal to save money.

When I return, I nearly drop my Sprite.

Someone has taken my seat.

Not just anybody, either.

Lincoln Chan—with his swoopy black hair, lavender bomber jacket, and long, oversize pink T-shirt—is seated beside Travis. The two make up 40 percent of the Fierce Five.

Believe it or not, Lincoln and I were best friends in grades six through eight, bonding over our love of the Whiskered Warriors series and *Dungeness & Lobsters* trading card game. One enchanting evening the summer after eighth grade, he made a move on me with a gentle peck on the lips—my first kiss.

We were walking through town at night, after all the shops were closed and not a car was on the road. A magical hour when it felt like the whole world was asleep. He had asked to walk me home. We were passing a construction site of a new house being built when he pulled me behind a crane and kissed me. Just when he ran his hands through my hair, a car passed by, startling us apart, and after a brief goodbye, we went our separate ways home.

At the top of freshman year, Lincoln stopped talking to me outright. To my horror and confusion, he blocked me on every platform—even Venmo—without any explanation, making me doubt everything I ever said and did. My first kiss. And my last.

Like with my other crushes, the reason behind Lincoln ghosting me remains a complete mystery. The type you might see on an episode of *Cold Case*. It's why I kind of hate his guts.

To make matters worse, Lincoln had a major glow-up since we made out. It's how he became the other half of Eastfield High's It Couple. It's also how Lincoln scored his spot among the popular clique that gossips about scandalous house parties, spreads juicy hookup rumors, and plans fancy group getaways.

Lincoln Chan was the first one who planted my seed of self-doubt, who made me feel like something was wrong with me. The first one who had me thinking about how I may not be boyfriend material after all. The first one who got away . . . with making me feel undesirable. He outright stole my heart. And now my seat.

"OMG," Katie says to her friends, all of them pretending I'm not standing here. "Last weekend was so much fun. I'm still dying over Eamon knocking that potted tree into your pool!"

"It was hell to clean up." Travis hides his face in Lincoln's shoulder.

I clear my throat. It's gone dry as dirt. "H-hey." I hope Lincoln can't sense I'm a bundle of nerves. We haven't exchanged words in three years.

Be cool, Leo. Stand your ground. Trust the process.

That's what the checklist would say, right? Or is standing here in silence the opposite of cool? I mean, what am I supposed to do? Keep staring at the single, dangly earring in Lincoln's lobe? I can feel my face turning darker shades of red by the second.

Those around him—like the rest of the Fierce Five—go quiet, eyes flitting, as he remains still. Eamon nudges Travis conspiratorially. Sakura and Katie seem to be on the brink of laughter.

"I—I was sitting there," I assert, wishing my voice wasn't so trembly.

Eamon bursts into laughter, revealing the big gap between his two front teeth. Eamon's never been particularly kind. He's from a huge family, and all of them have the same freckled faces and button noses. I remember he invited me over to his place once in fourth grade to make gingerbread houses, and his kitchen was chaos, with his brothers and sisters running helter-skelter, flinging candy at one another and screaming. Perhaps it's what's made him so scrappy.

Lincoln's expression is blank and uncaring. "Yeah. I didn't know that." His tone is irritated. Sure, he's hot now, but I bet he gets bad grades. At least I hope he does. I can't help noticing he still eats the same thing for lunch: turkey sandwich on rye, no cheese, extra mustard.

Not to mention the king-size Three Musketeers bar. Some things never change.

"It's okay." I pick up my backpack from the floor, failing to look as unbothered as possible. I feel the eyes of the Fierce Five boring into me and filling me with embarrassment, on top of the already awful feeling I have interacting with Lincoln after all this time. I hurry into the hall, feeling like I could burst into tears.

So much for trusting the process.

Recalling my last resort, I head for the school library, willing the red-hot fire in my face to cool. I just made a *complete* clown of myself. This Boyfriend Material Checklist was a bad idea. Dillon will be glad to hear that I will no longer be following it. That's a wrap, folks. Single forever, it is.

Lincoln Chan just reminded me that there's no hope for me. That I *am* hopeless.

No Non-Smile or Cool as a Cucumber attitude is going to be enough to get a boyfriend before graduation. I can kiss goodbye any lovey-dovey semiformal slow dance or Valentine's Day date fantasies.

"Chin-ups?" asks a marine, but upon seeing my expression, he looks away out of respect.

Chin *down* is more like it.

I just want to be alone.

Well, that's new.

Goodbye, Boyfriend.

A WAX SEAL OF AN ACORN HOLDING A PAPER WRISTBAND IN
place. The words Be Thankful stamped in black letters across
the top of the page. A picture of me holding a warty gourd in a
pumpkin patch.

It was a beautiful fall day, and I could smell the apple cider
and powdered donuts from the row of food vendors down the
hill. I loved that time of year, even if I *did* have to drag Dad to
take me. Dad had me wait for him on the long line at the hayride while he got a cup of coffee.

"Next up!" The man running the hayride ushered people
into the wagon of a tractor. He waved me forward, but I didn't
budge. I looked for Dad—he should have come back by then.
I texted him again, but there was still no reply by the time
another hayride rolled up ready to go.

Being that I was now the only person around, I climbed into
the wagon and waited for Dad as other passengers started piling

in. A guy my age sat beside me, and I froze. He was cute. He had on a red plaid shirt with blue jeans, chunky black boots, and sunglasses. He glanced over before diving into his phone. I stared at the stray pieces of hay on the wood boards at my feet.

I'd never seen him before. I wondered if he was local or just visiting town. I wished I'd had sunglasses to hide my eyes, which kept darting to him. His dad climbed up into the wagon and joined him, then more and more people filled in. Finally, Dad arrived, squeezing in beside me.

The man running the ride roped off the back of the wagon, and we began to move. Dad struck up conversation with the other guy's dad, and my cheeks turned as red as the fall foliage.

We reached a grassy field dotted with pumpkins and everyone hopped out to pick theirs. After poking around at half-rotted ones, I found a pumpkin with smooth, rounded sides and a sleek stem. I saw the cute guy lift a dented, barnacled gourd and recoil, so I offered him my pumpkin.

He gave me a smile, and I gave him a piece of my heart.

I start to close my scrapbook when I see some of Dad's arm in the corner of the photo. A blur of a brown jacket sleeve. It's the picture of him I have in my mind. A blur never really there.

UNFORTUNATELY, MY PART-TIME JOB MAKES IT IMPOSSIBLE
for me to be alone for more than a few hours.

When I enter Ye Olde Tea House for my after-school shift,
I'm hit with the smell of fresh-baked brownies. Ye Olde Tea
House may be the newest installation in town, but with its
gilded tea saucers and china plates adorning the shelves that
line mint-green walls, along with silver spoons tied with velvet
ribbons and glossy bows, you'd think this place has been here
since the ye olde 1840s.

"Hello, Leo," says the store's owner and my boss, Judy Spohr,
from where she stacks hats in the entrance. Judy has collected
teapots all her life. Cute, colorful ones with fun patterns and
shapes. Teacups too. Lo and behold, she found this quaint little
space in town and shined it up. Gran would have loved it.

Being here is typically enough to bring me out of any funk. It's right up my alley—made better by how I got the job after finding out Vincent O'Connor, Crush Number Three, was working here—although I knew none of that when I applied. He still does work here, if you can call it working. Being in constant, close proximity with another one of my crushes has been awkward at best. He never entertains me in conversation, usually giving one-word answers, which is annoying but somehow makes me want to keep engaging with him day after day.

"Hello." I wave at Judy and pass her extensive collection of fanciful hats that customers sometimes opt to wear. The hats have fake flowers glued to them along with feathers and plastic cherry bunches. They are pretty over the top, which is why I like them. On weekends, the place is overrun with five-year-old girls, who fill up every mismatched, wobbly table. Cool People come here too, to take pictures of baby-pink sugar bowls and teacups steaming on saucers. It's trendy and looks good on socials, aka the perfect place for people who try really hard to look like they're not trying hard at all.

I head into the toasty kitchen, where I find Vincent. His red hair and pale blemish-free face are complemented perfectly by his strawberry lip gloss and silky dress shirt with frills. I met him at a hayride two years ago. Separately, our dads brought us to pick pumpkins. I found the perfect pumpkin and called Vincent over to claim it as his own. He was elated. Meanwhile, I had to resort to a squirrel-bitten gourd. On the way back to the parking lot, my apple cinnamon donut fell into the dirt, and he handed me one of his donuts—along with a moist towelette and a pitying smile.

On my first day on the job, Vincent said it was nice to meet me when clearly we'd met. Sigh. I should add FORGETTABLE to my scrapbook on his page, along with UNLOVABLE. Though I wonder if he *does* remember having met me and just didn't want to admit it for some reason. I think back to what Vincent told me my first day on the job. He said I had "a lot of potential with the right hair, makeup, and styling." Now, it hits me even harder. I *am* a troll. And not like the cute ones with the neon-pink tufts.

Oh, well. I remind myself that any further boyfriend-material modifications are at a full stop. Especially after playing it cool with Lincoln went so well.

I wrestle my rumpled, flour-spattered apron on over my all-black ensemble, in no mood to greet Vincent.

Even though my crush on him is as faded as the paper wristband for the harvest hayride glued to his scrapbook page, I still can't seem to take my eyes off him, even during one of my funks. Meanwhile, his eyes have no problem staying far, *far* away from me. Like usual.

And like usual, he's too busy taking selfies to acknowledge me. Vincent is what Varsha calls "a vain #InstaGay." That said, he is really talented and resourceful, with a killer fashion sense, judging by his apron alone, which he's bejeweled and mono-grammed. As an aspiring costume designer, he elevates clothing and accessories whenever and wherever he can.

I bump into a sealed can of loose-leaf artisan tea, which falls to the floor with a clatter.

Oops. At least it wasn't Judy's bowl of handmade artisanal flower-shaped sugar cubes.

Vincent barely registers my presence before busying himself with his phone again.

I'm still too preoccupied going over what happened with Lincoln to care. I pick up the can, then get to work, starting by washing my hands. Lincoln is an Undeniable Jerk. Heck, Sergio too. The whole lot of them! My crushes *have* been terrible. Dillon was right about that. It's making me not feel compelled to engage with Vincent like I normally would. I don't ask how he's doing or bring up any new shows I've streamed. I don't ask him what kind of perfume he's wearing or what brand of suede shoe he's sporting. I keep my thoughts—and my eyes—to my dang self.

Soon, I'm taking down a couple's orders on my notepad. I can be shy, so this job presented me with a good exercise in human interaction. I think it's working. These days, I don't stammer as much. Luckily, the menu isn't extensive. People either order a zillion-dollar tiered tray of sandwiches and pastries, or a pot of tea for ten bucks. It's usually the latter. Like this couple's order—one pot of herbal lemon tea for two.

Shelves in the kitchen host a variety of pristine teapots, cups, and saucers. Part of the fun is picking out which to deliver to diners. Some teapots are chipped, and the teacups and saucers are mismatched. But that's what gives them their charm, like the hats on the rack by the door, or nice scraps of crafting paper. I consider a white teapot covered in strawberries, to match the woman's red nails and the man's crisp white shirt, but Judy hands me a cherry-red teapot shaped like a heart.

"Here you go. I think they will like this one. This is the very first teapot I owned."

I take it, noting it looks shiny as new. "Oh, very cool. Thanks."

After adding boiling hot water from the kettle, I steep in the diffuser, and revel in the fresh lemon aroma that wisps into the air. Then I select a white cup with a rose on it, and a pink one with a gold stripe, and deliver them, along with a sugar bowl and the teapot heavy in hand.

"May I?" They nod and I pour the hot water out in a steady stream. Some of it dribbles and burns my thumb, forcing me to recoil and shout. Hot water splashes onto the man's lap. He yells and pushes out from the table, which causes his chair to tip and him to fall.

The woman gasps and goes to stand, but her leg chair catches in the bunched-up lace rug, and she also falls. I move in an attempt to help catch her and miss, nearly dropping the teapot.

They stand, brushing themselves off, and all I can do is watch, stunned. Luckily, there's no broken china or broken bones from the look of things. After ensuring everyone is okay and apologizing profusely, I hide in the kitchen, feeling the heat in my face continue to boil.

"Is our shift over yet?" Vincent asks no one, with an air of boredom.

Still, I take it as an invitation to engage. "Fifteen minutes to go."

Vincent groans, then gets back to texting on his phone in its bedazzled bandolier. Hard as I try to resist, I can't help watching him in the reflection of the silver tray I'm polishing to soothe my shaking nerves. He has impeccable taste and a perfectly manicured look. What's his secret?

After checking in on the diners to ensure they're okay, I retreat back to the kitchen and hover over a giant baking sheet piled high with the crusts that Judy lops off various foodstuffs. If you ever wonder where the crusts of the crustless go, the answer is my stomach. I nibble on flaky bread crusts, some of which harbor the traces of egg salad or cream cheese and watercress. Or the shorn-off tops of vanilla cakes. The chewy edges of brownies. I never eat them while on a shift with Vincent, because it makes me look like a foraging raccoon. But screw it. I'm a lost cause, and it's not like he can think any less of me.

I bite into a particularly chewy brownie edge and let out a satisfied moan.

Vincent looks over and grimaces. "You're eating the garbage?"

Oh, so *now* he pays attention to me.

I feel the flush creep up my face despite myself.

He looks at me—and holds his gaze. "What's up with you?"

I freeze. Is he referring to my unsavory snacking habit?

"You seem super low energy today," he continues.

Oh. That. So, he *has* noticed. For maybe the first time in my life, I try a shrug, not wanting to get into it.

His gaze narrows further, but I don't care. I'm over it.

Judy steps foot into the kitchen, her silky gray hair pulled back in its signature neat ponytail with not a strand out of place. "All right, boys. The last table just left. You can go."

"Sweet!" Vincent sets down his apron and snatches up his purse. "Later, Leo."

My heart rate spikes, and I give an imperceptible nod.

Did he just bid me adieu? He *never* bids me adieu.

"Good night, Vincent." Judy snaps the lid onto a tin of powdered almond cookies and gives me a soft smile, watching me pick over the tray of crusts. "Leo, I really love how much you enjoy my baking."

"I really do." I smile, teeth full of brownie that I quickly rub off with a finger, then grab my hoodie. "Night, Judy."

"Good night, Leo," she says, blinking her big blue eyes behind her owlish glasses.

Before I go, I head back out to my table and find my tip waiting for me.

A quarter. Well, can't say I'm surprised.

Regardless, there's a skip in my step on my way to Mom's car, thinking of Vincent's goodbye. *Later, Leo* . . . Did he say it because I ignored him all shift? Is that what not trying—and succeeding—looks like? Maybe my Boyfriend Material Checklist is back in play. Maybe I *can* do it.

It's the first time a goodbye has ever felt so good.

5

"SO, NOT SMILING AND ACTING BORING IS MAKING GUYS
notice you," Varsha says. "Interesting."

Dillon cocks an eyebrow. "Is it?"

The next afternoon, Dillon, Varsha, and I take full advantage of senior off-campus privileges by getting a booth at Mike's Diner. It's a celebratory lunch, albeit a delayed one, to commemorate my small victory about how not trying too hard totally worked on Vincent. And just when I was going to throw in the towel on my self-improvement journey.

The whole place smells like fresh, fluffy waffles. I watch as a waiter passes by with trays of chicken tenders, hash browns, and fries. We settled on ordering pizza. The place is packed with seniors, filling the bar, tables, and booths. Some are even from Crestview, the private school in the next town over, the one that Vincent attends—and Enzi Aguta, Crush Number Five. I've spotted Enzi in here on a few occasions, and he sometimes shows up at the teahouse to visit Vincent, too. On those days, I busy myself by picking cemented food off dirty plates at the sink.

"So?" I waggle my eyebrows at Dillon and Varsha. "What's next?"

"It's obvious," says Varsha from across the table. "You need your next checklist item."

"Right. But what is it?"

"Julien?" she asks.

"Shh. Not so loud."

I take a moment to look around the place for Julien Ivanov. He was another one of my past crushes, and the nerdiest by far, with wiry eyeglasses and an off-kilter smile that lights up at talk of math. We don't have a cute code name for him.

Julien and his family moved next door when we were both fifteen. His older brother Roman became friends with my older brother, Silvio. Whenever they'd hang out, Julien and I would watch them play computer games or join their movie screenings. One day, Julien invited me over for tacos. I thought maybe he liked me. I went over, and we ate tacos and watched TV—nothing spicy in the slightest, in the tacos or otherwise. Just days later, I saw him making out with some girl under the bleachers. He and his family moved across town, and I never heard from Julien again. Though I *did* hear he'd dropped out of high school. Apparently, he'd skipped so many classes that he wasn't going to be able to graduate. At least he was able to get a job at the diner.

A waitress sets down our pizza—and the two sides of fried egg for Dillon and me to add onto our slices. It's delicious, but I'm having trouble enjoying it, since there's no Julien in sight. Now that it's all systems go again for my Boyfriend Material Checklist, maybe I could talk to him and get some information to add to it, like feedback on what he thinks of me.

"The thought has crossed my mind," I muse. "I mean, he didn't really *reject* me, and I'm not even sure he's into guys . . ."

"Okay, but what *would* Julien's item be?" Varsha asks. "Hypothetically speaking?"

Dillon slides a slice onto his paper plate. "That you no longer lived next door?"

"Could be," I say, picking a green pepper off my slice.

"Remind me again why you won't ask Vincent what he thinks of you?" Varsha asks. Another ex-crush without a cute code name.

"He refuses to engage with me so much that trying to get information is hopeless!" I grin. "That said, I still can't believe ignoring Vincent actually got to him!" I add in a low voice.

"I'm pretty sure that's always been a thing." Dillon chuckles. "Even *I* know that."

I spy Sakura eating a salad across the room with some of her pom squad pals. Dillon follows my line of sight, then quickly looks back at me. I catch Sakura glancing over at him.

"Clearly, ignoring someone really does draw them in deeper. You perfected the art, Dillon." I bite into my slice of hot, ooey-gooey cheesiness.

Dillon rolls his eyes.

"I'm serious," I say in singsong.

Varsha pulls another pizza slice onto her plate. "Speaking of serious, please tell me you started giving thought to college applications? Have you given more thought to signing up for clubs? Schools love that." Her face lights up. "And remember what I was saying! A club could also help you find this future boyfriend-to-be!"

"Yeah, I'm still not joining the Knitting Club."

Varsha reaches for some napkins. "Okay, then what about auditioning for the school drama?"

I'm not sure I need more drama.

"Before you tell me, 'Oh, but I'm not a Theater Kid,'" she continues, "consider this—your future boyfriend may be part of the production."

"Hmmm."

"A school play is a good way to get out of your comfort zone, too. And the only way to grow, as in grow into boyfriend mate-rial, is to step out of your comfort zone."

"Did no one hear me when I said Leo is *already* total boy-friend material?" Dillon asks.

I glare.

He throws his hands up. "Fine. I relent." He bites his pizza and his fried egg slides off. "So, why not just take public speaking?"

"We don't offer that," Varsha reminds him.

"Well, we *should*—"

"Focus." Varsha pinches her hand in a gesture that draws Dillon's eye. Then she turns back to me. "Leo, come on. Do the play. Meet a gay. Whaddya say? Hip, hip, hooray? Eh? Eh?"

I laugh. "What is the school drama this year, any*way*?"

"*Twelfth Night*," Dillon answers. "Haven't you read every Shakespeare play a hundred times?"

He's right. *Twelfth Night* is one of my favorites. It's about love, so obviously I'm a fan.

I blot egg yolk off my mouth. "But the only roles I've ever played were a nameless orphan in *Annie* and a nameless priest in *The Sound of Music*." I sigh. "My acting chops are lacking. Besides, just the thought of auditioning makes me feel sick. Are *you* going to try out?"

Dillon swallows. "Nah. I'm more of a musical person. I need a little song and dance."

"How did the visit from the Princeton rep go?" I ask Varsha.

"It went super well!" She narrows her eyes. "Don't change the sub—"

"And, Dillon," I say, turning to him, "how was the first meetup for Robotics Club?"

"Electrifying," he says, then laughs at his own pun. "No, it was really lovely. I mean, it was weird because Katie Cooper joined . . . I didn't expect to see her there."

"See, Leo? Everybody else is joining a club." Varsha gives a wide smile. "At least audition for *Twelfth Night*, Leo."

As promising as that sounds, and as naturally dramatic as my life is, I'm just not cut out for performing in front of crowds larger than two people. I took piano lessons for years, and when I had this big recital with my piano teacher Ayumi's other students and their families, I completely forgot how to move my hands across the keys. My embarrassment reverberated louder than the actual waltz.

I sigh, smiling. "Never gonna happen. We'll just have to keep thinking."

Coming up with the next checklist item and where to find a boyfriend is tougher than it seems, but I'm comforted thinking about how good it will feel to finally have true love. I imagine it like it's this magic spell strong enough to siphon all the sorrow from my life and infuse it with sunshine—just like I feel when I crush but permanent. It'll make all the hard and heavy things feel brighter and lighter.

The waitress places down the check and reminds us to pay at the register.

Varsha riffles through her fuzzy sloth wallet and groans. "I don't have cash. Venmo?"

"Sure. Yeah. Venmo works," I say, the app reminding me painfully and suddenly of Lincoln.

"Don't worry. We didn't block you on that one," Dillon teases, as if reading my mind.

I feign an amused laugh, then go to pay. I'm disappointed to find there's no Julien at the register, with his wiry eyeglasses and short, sandy-brown hair poking out every which way.

I'll just have to come back another day to talk to him for my information gathering.

One half a school day and a work shift later, I'm curled up in bed with tablet in hand, watching my favorite scene from *Little Women* and swooning over Timothée Chalamet for the umpteenth time. Maybe Varsha is onto something about widening my dating pool. If I were to be in the school play, maybe I'd capture the eye of a handsome new guy who comes up afterward with a bouquet of fresh red roses.

I shift my focus from where to find my future boyfriend back to how I can continue to draw him in—whoever and wherever he is. My hand smooths over the checklist. Varsha's right: I need my next action item.

Going through my scrapbook, I try to find any common threads among the six crushes, to see if there's one single thing about them that drew *me* in. But they're all so vastly different.

I pause on Vincent's page, with the wristband for the hayride, and an Instagram photo that I printed of him in a sparkling blazer and loafers, looking the picture of fashion-forward. Practically the only thing he's ever said to me was about my style—or lack thereof. If he didn't like my style, perhaps the others didn't, either.

"Leo, dear!" Mom calls from downstairs. "Dinner's ready!"

"Be right down!" I holler.

I watch as Timothée takes Florence Pugh's face in his hands and kisses her. He just goes for it at precisely the right moment. It's the kind of kiss that one gives when they love you so much, they'd put their own life above your own. That "catch a grenade" for you kind of love.

I'm bound to feel that before the school year's through. Right? The black hole starts to pull me in at the thought of not finding it.

There's one thing that my crushes all have in common. They're all so cute. How can I be cute, too? Or would they not be attracted to "cute" like how I am, in the same way I'd much rather a guy smile than put on a hot and serious smolder? Then again, *everyone* who experiences attraction is attracted to "hot." Maybe I'm the only one who thinks "cute" is a romantic thing and not a friend-zone thing. Maybe I'm already cute and don't even know it.

Then again, I think *Dillon* is cute.

I head down to the kitchen, where the marinara sauce bubbles gently on the stovetop. Mom's straining angel hair pasta into a colander at the sink. Steam billows around her face. Her thin arms struggle to tip the pot.

She lost so much weight over the past year. Unlike Silvio and me, when Mom is under stress, she tends to lose her appetite. I'm glad to see her cooking more and more these days.

I take a seat on one of the rickety wooden chairs with its slipping, untied cushion. The oak table feels so big for just the two of us. Mom sets the pasta and meatballs down on cozies as I dole salad out onto a plate. The TV hums with a game show announcer introducing contestants.

She slides a fried egg on top of my pasta, just the way I like it.

"Thanks, Mom," I say, breaking the yolk and letting it soak in.

I may no longer have a dad, but Mom more than makes up for it. I wonder if I *ever* had a dad. His greatest contributions to my life included reminding me to put sunscreen on my ears and to gargle with salt water for a sore throat.

After taking hot, steamy mouthfuls of pasta, I catch Mom gazing at me while sipping from her glass of red wine. She's wearing her favorite Christmas pajamas—green ones with puppies in stockings—although it's September. She always changes out of her stuffy suit jackets after work into comfortable clothes. On top of volunteer work, she's been putting in overtime all year since earning her license and starting her own psychology practice.

We sit in silence while the game show drones on. I get the sense neither of us cares who wins. I continue to ponder, itching to come up with the perfect next action item to add to the list.

Neither of us acknowledges the fact that the head of the table is empty.

"How was school?" Mom asks. "Any word from Sergio?"

"Ugh. No."

"Just move on, dear."

"Easier said than done." I try to tune out memories of sandy couch cushions, Sergio hosing off the deck, dangling on the swing set beside a trellis of honeysuckle that was as sweet as Sergio. When he still liked me. If he ever did.

Mom's voice cuts through my thoughts. "Did your senior portrait go okay?"

"Umm, I totally forgot about the fact that I chose black for my backdrop, and my shirt was black, so I'm pretty sure I'll look like a floating head."

She laughs. "I'm sure you looked handsome anyway."

I shove another mouthful of pasta in my mouth.

"Have you given thought to colleges yet?"

Not Mom, too. Crushes aside, senior year is the final leg of the race before I graduate, spread my wings, and go off to . . . college? Maybe? You know, once I figure out where and how to apply? Who am I kidding? How am I going to spread my wings if I can't even manage a flap here?

I should be ecstatic about a fresh new chapter. High school hasn't done me—or my love life, self-confidence, self-esteem, dignity, dare I go on?—any favors. Not to mention I've never been plugged in to the goings-on of clubs, activities, sports, or class get-togethers. I'm an outsider, for better or for worse. A scrapbooking bookworm with hobbies that I've only shared with Dillon and Varsha—and Lincoln, once upon a time. Though he doesn't know about my scrapbooking, something only grannies do. Not exactly "hot."

Whatever lies ahead can't be worse than high school though, right? My older brother Silvio's apparently having a great time at his first year of Boston College.

"I've given it a *little* thought," I reply.

She takes another long sip from her glass. "Well, that's good. You're so smart. You'll get in someplace. You just have to focus on applying."

I grumble. Talking about the future stresses me out, and she knows it. But it's true, I've always been a good student.

"How's work?" she asks.

"Better than yesterday's shift. I had someone order the Queen's High Tea."

"The one with five tiers?" Mom bobs her head. "Wow. Big spender. Good tip, I hope."

I smile. "Better than that twenty-five-cent tip."

"It all adds up." Mom sprinkles grated parmesan onto her pasta then mixes it in with her fork, sending steam dancing into the air. "Has Vincent said more than two words to you yet?"

I shake my head.

"Well, we can at least give him points on style. He always looks so fashionable."

"How about me?" I ask, tentative.

"I think the clothes we got on our back-to-school shopping trip look nice."

"Me too." I eye her wine bottle. When Dad still lived in the house, she started to drink a lot toward the end. She's been trying to cut back, but without much success. "How are you?"

"Well, your father's trying to take me back to court." She puts on an amused smile and takes another sip. Typical Dad. He's been trying to get everything in the endless shakeout, down to the last light bulb. When he shouldn't get one single thing after what he's done.

"Just Philth being Philth."

His name is Phil, which makes Mom's nickname for him a perfect fit. Even though she thinks of him as dirt, I can tell she's still hurting. Plus, it doesn't stop her from encouraging Silvio and me to have a relationship with him, despite the truth of the matter. He thinks she brainwashed us against him, but I want nothing to do with him. No Brainwashing Required.

He'd been cheating on Mom for a while. When she found out, he refused to stop seeing the secretary at his dental office who doesn't look much older than me. I met her the time Dad invited his employees over for a barbecue. Little did we know they were secret lovers. Thinking back, it was obvious from the way he looked at her and the way he started to change—buying a red motorcycle and donning leather jackets, wearing do-rags and snakeskin boots with shiny spurs, when before he'd been a doctor in soft cashmere cardigans driving a big gray minivan.

Mom figured it out eventually. It's not like he was being that subtle. She threw him out. We never heard from him again, except for when the courts arranged for my brother and me to meet him at Jake's Steak House, where he told us he was happier than ever, living with his new young girlfriend. The thought makes my stomach clench, and part of me holds on to the idea that maybe he'll change his stripes and come back before the divorce gets finalized.

"Sounds about right . . ." I trail off, not wanting to talk or think about Dad. "How's Silvio?"

"Well, your brother's pretty much all settled in at his dorm at school. He says hi." I doubt he says hi—Silvio's really stoic and doesn't do those kinds of mushy things. He's the opposite of me. He thinks sports are fun. He wants to skydive one day. He gets mad when I take too long to order at the bagel shop in town and gets embarrassed when I modify my sandwich order at the deli. But I smile anyway at Mom's continual effort to bring us closer together as brothers.

Mom lifts her pasta to her mouth and waits for it to cool. "How are *you*?"

I bristle. "Me? I'm good."

"I've noticed you've been acting a little off." She continues to stare. It's unnerving.

"Mom, quit trying to psychologicalize me."

"That's not a word, dear."

"I've just been busy with school and work and everything." Is it really that obvious? It must be, if even *Vincent* noticed I've been acting different. I don't want to tell Mom about the whole Boyfriend Material Checklist thing. I know she'd never stand for it. She thinks I'm perfect as I am. But moms are legally obligated to think that.

I wipe my lips. "Do you think a guy would ever want to date me?"

Mom screws up her mouth, thoughtful. "Are you talking about Dillon?"

I laugh. "What? No way. We're friends. I just mean in general."

"I think you're unusual," she says, her voice kind and careful. "You're not going to attract just anyone. That guy will come along, and when he does, you'll know it."

I can't help smiling at how hard she's trying. "You're right. Thanks, Mom."

I continue to eat. Dad also used to call me unusual, but not in a good way. He always wanted me to be a different kind of son. More outdoorsy and rough-and-tumble. He wanted me to "be a man," whatever that means. I'm not sure *he* knows. But I have to remind myself that this time, I'm not changing myself for him. I'm doing it for me. It's funny how one person can see you as nothing and another person as everything.

Thankfully, she turns her attention back to eating and the TV.

But what she said about Vincent being stylish . . . Maybe there's something there?

After dinner, I finish my homework, brush and floss my teeth, hop into bed, and pull out my phone. I head straight to

Vincent's TikTok. There's a Get Ready with Me (First Day of School) video pinned to the grid. He's a whiz at creating content, doing a voice-over while cutting together a seamless edit that shows his daily routine, from washing his face with sudsy water to dabbing on a scent.

I click on my own profile, peering at the tiny photo of me. I don't have many videos, and only a few friends. It never bothered me, but it does now. Maybe if I were famous or had a booming social media presence or had a different look, I'd get more attention. Make guys glue their eyes on me. Ask me out. Boldly take my face in their hands and kiss me midsentence.

Suddenly, the next checklist item becomes as clear as day.

Phone flashlight on, I drag my scrapbook over and add the second action item to the list:

2. GET A GLAM GLOW-UP.

BOYFRIEND MATERIAL CHECKLIST

1. BE COOL AS A CUCUMBER. ☑

2. GET A GLAM GLOW-UP. ☐

6

COME MONDAY MORNING, I HUNKER DOWN TO PULL TOGETHER
a new look for myself.

My tiny two-story house isn't secretly a Macy's, so when I dig
through my closet and come up with the same old brightly colored hoodies that Mom and I picked out during back-to-school
shopping, I stride into Silvio's room downstairs to see if he left
anything behind that's more neutral. His room is bare, with a
few rumpled shirts in the closet and tattered pants that he was
probably better off getting rid of.

Thirty minutes later, I stare at the getup I've pulled together
in my closet mirror. Silvio's brightly colored patterned dress
shirt with the sleeves rolled up. Green-and-yellow striped tie.
Snug blue jeans. And loafers with polka-dot socks. I wanted to
wear something casual, hence the jeans and rolled-up sleeves,

but also something more formal, hence the button-down and dress tie.

I tilt my head and squint. If I look hard enough, I can see the outfit start to come together, like those paintings Dillon's always talking about, the ones that look like a bunch of random tiny splotches of color until you pull back and see it's actually beautiful water lilies floating on a pond. The more I scrutinize myself, the more I'm not so sure this look is giving beautiful water lilies. Or that it will send my abstract boyfriend-to-be beelining his way through the universe to strike up conversation, hearts in his eyes and red roses in his hands, ready to confess his love.

Plus, there are stains in the shirt's armpits.

I'm afraid my hair isn't much better. Since I started growing it out last winter, it resembles a bird's nest when it isn't tied up—which is why it's usually tied up. I've had a vision for it, where it looks like Timothée Chalamet's hair, a long messy, effortless tussle. Currently, it's giving Wet Mop Flop™. I slicked its center part with an exorbitant amount of gel that's made it stringy. I guess it's better it looks greasy than frizzy. Honestly, I just want to tear it out and rip off this outfit and scream. But this is my year of pushing myself to be boyfriend material while pushing myself to also find a boyfriend. When Mom finally beckons, time's up and this is the best it gets.

Miss Tiramisu gives me a reproving look from her cat bed on the floor and meows.

It's not a good sign when Mom asks me if it's Fashion Faux Pas Day for Spirit Week.

"Nope. Just trying something new."

Once she drops me off at school, my insides writhe, and I'm feeling more exposed than I usually do. It's only a matter of time before someone from the Fierce Five says something about my new look.

Bracing myself, heart racing, I head through the main entrance and swipe my student ID card.

People are looking my way, which is new, but when Katie sees me, she giggles into her hand. Eamon straight-up confronts me on the stairwell.

"Dude, what are you wearing?" he asks with a cackle.

I blanch, suddenly realizing it's not an awesomely daring and stylish look at all. In fact, it clashes horribly. This is what happens when you try and copy TikToks. You come away looking like the janky *Nailed It!* version.

I give a blank stare, forcing myself to act unbothered, but his words make my face turn beet red and my entire body tenses up. Is he right? Do I look odd? Eamon isn't a fashion guru, so maybe it's too avant-garde for his simpler taste in attire?

But by the time it's advisory, I'm wishing I were back to being invisible.

At lunch, I slip into the cafeteria to find my friends at a table. Varsha's easy to spot in her fuzzy, Dalmatian-print bucket hat and pink cheetah-print T-shirt. "Hey, y'all."

Their eyes go wide . . . in judgment. Ouch.

"That bad?" I ask, plunking down. Their expressions are enough to make me sick.

Dillon looks me up and down. "It's a statement."

"I'm trying to be more stylish. As part of my checklist—item number two."

"So *that*'s what this is," Dillon says with a slow nod. "You really don't need a makeover. Maybe sleep on it, and if you're still feeling the same way in the morning, revisit it then?"

"It looks like Leo's already slept on it, though," Varsha says with a grimace.

"Varsha? Worse than Katie Cooper coming back from the Bahamas with cornrows?"

"It's not great," Varsha admits. "I think it's a good checklist item but . . . Leo. You may need some help."

"Amazing! I was hoping you'd say that. What are you two doing after school tomorrow?"

"*Us?!*" Varsha asks. "We aren't exactly fashionistas." She chuckles. "No offense, Dilly."

"None taken."

"But you're all I've got!" I whine. It isn't lost on me that Sergio and Zubin are watching me and chuckling from the gamers' table. I slide lower in my chair.

"I mean, anything has to be better than . . ." Varsha regards my outfit again. "Fine. I'm in."

"Yeah. Me too. Even though I'm no fashionista." He glares at Varsha in mock annoyance before looking back at me. "Makeovers can be fun. To be clear: not that you actually need one."

Varsha's hand shoots out with a hair tie. "But you may want to put your hair up."

I wrangle it into a bun. "Thanks."

"Not for nothing, but I've tried telling you that animal print is *always* in style. Just not real animals, obvi. I mean, take a look at me." She gestures to her pink cheetah-print T-shirt that complements her clipped-in streak of hot-pink hair.

I shudder. "Okay, I'm rethinking asking you for fashion help."

"Yeah, Varsha, I'm not quite sure pink cheetah print qualifies as fashion-forward," Dillon chimes in.

"Thank you, Dillon," I say, dunking one of his french fries into a plastic cup of ketchup we're apparently sharing. Dillon always looks so buttoned up, kind of like he came out of a J.Crew catalog, with his perfectly fitted sweater and its little bit of T-shirt peeping out from underneath; jeans that are not too light and not too dark; and a shoe that isn't a smelly running sneaker or beat-up Converse. Yes, I own dress shoes, but I only really wear them for stuffy dinners or somber events like funerals or that day Dad took us all to court to contest child-support payments and whether Red Bull merits being categorized as a meal. It's a long story. All of this to say, Dillon's style works for *him*, but I'm not so sure it works for *me*.

Still, he has that eye for looking nice.

I nosh on a fry. "Okay. So where are we going to have our fashion show?"

"Why don't we ever go to your place anymore?" Varsha asks me, but I ignore her.

"And you're positive you want to do this?" Dillon reaches for a fry the same time as me.

I snatch it and rap him across the knuckles with it. "Yes," I reply. "Come on. Remember, this is *me* we're talking about. I'm a far cry from your smoldering, serious type." As the words leave my mouth, I glare at Lincoln Chan from across the cafeteria, then sink even lower in my chair.

"Smoldering, serious type?" Dillon feigns a yawn. "Boring."

"I've never been in a real relationship," I remind him.

"*I've* never been in a real relationship," Dillon shoots back.

"Well, nothing's stopping you," I retort.

"Seriously. Sakura is *obsessed* with you," Varsha adds for good measure, nodding in her direction, to where she's seated alongside Lincoln and the rest of Eastfield High Royalty.

"The Sakura-Nakamura-is-obsessed-with-you theory again." Dillon rolls his eyes, then settles a little lower in his chair so that we're almost even. "Yeah, well, still not happening."

My friends were appalled at the Eamon stairwell moment. Every member of the Fierce Five is a bad egg. I still can't believe I ever had hearts in my eyes for two of them.

"*I'd* date you, Dillon." Varsha shakes her salad in its container. "You know, if I wasn't aromantic, and assuming you'd want to date me . . ." She stops shaking. "Did I make it weird?"

"Thanks, Varsha. Not at all." He blushes anyway. "All right, Leo, back to you."

"Okay, great, back to me. Wait. Would *you* date me?" I ask him.

He laughs, face-palming. "Uh, back to you."

"My goodness! I'm worse off than I thought!" I clutch my chest. At the same time, I notice Travis across the cafeteria holding Lincoln's hand. A reminder of the bounty a makeover can bring.

Dillon lets out a heavy sigh. "If this is really what you need to do to get through senior year and find yourself a boyfriend, then

I support you in whatever you decide. Begrudgingly."

I rest a hand on his shoulder. "Aww. Thank you, friend."

"But," he continues, "I'm not happy about it, because you know I know they know we know it's not you, it's all of them, and you just haven't found the right guy who likes you for you."

"Who likes me for me?" My eyebrows rise. "Scrawny, bug-eyed, goofy me-in-salt-water-taffy-pastel-colors me?" I gesture to myself, fighting a laugh. "No one's buying what I'm sellin', folks." Off their irritated looks, I add: "What? It's true!"

"Oh my gosh. Whatever." Dillon swipes another fry. "Shouldn't you get an actual meal?"

Varsha grins. "Makeover tomorrow at Dillon's place, it is!"

As excited as I am about being made over, I feel a twinge of sadness.

After all, I actually deep down like myself.

But what does it matter if no one else does?

The next evening, I'm regarding myself in Dillon's dresser mirror while he and Varsha look on from behind. She's in a sparkly orange headband and sweats, and he's in joggers and a plain T-shirt. One half of my shirt is tucked into a brown braided belt, and there's a neon-pink baseball cap on my head.

Judging from the looks on my friends' faces, I know I've failed. Again.

Varsha shakes her head. "That is *not* it. You want to look like you don't care—not that you've given up on life!"

I toss the baseball cap at her like a Frisbee, and she smacks it to the floor.

Dillon pats a pile of clothes on his bed. "Let's try something more subdued."

"How are guys going to see my 'special' if I'm not putting in effort to exude it?!" I try on khakis and a sweater that ages me about fifty years. A jersey for a sports team—football, maybe? And corduroys with a vest and suspenders that make me look like a newsie.

Varsha holds out Miss Tiramisu's knit frog hat.

I jam it on. "I think we've found our look, folks."

We all laugh.

After trying on a few more outfits, I settle on a plaid shirt and jeans with expensive holes. It's not bad. But I wouldn't go as far as saying it looks nice, either.

"On to hair?" Varsha unties my bun, and my hair loosely maintains its shape—looking as if an industrial fan were blowing at me head-on, sending my hair flying out straight behind me.

We all regard it in a moment of silence.

"On to hair!" I say with forced enthusiasm.

They help me wash it in the kitchen sink, then Varsha blow-dries it to a crisp, and Dillon takes her straightening iron to it after admitting he's always wanted to use one of those things.

How reassuring.

Some strands are definitely still wet judging by the sizzling steam coming off the iron.

"All right! The big reveal!" Varsha says twenty minutes later in the bathroom.

Dillon moves my hands away from my eyes. "And, open."

In the mirror, I find a literal scarecrow staring back at me, my hair pin-straight, long, and poking every which way, the plaid shirt not fitting quite right. All I'm missing is an old straw hat. Varsha and Dillon know it too, judging by their expressions.

"Well, I appreciate the effort, but I'm not sure the Vincents of the world would approve."

Varsha looks me up and down. "Maybe you should ask for *his* fashion help."

I laugh. "Who? *Vincent?*"

Varsha shrugs. "If he's the be-all, end-all of fashion, why not go straight to the source?"

"Me, asking a past crush who's made a habit of ignoring me and pretending I don't exist?" I blow out a stream of air, sending my flat hair fluttering.

"Let's not forget he acknowledged you the other day," Varsha says.

Dillon scrunches up his face. "Yeah, I'm with Leo on this one." He rests a hand on my shoulder. "You really want to reach out to a past crush asking him for help? That seems dicey."

"Right?! What if Vincent rejects me again? I can't handle that right now!"

"Hear me out." Varsha leans against the sink. "You just got Vincent to notice you with your Cool as a Cucumber act. Maybe now he'll take you seriously."

She has a point. "So I should just, what? Ask him at work? How do I say it?"

"Text him that you want his help giving you a makeover," Varsha insists.

"I can't just out of the blue ask him that. It's going to seem so random! Plus, he gave me his phone number at work under the condition that I'd only text him about important things."

Varsha crosses her arms. "This *is* important."

"Important *work* things," I amend.

"From how you've described him," Dillon says, "I don't think Vincent would view *anything* work-related as important."

My jaw goes slack. "Did he say that because he never wanted me to text him at all?!"

Varsha glares at Dillon. "Not helping the plan," she mutters. "I say text him, Leo."

My stomach pangs at the idea of Vincent denying me yet again, and asking him for a makeover seems antithetical to my no-more-trying-hard rule I've been implementing.

But, Leo, the checklist.

I groan, looking to Varsha. "Ugh. Fine. I'll do it." I start to scroll through my phone.

Varsha peers over my shoulder. "Umm, why does his name have a heart emoji?"

"No reason," I say with a sheepish smile.

"It's a miracle you never blew up his phone like you did with Speedo," Dillon remarks.

"You're tellin' me!" I pull up the first—and also last—text to him from May, which was just my name. After the NTB (no text back), Varsha and Dillon both threatened to delete his number off my phone when I was tempted to double, triple, and quadruple text him in hopes of starting a conversation. It really is a miracle I never did and left it at: Hey, it's Leo Martino!

Employing my Cool as a Cucumber method, I go to send

a casual text—with no punctuation. Apparently, exclamation points are a dead giveaway of a try-hard. And a simple emoji? 😊 Forget it! ☹ But I find myself frozen, staring at the keypad.

Finally, Varsha takes my phone. "Here. I'll do it."

Leo: Hey wanna give me a makeover

Dillon bites his bottom lip. "You don't think it's a little bit of a jump scare?"

"I mean, it is. But we're scientists collecting data!" My eyebrows dance as I take back my phone. "Now we wait. Cool as a cucumber." No sooner are the words out of my mouth when the three tiny gray bubbles appear underneath the text to him. "HE'S TYPING!" I hold my breath, white-knuckling my phone. "Please say yes," I whisper. "Please say YES!"

The bubbles vanish—along with all hope.

"Where'd he go?!" I scream.

"Is everything okay?" Dillon's mom's voice floats down from her lofted bedroom above.

"Yes, Mom," Dillon calls.

"Sorry," I whisper to him.

"He'll reply." Dillon checks his Apple watch. "Let's start on our homework."

In his living room with its tall ceiling and skylight giving us a view of pitch-black night, we spread out our homework on the low coffee table. Dillon brings out a bowl of Cheez-Its.

"I brought you guys a little something from the teahouse." From my backpack, I hand a plastic tub of almond cookies to

Varsha and a container of linzer tortes to Dillon. "Your faves."

Dillon sinks in his teeth and moans. He loves any dessert with fruit. I've yet to convince him chocolate desserts win out over fruity ones. It's one of our longest-running friendship wars.

"Think you can bring anything in from the teahouse for my bake sale?" Varsha asks.

"Sure. Judy always has extra stuff."

Varsha nibbles into a cookie, and her eyes light up. "These are good!"

"Just a little something for putting up with me. I know I'm a lot."

"You are not 'a lot.'" Dillon licks powdered sugar off his fingertips.

I arch an eyebrow and gesture at my lackluster outfit. "I rest my case. Plus, I mean, don't forget the egregiously long audio notes I leave for you that you've responded to point for point."

"True. Please never leave a ten-minute voice note for us again," Dillon says.

"See? I'm a lot. Point proven."

"We put up with you because that's what friends do, obvi," Varsha throws in.

"Yeah, totally," Dillon says. "You put up with me when I had a meltdown for a month straight after my painting didn't get accepted into that one exhibition at the Capitol Rotunda."

"I curse its name!" I yell.

"And you put up with me when I got the flu and was demanding company," Varsha says.

"Who knew forcing me to watch every animal attack movie would make me a stan?"

Varsha grins. "Wasn't *The Shallows* so good, though?"

"That adorable seagull stole the show. I loved him!"

It's true . . . the things some may consider a lot are just right with the right hearts. Dillon has a thing about making sure peanut butter coats the entire slice of bread, and Varsha has to put both sugar and salt on her popcorn, and I love them for it.

Once our snack break is over, we get back to our homework. My friends get lost in their textbooks and notebooks, filling the air with sounds of highlighter strokes and pen scribbles, but I'm having a harder time focusing on academics right now from where I'm perched on the couch. I sidle into a squashy pillow and puffy quilt, and stare at a gigantic painting of a graveyard on a grassy knoll—his mom painted it. She paints graveyards and cows. It's her thing. He gets his artistic abilities from her. My sights wander to the candles lining the mantel. I always love how cozy it is here, though it's putting me in the mood to nap. I get back to my Economics Government homework. At least for about one minute, when I check my phone again.

"Stop checking," Varsha says without looking up from her Calc textbook.

I groan and turn my phone face down on the coffee table, then shove it away.

"And stop clicking your pen," she adds. "Please."

"Sorry," I whisper into the pages of my boring Econ Gov textbook.

My phone dings. I scream and lurch for it.

"Everything okay?" Mrs. Noble calls down.

"Yes, Mom." Dillon buries his head in his hands.

"What did he say?" Varsha asks, looking like she'd rather get back to her homework.

Silvio: Hey u with mom? Tried calling and she didn't pick up

I roll my eyes. "Just my brother."

Leo: No. Why? All OK?

Silvio: Yeah. Dad called. He was going on and on and saying terrible things about her

Why is Dad always the one trying to brainwash us against Mom? Ironic. And why is he trying to reach out right now? I don't like it. He must want something. Maybe he's trying to extract information from Silvio that he can use against Mom in court.

Leo: Tell him you don't want to hear it!

Silvio: I try that all the time. He just keeps going

Leo: She's still at work. Don't tell her about the Dad thing. It'll only upset her

Silvio: K

Dillon catches my eye. "You okay?"

I freeze. I hadn't realized he'd been watching me, and my features definitely tensed up while texting. I shake off thoughts of Dad, which I'm good at, and smile. "Just family stuff."

He nods and doesn't push the topic, much to my relief.

By the time our homework is done and Mrs. Noble starts

frying chicken, it's Varsha's and my cue to go home to our own meals. Sleepy, I zip up my backpack and trudge to the door.

"Well, we tried." Dillon gives a sympathetic look, casting his gaze over my ensemble.

"Yeah. Thanks for your help, guys. I'm sure we'll come up with a good look eventually," I say in a sullen voice, then offer a grateful smile. I hug Dillon. "Bye, Dill Pickle. Thanks for having us."

Varsha hugs him, too. "Bye, Dilly."

I reach for the door handle when—

My phone buzzes.

Probably just Silvio again.

I will my scurrying heartbeat to slow.

But with my friends staring at me, egging me on, I open my texts. "HE REPLIED!"

"What he say?!" Varsha and Dillon ask in unison, squeezing in on either side.

I show them the screen. "He gave my text a thumbs-up—a *glorious* thumbs-up!"

Next thing I know, we're all screaming and jumping up and down.

"Talk about not trying hard, though," I stop to mutter. "A thumbs-up on a text is as little effort as humanly possible."

"Everything okay?" Mrs. Noble's voice calls out from the kitchen.

Dillon cackles. "Yes, Mom!"

"You guys!" I whisper, gripping their shoulders and grinning. "Trust the process! It's working!"

So, Vincent is going to give me a makeover. A *real* one.
Let's just hope I can pull it off—and that it feels right.
Glam glow-up, here I come.
Hang tight, Boyfriend!

THE NEXT DAY AFTER SCHOOL, I SHOW UP TO A MANSION
on Windmere Drive, located in an exclusive neighborhood.

I wait on the brick stoop of the house—huge and impos-
ing, with its steely-gray walls and forest-green shutters. Not
to mention its long gravel driveway cutting through the gigantic manicured lawn. It smells like fresh grass and even fresher
manure, and is just the sort of lavish place that I imagined Vincent would live as a private school student with style-icon status.

When no one comes, I use the lion-faced brass knocker again.
My beat-up sneakers idly stomp a few crispy orange leaves, the
first of the season to fall. Never in a million years would I have
ever imagined being here—in all senses. I'm still shocked that
Vincent agreed to help. He's not exactly the giving type.

The tall green door opens, startling me.

"Mr. Martino," says a man in a chef's hat. "Mr. O'Connor is expecting you."

Inside the exquisite mansion, a chandelier sparkles and a massive vase of lilacs rests on a mirrored table. The man, who must be a personal chef, leads me up a winding dual staircase onto the second floor and down a plush carpeted hallway. Life in the suburbs is worlds different from home. Though I wonder if things with Vincent's family are as messed up as they are with mine, and why he works at all, if he comes from such opulence. If I had to guess, Vincent's rich parents forced him to work at the teahouse to prove to them that he's "responsible."

The portraits in the hall show Vincent with his mom and dad. They're all smiles, from the days of Vincent as a little ruddy-faced tyke to a modern-day stylish Vincent, each iteration growing noticeably more fashionable, with the latest wearing a beret and a swoop-neck sweater. Seeing his family still all together sends a twinge of jealousy through me.

"Leo. Come on in." Vincent is seated cross-legged on a rich purple velvet armchair beside palm fronds sprouting out from a large urn. He holds a glossy magazine, and I can see his short nails are purple, which complement his violet pants, indigo blouse, and plum slippers. Pop music plays from his laptop. And an essential oil diffuser spits out wisps of smoke, filling my nostrils with the comforting scent of lavender. But it does little to calm my fear of him insulting my style again—or saying I'm hopeless and kicking me out. I can't handle another slammed door, another rejection.

"Make yourself at home." He lets out a soft hum. "Scratch

that. I don't want you leaving your things everywhere. And take off your shoes. Also, why are you still wearing your work clothes?" He studies my all-black ensemble for another beat, recycled from school picture day. I figured it was the least offensive look I could assemble.

He grimaces. "Oh, dear. This is what you wear outside of work too, isn't it?"

I give a little laugh. "Hence why I'm here," I say in singsong, kicking off my shoes and leaving my backpack by the door, all while contemplating how this is probably the most he's ever said to me. And he's noticed what I've worn to work?!

"So, what's the tea, sis? Why do you want a makeover, anyway?" he asks tartly.

"Well, I made this checklist and want to try and get my first-ever—" I force myself to stop in the name of all that is Uncool. My excitement and anxiety are already getting the better of me.

"I just want to explore my style and try on a new look this year, that's all. One that's naturally flawless and stuff." I leave out the part that's he's partially the reason why I'm seeking a new look, with his feedback from a few months ago.

Vincent shoots an eyebrow up. "So, *that* would explain the change in demeanor."

"I hope that's a good thing?" I ask with a sheepish laugh. Although it's only been a few days, I guess people really *are* noticing my newfound Cool as a Cucumber attitude.

"I think the best makeovers start inside us."

Wow. Profound coming from Vincent.

He gestures to his vanity with its bulbed mirror. "I got a whole bunch of stuff ready. So, we can definitely give you a new look. You *were* thinking a full makeover, weren't you?"

"A full makeover?"

"You know," Vincent presses on, "new wardrobe, haircut—"

"Haircut?" I blurt. "Sorry, it's just that I wasn't prepared for a haircut."

I need to get a grip, even though something bristles inside me. My inner Leo wants to jump for joy that I'm having this Cool Alone Time with Vincent at his amazing place. But I am slightly terrified.

"Umm, yes, my love. The haircut. Along with the makeup." He gestures to a box opened with ascending shelves like some sort of miniature staircase laden with brushes, blushes, and creams. "Anyone who's anyone wears makeup," he continues, "even if you can't tell that they're wearing it, to give them that polished look. And trust me, we're going to want to polish you up. No offense."

"That sounds good," I say, finding it increasingly difficult to take no offense.

"Great." He sets down his magazine in its rack. "So, what's our budget?"

"Uh, well, I thought that might come up, so . . ." I reach into my pocket and pull out a handful of lint and a wad of cash— money I saved up from over the summer.

Vincent clocks the lint and grimaces in disgust, but takes the money anyway. "Okay." He counts it. "So, we'll have to do all of this at a bargain rate. Not a problem. Like I said, I'm prepared."

He pockets the money and grins. "I have turned paupers into princes."

"You have?" I ask, smiling. How many people have come to him for a makeover, anyway?

"I was referring to myself. You didn't think I always looked this glamorous, did you?" He gestures from a framed photo of a freckled little kid with a frizzy bowl cut and suspenders to his current self with his dewy freckle-free face and styled red hair that's short on the sides with longer, tousled pieces on top. "To look this good takes effort. And a lot of laser hair removal, which you don't need to worry about because you probably couldn't afford it. No offense."

"None taken." I swallow hard, studying his plush carpet. "Thanks for agreeing to help," I add, trying not to sound *too* thankful in the continued spirit of coolness. So far, I think I've been chill. Yes, Vincent's big personality brings out the shy guy in me, but while I feel myself freezing up, at least it's coming across as Cool as a Cucumber rather than Eager as a Beaver.

"See? I'm not just good looks. I'm also charitable, and this is going toward a good cause. Besides, the thing about a full make-over is that it's as much a gift for you as it is for me. I'm the one who has to see you on the regular." He grins, claps his hands, and stands. "Let's begin!"

Despite his harsh approach, I know he means well. And I'm ready.

I sit in a chair with newspaper spread out around it.

"A full makeover is all about exploring a different side of you. First, let's see what we're working with." Vincent sizes me up in the vanity mirror, then fixes me with a sympathetic smile. "If it wasn't clear from my reaction a few moments ago, your outfit is giving crypt keeper. Your hair is giving mop. And it's obvious those eyebrows have never once been laminated."

Focusing on how he may have a point helps the hurt of his words subside. *"Laminated?"*

"Oh, calm down," he commands. "So, very important, if not *the* most important question: Who do you want to be? How do you envision your style? Fem? Masc? Neither? Any comps?"

"Hmm." I bite my lip, realizing I should have given this part some deeper thought. I'm far from masculine, but I'm not exactly feminine, either. I'm kind of my own gender, and possibly my own species, and I'm not sure I could pull off anything other than just Leo.

"I mean, I could always surprise you," he offers.

My heart begins to race. "As long as we don't do anything too—"

"Attractive?" Vincent raises a sarcastic eyebrow.

"*Extreme*. I'm just not that kind of a person."

"And how's that working out for you, sweetcakes?" Vincent takes my hair out of its topknot, and it explodes in every direction, making him leap back.

I let out a little chuckle in embarrassment. "Hence why I'm here, remember?"

"I mean, this in-between growing-out-your-hair look where you wear it in a high bun? No, no, no, no, no. It's not doing you *any* favors. You don't have a forehead—you have what we call a *five*-head. We need to hide said five-head while not dragging down your long face any longer." He pulls the hair down on either side of my cheeks, causing me to cringe at how horselike it makes my face. "We need to make you look the best that you can. Hence why you're here, right?"

My eyes dart, my heart protesting in my chest. I have the urge to call the whole thing off, to tell him that I'm fine with how I look and that I don't want to change. Maybe looking like a vampire from the year 1865 is attractive in its own special way that I just never appreciated before.

But I think of that feeling of rejection, and how much I want love from a future boyfriend, and combat the conflicted, messy feelings making me want to flee in frustrated tears. This makeover is a step forward in the name of love. I think of the checklist.

Trust the process . . .

"Right." I smile, releasing a puff of air.

"So? What'll it be?"

"Something like this?" I turn my phone to show him Timo-thée Chalamet.

"Hon, I'm good, but I'm not a miracle worker. We gotta work with what we've got." He moves the hair around on top of my head, further assessing it. "You have nice eyes," he admits.

"I *do*?" I let out a sigh. It helps me relax—a little. "I want to enter a room and turn heads."

"Okay. If you want to turn the *right* heads, you have to *be* that person yourself. If you want sporty, be sporty. If you want glam, be glam. Get it? Embody who you're attracted to."

He must be able to read my puzzled expression, because he

keeps talking. "If there's one thing I've learned about the gay dating world, it's that gaymers like other gaymers. Jocks like other jocks. And so on and so forth. Not being any of those things has likely put you at a *serious* disadvantage. Is there one person, maybe at your school, who makes you stop to pay attention?"

For some irritating reason, Lincoln Chan springs to mind, followed by the slew of others. "I think a lot of people make my head turn," I admit, feeling myself blush at the confession. Little does he know he's one of them. "I don't think it's just one look I can copy and paste."

Vincent blinks. "I don't have all day, hon. There's a *RuPaul* episode waiting for me."

"I want to look so different from how I usually do, that I won't even recognize myself." I've never admitted that aloud. "I want to look like a handsome hottie. But pretty, too."

Vincent cocks his head. "So, like me?"

The blush returns. "No—I mean, yes—kind of?"

"'Handsome pretty hottie who turns heads,' coming right up." He smiles. "Before we get started, give me your phone. I'm taking a 'before' video." He aims my phone at me. "We want to show people the old you before we show them the new you. So, do whatever the old you would do. In three . . . two . . . one."

The old me? I think about the beaming try-hard who's still in here and let him out, grinning and waving to the camera, feeling my eyebrows skyrocket before I let out an excited dolphin squeal. "Hi!"

"Hoo-boy." Vincent sets aside my phone then runs his fingers through my hair again, sending me tingling. "When in doubt, go short and blond. I have all the things ready for us."

I gawk, any relaxing vibes shot. *Me? Blond?*

Coming from Vincent with his natural red hair. At least I *think* it's a natural red. I'm starting to question everything. His hair is gelled up and combed sideways into a swooping sheen of perfection, held in place as if by gravity-defying physics. Why hasn't he done anything that drastic to *his* hair?

He catches my expression. "Trust the process," he says in singsong.

Trust the process. Right.

"Okay. I'm all yours."

And with that, he gets to work. After tucking a towel into the collar of my T-shirt and tying an apron around my neck, he takes a spray bottle to my hair, dampening it to comb it out.

He clips and snips; I squeeze my eyes shut as I mourn each piece that falls. All those months of growing it out were for naught. No. For *this*. I can trust Vincent. He knows what he's doing.

"Where did you learn how to cut hair?"

"Shh! I can't talk and cut at the same time."

Well, *that's* a bad sign.

As he uses a buzzer by my ear, I try peeking in the mirror.

"Nope!" He moves around to block my view. Then he snaps dozens of clips in my hair, along with tiny sheets of aluminum foil. Wearing gloves, he brushes a blue-white paste onto various portions of my hair, then tucks them into the foil sheets. Brush and tuck and repeat.

"This reminds me of the time I went platinum for Halloween," he says. "I was Ken."

Halloween gets me thinking. "Going pumpkin picking this year?"

He lifts an eyebrow. "It's not really my thing."

"It's not? Not even a little bit?" I ask, unable to stop myself from going there.

He gives me a blank stare. "Should it be?"

"You really don't remember? Our dads took us pumpkin picking two years go."

He gives me a blank look then continues to paint on the goo. But I catch something in his eyes that tells me he remembers. Maybe this is *his* way of not coming across like a try-hard himself.

When he pulls off the foil, I catch a glimpse in the mirror. It looks like the top of my head is slathered entirely in gunky toothpaste. *Trust the process, Leo. Trust the process. Do not panic!*

I'm totally panicking. As we wait for the dye to take, he switches from the pop music to an episode of *RuPaul's Drag Race*, then takes a file to my nails to sand down any jagged edges.

"You can tell everything about a person just by looking at their nails."

A man with salt-and-pepper hair pokes his head into the doorway. He's in a bulky white cardigan and has on a pair of tortoiseshell reading glasses. "Hey, boys. Good to see you again, Leo!" His smile feels like a dagger, reminding me of Dad and how he used to look more like Vincent's dad before his transformation into Motorcycle Dad.

"You too," I say.

"Vincent, you may want to crack a window in here. It smells

like chemicals."

Vincent rolls his eyes. "Thanks, Dad. Will do."

"Excellent." Mr. O'Connor beams and his sights sweep back to me. "Leo, how's your dad doing? I haven't heard from him in a while. He doing okay? I heard he started a rock band."

My insides prickle as I grapple with how to answer. I don't want to admit the truth—that Dad is a monster who left us for a new life with a girl practically my age. It's far too embarrassing. I want Mr. O'Connor to think of us as how we used to be, just like Dillon and Varsha do.

"He's good. Better than ever," I say, and it's not entirely a lie. "Yeah, I think he's in a band now." It's too humiliating to reveal more details.

Mr. O'Connor studies me, smile unwavering. "Wonderful. I hope he'll like the brand-new look Vincent's giving you," he says before ducking out.

Thoughts of my dad swirl in my head, and I'm suddenly wondering if my transformation is a good idea after all. I mean, Dad transformed, and not for the better. Maybe I'm fine the way I was? Is it too late to turn back, for either of us?

Not wanting to dwell on the matter, I shift gears and shoot Vincent a teasing look. "Seems like *your dad* remembers me from pumpkin picking."

Vincent squints, head tilted. "Your dad's in a rock band? He seemed so vanilla."

"Aha! I knew you remembered." Then I register his question and feel my light dim. "Yeah, he is," I say. "I mean, I haven't spoken to him in a while, and he's not the best dad in the world, but—" I force myself to stop talking. Only a try-hard would trauma dump on someone.

Vincent blinks, then continues filing my nails. I'm glad he doesn't care to know more.

We break for pesto and goat cheese flatbread, then get back to watching *RuPaul*. One hour becomes two. Two become three. The daylight in Vincent's bedroom fades. Eventually, after he washes my hair in his bathroom sink and blow-dries it, he fine-tunes my haircut, then steps back to admire his work.

"Okay. Want to see?"

"I'm terrified," I admit, heart racing. "But yes."

"Too bad. You have to wait." He sticks out his tongue. "Ready for the nostril waxing?"

"The *what*—?"

He grimaces, pointing to my nose. "No one wants to see hair poking out of there."

I reach up and graze my nostrils. "Can't I use scissors or something?"

"Scissors? See, this is why I'm the expert here."

Within moments, he applies globs of hot wax on Popsicle sticks into each nostril, then rips them out, taking any hair with them. He goes from nostrils to eyebrows, starting by shining his phone flashlight at my face. His fingers trace over my eyebrows as he murmurs to himself.

"Everything okay?" I ask.

"This might take some time." He views me through a TikTok filter on his phone, one that he says shows anatomical lines to help guide him on how to shape the brows. It stings with each yank, especially when the sticky strips pull the hair out just above my eyelid, which makes my eyes water. But I clench my fists and grit my teeth. Then he puts glop on each brow and brushes them up before snipping the long stray hairs coming off the top. He uses a razor for cleanup. Once that's over, he sticks a mask under each eye while we wait ten minutes for a blackhead-removing strip to harden on my nose.

"This seems a little . . ." I trail off, then we speak at the same time.

"Necessary?"

"Excessive?"

He pauses, pinching an edge of the nose strip to give me a patronizing look.

I avert my eyes. "As you were," I whisper, and let him finish tearing off the strip.

"There," Vincent says dogmatically. "The worst is behind you."

He proceeds to talk me through a full skin-care routine, teaching me the importance of cleansers, toners, sunscreen, moisturizer, and undereye cream. And to think I used to just wash my face with soap and water! My only other skin care was the expensive moisturizer I'd steal fingerfuls of from my brother over the years without him noticing, along with his fancy cologne (that one was harder to keep secret).

Vincent walks me through a makeup regimen that will have me looking like a "glazed donut." After blotting sponges, tickling brushes, and aromatic powders, he announces my polished makeup look is complete. He finishes it off with strawberry-scented setting spray.

I smack my lips. "Tastes good!"

"I'm not sure that's edible."

In the walk-in closet, he's draped the mirror with a few bathrobes to keep my look under wraps.

"Wow, this is a lot of clothing."

"Yeah, well, you have to keep up with the times." He gives me a tight smile. "And we need to bring some color to your palette. Oh, but not too much color. Stay away from white, yellow, beige, and pink. With your skin tone, those colors are *not* your friends."

The next forty-five minutes are a dizzying array of trying on garment after garment. Everything from a jean jacket ("The correct term is 'chambray'") to shirts with ruffles, cable-knit turtleneck sweaters, and sweatshirts paired with overalls with one of the straps undone.

Everything is oversize, despite Vincent stressing the importance of simplicity and a good fit. Everything is making me feel super tiny, because unlike Vincent, who's tall and lean, I'm more short and squat, and all this oversize clothing feels ridiculous on me, like I'm a child swimming in adult clothing. Each item is met with either a yay or a nay. Mostly nays, though.

"Who knew my color is forest green?!"

He strangles me with a thin scarf. "Watch your makeup."

"Are you sure I don't look like Oliver Twist?"

He hands me a green flannel shirt. "Try this on for size."

I button myself into the shirt.

"Never mind. You look like that one rancher prince from

Montana."

"Who?"

"No one. Here try this." He dumps more clothing in my arms, like lacy shirts with ruffles off the shoulder. Floral button-downs and cardigans. And fleece jackets and slick bomber jackets.

I try on a few combinations until he rests his hands on my shoulders.

"That's it. It's trendy. It's fresh. It's today," he says at last, clucking in approval. "Handsome pretty hottie. But try not to let the clothes wear you."

I have on a forest-green crop top with wide green corduroy pants and a pair of sneakers that are so white, they hurt my eyes. The pants are short, exposing long black socks. Atop it all, there's an oversize button-down short-sleeve shirt. My midriff is on full display above a belt with a sleek silver buckle.

"Your look is complete." Vincent reaches up toward the bathrobes hanging over the closet mirror. "You wanted unrecognizable? Here you go. Bam!" He rips down the bathrobes.

I gaze at two impeccably arched eyebrows. I never knew they needed waxing, but they now look like two distinct entities versus the fuzzy natural shape they once were. They make my chocolate-brown eyes more pronounced, and I'm no longer staring into the eyes of a bullfrog.

Seriously—no *wonder* no one's wanted me! Could it have been my eyebrows alone that deterred them? The skin-care products and makeup give my face a healthy glow while hiding any imperfections, with not a blemish or blackhead or dark undereye. And then there's my hair. Not only has my hair been shorn off, but it's also been dyed a pearlescent white. At the top, it's spiky in parts, then curls in a soft wave above my forehead. It's all a lot to take in—I look like a different person.

Is this the real me?

Vincent flashes a smug smile. "You look *snatched*."

"Hello, Handsome Pretty Hottie." I run my fingers down my cheek.

"Don't touch your face." Vincent winks. "I told you I'm good."

This new look is certainly going to turn heads. Maybe I *should* trust the process. Maybe all this time I've spent agonizing over my old hair "style"—if I can call it that—was in vain, when all along I needed something drastic. I wonder what Dillon would think about my appearance. Probably that I looked better as I was with my natural brown hair, like something Mom would say. Varsha would think it's a good idea to try something new in hopes of yielding a different outcome. And I agree—I'm glad I took the risk. But it's still peculiar not recognizing myself.

"I like it," I reiterate, more confident this time. For some reason, I'm thinking about Lincoln Chan again, and wondering if he went through a similar process, and how it made *him* feel.

"I think you look good," Vincent says.

I run my tongue over my teeth and wink at my reflection, trying it out.

Vincent blinks. "Never do that again."

He uses my phone to record the "after" video for my TikTok, and I strike a fierce pose, working overtime to keep my face relaxed. Then he edits the video together set to Doja Cat's "Need to Know." In the video, I go from Old Leo to New Leo, aka Handsome Pretty Hottie.

"Aah, this is so awesome!"

Vincent rubs his ear closest to me, staring daggers.

"Sorry," I say, quieter.

He saves the video in my drafts folder. "Post it first thing in the a.m."

"Okay." I study my new hair in the vanity mirror again.

"You know," he says, "I can see the change in you already."

"You can? Even though it's been, like, five minutes?"

"Yeah." Vincent gives a genuine smile. "The most important thing to looking attractive is protecting your energy. Walk around like you're wearing armor. People can't put a dent in you no matter what they do. Got it?"

"That's genius."

He purses his glossy lips. "You know, I accept tips on Venmo."

I laugh. Of course, Venmo makes me think of Lincoln, and I stop laughing.

"Okay, so, you have homework. Practice better posture and smiling with your eyes." Vincent's sights land on my hands. He digs in his pants pocket, pulls out the linty wad of cash I'd given him, and slaps it on my palm. "And spend it on a proper mani-pedi," he says. "While your bleach was setting, I scheduled an appointment. It's tomorrow evening at Patty's Nails."

"Thanks." I pocket the money, curious how much more finessing my nails require.

"And drink lots of water if you want that skin to glow," he adds.

"Lots of water." I nod. "Nails. Smiling with my eyes. Got it."

He hands me a parting bag full of samples—pots for clay masks and tubes of caffeine cream to reduce my undereye puffiness. I notice he included whitening strips.

I gasp. "Do I have yellow teeth?"

He dons a patronizing smile. "Most people do."

Yikes.

"Lastly, clothing. I know you're pressed for money, so here's a little tip: Buy and return clothes. Just don't stain anything. I've seen you pour tea. You don't have the steadiest hand."

My eyes widen. *"Buy and return clothes?* You can *do* that?"

"You did *not* just ask me that." Vincent smirks. He steps closer to me until we're face-to-face, and my palms turn sweaty. "You look so good."

I look away, then back into his eyes. "Thanks for taking the time to help me."

He scans me from head to toe. "Worth it." His mouth quirks in thought. "And fun."

I bite my lip. "It was, wasn't it?"

"Who's this makeover all for, anyway?"

"No one," I say, my heart thumping. I hope the blush is hiding my blush.

Vincent laughs. "With the way you look now, they're about to be a someone."

"LEO, LET'S GO!" MOM CROAKS FROM THE BOTTOM OF THE
stairs the next morning.

In the narrow mirror stuck to my closet door, New Leo in
full hair and makeup gives a quizzical look at the green ensemble. When Vincent had chosen it for me, I thought the outfit
was amazing, but seeing it now, I'm questioning whether I can
pull it off. My insides flutter with fear at the thought of revealing my new look to all of Eastfield High.

Trust the process, right?

Taking a deep breath, I carry out posting the before/after
video to TikTok (check), then close out the app, not wanting to
obsess over who's viewed it, even if I *do* only have a few followers.

I glug down a cup of tap water and take a steeling breath.

Downstairs, the whole house is quiet. But the thoughts in
my head are loud. What are people at school going to think of

my new look? What are my ex-crushes going to think? Are they going to laugh? Or ask me out on a date?

I stop at the framed family photo propped up by the front door. Two boys huddle between their beaming parents against a clean white backdrop. Their eyes are bright. I don't recognize us even though we're only a few years younger. Mom must be moving things around the house, like usual.

Giving myself one last look in the hall mirror, I no longer see eyes trapped within dark, discolored lids or a mess of hair. I appear well rested and dewy, like I'm ready for a red carpet.

Mom honks the horn. What is she going to think of my new look?

I sling my backpack over my shoulder, then open the door and head down the steps to the car fuming in the driveway.

Mom pulls away from our tiny two-story home, staring straight ahead. She looks nice in her suit—it reminds me of the one she wears to a majority of the divorce hearings, where Dad contests every single possession and fights everything to make reaching a settlement impossible. Silvio and I even had to take the stand to prove child-support money was going to food (aka the Red Bull Incident). Dad doesn't want to pay child support, *pendente lite* (which is *not* a pasta dish), and now he's trying to get out of paying for Silvio and me to go to college, despite having the amount saved up for that very purpose since we were young.

During the separation, Mom studied and passed her licensing exam, which she'd put off doing since I was born. Now, she practices as a psychologist and even makes time to volunteer at bereavement support groups at our local hospital. I think by giving back, she was able to start her own healing. And I think she's doing great. Or at least better.

I tell Mom she has Pepto Bismol smeared on the side of her mouth, and she wipes it away. Her face is blanched like she has the flu, tipping me off to her hangover. Sometimes, she starts thinking about Dad and how much he hurt her, resulting in a sleepless night of wine and tears. Maybe he set it off by reaching out to her again about something, like when he texted her demanding the vintage toy train set from his childhood that he'd accidentally left in the attic. I wonder if that's why he was contacting Silvio. I'm just glad Mom's trying-to-look-young phase is over, which took up a majority of the year and involved lots of clip-in ponytails and press-on acrylic nails.

She smiles vacantly. "Do you have everything you need for school?"

"I do." My voice cracks. I wonder if she's going to acknowledge my new look.

"Great!" Mom says, keeping her sights trained ahead.

I stare at the road. The hood of the car devours rushing gray pavement.

My heart drums against my rib cage.

I imagine it as something that wants to be free of my body, the way it hammers.

I fumble with the car lock. "Have you heard from Silvio?"

Mom shudders then composes herself. "Yes. He told me Philth was bad-mouthing me again." Hearing his nickname makes me wince. The passing of time has helped dull the edges of the bad memories with Dad, like the time he spit in my face so hard that his gum stuck to my cheek, but sometimes, the memories are still sharp enough to cut.

"It's okay. That's just what he does," she adds in a quiet voice.

I shoot her a sympathetic smile. "Sorry, Mom."

She brightens. "Anyway, you look very nice today!"

So, she *has* noticed. "Thanks." I wish she had more to say on the new look, but a part of me is glad there isn't some big fuss over it. In the past, she's been pretty conservative about gay stuff, and I used to be able to quote her on how just because someone's gay doesn't mean they need to broadcast it to the world. ("I mean, straight people aren't going around telling everyone they're straight!") Even then, I knew she meant well. Since, she's come around to full love and acceptance, but her greatest fear is still for haters in the world to hurt me simply for being gay.

We don't have time for me to snatch up iced coffees for Dillon, Varsha, and me, since I was running late, so I spend the rest of the drive practicing smiling with my eyes on Snapchat. I also practice an actual *smile* smile. Not a needy smile. A "cool" smile. I send a selfie to Dillon and Varsha—a sneak peek without spoiling the surprise. They've been hounding me all morning wanting to see.

Dillon: Looks good! Love the filter.

Leo: It's not a filter!!!! 🙄

Varsha: !!!!!

Varsha: Remember my bake sale is today! Did you bring the goods?

Leo: Yep! There will be more than one new snack at the table... 😏

I'm meeting them during our lunch period to help Varsha set up for her bake sale fund raiser for E.R.A.S.E.—aka End Racism and Sexism Everywhere. I promised I would sit with her and be the cashier. My backpack's stuffed with chocolate chip biscotti, courtesy of Judy.

Mom pulls up to Eastfield High and gives me a few short pats on the back. "Love you." Her breath reeks of sour stomach. The kind she gets after a night of drinking too much and not eating from stress.

I angle my head away. "You too." The "I" and the "love" get caught in my throat. Just like how my family was never one for hugs, we're also apparently incapable of stringing the "I," the "love," and the "you" together in one nice clean normal sentence. Even me, Leo who loves love. Although Dad has only been gone for six months, the phrase is practically a forgotten relic.

But I do love Mom. I love her so much I could cry—except not right now because it would ruin my makeup.

Ducking my head, I scuttle into school, feeling the confidence I'd mustered start to dwindle.

Walk around like you're wearing armor . . .

I hasten my steps to first-period Calc. Other students look my way, but seemingly more out of curiosity, like "Who's this new guy?"—versus "Wow, Leo looks famous!"

I steer myself into class and remember to sit toward the back of the class instead of my usual front-row seat. Instead of hiding behind my phone to watch videos of sea otters holding hands, or hiding behind my copy of *Mice of Flame and Paw*, I lean back in my chair and gaze just above the chalkboard like I'm bored.

People flit around, continuing to chat and take their seats, but I act too tired to notice. Inside, though, I feel like the floor could drop out at any moment.

People can't put a dent in you no matter what they do . . .

In my periphery, I catch Lincoln across the aisle. He's in a light blue jersey, and the whiff of his Fierce by Abercrombie cologne wafts my way like an aromatic siren call. My first ex-crush sighting of the day. Ugh. Why'd it have to be him?

Don't look at me. Please don't look at me.

I chance peeking over at him, forcing my expression to remain neutral. As if I'm wondering where Ms. Domingo is and Lincoln just *happens* to be in my line of sight.

His quizzical expression turns to one of boredom. The opposite of the cute mischievous smile he used to give me back in the day when we'd watch movies at his place and talk about our favorite parts for hours. The one he flashed at me after the bed-sheet hanging off his top bunk caught on fire from the lamp on his nightstand and his panicked parents rushed in to put it out.

That one mischievous smile would have made this whole extreme makeover worth it.

I'm starting to feel silly, like I dressed up for Halloween on the wrong day.

"Hey."

I can't help doing a double take. Did Lincoln Chan just *talk* to me?

"Oh, hey!" Oh, no. Did I just hit a high C?

Cool as a cucumber, Leo!

He runs his hands through his shock of jet-black hair, and

the way his eyes widen makes him seem a bit breathless. "You dropped this." He hands my ballpoint pen to me.

I feel my insides wilt. "Thanks." So, not awestruck by my good looks. Cool, cool.

In fact, he can't tear his gaze away from me any faster.

The morning announcements mention auditions for *Twelfth Night*, and I get a flutter in my stomach at the mere thought of trying out like my friends suggested.

"All right, everyone, let's begin." Ms. Domingo shuts the door and strolls into the room.

After she takes attendance, I chance looking back at Lincoln out of the corner of my eye.

He's listening to today's lesson, totally engaged, like the good student I remember. He reaches up and locks his fingers together at the nape of his neck. He has big strong hands, with short fingernails and long, smooth fingers. It's funny to think those hands were running through my hair once upon a time.

I remind myself that he's a completely different person now. We used to be friends. But now he laughs at fart jokes, and drinks alcohol mixed into Snapple cans at house parties, and thinks he's the coolest guy in school. He grew into his good looks, but then he *became* his good looks and his personality vanished, flushed down the proverbial toilet. The fact I'm fawning over a handsome husk of a human makes me mad for being so shallow, and I tear my gaze away.

A few minutes later, his look of concentration has vanished. He makes a paper airplane and throws it at Tré Gooding in the front row. It hits the back of his head, but Tré doesn't notice. A few students stifle laughter. A real class act. God! Why am I so drawn to these terrible guys?!

When class ends, I'm stepping out of the room at the same time as Lincoln—unplanned, I swear. He gestures in front of him to let me pass, his other hand holding his textbook by its top and down at his side like one might hold a briefcase. I always liked that quality about him: always doing something a little offbeat like that. Even the way his backpack's slung over one shoulder is charming. I duck my head and involuntarily flash a tight smile.

Stop smiling!

"I wanted to apologize," he whispers, "for taking your seat at lunch the other day."

I push through the stunned sensation. "Okay. Yeah," I say in a put-on deep voice.

"Cool hair, by the way."

"Thanks." I blush despite myself.

There it is. That old familiar smile. I didn't realize how much I've missed him until I saw it. "Later," he says before spinning and dashing off down the hall to wrap Travis in a bear hug.

And just like that, my skyrocketing heart rate stalls out before crash landing.

Hey, it's a start?

After fourth-period Econ Gov, I'm still in shock over Lincoln both apologizing *and* complimenting me. Not to mention I've been checking who's liking my TikTok so frequently that my phone dies. Spoiler: five people liked my post, all bots. But nothing can dash my spirits in the aftermath of how the school's Most Popular acknowledged me.

Lincoln's as big a jerk as they come, but . . .

If I've caught Lincoln's attention, that means the Boyfriend Material Checklist is working.

I pop into the bathroom for a makeup touch-up and am still just as mystified by my reflection as I was the last time I saw myself. The makeup's holding up, but I blot my forehead with a paper towel anyway before heading to the cafeteria for the last few minutes of lunch. Dillon and Varsha have something during lunch today, so it looks like a solo library lunch again—

I stop midstride.

Varsha's bake sale!

I slam my palm into my forehead. I totally forgot. I race ahead, well aware that running helter-skelter is definitely something a try-hard would do. Oops. Not to mention each step aches from heel blisters from breaking in these stiff new shoes.

Students stand in a long line in the hall outside the cafeteria. Talk about a turnout!

I circumvent the line, squeezing behind the table heaped with brownies and lemon squares. Varsha must have recruited Dillon when I didn't show. His hands fly to the lockbox, fumbling to hand change to Nancy Tambor. Varsha tucks an empty serving platter caked with orange frosting under the table. My friends each acknowledge my presence with a cursory glance. I quickly unload my biscotti.

"I am so sorry! My phone died, and I totally forgot because—" I gesture at myself.

"Who even are you?" Varsha says. "What have you done with Leo?!"

After ten minutes, students wipe the remainder of the baked goods. Sergio is the last to walk off with a napkin laden with frosted cookies. But not before casting a look back at me.

Yes!

Dillon examines me, clasping the lockbox shut. His expression is thoughtful. Not mad, thankfully.

"Well? Think it's a good look that's gonna get me my first real boyfriend?" I whisper.

"Uhh, yeah!" Varsha crumples up the bake sale sign. "But it wasn't a good look leaving me high and dry! You promised to help, and that? That was a lot." She throws the balled-up paper my way. "To make it up to me," Varsha continues, "next movie night, we're watching *Lake Placid*."

"Deal. I'm so sorry again."

"It's okay. Dillon here pulled through because he's the best."

At his name, he starts, interrupted from tallying numbers on a clipboard.

"Well?" I ask, taking a step back to show him how I look from afar.

"You know, I never pictured you as a blond."

"Any other thoughts?" I implore.

"I never appreciated your bone structure until now," Varsha muses.

"When you said Vincent was giving you a makeover, I assumed he'd lend you a shirt. But this is like a total overhaul," Dillon says.

I narrow my eyes. "You say that like it's a bad thing."

"Not at all! I think this new look is definitely going to get attention."

"I hope so!" I say, even though it's not the rousing endorsement I wanted. Still, I give them a subtle twirl. "Speedo just checked me out. And guess who looked my way in Calc?"

"Everyone?" Dillon asks.

I give a playful laugh. "I mean, probably. But also Abe." Aka Lincoln.

"Oh, that jerk face?" Dillon says.

I nod. "If I caught *that* jerk face's eye, imagine all the *other* jerk faces!"

Varsha grimaces. "Yeah, not who we're trying to reel in here, remember? Besides, Abe is taken. Plus, he totally stole your heart. Like, worse than the rest. He's the Jaws of the crushes."

"Fine." I help her fold up the plastic tablecloth. "He also apologized."

"For ghosting you?" Varsha asks.

"No. For taking my seat."

Dillon breaks into a laugh. "Well, isn't he a saint?"

Varsha studies the clipboard. "We're a few dollars short of our goal, but we basically reached it. I'd say this bake sale was a success. Even *with* Leo leaving us high and dry."

"I guess you could say this bake sale left no crumbs." I root around in my pocket and procure the wad of cash that Vincent gave back to me to spend on my nails. "Here. Least I could do."

Varsha pinches the cash from me and counts it. "Goal reached! Thanks, Leo!"

"I didn't think you'd actually—" I watch as she hands the cash to Dillon, who pops it into the lockbox before I can reach out to snatch it back.

Then he passes me a powdered donut in a napkin. "Here. I saved this for you."

I take it. "Yay! You're the best!"

Varsha slips her arm through mine, and her other through Dillon's, and we're off. As we head to class, I take a deep, cleansing breath, filling my lungs with unstoppable, invincible energy, my besties by my side. New Leo is ready to rock and roll. Glam glow-up? Check.

Now, what's next on my checklist for love?

THE PAPER PUNCH NAPKIN WITH THE COUNTRY CLUB LOGO.

Glitter and sequins in purple, yellow, and green. The photo-booth pictures of my friends and me, big goofy smiles on our faces, with a heart drawn around the panel of when Enzi slipped into the booth.

Enzi Aguta had been friends with Nancy Tambor for years. She'd always bring him around to class dances or other school functions. From the second I saw his face on her socials, with his braids that kissed his plump cheeks, his glowing smile, and his dreamy brown eyes, I knew I was smitten. So, with junior prom on the horizon last spring, I thought Enzi would be the perfect person to ask: everybody knows there's no better date to a school dance than a dreamy out-of-towner.

Of course, when I asked him during a game of capture the flag at Cougar Field (don't ask me how I ended up at a group event outside of school, it's beyond me), he laughed and gave me a flat-out no. As it happens, Nancy had already asked him. Even thinking back to that moment, standing in the tall grass at twilight while watching him stride away, mosquito-bitten and sweaty, my cheeks burn as red now as they did then. It's one of those moments that never lose their cringe, no matter how much time has passed.

While Dillon and Varsha flitted around the ballroom on junior prom committee duty, with Dillon helping out with taking photos for the yearbook, I sat at the table all night, watching Enzi make Nancy laugh and feeling like a turtle retreating further and further into his shell.

Enzi kept giving me the eye, with that wolfish grin, and repeatedly beckoned me onto the dance floor. I laughed, staying put. I didn't want to embarrass myself further with questionable dance moves, and I was confused if dancing together was a joke to him. Rumors had already spread that I'd asked him to the dance, and most people found it funny. Why? Because most people thought he was straight and that poor Leo was going after the wrong guy? Or because it was just yet another public flop of mine in the Romance Department after Lincoln—assuming people even *knew* about that stint. I wasn't in the public-school zeitgeist to know.

Enzi didn't take no for an answer and kept trying to reel me onto the dance floor like a fish on a line. He couldn't take his eyes off me—even as he did the worm inside a dance circle.

When he saw me reach the bottom of my water glass, he came by to fill it from the pitcher. On my way back from the bathroom, he pulled my chair out so that I could sit. And he kept summoning me to dance, and I kept refusing. He popped into the photo booth with Dillon, Varsha, and me to take a photo. At one point, he tossed his boutonniere to me and winked.

Then, while we stood in line at the snack table, Enzi asked me if I was dating anybody, to which I nearly burst out laughing with an eye roll—*me?! Dating anybody?! Hilarious!*—but to which I *actually* replied with a cheeky shake of my head. And I thought he was going to ask me for my number or something as we shuffled down the table, filling our plates with cheese and stale crackers—that is, until Lady Gaga began to play and I started to sing along, something I tend to do when I'm feeling myself. And I was. I could tell he liked me.

Then Enzi told me I had a bad voice . . . like a dying cat. Remember that? Which I confess was true in that moment. I was nervous, which made my voice tight and croaky.

His boutonniere, now just crisp, crinkly pressed flowers that flake apart with every page turn.

Where did things go wrong?

9

IT TAKES FOUR WHOLE DAYS OF WAITING BEFORE I GET AN
answer to that question.

After school, I'm on my way to pick up my paycheck at the
teahouse when I pass the pet store on the corner and stop short
to look at a cute puppy in the window—when someone slams
into me on the sidewalk.

His scoop of chocolate ice cream ruins his cream knit sweater
vest. The woven fabric is embellished with a torch and scrolls of
parchment. Crestview's prep school crest.

"Oh, my gosh! I am so sorry!" I blurt, horrified. It takes a
second to realize I know him. Then the laser-lit image appears
in my mind: Enzi Aguta, throwing me his boutonniere at junior
prom, which is now preserved in my scrapbook. It's like he
stepped off the pages and is now standing before me. Except

now he's covered in frozen dessert.

Enzi wipes a glob of ice cream off his barrel chest. "It's all good, Leo." He starts dabbing at himself with a napkin.

"Can I help?" I ask.

"It's fine." He holds up a hand signaling for me to leave him alone. Not quite the lovable ball of energy I last saw doing the worm across the ballroom.

"It's been a minute," I start. "Sorry our reunion had to be so . . . creamy?" I let out a little laugh to try and cover up my awful word choice. No. Atrocious.

"Yeah. Same." He levels me with a friendly smile. "I dig the look. Barely recognized you."

Before I can thank him, he salutes me, turns, and walks off.

But then I realize we're walking in the same direction. He's probably going to visit Vincent at the teahouse. I follow a few paces behind him, feeling like all I'm missing is a trench coat and a top hat to embody the full creeper vibes I'm unwittingly emitting.

I veer into the deli next door as I wait for Enzi to leave the teahouse.

When he does, we lock eyes through the glass, and he starts, alarmed, then bolts.

One point for Enzi liking my new look.

Minus two points for literally everything else.

I belly flop onto my bed and open my various social media accounts, checking my before/after video on TikTok again now that more time's passed. Can't be a try-hard if no one can see you being one, right? The post has thirty-one views, and the same handful of people have liked it since I posted it. So, not the big splash I was hoping to make on socials—but Lincoln's, Sergio's, and Enzi's in-person reactions more than make up for it. Even though I still hate Lincoln's guts.

People are noticing my new look. Now I need to figure out how to get the flirtations to come too.

I shift over to Instagram and archive all my old photos (check), then post a photo that Vincent begrudgingly took in an alley by the teahouse. I'm leaning against the brick wall, looking, you guessed it, bored.

Next, I set up a ring light I ordered from Amazon. I switch it on and pose for a few selfies, then download the Facetune app and rearrange my features slightly—making my head less long and narrow—until I remember Vincent telling me that selfies may qualify as try-hard behavior, so I do away with them altogether.

I check back through my likes and can't help but notice Lincoln's name isn't one of the contributors. Why would it be? My thoughts wander to the way he looked at me. He didn't have to apologize, or talk to me at all, but he did. And was . . . nice.

It's painful, that shift of going from so close to a no one. I should really be used to it by now but . . .

A like on my latest photo causes me to spring up. *Enzi*.

Enzi must *really* like my new look—and maybe he wants me to know it? My cogs start turning about my next step in my Quest for Love. In thinking about how to turn my disastrous run-in into a blessing in disguise, I wonder if there's some feedback from him that I could get to distill into my next action item. Being a bad singer is *no* reason to drop someone, right?

Heart racing, I pull up his profile on Instagram and message him.

> **Leo:** Hey
>
> **Leo:** Cool running into you today

It's still agonizing not being able to use punctuation. I wait a few minutes, but when I see he still hasn't messaged me back, I remove my makeup and run through my new skin-care routine. I slather some sort of creamy avocado nourishing hydration mask all over my face. While it dries, I keep refreshing my Instagram to see if he's seen my DM yet.

I check my messages until I'm tilting over onto my pillow in exhaustion.

TikTok acts as a welcome distraction again, though I stop scrolling when a video pops up of a bull shark eating a man in Egypt. Damn algorithm. Probably overheard the conversation about that alligator attack. Thanks for that one, Varsha.

> **Vincent 🖐:** Patty's Nails called. You didn't go?!

Ignoring Vincent's text, I return to Instagram and my eyes flash open. Enzi replied!

I roll onto my stomach, holding my breath.

> **Enzi:** "Cool" is right 😊

Uh, that's it? Cute, but a bit anticlimactic. What am I supposed to say to that? I wait for more.

Nothing.

Time to butter him up a little.

Leo: Well minus the ice cream thing did your vest survive
Enzi: He'll live lol
Leo: Good you looked really nice
Enzi: Yeah thanks you too

As happy as that makes me, I realize this is going to take some finessing. Which might mean getting straight to the point?

Leo: Hey random question
Leo: Did I do something at junior prom

He sees my DM and takes two whole breathless minutes to reply.

Enzi: Huh?
Leo: Yeah idk we had fun but then stopped talking after junior prom
Enzi: Oh. Nah, you good
Leo: Hmmm I am doing some self-improvement project
Leo: So any feedback is welcome
Leo: Srysly

This time, it takes fourteen minutes for him to reply, and

I'm fighting sleep hard. I watch Rat Tok and NPC tavernkeep role-play before skipping around the streaming networks until I land on a favorite *SpongeBob* episode where Mrs. Puff is incarcerated.

Enzi: I mean you were hella quiet lol

I *was*? I suppose I *can* be "hella quiet" at times, but I'm still confused.

Leo: What do you mean?

I'm so perplexed, I even dare a question mark.

Enzi: You were kinda invisible
Enzi: You didn't dance or anything

I groan, flinging myself backward onto the bed, and Miss Tiramisu comes over to me in her frog hat—only to lick my avocado mask. I still can't believe she wears that hat. Varsha always knew Miss Tiramisu would.

I think back to junior prom. I remember sticking to my seat at the table in the ballroom, downing glass after glass of ice water, and picking over my plate of salad, chicken, and cake. It's true—I mostly watched other people shake on the dance floor from behind the floral arrangement on my table. But it was hard to converse over the loud music, and I've rarely shown off my dance moves outside the comfort of my own home. Plus, I can't project my voice for squat diddly.

I guess letting my introverted side win out *was* the pitfall.

Leo: So if I danced maybe you would have kept in touch
Enzi: It's about having more of a presence I think

"Hmm." I chew the side of my mouth. Wasn't the point of my makeover to give me a presence, more or less? Is *that* what Enzi means? My new look is working, but it can only take me so far.

This time, I make sure I don't reply so fast. I toggle back to TikTok, where I find I'm down a follower. Trying to track down who it is takes up time. When I still can't crack it, I reply.

Leo: So less of how I look and more of how I command a room
Enzi: Yeah. I'd say that's pretty accurate. That help?
Leo: Yeah thanks

Enzi hearts my message.

After some processing, while watching *Twelfth Night* on my tablet, I scribble a note onto my checklist in my scrapbook.

3. HAVE A POWERHOUSE PRESENCE.

At this rate, someone just *has* to give me their heart soon.

Their *real* heart, not a hearted message on Instagram.

And I have just the thing to get me that powerhouse presence.

BOYFRIEND MATERIAL CHECKLIST

1. BE COOL AS A CUCUMBER. ☑

2. GET A GLAM GLOW-UP. ☑

3. HAVE A POWERHOUSE PRESENCE. ☐

SO, AS IT TURNS OUT, I GUESS I *DO* NEED MORE DRAMA— of the theatrical variety, that is.

Two days later, I'm standing before Dr. Horan and Ms. Kennedy in the auditorium, hoping the hours spent rehearsing in front of my closet mirror are enough to ace this audition for the school drama.

Never in a million years could I have imagined myself reading out lines onstage without fainting on the spot. Well, I haven't read them—yet. But like some sort of power-up potion, my new look has given me the boost of confidence I've needed to follow through on the advice from Enzi.

"It appears you're auditioning for the role of . . ." Dr. Horan consults his clipboard. "Duke Orsino, our lead. Excellent. We love to see fresh faces here."

I gulp. Maybe I should have set my aims lower. I gaze down through the dim light at Dr. Horan and Ms. Kennedy, who are practically invisible in their all-black outfits. His gleaming bald head and her spiky, silvery hair stand out in the room draped in a velvety gloom.

Ms. Kennedy knits her fingers together. "Whenever you're ready."

My knees start shaking, and it feels like the stage sways. I focus on a little orange strip of tape at the edge in order to keep myself from believing the room is actually pitching sideways.

Think of the checklist, Leo. Be cool as a cucumber.

Clearly, if I can't even audition without having a meltdown, what chance do I have of landing a role? And a *lead* role at that? Forget about landing a *boyfriend*! And am I really opening myself up to yet another rejection? What else is new?

Push through. Remember your glow-up.

I force my breathing to become incrementally more even. I tell myself that cool cucumbers don't faint in school auditoriums. Vincent appears like a little bedazzled angel on my shoulder, reminding me to straighten up, smile with my eyes, and take a wide, commanding stance. I think of our impromptu photo shoot after work when he said: "You look the part. Now you have to *be* the part."

You've got this, Leo. Powerhouse presence, let's go!

"'If music be the food of love, play on,'" I begin, trying to ignore my inner critic screaming at me, telling me how high-pitched and annoying my voice sounds. "'Give me excess of it, that, surfeiting . . .'"

I keep going, walking a bit to the left and a bit to the right, to show that I'm comfortable moving around, which—spoiler alert—I'm not. In fact, I'm very *un*comfortable. Miraculously, though, with each verse, I can feel myself beating back the usual hot creep of blush.

"'Even in a minute: so full of shapes is fancy, that it alone is high fantastical.'" I return to center stage and bow as I finish. My heart pounds in my ears, yet I could jump for joy that I was able to memorize nearly every line and only had to consult the script page twice.

The directors clap out a polite round of applause. Dr. Horan scribbles something onto his clipboard. "Very well done."

"Indeed." Ms. Kennedy lowers her bold-frame glasses with a clacking from their beaded eyeglass chain and rubs the narrow bridge of her nose. "The cast list will be announced next Friday."

I nod, playing it off cool while I'm screaming inside with both excitement and relief. With any luck, maybe I'll get *a* role, one that will help combat my lack of presence.

I trip down the stage steps but catch myself, give a bashful chuckle, and hurry to class.

The next few days are a waiting game, with one stylish outfit after the next, and many Band-Aids on my heels from new-shoe blues. Luckily, I think I've been getting the knack of pairing which shirt goes with which pants, and I've been able to mix and match with none the wiser. Sergio and Travis watch me when they think I'm in a bored malaise and not paying attention. Sergio holds the door for me in Lit, and Travis skateboards past me in the hall and gives me a spirited fist bump.

I haven't drawn Lincoln's eye again, not since that one time nearly a week ago. Maybe if I keep going with getting a stronger presence, it'll only be a matter of time before he and others fall prey to the checklist.

What I really want is for someone to flirt with me. Is my Future Boyfriend in a café sipping a latte? On the train into the city? In the dentist's office getting his teeth cleaned?

By Monday, word gets out that I auditioned for *Twelfth Night*. Emily Sharpe and Anne DeClerk, two of Eastfield High's best-known Theater Kids, even approach me in the hall to ask which part I tried out for, heads cocked and curious. Both girls always wear all black, which makes me think of my own all-black ensemble. Maybe I've been a Theater Kid all along and never knew it. Emily is notorious for posting photos of her albino pet rat—mostly snapshots of the two of them snuggling in bed. She and Anne tell me there's talk that my odds are good, that there are always surprises in casting, with Non-Theater Kids getting roles. They regard me like how my cat regards me when I start to belt out show tunes. But at least I'm getting noticed?

By Friday, everyone's champing at the bit to see who got which role. Especially when Emily's voice comes through the intercom during morning announcements to let the whole school know that today is the day. I'm so tense, I bend part of my pen cap until it snaps.

I try to play it cool when later, people nearly leapfrog over each other to read the list posted to Dr. Horan's office door.

Calmly, I push my way to the front of the mob pit and survey the list. There, about halfway down the page, is my name.

I actually got cast?

I'm vibrating with pure glee—and something like fear. Being cast means my next several weeks are going to be spent with people I don't know, doing something I've never done. I have to remind myself it's all in the name of my Future Boyfriend goal. Like Varsha said, maybe I'll find my Future Boyfriend backstage. Because he sure as heck hasn't made himself known yet!

I refocus on the cast list. Now, as for the character I'm playing. It isn't Orsino. I'm not surprised, but still, something in me deflates. I was cast as Sebastian, the twin of the character Viola. He's lost at sea in a shipwreck with only a few lines. Not the surprise casting I was hoping for, but I'm comforted that I can likely handle such a small role. And though it may be a small role, I'm going to act the heck out of it. I'm going to have so much presence that I'll be a crowd favorite. Dare I say, a star? "Hella quiet," who?

Emily and Anne stand on their tiptoes in the clump of students at the door.

"Who's playing Orsino?" Anne asks.

My eyes comb the list. There, at the top, is . . .

LINCOLN CHAN.

"Sweet," he says from my left. "I got the role." He doesn't say it to anyone in particular, and then he strides off with a self-congratulatory smile, his one cross-shaped earring twinkling.

Emily gasps. "Now *that's* what I call surprise casting."

Moments later, I let out a subtle squeal (or as subtle as a squeal *can* be) when I meet my friends by their lockers. "I did it! Say hello to Sebastian!"

"The crab?" Varsha hands my AP Bio textbook to me, then slams her locker shut. Today, bright orange clip-ins streak her thick black hair, in honor of Spooky Szn almost officially underway.

"Wrong production," I say, even though I know she's only joking.

Dillon smiles. "Amazing!" Today he's in a fuzzy, huggable sage green sweater. I make a mental note to borrow it.

"Thanks. I only have a few lines, but that's not the point. I will be in rehearsals! And that's not all." I pull my friends in close on either side of me. "*Abe* is in the play too!" I hiss.

Dillon frowns. "What? He's not even an actor."

"Well, neither was Leo until about thirty seconds ago," Varsha says.

"Touché."

Dillon chuckles. "Can't say I saw *that* coming."

"Big same, fam." Varsha rests a hand on my shoulder. "P.S. I love how *we* suggest auditioning for the school play, in one ear and out the other. Then some fleeting crush from yester-year says you lack presence, and you're practically signing up for MasterClass."

We start off down the hall to next period. "I'm deriving my checklist items from ex-crushes. What more can I say?"

"Please don't tell me you asked Enzi why he turned you down," Dillon says.

"How else is Leo supposed to keep pulling his checklist together?" Varsha shoots back.

"Yeah! This half-baked checklist isn't going to fill *itself* out!

We know why Speedo turned me down. Now we know why Enzi ghosted me. And at some point, I need to find out why Mary Todd"—aka Travis—"rejected me. The only data point is when he said I shouldn't smile so widely because it makes me look goofy." I laugh, then cover my mouth. "Oops. Still working on it."

Dillon groans. "For the bazillionth time, you have a *great* smile."

"If I'm going to course-correct things about myself to find true love, then it doesn't hurt to take their advice. Well, it does hurt. But that's not the point here, people. I'm in my Hot Gay Era."

"Are you going to get advice from every old crush? Like, even from Abe?" Varsha asks.

I grimace. "Ugh. I guess so." The thought makes me queasy. "Y'all, the fact that Abe auditioned is super sus. Maybe he's doing a checklist, too?" I laugh weakly and don't say more. But thoughts start gathering speed in my head, like how perhaps these coincidences, the crumb of attention from Lincoln, mean that maybe things between us aren't over for good. Maybe a rekindled romance between us is meant to be . . .

"Oh no," Varsha cuts through my thoughts. "You're thinking maybe it's meant to be, aren't you?"

"No!" I protest.

She pinches her lips together in skepticism.

"Maybe Abe auditioning makes sense. Not the New Abe, but the Old Abe, the one from the days when we used to be friends. He *was* a theater nerd," I say. "He loved *Hairspray*!"

"You still think it's fate, don't you?"

"No," I lie. "I think maybe he figured that this was his one chance to be a part of a school production before graduation. Or maybe he auditioned to round out his college apps."

"Speaking of which, mine are pretty much done," Varsha says with a smile.

Dillon high-fives her. "Nice."

Varsha gives me a knowing look. "You're totally hoping Abe falls for you, aren't you?"

I fix her with a withering gaze. "Shush." Sometimes, I hate how well she knows me.

"You're sure you can commit to being in the play?" Dillon asks as we turn a corner.

"Yep! What else am I doing? Watching TikTok? Which reminds me . . ." I take out my phone and check the view count on my before/after video, which is still nothing groundbreaking to report.

"How many times have you watched your own video?" Varsha inquires.

"That's none of my business," I quip, tucking my phone away.

Dillon beams. "Well, I am just so glad you're a part of something now."

"Unless," Varsha intercedes, "the fact that Abe's there consumes your every waking thought, which is kind of the opposite of what you joining something was supposed to achieve."

I gape, not wanting to admit that the scenario she described seems highly probable. "That's not the point," I counter. "I'm going to work on my presence to find my Future Boyfriend."

"Who *isn't* Abe," Varsha reminds me.

I feign a shudder. "Definitely not. No second chances for him."

"Great!" Varsha pulls a thick white business card from her jacket pocket. "While we're sharing good news, the Princeton rep who came in again gave me her card, asking me to email her!"

Dillon inspects the card. "This is awesome!"

She grins. "Yeah. I know."

"And guess who got into the all-state chorus?" Dillon asks with raised eyebrows.

We all cheer for him, jumping up and down. "Way to bury the lede, Dill Pickle!" I say, giving him a playful nudge.

"Shall we visit the snack locker for some celebratory nibbles, Leo?" Varsha asks.

I light up, then wipe the expression from my face. "Vincent told me it's not stylish to be seen scarfing down Cheetos in the hall, so I've been avoiding it all week. But we can go there if you want."

Varsha cocks an eyebrow, nostrils flared. "Dillon, I'm starting to agree with you that maybe the checklist is creating a monster."

"I never said that!" Dillon retorts, returning the business card.

"You were thinking it," she says dryly, snatching it back.

I nudge his soft, fuzzy sweater arm. "Dillon would never."

"Congrats on your new role," he says. "Just be careful."

There's no way I'd crush on Lincoln again, even if we *are* pushed to work in close proximity.

No. Way.

A BOOKMARK OF A MOUSE HOLDING A MEDIEVAL SWORD.

Stickers of a puppy and paw prints. Doodles of roller skates and rainbows and exclamation marks. A sticker of a lipstick kiss.

I love Lincoln Chan. Or, I did.

Sixth grade. The night of Jaclyn Anderson's birthday party at Moonlight Rollerway in Florham Park. Lincoln asked if I wanted to carpool with him and some friends, and I said yes. We hadn't really talked all that much since starting middle school, but soon, we were sitting next to each other at lunch and walking together through the halls, two magnets of opposite charge.

He didn't seem to mind that I was friendless—this was before Varsha and Dillon, when I had a different best friend every week. Lincoln was just a regular kid, like me, but there was something special in his eyes. A kindness when he spoke to me.

During the car ride to Jaclyn's party, I sang my heart out

to Ariana Grande, and he and the other guys barely batted an eyelash, though it got an enthusiastic rise out of Mr. Chan, who egged me on. Lincoln smiled back at me from the passenger seat, and I was grateful the darkness concealed my blush.

At the roller rink, all the girls were abuzz about Jaclyn confessing her love to Lincoln, urging her to talk to him, and the guys were doing the same to him. I slid onto the rink and saw how fast I could go.

By the time ice cream cake was served, Jaclyn asked what Lincoln was doing the upcoming weekend. He looked at me and said: "Leo and I are going to this thing. Sorry."

What was he talking about?

Once she'd skated away with her head down, likely hiding tears, I asked what he meant, and he asked if I wanted to come over to watch a movie at his place next Saturday. I said yes.

He had chosen *me*.

The movie night at his place was a hit, followed by many more movie nights, including bowl after bowl of Three Musketeers bars. We went to a Whiskered Warriors midnight release party together where the author showed up at the bookstore to sign copies, and spent days drawing and sketching fantastical things on the heated granite tile floor of his kitchen while we'd both sing along to Broadway show tunes. We danced to Dua Lipa in his bedroom, went sledding down his driveway, watched *Hairspray* (the Zac Efron edition) again and again, and played with trading cards. That's when I met Junior, the cutest dog in the world. I wanted to squeeze him and kiss his cheeks—both Junior *and* Lincoln, honestly—but Junior had a vicious bark from a sad shelter-story trauma. Lincoln insisted he was harmless and wouldn't bite me, but his tiny, bared teeth said otherwise, and I had to keep my distance and watch as Junior flopped down beside Lincoln to sleep. I wished I could have waved a magic wand and just gotten rid of that bite, that bark. Then he'd have been the perfect dog.

Sixth grade turned to seventh, then eighth.

The start of the summer after eighth grade, Lincoln asked me on a walk around the neighborhood one night. He was leaving for China the next day for the whole rest of the summer to visit family. We walked and talked, while crickets and sprinklers sounded around us, until he pulled me in for the kiss, his hands running through my hair. The kiss was sweet. Perfect.

Then he told me he'd see me in high school that fall, that he was going to miss me.

My lip quivered. I didn't want him to leave. Things were just getting started.

I didn't realize that'd be the last kiss, the last time he'd want to hang out with me.

SOME PEOPLE DON'T LIKE CHANGE, BUT I'M LEARNING I MAY
be one of the few people who *does* like change, especially when
of my own making. Over the weekend, I'm honing my makeup
skills, and at the start of the week, I'm walking taller through
the halls. Candace Jones offers me a stick of gum in AP Bio.
(People usually ask *me* for gum!) I'm not picked last for vol-
leyball in Phys Ed. (Second to last isn't last!) And it's taking
less effort to keep my mouth set in a perfectly straight line
while bumbling around with Dillon and Varsha in the morn-
ings, iced pumpkin spice lattes in hand, me in a fashionable
new scarf (with price tag tucked beneath it).

Wednesday morning, Mom walks into the kitchen with a
stack of mail while I'm pouring pumpkin-flavored creamer into
my tall glass of cold brew at the table. "What's that smile for?"

"Nothing. Was just thinking about the school play."

"Speaking of smiles"—Mom sets down a thick white packet—"looks like maybe your yearbook photo is in."

After blotting grease off my fingertips, I reach over my plate of fried eggs and buttered toast and tear it open, then carefully pull out the glossy photographs—and wince at what I see.

There I am in all black with the black background, like one of those singing heads at the Haunted Mansion at Disney World.

"Well, I knew it wouldn't be pretty," I admit with a sigh, holding up the photo to Mom. "Pre-makeover and pre-learning-how-to-form-cool-facial-expressions."

"And pre-all-those-outfits-Vincent-lent-you."

For the past three weeks, I've kept up the charade that Vincent's been the sole source of my nice new clothes when she asked where it was all coming from. She doesn't need to know about my little mall trips or about the T-shirt I bought from Balenciaga for $690.

She regards the photo more closely. "You look great."

I snort.

"I'm still not sure why you chose to wear black with a black background, though. But you yourself look very nice."

"Thanks," I relent. "I think I'm still going to want to do a retake, if that's okay."

Mom takes the packet and reviews it.

"Please," I plead, wringing my hands together. "I want to show off my new look."

"As long as you don't blend in with your background."

"Hooray!"

She smiles. "Excited for your first day of rehearsal?"

Just the thought of it makes my insides wriggle in delight. "Very."

Mom checks the clock above the table. "I can take you to school today, if you want to let Varsha know. I don't start at Saint Barnabas until ten."

"Okay. Cool. Thanks, Mom." I gulp down icy pumpkin spice goodness.

Ding!

A notification pops up on my latest Instagram post, and I click to see who liked it.

Lincoln Chan.

"Lincoln liked my photo." I cock my head in confusion. "He . . . unblocked me."

I tap over to his profile, my heart thumping. *He unblocked me.* Sure, he didn't follow me, but he *unblocked me.* My heart rate spikes. What does this mean? Is it possible he's excited to be in the school play with me? Or is it just that he knows he'll have to be in close proximity with a spurned ex-crush and feels obligated to let me out of internet prison?

I scroll through what feels like years' worth of new photos. New to *me*, that is.

Lincoln with the rest of the Fierce Five on a football field. A shirtless mirror photo. (Those abs! That six-pack!) A photo of him as a baby with his mom for Mother's Day. His hand holding a water glass raised to his face. A random bowl of spaghetti.

There's a candid of Lincoln walking next to a palm tree at the water's edge, a setting sun lining a distant mountain across the sea. Lincoln walking through a flower field in white pants and a beige mesh tank top.

And last but not least, Lincoln shirtless in a baseball cap with pants that say PLAYER on the side, and white socks in sporty striped sandals. Swoon. He can do no wrong. Each picture is capital-C Cool.

And none show him with his short, spiky hair, Invisalign, or blemishes from yesteryear.

I watch a few reels, one of which includes him lip-syncing to Bruno Mars in his bathroom mirror, with his perfect tousled black hair, perfect white teeth, and perfect bare chest peeping out from an open zip-up hoodie that makes me want to zip the rest of it not *up* but *down, down, DOWN!*

And of course, the zillion couple's posts of Lincoln and Travis. *Blech.* Total buzzkill.

He has 103k followers, but only follows 850 people. Sadly, I'm not one of them.

I hate how much it makes my heart swell. Reminder to self: He was the original Terrible Guy. No matter how much I'm struggling with ideas of fate bringing the two of us back together after all these years.

"Be careful," Mom warns from the counter, where she pours hot coffee into her mug. "He's broken your heart before."

How does everyone have this bizarre ability to know what I'm thinking?

I shrug off her words, fighting the thrill of thinking about our first rehearsal together.

And wondering why he unblocked me.

After the last bell, I enter the dimly lit school auditorium, sashaying down the aisle in sunglasses, full face of makeup, and an oversize suit jacket over a white tank top paired with wide-leg pants.

"Slay," Emily chimes in from an aisle chair.

I resist cracking a smile.

The first few rows are filled. The auditorium hums with excited chatter. I follow other students to the stage, where we pluck a copy of the script from a pile before taking our seats.

Several chairs away, I spot Lincoln, leaned back with one leg resting on the other, looking every bit a leading man in his lavender bomber jacket and trendy ash-gray jeans with his hair tousled just so as he talks to a few bright-eyed Theater Kids. How is it the two of us are the only Non-Theater Kids here, and he's already in with them? I remove my sunglasses, hoping to share an exchange with him now that I know he no longer hates me to the point of blocking my Instagram, but he doesn't look over. And I'm pretty sure my sunglasses left nose indents. Great.

"Welcome, everyone," Ms. Kennedy says from onstage, "to this year's production of *Twelfth Night*."

Everyone screams and claps and whistles. Everyone except for Lincoln, who plays it cool. And me. Two can play at this game.

Ms. Kennedy grins. "We are delighted to have each and every one of you as part of the show. It's going to be a great one for Eastfield High."

The Theater Kids around me sit up straight at attention, and even though Ms. Kennedy continues to speak, I can't seem to stop staring at them. They hold their chins high, their expressions serene and studious, chests up, like they're proud of being among the chosen few. And the way Ms. Kennedy stands, back ramrod, with so much poise, holds everyone captive.

Talk about *presence*!

I sit a little taller myself. I start to feel all warm and fuzzy, and it takes a moment to wonder why. For once, I'm part of something special. I'm among these proud, talented people, which means I must have what it takes, too. To think, if I'd never started my Boyfriend Material Checklist, I wouldn't be here. By the time opening night arrives, I'm going to have such a presence, I can check that box off too. And maybe, just maybe, find my Future Boyfriend somewhere along the way. The possibilities of what the play may bring keep swirling in my chest.

We start off rehearsal by playing an icebreaker-type game called Pass the Pulse, forming a giant circle onstage. While Ms. Kennedy goes over the instructions, Lincoln steps into the free spot beside me. Which is whatever. Until we're told that everyone must hold hands. I've got Hannah Livingston's hand gripping my left, and Lincoln's hand sliding into my right.

Why did he unblock me?

We don't bother acknowledging one another as we try to form a passable grip—one that's not too tight to imply romantic interest, and not too loose to imply complete and utter disgust for one another. It's a combined effort, that's for sure.

He must like me again to *some* degree, right?

I wonder if his hand was always this smooth, his grip always this sure. . . .

Closing my eyes, I shake away any lingering thoughts of fate and destiny. That is, until we all close our eyes while Ms. Kennedy begins a pulse by lightly squeezing the hand of one of the students, who, in theory, will then squeeze the hand of their neighbor, and so on and so forth until the pulse returns to Ms. Kennedy. All of it in complete silence. All my focus on Lincoln's grip.

I hope my palm isn't sweaty. It's hard to tell if it's mine or his that's getting clammy.

And just like that, he squeezes my hand, sending the pulse directly into my heart.

I giggle, feeling a giddy ticklish flutter in my neck.

"Leo."

I open my eyes to find Ms. Kennedy looking down her long nose at me. "Because of your little outburst, we'll start again. It's okay. Please, everyone, close your eyes once more."

This time around, when Lincoln squeezes my hand, I clamp Hannah's hand hard to keep the energy moving. Judging from the wince I hear, potentially a bit *too* hard.

The games continue with Zip Zap Zop, an exercise that requires us to pass the energy across the circle. Fortunately, I give the energy and the eye contact to a person who isn't Lincoln.

When all the fun and games are over, we sit in a circle onstage and read through the script, with each person speaking their lines. Everyone has the jitters at first, but eventually the energy grows more somber as we settle into the story, one I know and love well.

People chuckle at a few lines delivered, like "He is gagged" and "Wilt thou set thy foot o' my neck?" Of course, not so much as a smile from Lincoln. I survey the others, my eye landing on three cute *smiling* guys, aka potential new crushes, who seem to eat up every line.

"Lincoln, that's your line," Ms. Kennedy instructs, keeping her eyes trained on her script.

By the time it's my turn to read a line in response to Lincoln's, I just want it to be over with as soon as possible, despite it being the part I've been looking forward to the most. I deliver it without so much as looking his way, and in a voice that makes me reconsider my whole try-hard angle. If I sound any more "cool as a cucumber" reciting my line, I'm going to put the audience to sleep. Red-hot heat crawls into my cheeks.

How am I going to have a presence *and* play it cool?

It's Lincoln's turn again, and I chance looking his way. As he reads, his sparkling brown eyes lock on mine, and even though it's an adjacent romantic moment in the play, it feels like a head-on romantic moment in real life. My heart is racing, the blush is deepening, and I force my sights back on my script, staring so hard that the letters begin to swim together.

All during the rest of the read-through, however, I notice Lincoln's eyes keep darting to one of the other guys in the cast.

Tim Connelly. Plays acoustic guitar at coffeehouses and has a soft smile. His mom's some super executive at the World Bank, and he spends every summer somewhere overseas, like Tokyo or Dubai. His dad owns the golf course in town, plus a bunch of high-end restaurants. He's the sort of guy who really should be at private school with the likes of Vincent and Enzi, but his parents wanted him to have a normal existence to "keep him humble."

"We should hang out sometime," Lincoln whispers to Tim. "I host a movie night."

Jealousy socks me in the gut. So, I guess he goes around inviting just anyone to movie nights. I guess I was nothing special. I guess unblocking me on Instagram meant nothing.

Is that why Lincoln auditioned for the play? For Tim?

Tim brightens at Lincoln's words. Either Tim is naive and thinks Lincoln is just being friendly, or Tim, whose other claim to fame was dating Katie Cooper in sixth grade, has also noticed Lincoln's high cheekbones. Lincoln likes *Tim*? *Tim*, whose cool factor, looks, and presence are all a bit questionable? By no means has he achieved checklist-level status of Boyfriend Material.

But if he's the type who's making Lincoln keep doing double takes, then I need to figure out what Tim's got that I don't. His renowned reputation as the son of rich, powerful, learned parents? I don't have power or wealth. The thought makes my energy dim and my whole mood darken. I chew the inside of my cheek, eyes lowered. I just want to go home to my squat two-story house overlooking the trash-filled turnpike and eat donuts.

Keep going, Leo. Trust the process.

Making a zillion dollars and traveling the world isn't something I can add to my checklist. But I can still take my transformation further.

Yes, I've got to finesse my presence, but perhaps something else too.

As more people take turns reading their lines, Lincoln leans in and whispers something to Tim, who guffaws in an amused, open-mouthed grin. Lincoln leans back, arms spread behind him, legs bent out in front of him, totally carefree.

I strike a relaxed pose, too. I have to remind myself that no matter how many times Lincoln looks Tim's way, Lincoln's dating Travis. Which actually makes me feel *more* jealous. And why are *all* the Theater Kids ogling Lincoln? Him and his dang superstar presence. Is rehearsal over yet? Is it too late to quit? Quitting can be a good thing at times, right?

After we're done, Dr. Horan works on blocking a few scenes as I watch from backstage, where Theater Kids are playing pattycake-esque games on the dusty floor, or braiding each other's hair on folding chairs, or sharing music via their earbuds. The previous magic has fizzled and, suddenly, I'm feeling like a big outsider again. And drained.

"This is so fun," I lie, turning to Emily and Anne.

Emily's clear blue eyes lock on to mine. "Yeah, it's fun to have new people."

Anne comes up beside her. "Yeah, like you and Lincoln." She looks at me, unblinking.

"I wonder why he tried out anyway," I muse.

"We have our theories," Emily whispers, shooting Anne a conspiratorial glance.

I cock my head. "Oh, yeah? Like what?"

"Well, we have our theories on why you tried out too," Anne cuts in.

"Me?" I laugh. "Okay, let's hear it."

"We think you want to be a famous Hollywood actor or something one day," Anne says.

I let out a high, contemplative hum. "What makes you say that?"

"Well, you changed your look," Emily says. "It's very Hollywood."

"Yeah, but you have no acting experience," Anne concludes.

So, they think my look is Hollywood? I'll take it! "Thanks. Do you think Lincoln is in it for the same reason?"

"Nah. He gives off more model vibes than actor vibes," Anne says.

"What's the difference?"

"One is all about looks, and the other is about personality," Emily says.

"Okay." I'll try not to take that personally. In fact, I'm glad to hear *someone* still thinks I have a personality, given that following the checklist has watered it down to practically nothing. "So, why do you think he tried out?" I press. Surely, it's not to flirt with Tim when Lincoln has Travis.

"Well, our theory is more of a fact than it is a theory," Emily confesses.

Anne nods, her dark eyes sparkling with mischief.

I let out a little laugh. "On the edge of my seat here."

"What will you do for us if we tell you?" Anne asks.

I purse my lips. "What do you want?"

"Would you hang out with us sometime?" Anne asks.

Emily grins. "Yes. We'd like that. So would Clod."

I arch an eyebrow. "Clod?"

"My pet rat."

The albino one. I shudder.

They can't be serious. But if hanging out is the condition for sharing why Eastfield High's Most Popular is starring in Shakespeare's *Twelfth Night* . . .

"I'm in," I say. "But no rat, please. I have a fear of vermin."

"*Vermin?*" Emily looks outraged, then she pouts. "Fine."

I shrug. I really don't want to have to get into how I watch Rat Tok and silently root for the exterminators, or about how I think that mice are just tiny rats, and squirrels too, for that matter—rats with bushy tails. And then there's the whole irrational fear I have of any rodent from the days of hearing the erratic flutter and scrape of mice on glue traps at night, and Dad carrying them out of the attic through my room, their still-screeching bodies visible through the white plastic of the garbage bags as he'd shine his flashlight on them for me to see. I'd watch from my bed, covers gripped tight around my neck as he'd snicker at seeing me squirm.

"Clod will be disappointed, but he will understand," Emily adds.

"Well?" I ask, peeking around to make sure Lincoln hasn't wandered in.

"He and Travis broke up," Emily whispers.

"Yeah. We think he's doing the play to distract himself," Anne chimes in.

"Yeah. Or to win him back," Emily says.

"What?!" Here I was just thinking he was tapping into his old theater-nerd roots. But if Lincoln and Travis broke up . . .

I *knew* it. Lincoln is *most certainly* pursuing Tim in a romantic fashion. Is it to take his mind off the breakup or to win Travis back?

"Yeah," Anne says. "Hannah told us."

"They broke up?" My heartbeat accelerates, and my mind reels with possibilities. Like if Lincoln is single now, then maybe it really is fate drawing us closer together. Or, he and Tim. Or even if our romance were to get rekindled, would I even want to be with someone so . . . terrible?

But then I remember the movie nights and homework sessions and Whiskered Warriors midnight release party and his adorable pup and that kiss under the moon.

No second chances, remember? Not even after the unblocking.

Besides, it's not like he followed *you.*

Emily shrugs. "Apparently."

Anne nods. "And Travis was kicked out of the Fierce Five. Now it's just the Fierce Four."

For a long moment, I stare into the folds of the dark velvet curtain, mind still reeling.

Emily sidles up close to me, breaking my trance. "We like you."

Anne sidles up on my other side. "Yeah, we like you."

I grin, despite my state of shock. "I like you, too."

Emily blinks. "I think Clod would like you, too. If you'll have him."

I offer a pained smile. "Maybe someday."

It's late by the time we all take the stage again and receive notes on the read-through, but everyone's still just as excited as when we first began rehearsing, and we give ourselves a big old round of applause. Even Lincoln, though a smaller round.

While everyone disperses, I catch Lincoln whip out his phone and approach Tim with a smoldering, hungry expression. "Hey, let me get your number."

"Yeah, man! Sure!" Tim takes his phone with an easy grin.

I tear my gaze away before they see me watching. Let them flirt. Tim can have him.

Leo, you can't stand Lincoln, aka Public Crush Enemy #1. Remember?

Exactly.

Once I've packed up, Lincoln is nowhere to be found, and neither is Tim. My mind crawls with visions of them making out in a costume closet somewhere, and I force myself to stop thinking about it so that my heart doesn't keep squeezing. I don't even *like* Lincoln. I don't even know who he is anymore. I just want someone to want me the way Lincoln apparently wants Tim. And maybe, by adding more feedback from past crushes to my checklist, I can make it so.

In moments, while I'm waiting for Mom to come pick me up outside of school, I peek at Lincoln's Instagram. All the photos of Lincoln and Travis are indeed now gone, confirming what Anne and Emily told me must be true.

I text Dillon and Varsha the juicy news.

And then the thought comes to me once more, one that I *won't* be texting them:

What if Lincoln's the Future Boyfriend who I've been look-ing for?

Again?

TACO STICKERS. JOLLY RANCHER SKETCHES. MATHEMATICAL
equations forming the shape of a heart.

Julien Ivanov and his family rented the house next door the
year I turned fifteen. Lo and behold, he was fifteen too, and we
both had older brothers who ended up hitting it off.

It was common to hear Silvio and Julien's brother, Roman,
playing online games at home or skateboarding down the street.
When Roman came over to our house, Julien would tag along
too. Silvio would bring out a big jar of Jolly Ranchers, and we'd
all eat them as Julien and I watched them play trading cards or
paint diecast figurines.

Sometimes, I wouldn't know Roman and Julien were over at
our house, and I'd be in the kitchen, singing Ariana Grande at
full volume when Julien would push through the swinging door,
stopping me in my tracks. It always felt like he wanted to compliment me on my singing, but he would never say anything.

During movie screenings, Julien and I would sit next to one another on the couch as Silvio and Roman laughed and threw popcorn at the screen. Julien would make quiet comments to me about the movie, picking up on all the little details I'd never noticed before, like he was trying to connect with me.

Whenever I asked Julien to come over and hang out with me, I felt like he held back.

Until one day, Julien called saying he'd made tacos and invited me over. Just me.

We ate tacos and found our footing in conversation, talking as if meeting for the first time. He asked me about school and little things he had picked up about me, good things like how I'd volunteered at the animal shelter, much to my surprise.

And I found out he was a math whiz whose favorite equation was Euler's identity, and that he thought school was a waste of time.

Then he said he had fun and the two of us should hang out again sometime soon.

But we never did.

I found him making out with a girl under the bleachers a few days later.

The next month, Julien's family moved to the other side of town.

A photo of Julien at our house eating Jolly Ranchers and laughing.

Just another crush Old Leo failed to reel in.

"DON'T EVEN THINK ABOUT IT," VARSHA SAYS FROM ACROSS the table at Mike's Diner the next day.

"Think about what? All I said was that it's *confirmed* that Abe and Mary Todd split up."

The news broke this morning, confirming the It Couple has officially called it quits. Varsha heard about it from Kasey Maplewood in Finance Literacy. Dillon even heard about it from his friends in Robotics Club.

"I know what you're thinking, Leo, and I don't like it," Varsha hisses.

I take a long, innocent sip of Sprite.

"Your goal is to be the best version of yourself to attract a future boyfriend. Key word: *future*. And I don't think that includes jerky crushes of the past."

"I know that," I say airily, adding the side of fried egg onto my pizza slice before taking a bite. "Which is the reason why we're here today, so that I can find Julien and strike up a conversation in hopes of getting more intel for my checklist for said future mystery boyfriend." I nod toward where Julien is working the register, handing change over to a few seniors from my school. He looks chipper and smiley with his adorable scruffy chin.

Varsha gives me a soft kick under the table. "He keeps checking you out."

I sit up tall and blot yolk from my mouth. "He does?"

"The checklist is working," Varsha says.

"We don't know that for sure yet," Dillon adds.

Cucumber cool, glam glow-up, and powerhouse presence are still very much works in progress. But still, I need more. Julien and I hung out one time alone, but it never progressed further.

"Back to Abe and Mary Todd." Dillon reaches for a fried egg. "Do we know who broke up with who?"

"Details are murky at best," I share. "I heard Becky Van Neil tell Lu Lockheart that Mary Todd has been moping around all morning. Y'all, Abe looked right as rain during rehearsal." I can still feel his energy pulse squeezing into my palm.

"Leo." Varsha tilts down her chin to fix me with a death stare. She studies the mischievous smile spreading across my face and whacks Dillon. "Do you see this? He's scheming ways to win Abe's heart!"

"Shhh, I need quiet. All this talking is making it hard to scheme."

"Didn't you have literal nightmares about Abe for, like, the past three years?" Dillon asks. "Where you'd wake in a cold sweat?"

Yes. Yes, I did. Leave it to Dillon and Varsha to bring me back down to earth.

"Who ever said anything about Abe? Mary Todd's back on the market, too!"

Now they're both giving me a death stare.

"Kidding, kidding." I laugh, then sigh. "No, they're both duds. You guys are right." I want to tell them that only one half of said broken-up couple is going to be in play rehearsals with me the next several weeks, and fate and destiny and blah-blah-blah, but I don't want them to get on my case any more than they already are. And they're right to be on my case. Lincoln broke my heart. I'm not going to give him the chance to do it again . . . which would require him to like me . . . which maybe I can get him to do . . . through my expanding checklist.

No. Bad Leo. Bad.

Besides, Lincoln clearly likes Tim.

Sometimes, I wonder if I'm trying to torture myself on purpose.

And I'm embarrassed just thinking about telling my friends about that, which is a first for me. I usually tell them every-thing crush-related. But they'll judge me so hard, even more than they have been. Which I get. I mean, it's Lincoln "Heart-breaker" Chan. It would be unwise to fall for him again, and even more unwise to let on that my crush on Lincoln is slowly returning like a dormant volcano rumbling awake. Forget shar-ing about how good I think our names sound together! And how I can't believe that he unblocked me and talked to me.

It hits me: I never viewed my friends as judgmental. But maybe they are. Then another thought hits me. Is *that* why I never told them about my parents breaking up? All this time, I thought it was because I was embarrassed about it in comparison to their picture-perfect families, but deep down, is it actually because I thought they'd judge me? I brush the thought aside like the cobwebs strung up around the diner now that Halloween's hovering on the horizon like a blood moon.

Time for a topic change. "What did the Princeton rep say?"

"Yeah, is she going to pull a few strings for you?" Dillon asks.

"She just asked for me to let her know when I apply, and if I have any questions in the meantime." Varsha stifles a smile. I can tell she's super excited at the promise of getting into her dream school. "Oh!" She reaches into her bag. "This is for you." She hands me a large frog hat that matches the one she knitted for Miss Tiramisu.

"Thank you! It's so cute!" I squeal, admiring it under the table. "How do you have time to be a straight-A student running all sorts of clubs and still have time to do this stuff?"

She shrugs. "I just do."

"Same," Dillon shares. "My glassblowing project is so fun."

"Glassblowing sounds hard," I say. "And hazardous."

He laughs. "It's not bad once you get the hang of it."

How are my best friends both so effortless, and here I am, struggling to put makeup on and Facetune a photo? It's times like these I feel downright silly. All I have is a glow-up checklist.

I zip the hat into my backpack.

"We should head back to school," Varsha says.

"We still have to pay. And we can't leave before I have my chat," I remind my friends.

Dillon glances in Julien's direction over the top of his

milkshake. He's leaned up and texting on his phone behind the counter. So, Julien *is* capable of texting . . .

Varsha riffles through her wallet and groans. "I don't have cash. Venmo?"

I look to Dillon, who nods. "Venmo works," I say.

"Has Abe unblocked you from Venmo yet?" Dillon asks.

I shake my head, eyes downcast with a sheepish smile. "No, I checked. A guy can dream."

My friends look at Julien, then back to me.

"Good luck over there," Varsha whispers. "Get that data."

"And remember, don't just ask him what he didn't like about you," Dillon adds.

"Obviously." I roll my eyes, then head over to the counter, where Julien's waiting.

My heart feels like it's going to pound out of my chest. Julien's looking cute as ever in his wiry eyeglasses, neatly combed hair, and white T-shirt with a red apron tied around his waist. He's wearing a glowing spider pin.

"Julien," I say, reminding myself that I look good and to stand tall. "Nice pin."

"Hey, Leo." Julien takes my receipt. "Thanks. Long time no see. How's Silvio?"

"Good. I didn't know you work here," I fib.

"Yep." He glances at the receipt. "Cash?"

"Oh. Right. Yes." I hand him the cash, and he digs around for change in the register. "Here you go." He places a few dollars and coins in my hand, but he has the jitters, sending a few coins to the floor, bouncing and spinning and rolling away.

But I'm too cool—and wildly rich?—to go hunting them down.

"Thanks," I say, trying hard to maintain eye contact, even with Julien looking around the diner as he shifts from foot to foot. I can't tell if he's nervous because this is the first face-to-face we've had since he invited me over to his house that one time. Or could he possibly be into my new look? My delusional guess is yes.

"Sure thing." He pushes his wire-frame glasses up the bridge of his nose. "Have a good one."

My heart starts up again, like a snare drum in my chest. Time to seize the reason I came to the diner in the first place. "Hey. Not to be awkward, but that girl you made out with under the bleachers. Are you still together?"

"Rachel?" Julien recoils, taken aback. "I mean, that's long over. Why?"

I chew the corner of my lip. "Can I ask what it is you liked about her? I'm doing a self-help survey thing for this . . . psychology class."

Julien cocks a sandy-brown eyebrow over the silver rim of his glasses. "Well, okay. Sure. I mean, she was the most gorgeous girl in our grade. Of course, it's easier to be gorgeous when you can drop that kind of money." He lets out a nerdy laugh. "Honestly, the fact that she was rich made her even hotter."

"Interesting," I reply, mulling it over. "Well, thanks. Good seeing you." I take my time to pick up the fallen change and drop it into the little jack-o'-lantern tip jar next to the register.

For your services, good sir.

I speed-walk to my friends waiting for me at the door, heart still racing.

"How'd it go?" Varsha asks as we climb into her car.

I buckle my seat belt and grin. "Data acquired."

A few hours later, I'm home trying to style myself for tomorrow and failing miserably. I'm fresh out of new outfits. I've exhausted every combination of shirt with pants. I lay out my borrowed pair of shredded jeans, white crop top, and a gold choker with a baseball cap—my last new look. Meaning I should pay the Short Hills Mall a visit and return these and buy—only to also later return—some newer outfits. Including the Balenciaga T-shirt I decided to splurge on.

Miss Tiramisu meows, and I shake her feather wand for her. "Mushy squishy!" I squeal.

When she gets bored of pawing at the wand, I take out my phone and pull up Lincoln's contact. I wonder if he unblocked my number. I wonder if he ever ended up doing the things with Travis that he and I spoke about doing years ago, like going to Mountain Creek Water Park and spending a day at Six Flags Great Adventure. I check TikTok, where I like Varsha's latest post of her knitting a pumpkin in a witch's hat for Halloween. Then I toss my phone to the opposite side of the bed.

As for Julien's feedback . . .

In my scrapbook, I add my next checklist item:

4. FAKE BEING RICH.

BOYFRIEND MATERIAL CHECKLIST

1. BE COOL AS A CUCUMBER. ☑

2. GET A GLAM GLOW-UP. ☑

3. HAVE A POWERHOUSE PRESENCE. ☐

4. FAKE BEING RICH. ☐

"HOW HAVE YOU MADE DIVISION OF YOURSELF?" ASKS TIM, who's playing Antonio.

The next day, I'm sharing the stage with Lincoln, Janine Churchill, and a few others. We keep going with our lines, but all I can think about is testing out my newest checklist item.

"'Pardon me, sweet one, even for the vows, we made each other but so late ago,'" I say.

Lincoln strides past me toward Janine. "'One face, one voice, one habit, and two persons. A natural perspective, that is and is not!'"

Most of the cast fills the stage for this final scene, and while my line isn't delivered to Lincoln and vice versa, I still look at him when I say it. Is this truly fate, like something straight out of one of my favorite romantic comedies? Two lives, intertwined . . .

"Leo," says Ms. Kennedy. "Look at Olivia when you deliver the line, not Duke Orsino."

Lincoln scrutinizes me for a long moment, and I try not to blush. The pink prevails.

Today, there's a piano onstage, along with a few other props: an accordion, a sundial, hedges, wooden swords, and real-looking marble statues made from Styrofoam.

Tech crew is painting one of the flat sets green, while Dr. Horan calls students back to get fitted for costumes. Apparently, most of us will be wearing bowler hats and three-piece suits, and there's going to be a big ballroom scene at the end of the play with fancy garb.

"Cut," says Ms. Kennedy. "Let's move you over there," she says, instructing the Fool. (No, that isn't me. Yes, that is the name of a character.)

As they talk, Emily and Anne begin waltzing together. Emily spins away from her and clasps my hands. Before I know it, I'm twirling with her, gliding like we're at a royal ball. Not sure this qualifies as having a powerhouse presence. In fact, it's giving try-hard and goofball energy, but I'm not sure how to disconnect from her without sending her spinning off the front of the stage. A few of the other students start to chuckle. I catch Lincoln laugh and look away, and eventually Emily's grip loosens.

Ms. Kennedy claps her hands. "All right, let's take the scene from the top."

We run the scene again until we're instructed to exit stage left as the Fool reminds everyone that it "raineth" every day. Ain't that the dang truth?

"Lincoln. Leo. Can you please come here for your measurements?" Dr. Horan asks.

Lincoln's busy talking with Tim. See, I was right—being rich *is* attractive. This is why the newest item on my checklist is *Fake Being Rich*. Time to start working on it.

We make our way farther backstage, where a rack of clothing awaits us beside a table heaped with props.

Anne and Emily also come back here and sit in folding chairs against the wall, eyeing something on Anne's phone. When Dr. Horan begins taking Lincoln's measurements, I mosey over to the girls.

"Hey. How's it going?"

"Good." Emily blinks her clear blue eyes at me. "It's Clod's birthday." She angles her phone to show me a photo of her albino rat in a photoshopped party hat with balloon stickers. Talk about a jump scare.

I resist shuddering. "How cute."

Lincoln's well within earshot. "Are you going to have a birthday party for him?" I ask, seizing the opportunity. "He deserves something big, like this birthday party I threw for my brother last year. We had three hundred people over to our house. It was the best."

"Wow!" Anne's eyes widen. "Do you live in a big house?"

I nod. "Yeah. It's a mansion."

"Where?" Emily asks.

"Short Hills," I lie, naming one of the nicest neighborhoods in town.

Anne and Emily both *ooh*.

"Short Hills?" Emily asks. "We hear it's spectacular."

"Yeah, we hear it's spectacular," Anne parrots, craning her neck closer to me, eyes unblinking.

I feign a stretch. "Yeah, well, you know. It's nice. Reminds me of a neighborhood in Switzerland I visited last winter."

Lincoln glances my way, confirming that he's heard me. Dr. Horan motions for him to extend both arms out to the side as he takes measurements.

"Travis lives in that part of town," Emily says. "But he has a job at the mall there."

"Yeah," Anne whispers. "Is that weird? Why would he need a job?"

"Wait. You saw Travis working at the Short Hills Mall? Which store?"

"Hot Button."

"Oh. Does he now?" I ask. It's time for me to extract myself from this conversation. I've gotten what I needed out of it.

I bid adieu to the girls, then mosey back to Dr. Horan and Lincoln. "I'm excited for our costumes."

"Indeed! We've got a lot of fantastic looks this year," Dr. Horan says. He clicks and unclicks his pen, scratching its tip against his clipboard. "Hang on. My pen's out of ink. I'll be right back." And he vanishes through the curtain, leaving me alone with Lincoln.

It's dusty and dim. My eyes flit down at my white shoes, wondering where else to look.

"Smooth moves back there," Lincoln says.

I quirk an eyebrow. "Yeah? Thanks." I wonder if he's

remembering when we'd dance to Dua Lipa in his bedroom.

He nods. "Yeah. For sure." He regards me for a long moment. "Liking rehearsals so far?"

"Yeah!" I cheer, reminding myself to play it cooler. Much, *much* cooler. "Yeah," I say again, this time in a low bass grumble. I can feel his body heat. I want to lean into it.

There's an awkward silence.

"I didn't know you've been to Switzerland," he says.

Aha. So he *was* listening. And he *does* care. Maybe.

"Where in Switzerland? My aunt used to live there."

I freeze, a cold sweat gripping me.

Think, Leo, think!

"Arendelle," I blurt.

He hums. "I don't know it."

"I mean, I've been to . . . Salzburg," I utter, then gulp and force a faint smile. "I mean, Geneva. Have you ever been?"

"No. But that's really cool *you* have." He hums again. "You're in Short Hills now?"

I nod. Does he recall where I really live? "I moved," I croak.

He fixes me with an appraising stare, then nods. "Cool."

Cool? Coming from Lincoln Chan, that's a Big Stinkin' Win in my book.

"Here we go!" Dr. Horan emerges from the curtains, a new pen in hand. He scribbles down the rest of Lincoln's measurements. Once he's done, Lincoln gives me one last lingering look before he ducks through the curtain and out of sight.

"Is it hot back here?" I ask Dr. Horan as he measures my chest. "Or is it just me?"

I know it sounds wild, but I feel like there's something there with Lincoln.

Does this mean he has Future Boyfriend Potential?

If so, what do I need to do to keep reeling him in?

Travis comes to mind. He made the comment about my smile, but as for the other thoughts he's hiding about me? I still don't know for sure.

Maybe I need to pay the mall a visit for some intel.

Plus, my nice new clothes aren't going to return themselves.

DOODLED GUITARS AND SKATEBOARDS. A PHOTO OF TRAVIS eating a croissant. A smiley-face sticker that says Muy Bien!

Travis Matthews. I can still hear the familiar scrape of the chair legs as he inched his desk over to me during class when Profesora Jiménez would tell us to pair up for group assignments. I'd fill out my worksheet, and Travis would copy down what I wrote. He'd glance up through his locks, blessing me with a dazzling smile, before asking if I had any gum. Which I always did. Which I always handed him. Two sticks. One is never enough, you know?

He'd text me, asking to meet up to do our homework together in the library. A few times, he had even invited me to his place. He'd get awfully close to me at his kitchen table, elbows touching, before pulling away. Somehow, he'd always end up on his couch with his socked feet up to text on his phone while I finished our worksheets.

One night, we did homework in his garage while he tuned his electric guitar, then played a few songs. He was practicing for a show he and his band were going to put on at a coffeehouse.

In class, I touched his leather wrist cuff and asked where he got it.

He removed it, offering it to me to keep. I refused, blushing.

Then the bell rang, and he hollered to Fraiser Hewitt across the room, asking if he'd be at the coffeehouse. Fraiser would be there, along with a few other classmates.

I wondered why he hadn't invited me, and if my friends could be right, that all this time, Travis was just using me for homework and classwork help. Why he only ever seemed to ask me for gum and never to hang out.

When the semester ended, I saw him coming toward me in the hall with a group of friends, and when I waved, he looked right through me, like I was a complete stranger.

Chewed up and spit out, just like all that gum.

COME SATURDAY, THE SHORT HILLS MALL IS THE PERFECT place to walk in search of cute guys.

Not that that's what I'm doing today. Not really. It's what I did over a majority of the summer. I kept finding myself back here, as if on autopilot. I'd stroll into as many stores as possible before I'd find a cute guy my age perusing the racks and try my hardest to give him the eye. No such luck.

Still, I make time to return some of my outfits with tags still intact, and stop at Pax Johnson to buy some new ones. I'll return those next week. I breeze out in a fresh pair of slacks and camel cashmere sweater, hands laden with heavy shopping bags.

Varsha, on the other hand, wears full weekend attire: sweats and an oversize sweater that has a gigantic smiling gecko on it. Her earrings are shooting stars and rainbows. It's very cute—and very Varsha. So is the skeptical expression she wears as she eye-balls my newest garb. It's the exact same look she gave me after seeing the new photos I posted showing me in the Swiss Alps, tagged #ThrowBack #WinterBreak. (Thank you, Photoshop.) She doesn't think the whole buy-to-return clothes plan is very ethical despite me insisting it's harmless.

Which is why I can't tell her that I couldn't get a refund for the $690 Balenciaga T-shirt. I didn't know it at the time, but returns are for store exchange or store credit only . . . Crap. So, I'll have to work more shifts at the teahouse to make up for it. I exchanged it for another T-shirt. This one's oversize, camou-flage, and covered in sequins—well worth the $530.

We breeze through Läderach for free samples, leaving to "think about it" after the chocolatier asks us which we'll be purchasing.

"Let's go to Game World next," I say, thinking of the new issue of my favorite manga comic that just came out.

"And then Yarnland?" Varsha replies hopefully.

I nod, distracted, leading her across the glossy tile floor.

A few moments later, a lady rings me up at the register in Game World, a place I haven't been since the whole Sergio inci-dent when I returned the PlayStation. I shake the thought away.

Varsha steps up beside me, holding up a pack of trading cards for *Dungeness & Lobsters: 2 Clawz 2 Crabz*. "Have this one? Looks very you-coded."

"Of course," I say.

She sets it back down and plucks a plushie from a spin rack. "How adorable is this?!" It's a fluffy panda from the game

Pandanger Pandventure. "You could add this to your plushie collection!"

As much as I am a Plushie Aficionado, I don't think adding more to my collection is part of my whole new Cool Prescription. Even though that panda is stinkin' adorable.

"Meep wouldn't like him."

Varsha fixes me with a stare. "Meep? Your stuffed unicorn?"

"What?" I say defensively. "Meep feels very strongly about these things."

She laughs. "Well, Mr. Panda feels very strongly about attacking you right now." Then she smashes him into my face. I can't help it—I scream and run, dodging around an aisle of video game figurines as Varsha mashes the plushie into my shoulder.

I grab a plump anime duck plushie and bop her on the head with it, and she comes at me swinging. We're both bursting with laughter, cackling and screaming and running all around.

But the fun and games stop when I barrel into someone—Lincoln.

What is *he* doing here?

I fling the duckie over my shoulder and strike a sophisticated pose. "Hey. What's going on?" I say in a low tone. Thank god I'm in a fresh new outfit!

"Just doing a little shopping. You?" I notice the bag in his hand is from Hot Button. Did he go there to hang out with Travis? My stomach squeezes.

"Yeah. Same," I say, focusing on forming a serene, somewhat tired look. It's odd not seeing him with his whole crew out in the wild. "Just heading over to Tiffany's to pick up a new watch."

I point down the crowded, echoey passage.

He quirks an eyebrow. "Tiffany's is that way," he says, pointing in the opposite direction.

I nod. "Oh, right, right."

Play it cool, Leo. You've got this.

He starts to smile at me when—

Something smacks the back of my head.

It's Varsha, wielding Mr. Panda. "Got you!" she screams giddily.

I give her a pained smile and jerk my head, eyes wide, as if to say: *Not now!*

When she sees Lincoln, she freezes. "Howdy!"

Lincoln doesn't respond. Instead, he says, "Catch you later," then strolls away without another word.

When he's fully gone, I spin to Varsha, my face burning red. "You just totally embarrassed me," I blurt out. The words come out harsher than I intended.

She recoils, pulling the panda close. "Oh. I'm sorry. I didn't realize you were—" She shakes off her look of upset. "Wait. You *are* crushing on him again!"

"SHH!" I hiss, looking to see if he's lurking nearby and grateful to discover he's not. I try to calm my nerves. "Let's go to Hot Button now."

"What about Yarnland?" She looks stung for a moment, lips thin, eyes thoughtful, then nods. She's totally shutting down, and I feel bad for souring her good spirits.

I suddenly remember she needs yarn for the rest of her Halloween costume. "We can go after," I say.

As we head down the hallway, which is festooned with black bats and giant candy corns, I can't help but wonder what Lincoln thinks seeing me hanging out in a video game store with a girl who bops stuffed animals against my head. The old me wouldn't have cared. But the New Leo? Mortified. Because now I have the glow-up checklist. A different set of values and standards that doesn't involve being silly, goofy, or awkward, if it can be helped, even if it's with a friend.

I'm not sure how to reconcile that thought with how my friends are the same old friends I've known. I'm changing. They aren't. And I don't want them to. But I'm still beet red from what just happened. I hate myself for thinking it—but does being cool mean not being seen with them?

Finally, we step inside Hot Button and peruse the goods, keeping a lookout for Travis.

I find him folding a graphic-print skeleton T-shirt at a display table.

"Hey," I say with my Non-Smile™.

His braids are pulled back in a loose pony, and he's wearing all black except for an open plaid button-down with torn sleeves. "Hey, hey! What's good?"

"Nothing much. You, uh, doing okay?" I prompt.

"Yeah, why wouldn't I be?"

I feign interest in skateboard decals. "I heard about what happened."

"Oh. The breakup?" He shrugs. "Yeah. Thanks."

"Hey, I've been wondering," I start to say. Out of the corner of my eye, I notice Varsha, bored, disappearing into the aisle of chains and bracelets. I ignore a jolt of guilt and refocus on Travis. "Are we cool?"

He rubs the back of his neck. "Uuuh." He laughs. "What do you mean?"

"I don't know. We used to talk all the time. Then I never heard from you again."

"Oh." He wrinkles his forehead.

"Was it something I did?" I ask, then quickly add, "I'm working on this project about self-discovery, and I've been asking people for feedback on how they perceive me. You know. For the project."

He lets out a laugh, but it dies down, and he looks off into space, growing more serious. "Well, I don't think so. Yeah. You're a nice guy." He shrugs. "I just got busy."

As *nice* as that is to hear, I have a checklist to feed. I spent all semester doing his Spanish homework and didn't hear from him after, and when I saw him again in the hall at school, he didn't even acknowledge me. Plus, he started dating Lincoln soon after that. I know there must have been something more at play.

I need to change tactics. "What is it you liked about . . . you know?"

He considers me for a moment. "I mean, I really liked how he had a good friend group. I could never date someone with only two friends." He laughs, then his eyes flit to Varsha, who's pretending to consider a pair of jeans. Travis swallows hard. "Not that there's anything wrong with that."

"Totally," I say, though his words cut deep, being that I'm

a Two-Friend Loser. But I have my answer. I *knew* there was something more at play.

"Luckily, I've got tons of awesome friends who have my back, like Katie Cooper." He spots a customer flipping through T-shirts on the display table and waves at her. "Hey, hey, can I help you?"

The woman starts to respond, and he fist-bumps me good-bye before he goes to assist her.

Varsha strolls over. "Well, that's questionable advice."

"He just meant I should expand my friend group a little. You and Dillon are obviously the core two." Basically, the more popular I am, the more desirable I am. Which makes sense. Which means I have to *lightly* befriend some new people. Like Katie Cooper.

I try to smile at Varsha. "Any feedback is good feedback . . . right?"

She balks. "Seriously?"

I bop her with a pumpkin plushie. "In the name of the checklist."

In my mind, I add my next checklist item:

5. WIN POPULARITY CONTEST.

BOYFRIEND MATERIAL CHECKLIST

1. BE COOL AS A CUCUMBER. ✓

2. GET A GLAM GLOW-UP. ✓

3. HAVE A POWERHOUSE PRESENCE. ☐

4. FAKE BEING RICH. ☐

5. WIN POPULARITY CONTEST. ☐

"THANKS FOR JOINING US TODAY, LEO," BRENT UNDERWOOD
says, standing at the front of the library. He's the president of
Robotics Club. Dillon stares at me from one of the chairs, looking
like he's just seen a ghost. I may have dropped in unannounced
to try Operation: Win Popularity Contest, aka Befriend Katie
Cooper. Sure, my other checklist items still haven't been com-
pleted yet, but checklists aren't always linear, you know?

"Thanks." I give a friendly nod to the seven other students
who are seated in the semicircle of desk chairs and relax into
my seat. There's a robot at the center of the room that looks like
a metal tortoise with white plates and wheels. Katie flips her
ironed-straight ponytail over her shoulder and flashes a small
smile at me. I smile back. She has no idea that she's square in the
crosshairs of the next item on my checklist. If I get in good with

her, I'm practically one of Eastfield's Most Popular.

Brent runs through announcements, spouting information about line sensors, microcontroller boards, and control loops. Whatever any of that means. I share a glance with Dillon, who mouths: *"What are you doing here?"*

I pantomime checking boxes off a list into my palm.

He fixes me with a skeptical gaze.

"All right, everyone," Brent says. "Let's divide up into our groups for our coding exercise. Leo, you can join Katie and Dillon."

"Cool." I scooch my chair toward them. "I'll just watch."

Dillon looks wide-eyed at me, like he's trying hard to just go with things.

"So, we need to write a formula to control a line-following robot," Katie says.

Dillon pulls out a wooden car with wires coming off the top—I'm guessing that's his robot.

"What do you have for the main control loop?" Katie asks him.

Dillon turns to his laptop, which has lines of code running down it. "We should follow this one."

Katie shows him the code on her screen. "I think we should follow mine."

"I agree," I chime in, and Katie beams at me.

Dillon shoots me a look, as if to say: *Really?*

I spend the rest of the hour trying to keep up with conversations revolving around programming skills, engineering challenges, and robotic systems. They throw the words "CAD" and "neural chips" around a lot. Honestly, I can't follow much.

It's like when people try to explain sports to me. Good thing I know how to nod along like I'm comprehending stuff, as tiring as it is.

After the meeting, Dillon walks me out to the senior lot. "I'm so glad you decided to join a club. I just didn't think it would be Robotics." He laughs.

"Yeah, well, who knows? Maybe it's my thing," I say. "Plus, it's a great way to meet new people. Maybe get on Katie's good side."

He stops walking. "Do not tell me you joined Robotics just to befriend Katie Cooper."

I shrug. "I mean, would that be the worst thing? Weren't you and Varsha on my case to join a club?"

"Yes, one that you're actually interested in," he says. "Is this about getting more popular? Or about getting closer to Lincoln?"

I wince. Of course Varsha filled him in. I glance around to ensure the coast is clear. "You mean *Abe*," I correct him.

He rolls his eyes.

"No. It's about my popularity goal."

"I can't believe you're trying to be popular."

"Trust the process, remember?"

He peers at me. "I'm beginning to regret encouraging you."

"I can't get over your new look. You're maintaining it way better than I thought you would," Vincent says later that evening at the teahouse. "Have a boyfriend yet?"

"Nope." I'm taking cookies and tiny pastries from trays and arranging them on tiered plates. With Halloween around the corner, Judy's whipped up werewolf cupcakes, monster-eyeball macarons, and Frankenstein's finger éclairs. I pop a broken cara-mel apple tartlet into my mouth from the scrap pile.

Vincent examines his latest manicure: Barbie-pink nail polish. "Like Mariah Carey once said, love takes time. And like Judy once said, you're not going to be everybody's cup of tea."

But I *want* to be everybody's cup of tea. Which is why I need to focus on my new checklist item: *Win Popularity Contest.* Maybe love is just a numbers game.

Judy steps into the kitchen. "Hello, gentlemen. We have two people front of house." She looks at my hair. "That color really does suit you, Leo."

"Thanks." I turn to Vincent. "I'll take care of them."

He blinks at me. As if he were going to offer.

I stride through the curtain and into the dining room, then stop short.

Dad. And his young girlfriend, Margot. She's more blond than I remember and looks only a few years older than me, wearing a denim corset top, hoops, and a glittering choker. They're seated by the window. They don't see me.

My heart falls through my stomach.

I pivot on my heel and fly back into the kitchen. "Hey, do you mind?" I ask Vincent, realizing I'm panting in a total panic. I don't even give him the chance to reply as I close myself into the single-stall bathroom and lock the door.

I sit on the shut toilet, shaking. Dad is awful for everything he's put us through. This whole separation thing has been a game of picking sides, and Dad is definitely winning. He spread lies about Mom while he can't stop raving about Margot, who's apparently an excellent baker and cook. Even my mom's sisters—her best friends—have stopped talking to Mom completely. She has no clue why. The sad thing is, by ghosting her, they've ghosted me, too. And Silvio.

What did *we* ever do to deserve that? They used to come over every Sunday evening, bringing my cousins for a pasta and movie night. Now, I don't know if I'll ever see them again.

Like so many other people in my life.

Family friends. Uncles. Gran.

Vincent texts me asking if everything's all right. I can't bring myself to respond.

Finally, Vincent texts saying the coast is clear.

When I eventually emerge from the bathroom, Dad's gone.

Still trembling, I hang up my apron and leave.

At home, I'm finding it hard to focus on my homework because of how miserable I feel about seeing Dad. Not even rewatching *Hocus Pocus* for the umpteenth time is working to soothe my unsettled spirits.

After twenty minutes, I go to the kitchen to get cookies from the chicken-shaped cookie jar. I find Mom slumped at the table, still in her work attire and clutching her usual glass of wine.

"Hi, dear."

"Hi, Mom."

She smiles, revealing wine-stained teeth. I've never seen her look so defeated. There's a box of Pepto Bismol resting on the table. She eats those chalky tablets a lot these days.

"I'm going to a work conference on Friday the thirty-first in

Chicago, leaving that afternoon," she says. "So it'll be just you here that weekend. I'll make sure we food shop before I go."

"Sounds good," I say quietly. The cookie jar is empty, so I take out a pint of mint chip ice cream from the freezer. It was always Silvio's favorite flavor. It makes me miss him.

Mom sets down her glass and refills it, the wine glugging loudly from the bottle.

"Philth came into the teahouse today. He was with—"

Mom holds up a hand. "Please don't tell me. I'm trying to unwind. It was a long day at work."

I bite my lip. Of *course* she doesn't want to hear about it. I nod and get out a spoon. "Any news from Silvio?"

"He's enjoying Boston."

"Oh, good."

"Have you been working on your college apps? The deadlines will be here before you know it."

I stab my spoon into the pint. "I don't know about college. Maybe I'll just work full-time at the teahouse or something."

Mom looks at me long and hard. "You would do great in college. Apply. You can do it. I can help you." She doesn't say another word, so I head back upstairs with the pint.

Two and a half weeks fly by, helped along by senior portrait retakes, fine-tuning being cool, getting more face time with Katie in Robotics, and going to endless *Twelfth Night* rehearsals with Lincoln (no, it's not creepy that I stare at him from the wings whenever I'm not onstage).

In the cafeteria on Friday, Emily and Anne flag me down, but

I mime that I need to get food and keep walking. The Robotics Club table beckons me over with smiles, and I take the same tactic. But unlike Judy's werewolf cupcakes, my plan on how to become popular still isn't fully baked. Joining Robotics Club is nice and all, and so is having an in with the Theater Kids, but that can only get me so far. I need to be more strategic.

I've been ready to tackle my popularity action item full-on, taking it further by getting in with each clique—or at least the ones who'd help give me enough clout to make the Fierce Four into a Fierce Five again.

Instead of eating lunch in the library while Dillon and Varsha are off at their club meetups, I decide to try to join a new table. I give a nonchalant scan of the room. I contemplate plunking down with the jocks, who sit at the same long table as the Fierce Four. There's truly no Travis in sight.

I see Lincoln, who's waving me over and gesturing to an open seat.

My heart rate skyrockets. I give a slow nod in response, then buy my chicken tenders and fries like I'm in no rush to sit down.

When I finally plunk down, I get a few curious looks from guys in sports jerseys, baseball caps, and varsity letter jackets, but manage to latch on to the scrap of a conversation happening to my left that has nothing to do with lines of scrimmage or away games.

"Leo's in the play with me," Lincoln says, as means of responding to his friends' confused looks.

"Yeah, and Robotics," Katie adds.

"Hey, man," Eamon Troy says through a mouthful of tater

tots. "We were just talking about how there haven't been any good senior house parties this year."

"Yeah?" I ask, trying not to sound too interested in what he has to say. Nobody likes that.

Lincoln doesn't miss a beat. "Nah. It's wild, right? I mean, Tim Connelly tried throwing one, but it was a total fail because Pepperoni Nips showed up plastered and yakked on the stairs outside his house and then just left."

I make a passable attempt at rolling my eyes, not bothering to ask who "Pepperoni Nips" is. I think about how Dillon, Varsha, and I have never even been invited to a house party, let alone a good one. We haven't even tried alcohol. But the Fierce Four doesn't need to know that.

Eamon flicks a paper football across the table. "We hear you have a mansion," he says, exchanging a look with Lincoln.

Lincoln gives a toothy grin. "Yeah, Leo. Maybe *you* should throw a party."

I nearly choke on a fry. Is he calling my bluff?

"And not a boring one," Eamon chimes in. "A *good* one."

Their comrades murmur excitedly in agreement.

I catch Dillon and Varsha ogling me from the next table. My stomach sinks. I thought they had extracurricular lunch meetings to run? Or was that another day?

But something tells me this might have been for the best for Operation: Win Popularity Contest.

"Well . . ."

My thoughts race. Could I ask Vincent to host a party at his mansion? No. The makeover was one thing, but I wouldn't rest my Future Popularity on him. My place *will* be unoccupied when Mom's away at her work conference in Chicago. But it's a far cry from a mansion, even if I *did* rename my Wi-Fi "Leo's Mansion."

"My aunt's out of town," I fib. "Maybe I could host it at her place. It's small, though."

"That's okay," Sakura says. Her eyes glint.

"Yeah," Katie agrees. "As long as there's booze."

"Obviously." I gulp.

Eamon goes in for a fist bump, which I reciprocate. "Bro!" he hollers, everyone around us nudging each other and shaking my shoulders and arms—including Lincoln.

I ignore Dillon's and Varsha's mystified looks and smile at the Fierce Four.

Me? Throwing a house party?

Now *this* is a way to get popular.

16

THE NEXT WEEK IS A FLURRY OF AUTUMN LEAVES AND AN increasing amount of Halloween spirit in the air. Decorations are strung up all over the neighborhood, from pumpkins lining walkways to gold-and-yellow flowers springing out of window boxes.

It's time to initiate Operation: Hide Any Signs of Old Leo for my house party.

I stash anything that no longer fits with the new me. Celebrity photos and to-do lists and the vision board pinned up to my corkboard. All my stuffed animals. Sorry, Meep! My supply box goes under my bed, along with my framed photo of Gran, and my scrapbook is securely stashed in my desk drawer. After all, anyone could just wander their way up here. I've heard enough about house parties to know that people tend to give themselves tours aimed at make-out sessions on beds. Hopefully, that doesn't involve opening closet doors and desk drawers.

Even though Dillon and Varsha are still salty from recent events, making them even more wary of my house party, they agreed to come and support me anyway.

By the time Dillon and Varsha arrive to help decorate more, my room looks like a prison cell with just a bed, dresser, and lamp. All it's missing is the in-cell toilet. But it beats a unicorn plushie presiding over the room like the Mayor of Stuffed Animal Town.

I find my friends in the foyer dressed up—Dillon as Edvard Munch's painting *The Scream*, and Varsha as a lion carrying . . . Is that a knitted human arm?

"You guys look amazing! Varsha, you knitted an *arm*?"

"Of course!" Varsha holds it up so I can get a better look at her attention to detail. "I'm a lion who's sought revenge on the poachers who took my cubs." Then she aims the arm at me. "Umm, why aren't you in your costume?"

Oops. I suddenly realize that I forgot to tell them Vincent had talked me out of dressing up. According to him, Cool Kids don't wear Halloween costumes.

"Sorry. I forgot to get a costume," I say, not wanting to hurt their feelings. Time to change the subject. I gesture to the intricate sculpture in Dillon's arms that's shaped like a detailed model of a DNA helix. "What is that? It's so cool-looking!"

Dillon starts talking a mile a minute. "It's my art class midterm and it's due Monday, but I have to work on it tonight after the party because it's *still* not done and it has to look *perfect*, but Varsha's mom took the car so we had to catch an Uber here and—"

Varsha cuts in. "Dillon, everything's going to be fine. And honestly, it already looks great and you should have left it at school, where it would have been safe."

"No, no, no. It has to be *perfect*," Dillon insists.

"It's beautiful," I pipe up, hoping to distract him from spiraling.

"Really?" He blinks, then grins. "And you haven't even seen the best part." He flips a little switch and the whole thing lights up. "I used my electrical know-how to really make it shine."

I stare at it and suddenly have a vision of Lincoln and me gazing into each other's eyes in the glimmering lights of the DNA helix. It's like a scene from a romantic movie. . . .

"Dillon!" I say, pretending I'm struck with inspiration. "Let's put it on display!"

"I was hoping we could tuck it safely away in one of your bedrooms."

"You mean one of my *aunt's* bedrooms," I correct him with an exaggerated wink. "And anyway, it's too amazing to hide away. We need to show this off! I really think we should put it some-place where everyone can admire it!" I lead him to the corner of the foyer where Mom puts our Christmas tree each year. I'm already plotting how I'm going to get Lincoln over to this location when the opportunity is right for a dreamy, twinkle-lit moment.

Varsha's already in the kitchen setting up. Once we position Dillon's sculpture in the place of honor, we get to work taking another sweep of the house.

"Your room is sad," Dillon says from the doorway. "Where's all your stuff?"

I indicate the closet. "In there, where it's going to stay."

Varsha calls up from the kitchen. "Where's your chicken cookie jar gone? It was so cute!"

"Mr. Chicken had to go. It didn't pass the cool test." I pretend I don't catch Dillon's unamused side-eye, and check the time. "All right, we have T minus forty minutes before people start showing up. Let's set out the snacks and drinks."

I close the door on Miss Tiramisu. She's better off in my bedroom come party time.

While Dillon and I head into the kitchen, Varsha gets to work decking the halls with orange-and-black streamers and balloons.

We're in a rush because we had to wait until Mom left for Chicago to start the decorating. My insides flutter with nerves and guilt. A Halloween house party with potential underage drinking would only stress her out more than she already is these days and, besides, I'm responsible. Nothing will go awry. Mom will return from Chicago, not being able to tell a thing. Still, I feel rotten about keeping it from her.

Dillon sets out a clear, goo-green plastic punch bowl on the polished countertop while I place pumpkin-shaped sugar cookies in a neat, spiraling arrangement on a platter, compliments of Judy. Of course, I spared her any party details.

I snip open a big bag of individually wrapped chocolate bars and pour them into the bowl. Spooky tunes float out from the portable wireless speaker by the sink. Outside, the sun casts

long, orange streaks through the kitchen windows. The Halloween feeling is starting to set in—along with the panic.

Earlier this afternoon, practically the whole school was buzzing about the party. Apparently, after I invited the students in
the play and the Fierce Four, word started to spread, and then
next thing I knew, one person's plus-one was inviting another
person to also bring a plus-one. I have no clue who's actually
going to show and I'm horrible at math. I just hope the party
incites juicy tales come Monday to aid me in my quest for popularity. Though not too juicy. I hope no one barfs on anything.

I'm buzzing with excitement—and nerves—that Lincoln
might be coming.

"I still can't believe you're hosting a house party while your
mom's out of town." Varsha centers the platter of cookies on the
kitchen table beside a plastic cauldron. "This is so not like you.
Aren't you nervous?"

"A little," I say, lighting an acorn-scented candle. I don't mention that some of those nerves are Lincoln-related. Okay, *most*
of those nerves?

"What if someone drinks too much and needs their stomach
pumped?" Dillon asks.

"I have you two here to help me if anything goes sideways."

They exchange wide-eyed looks.

"Right?" I prompt.

Dillon gestures to himself then Varsha. "What about us says
Stomach Pump Experts?"

The doorbell rings.

I gasp, and Dillon and Varsha jump. "OMG!" I hiss.

"Someone's here?" I dim the chandelier adorned with fake cobwebs and give myself one last quick check in the mirror. I'm in a green button-down shirt with the sleeves rolled up high, trendy jeans, and pointed suede shoes.

I take a deep breath, inhaling the smell of pumpkin and cloves, and open the front door.

"Hey, Leo!" Anne and Emily are standing there in their typical all-black ensembles, except with vampire fangs. "Thanks for inviting us!"

"Hey." I wave them in. "Happy Halloween."

"Meet Clod," Emily says as she steps into the foyer. I notice, with a sinking stomach, that a rat is perched on her shoulder. Chills run down my spine. *Play it cool, Leo . . . Play it cool!*

Anne spots Dillon and Varsha huddling at the bottom of the stairs. "Nicely done," she says to Varsha.

"Thanks," Varsha says, waving her knitted arm.

Next, I usher in a group of burly jocks. They're all dressed in inflatable apple costumes and carrying bottles of apple vodka. Wait . . . are costumes a thing after all? I'm a little nervous about all the alcohol, but I show them in anyway.

As I'm about to close the door, I spot more people walking up the path, so I keep the door open and remain in place, welcoming more and more people inside in a steady stream. Every single person is wearing a Halloween costume. I'm starting to sweat.

Glancing over my shoulder, I can see that no one's been shy about getting the party started. Jake Hubbard pours drinks and passes out cups at the kitchen table, and someone's changed the music to rap and cranked it up to the point where I can see the mirror and the coatrack start to shiver.

Sakura and the pom squad arrive as the Spice Girls and breeze past me without even glancing my way. When I turn to see why they're laughing, I notice Varsha and Dillon still huddled at the bottom of the stairs.

Varsha gestures at me, and I hurry over. "How big is this thing going to *be*?" she yells over the thumping music.

I shrug, even though I'm getting more and more worried about how many people are showing up. "Big enough so that the whole school hears about what a huge success it is?"

Dillon pulls at the collar of his costume. "I thought it was only going to be you, me, Varsha, and, like, two other people. Not an actual rager with half our grade!"

"Yeah," Varsha says. "We hate seventy-five percent of the people here. No offense."

Why are my friends yucking my yum right now? Don't they know how important this house party is for my checklist goals? Not to mention they're giving off major icy vibes. Maybe they just don't know how to be fun and awesome.

"You guys know all that matters is that we have a good time."

Varsha winces. "So far, Leo, we're not."

"But we're here for you," Dillon reassures me. "Even if we're not thrilled about it."

"Yeah. What he said."

But the looks on my friends' faces make my stomach sink. They're miserable.

Excited voices at the front door pull my attention.

"Hi! Come on in," I say, ushering in the next wave of guests.

Tim enters with some prep school friends—including Enzi, dressed as a park ranger.

"Hey, Leo! Sweet place!" Enzi says. "For a sweet guy. Makes sense!"

"Aunt's place. And thanks." Is he *flirting* with me? And I wouldn't exactly call my place *sweet*, but the little the house party is doing for *Fake Being Rich*, it's sure to score big points for *Win Popularity Contest*.

After Enzi and company pass by, I gaze out into the dark front yard, then gently close the door. No sign of Lincoln.

"Want us to scope out what's going on in the kitchen for you?" Dillon asks.

"Why? Because that's where Sakura just went?" I tease.

"Ha, ha. No."

"Actually, do you mind being on door duty? I could really use a drink."

Varsha shoots me a concerned look, like suddenly I'm going to take up drinking when the three of us made a pact that we won't have a sip of alcohol until we're of legal drinking age.

"Of *Sprite*," I clarify, feeling a twinge of annoyance.

I'm squeezing my way into the kitchen past members of Robotics Club when I bump into Travis dressed as some rock and roller in a jumpsuit and gold sunglasses. "Leo! This party is dope!"

"Thanks." What I want to say to him is: *Remember when you said you wouldn't ever date someone if they only had two friends?* My eyes swivel around, taking in the jam-packed space, and a sense of triumph floods through me. With Sakura, Travis, Katie, and Eamon in attendance, I wonder if Lincoln's on his way . . .

"You look great." Travis brushes the top of my hair. "This hair color is sick."

"Thanks," I say again. All this flirting is nice. I could get used to it.

Travis fixes me with a big, dreamy smile that shows every tooth in his mouth—ironic.

Then a new song starts, and he takes my hand. "Come on. Dance with me!" His breath reeks of alcohol.

I laugh and let him twirl me.

By the time he pulls me in so that our chests touch, I'm hardly paying attention to anything else—which makes it the perfect time to catch none other than Lincoln staring at me from across the room.

Seeing him puts my flirt mode on overdrive—checklist item number 1, *Be Cool as a Cucumber*—and I wink at Travis before I gently shrug him off with a slight smile as I go to pour myself a cup of Sprite.

Leave him wanting more, am I right?

I pause for a second to take it all in. I used to think of school as a haunted house of past crushes, but now, my house is quite literally a haunted house of past crushes. In addition to Travis, Sergio (covered head-to-toe in vivid red body paint with menacing black horns . . . and a Speedo) is turning on the TV with Zubin and some swim team buddies to hook up a game console they brought. I turn to give Lincoln another flirtatious glance . . . but he's gone.

Everyone is engrossed in conversation, shrieking in laughter, shoving their faces full of cookies and cupcakes. No sign of Tim, thank god. I collect trash and sweep it into a garbage can, despite it looking uncool. My worries about leaving this place a mess are winning out some.

Katie's giggles draw my attention, and I find Travis and Eamon tossing Mr. Chicken back and forth. I nearly squawk at the sight, and race over and ask for the fragile ceramic cookie jar back before shoving it inside the snack cabinet. I hope no one's exploring in my room.

I'm weaving my way back out from the kitchen when—

"Lincoln," I say, taking in how his steamy firefighter costume, with its revealing vest and very short short-shorts, shows off his smooth, broad chest and strong legs. "You're here."

I feel extremely flustered by how good he looks and also foolish for rolling the dice wrong and not wearing a costume.

It takes me a second to register that every former and present member of the Fierce Five came to a party that *I* threw.

I've officially made it as Mr. Popular.

Travis gives me a dazed smile, but I simply nod in acknowledgment. Then he glances at Lincoln and backs into the crowd, clearly not wanting to have a run-in with his ex. A small part of me wants to ask Lincoln why they broke up in the first place, but I decide against seeming like I care.

Lincoln gets to opening the vodka, and I slip back into the foyer, where I find Dillon and Varsha standing by the front door. They have their backpacks on, looking like they're ready to leave.

"Hey. What's going on?"

"Varsha has a headache," Dillon says.

She looks down at her phone, tapping at the Uber app.

I peer at my friends. "Is there something you're not telling me?"

Varsha rolls her eyes. "Leo, you know we can't stand the Fierce Five."

"They're the Fierce *Four* now."

Dillon winces. "Not helping your case."

"Plus, I really don't want to risk getting in trouble and putting my future in jeopardy," Varsha adds. "So, we're gonna go." She pulls her bloodied lion mane down snug around her ears. "And I really do have a headache."

I take a moment to think of what to say. I thought we were all in this together. But seeing their arms crossed, I can't help but feel a little . . . guilty. So, if they want to go, they should go.

I let out a heavy sigh. "Fine. I'll talk to you guys later." I give them each a hug, then Varsha steps out the front door. But not before Dillon gives me one hard look, his eyes swimming with something I can't quite place.

I peer after them in the darkness and down the street at the houses lit with jack-o'-lanterns and blow-up skeletons. I'm honestly surprised they left. The biggest disagreement we've ever had was whether Central Jersey exists or if it's only North Jersey and South Jersey.

After I close the door, a strange sensation passes over me. As much as I hate to admit it, I feel like I can be more of my new self without Varsha and Dillon around watching me and thinking to themselves that what I'm doing is all just one big act. No one here can see through me now—plus, I actually *like* the new me. Or *parts* of the new me.

"Drink?" asks a voice.

I spin around.

Lincoln offers me a cup of fizzy brown liquid.

I shake my head. "Nah. I'm good. I'm playing responsible host for the evening."

"Oh, so that would explain the responsible host costume you're wearing." He winks.

I laugh awkwardly. "Oh, yes. It was a popular one at Party City this year." Ugh. Why didn't I dress up?

A stream of people flows from the kitchen, through the foyer, and into the living room. Someone falls, sending a clump of people pushing Lincoln and me toward the steps.

"Whoa," I say, steadying myself on the banister.

More seniors are pressing in on us.

"Maybe this isn't the best place to stand," I shout, even though he's only a foot away.

He lifts his cup overhead to avoid knocking into someone and gestures for me to head upstairs.

My chest goes tight. Does Lincoln remember that this is *my* house and not my aunt's? As good as this party may be for my popularity checklist item, I'm not sure it's doing much for pretending I come from wealth, but hey, it helps? I maneuver through a cluster of people and pad up the steps at his heels. Even though I had made a point of letting people know that upstairs was off-limits, we're only halfway up the stairs when I see two seniors making out in the second-floor bathroom.

Sergio and Mary Allison Pointer?!

When Mary Allison sees us, she lets out a raucous giggle and shuts the door.

Lincoln cocks an eyebrow at me, and now I'm leading him to my room. I'm leading Lincoln Chan to my room? Never in a zillion years would I have imagined thinking those thoughts and having it be reality since our old days of hanging out. My heart beats with every step, in time to the blaring music from downstairs.

I'm relieved to find my room just as tidy and empty as I'd left it, no stuffed animals, celebrity photos, or scrapbook in sight. Not that I was expecting said possessions to have broken free of their own accord, but my nerves are tense and my mind is playing through any possible scenario that could go wrong—all ending in my complete and total embarrassment.

Miss Tiramisu appears from under my desk, coming toward us.

"Mushy squishy!" I coo at her like I'd normally do. Then I freeze. Did I really just say that out loud?

Lincoln gives me an unreadable look.

I lean down to pick up Miss Tiramisu. "Come here, you," I say gruffly. It feels strange not talking to her in my usual squeaky baby voice. I put her into my bathroom and close the door behind her. *I'm so sorry*, I say to her silently.

Then I notice Lincoln has wandered over to my closet, hand on the door, where behind it, I've piled all my plushies that will come tumbling down in an avalanche.

"No!" I cry out. "Uh, wait. Come sit with me." I sit on the

edge of the bed and pat the spot beside me, forcing a smile to mask my terror.

He joins me on the bed and takes a little sip from his cup. "Your aunt's house is nice." He looks at me, a smirk in his expression.

So he's not letting it go.

"Oh. That," I say, grappling to find the words.

"Her house looks an awful lot like the house we used to hang out at in eighth grade."

"Yeah. We sold it to my aunt before we moved to Short Hills," I fib.

"Care to explain why I'm getting prompted to sign into 'Leo's Mansion' Wi-Fi?" He indicates a pop-up on his phone.

I face-palm, letting out a disgruntled groan. "I'm sorry I lied to you."

He fixes me with a curious stare. "Why would you make up something like that?"

Then, suddenly, it's like he can see straight through me, the same way Varsha and Dillon can. I wrote it off at first, thinking he doesn't care about me enough to remember coming here to hang out years ago—but he does. Apparently, he doesn't have *amnesia*. What do I tell him? That I made it up because I'm ashamed that I don't actually live in a big fancy mansion like Tim, Lincoln, and his friends? That I feared people wouldn't like me as much? That *he* wouldn't like me as much?

Think of the checklist, Leo!

I choose my words carefully. "Just 'cause."

"Yeah?" he asks, leaning toward me slowly, enrobing me in

his musky cologne and the intoxicating scent of a dark, woodsy shower gel. "And why's that?"

I shrug, feeling my throat go dry. I lean toward him slowly, incrementally, despite myself. It's like I'm being drawn in by his gravitational pull. I can feel the heat radiating off him, and my heart beats loudly in my ears.

"Who cares?" I say with a sly smile. "You're here, aren't you?"

He lets out a deep, quiet laugh. "Your secret is safe." Then, he asks, "Have you read the new Whiskered Warriors novel?"

I'm taken aback. Before I can think better of it, I tell the truth. "Yeah. You?"

"I did. I liked it," he says.

"Me too."

It feels like we're slipping back into our old rapport. "I'm glad you came," I utter. I'm suddenly acutely aware of my breath and hope it doesn't smell bad. What I'd do for some gum right now. Do I ask him how he's been? Or mention how I've missed him? So much? Do I ask him why he abandoned me? Questions for the checklist, of course.

"Got any Halloween candy? I'd kill for a Three Musketeers bar," he says with a smile. "It's my favorite."

"I know," I blurt, then stop myself from telling him how there's a whole basket of them in the living room and I can go get them right now for him. So glad the checklist reeled me in. Thoughtful gifts equal creepy and needy. "Creedy." And my days of being a "creedy" try-hard are over. Although just admitting I recall his favorite Halloween candy may have set me way back.

"Of course you know." He laughs. "We only ate our weight in them during my movie nights."

I go in overdrive to hide a bashful smile. "You remember."

"I do." He leans closer to me. Every part of me wants to kiss him, and all I can think of is the time we kissed before. It was just like this—that mesmerized way he's looking at me—but there's no way I'm making the first move. The checklist would say to let *him* come to *you*. But I can't let him. Not Lincoln Chan. No second chances.

Unless . . .

"Do you want to hang out sometime? You know, just the two of us?"

He blinks. "Isn't that what we're doing now?"

I shouldn't have said it. I ruined the vibe.

I laugh, turning red. "I mean, like . . . a without-a-house-full-of-people kind of thing."

He chews the corner of his lip, looking thoughtfully at me. I blew it. I blew it!

Then he nods. "Okay."

"Okay?" My breath comes out shallow. My heart feels like it's going to leap out of my chest. What is happening? Is it because he's tipsy? Or is my checklist working its magic?

"What's this?" Lincoln moves the sheet aside to reveal my beloved stuffed unicorn.

"Meep!" I grab his horn, and fling him into my hamper.

Lincoln quirks a thick black eyebrow. "Who now?"

"Oh. It's just my—I mean, *my cat's*—toy."

He sits back. "I won't tell." Maybe he still knows me, even if after all this time it's felt like he'd forgotten me.

I just grunt in acknowledgment.

"Sure you don't want a sip?" He offers me his cup.

I gesture to myself. "Responsible Party Host here, remember?"

"Is that so?" He takes Miss Tiramisu's feather wand and tickles the tip of my nose, and I shove it away and stifle a giggle.

In a moment of silence, I hear a terrible crash from downstairs.

I bolt up, suddenly full of dread. "That didn't sound good."

He rises. "After you."

I race down the stairs. What just shattered?

The foyer's packed, and everyone's facing the corner.

The corner where Mom puts our Christmas tree each year.

The corner where a million tiny pieces now cover the floor.

Dillon's sculpture. Shattered.

"*Oh, no,*" I whisper.

"Well, that's not good," Lincoln says from beside me, breaking into a laugh.

All the heavy, awful feelings related to my friends leaving come pouring back, joined by a fresh new wave of upset. People giggle nervously, turning away and resuming their chitchat while others have their phones out to record the mess.

My stomach sinks. Who did this? There are no obvious perpetrators. But also, what does it matter? The damage is done. I stoop down and pick up a jagged glass shard, eyeing what's left of the statue. There's no way to piece this thing back together. Dillon's going to be beside himself.

People clear out of the way as I book it toward the kitchen and return with a broom and a dustpan, and I begin sweeping up the mess, my mind racing with a swarm of worries. Lincoln stands by protectively, making sure no one accidentally walks into me where I'm kneeling.

Suddenly, police lights flash through the front windows.

A scream cuts through the air. "The cops!"

"Don't run!" a police officer's voice booms from a megaphone. The front door flies open, and he steps inside.

People trample in every direction, and I fall over from where I was kneeling. A sneaker steps on my finger and I shout out in pain.

"Everyone, stay where you are!" comes another police officer's voice.

My head is spinning. More people shove past me, racing out the back door. I can hear them yelling at each other.

This is just what Varsha was afraid of.

When I manage to stand, ready to flee with Lincoln, I find he's already gone.

But a policeman is gazing right at me.

17

"WHAT MADE YOU THINK THROWING A PARTY WOULD BE
okay?" Mom asks me the next morning. She was so mad when
she got home that she wouldn't even look at me.

She's seated at the kitchen table in her bathrobe with her cup
of coffee and the morning paper spread out before her, gazing
up at me with a disappointed expression that douses me in a
layer of ice-cold guilt. Fortunately, she seems to be blaming my
"bad behavior" on the divorce. I'm playing along since I haven't
exactly told her about my Boyfriend Material Checklist.

"You know you're going to get community service for this,"
she says. "For providing alcohol to minors." She shakes her head,
her brown ponytail swinging.

I moan. "Even though *they* brought it?"

Mom's sharp look makes me go silent.

The house phone rings.

Mom glares at it, then takes a long swig of coffee. She's been avoiding endless calls from disgruntled parents.

The phone finally stops ringing while I finish scraping butter on my toast.

Miss Tiramisu pads in and meows. We both ignore her adorableness.

Mom shakes her head. "It's my own fault."

"What?" I toss the butter wrapper into the trash.

"I've been too busy thinking about myself, and obviously I haven't been paying enough attention to you if you thought that throwing a secret house party was a good idea." She dabs at the kitchen table, and I see there's still something sticky on it. "I thought you said you already cleaned this."

I grimace. "I'll do it again." I spent all morning vacuuming, mopping, and cleaning every square inch of the place, but I guess it needs another once-over. "Well, I have the whole rest of the weekend. It's not like I'm going anywhere, since I'm grounded."

Mom picks up the newspaper and stares at it morosely, deep in thought.

I stay rooted to my spot at the counter, staring at the Three Musketeers bars and planning to take some to Lincoln at rehearsal next week. Lincoln, who sat beside me on my bed, who smelled like that fresh, musky cologne, who made me want to pull him in for a kiss and run my hands through his glorious, perfect swoop of black hair. I'm glad Mom hasn't threatened to pull me from the play.

In my pocket, my phone dings with a notification. My heart

leaps, hoping it's Varsha or Dillon. I haven't heard from them since last night, and I've been trying not to feel hurt.

I fish it out to discover Lincoln followed me on Instagram.

I squeal and fight the try-hard urge to immediately follow back. Then I realize Mom is pulling my phone out of my hand.

"I said no phone." She puts it in her bathrobe pocket.

"Mom!" I moan. "Lincoln followed me on Instagram." I see how she's looking at me and gaze down guiltily at my hands. "I'm really sorry, Mom."

"I know you are. I was young once too. But rules are rules and you're going to have to learn your lesson." Then she turns and walks out of the room, her slippers making a sticky sound against the floor.

"And mop the floors again!" she calls over her shoulder.

It feels like I've ruined everything.

Then I think of that notification of Lincoln following me.

Well, maybe not *everything*.

Monday rolls around. Ever since Friday's police raid fiasco, I've been dreading going into school. After Mom drops me off, I dodge past swarms of girls in sweatshirts with leggings, North Face backpacks with Hydro water bottles in the side netting, and Starbucks cake pops.

I swipe my student ID and enter the musty halls. Usually, I do coffee laps with Dillon and Varsha, but today that doesn't seem to be an option. As soon as Mom gave me back my phone this morning, I checked immediately, but I still had no messages from them. Where are they? I need them more than ever to face the day ahead. I'm still shaky from this weekend and worry that the party had the opposite effect of its intended one: to make me popular and beloved by all of Eastfield High.

Even *if* Lincoln Chan now follows me on Instagram. Police raids on parties aren't cool, right? Especially for any others strapped with repercussions.

I still haven't followed him back, BTW. It's too needy to follow back right away, right? I'm going to wait.

With my head down, I stop in the library to kill time by quietly scrolling on my phone—and instantly regret it. The place is loud and packed. As I move past tables to look for an open seat, I realize people are talking about my party.

"I am *still* hungover," someone whispers with a laugh.

"I think I'm still drunk," someone else says in a giddy voice.

"Dude, look what we broke," one guy says, showing a photo on his phone to another guy.

I've never seen those guys before in my life.

Lu Lockheart shows off her pair of muddy boots to Mary Allison. "My boots are ruined!"

Mary Allison's eyes bulge. "Oh no! What happened?" she says, and I recall her smooching Sergio. I'm still not over that revelation.

Lu's face lights up. "I was also at Leo Martino's Halloween party. When the cops showed up, I booked it and escaped out his backyard. *Barely.*" The way she says it, with a smug smile— she's actually showing off that she was in attendance. She could have cleaned them, but she's keeping her battle scars.

Hers aren't the only muddy shoes I spot, either.

"Here's the man now!" Eamon cheers, fist-bumping me. "Dude, you're a legend."

"Yeah, Leo," says Lincoln. "Your party was *epic*."

I feel my nerves begin to dissipate, replaced by Lincoln-induced heart palpitations. "Thanks," I say with a slight smile. The memory of our time on my bed, our faces moving close to each other, sends a thrill through me, and suddenly the thought of Lincoln Chan as my Future Boyfriend no longer gives me the complete ick. Without Dillon and Varsha spilling doubt into my ear, I allow the idea to grow. Suddenly, it's easier to bat aside the hesitation.

Do you want to hang out sometime? Just the two of us?

Okay . . .

And then there's the whole Follow Situation.

I wonder if it's possible that he's secretly squirming that I haven't followed him back. His expression only gives off calm, cool energy, but it could be a front.

"Join us!" Sakura gestures with one perfectly manicured hand to an open seat.

Normally, I'd flinch, thinking the chair would be pulled out from underneath me the moment I started to lower down. But I think it's safe to assume the days of people making my life miserable are over. Or at least on pause?

I unsling my backpack and sit.

"I'm so glad we escaped in time," Katie says.

"Dude, did you get busted?" Eamon asks.

"Yeah, but it's all good."

"Hooray," Katie says in a quiet, even voice.

Sakura tucks a long strand of hair behind her ear as she leans in to whisper. "Hey, did you hear Zubin got caught and his parents grounded him till the New Year?"

"Oh." I cringe. "That's not good."

"Worth it!" Eamon yells, and high-fives Lincoln.

As everyone continues to bubble over with more talk of the party and who narrowly escaped the clutches of the cops, I glance at the back of the library to where I used to eat lunch.

There's Dillon and Varsha. The second we see each other, they give me a curt wave, then stare down at their textbooks. The move makes my stomach churn. I tune out the chatter around me. They're ticked off at me. It makes me feel sick that there's this rift between us.

The bell rings, and the air fills with rustling pages and zipping bags.

"I'll catch you later," I say to Lincoln and his friends. Then I wait until Dillon and Varsha approach. They have to pass me in order to leave the library, so technically I've trapped them.

"Hey," I say with a bashful smile.

"Hey."

"Hey."

They keep walking past me, but I follow in lockstep. I can practically feel the chill coming off them. Both have an iced coffee. It sounds silly, but I feel left out. Iced coffee is our thing we all do together.

"Listen, I know the party was a disaster, but luckily you two left when you did!"

"Yeah, because we actually care about our futures," Varsha remarks.

Ouch.

Varsha whirls on me. "You didn't even dress up!"

"Dillon, I'm really sorry again that your sculpture broke," I say, thinking of how awful he must have felt after Eamon posted it on Instagram with the caption: It's not a real house party unless you break a big piece of junk.

He makes his lips skinny and shrugs.

"And I'm sorry you guys weren't comfortable," I continue. "Are you mad at me?"

"Were your parents mad at you?" Varsha asks.

Parents. It's still hard to figure out how to navigate telling them what happened with my parents, but I just feel like it's a detail that's totally irrelevant to anyone, and I don't feel like correcting her. Especially not right now.

"I'm going to be grounded for a while," I add.

Varsha shrugs. "But you're a homebody anyway, so does it really count as a punishment?"

"No. Not really."

"What about the play?" Dillon asks.

"I can still be a part of it and Robotics Club."

"Honestly . . . I don't think you should come back to Robotics Club," Dillon says slowly.

"Oh," I say, flushing. "I get it."

We reach a busy intersection. Varsha heads to the stairwell while Dillon turns right, leaving me in the center of the morning rush. I can't believe they're *this* upset with me. I can understand

Dillon being mad because of his broken sculpture. But Varsha? I didn't even really drink anything. And I haven't told them about Lincoln. Now I *know* they'd never let me hear the end of it. Especially if they heard I'm daydreaming about him being my Future Boyfriend, which does feel like a cardinal sin, the more I think about it.

"Bye," I whisper to no one, then sigh and head to class.

The PA system's starting to blare the "Superstars" theme song from *Super Mario Bros.*, their not-so-subtle two-minute countdown to get students to hasten to class.

There's Lincoln, walking toward his locker. I swing my backpack around to my chest, fingers pinching the zipper, prepared to give all the Three Musketeers bars to him right now. Why wait for rehearsal?

Don't be a try-hard, Leo . . .

At the last minute, I chicken out and wave instead, veering toward my own locker. I'm practically using the door as a barrier to hide behind as he strides past me and down the hall.

Hmmm. An idea pops to mind.

I unzip my backpack and unload the dozen or so Three Musketeer bars into my locker, then close it. What if my snack locker becomes my "do not gift this item" storage locker?

Take that, Sergio.

"Hey."

I turn. Lincoln is standing there. We lock eyes and my heart starts to race, thinking about the Instagram follow and how we agreed to hang sometime. Not to mention the Near Kiss.

He smooths down his oversize T-shirt. "Want to go over

our lines tomorrow? At lunch?"

I feel as light as air. "Definitely."

"Cool." A soft smile breaks over his face. "You still have my number?"

"Yeah," I say, trying not to sound too eager. "But . . ."

"I unblocked you," he says with a wry smile.

I give a little laugh, playing it off cool. "How kind." I still don't want to outright ask why he blocked me in the first place, for fear of ruining this moment.

"I hope that'll get me that follow back on Instagram."

I smile, despite the whirlpool in my stomach. "Maybe. I'll have to think about it."

If only he knew the restraint it's required of me not to follow him back yet.

He looks at me long and hard—it's unnerving, and I fight the urge to fidget with my backpack straps, rolling and unrolling them at the ends. "Dorrio's? Tomorrow at noon?" he asks.

"How about Mike's?" I ask. Let Julien see me living my best life.

"Sure."

"Cool. Let me check." I glance at my phone and pretend to look at my calendar, which is blank across the board. My stomach is doing cartwheels. I look up casually. "Sounds good."

"Great. I'll see you at noon."

"Yeah, sounds great."

He shrugs his slick bomber jacket over his big broad shoulders and smiles that wide, mischievous smile. Then he runs his fingers through his shiny black hair and takes his backpack by its handle.

Before I can gawk any further, he's off. But not before giving me one extra over-the-shoulder smile.

A small, nagging voice in the back of my head says: *Don't you miss your best friends?*

I do. But the one thing I haven't had—haven't *ever* had—this whole time was somebody who took a romantic interest in me. Who liked me. And not only did I find somebody who might like me, but I also liked him first. The odds of that happening have always been a million to one.

Varsha and Dillon will understand. They have arts and smarts, and I don't have anything.

Later that night in bed, I follow Lincoln back on Instagram. And pull up our old text history, the one I never had the heart to delete or the stomach to reread.

Forging ahead, I send a new text.

Leo: Testing 1 2 3
Leo: Blocked still?

He replies instantly.

Heartbreaker: Def still blocked :P

I crack a smile.

Is it really so terrible that I've dipped back into an old crush? Varsha was wrong. He's not the Jaws of the crushes. He's the *Moby Dick* of the crushes. This is a *good* thing. Not that I support whaling. But I know him, and he feels like home in the way the others could never.

Plus, my checklist needs its last item. Which means it's time to toss the metaphorical harpoon to get that feedback from Lincoln.

THE NEXT DAY DURING LUNCH PERIOD, I STAND OUTSIDE

Mike's Diner with my heart pounding out of my chest.

I check the time on my phone. Lincoln should be here by now . . .

Right on cue, Lincoln pulls up to the diner in his Mercedes-Benz beneath an overcast November sky. He parks it and steps out, hair billowing like something out of a romantic comedy. I've been waiting for this moment all day. Quite possibly all my life? And I feel like I'm going to pass out with nerves. I guess this is what "weak in the knees" feels like. I don't know where to look as he approaches.

"Hey. Hungry?" he asks.

"Definitely." I open the door with its jingling bell. "After you."

The hostess brings us to a cozy corner booth.

I was hoping Julien would be the one to greet us, but he's at another table taking down an order, looking over at us. He's clearly in awe.

Jealous, Julien?

"What's so funny?" Lincoln asks.

I didn't realize I was smirking.

"Oh. I . . . I'm just happy to be here with you," I blurt.

Did I *really* just say that?

He says nothing and looks down at the long, laminated menu. Meanwhile, I try to harness some of the "presence" I've learned for the play, sitting tall, chest up, legs spread wide.

Other students file in, taking note of us while they move to their tables. I know it's just a matter of time before people start talking. Could Lincoln and I become the new It Couple?

"Do you know what you're getting?" he asks, setting down his menu.

"Not sure yet," I say, although I spent all night picking out what to order. "You?"

Lincoln gestures to the collar of my new shirt. "Your . . . *price tag* is sticking out?"

I stiffen in horror, then unfreeze and quickly tuck it away.

Thankfully, Julien walks over to us in his red apron. "Hey, gentlemen. What can I get for you today?"

"Caesar salad and a Coke," Lincoln says.

"Make that two," I add. Forget the pancakes I've been craving.

Julien smiles. His eyes sparkle when he looks at me. "Great. I'll be back."

A waitress passes by with a towering stack of pancakes slathered in whipped cream. She drops it off at the table next to ours, where a girl breaks into a grin at the sight of the yumminess. I'm having major food envy and regrets.

"Woof, that's a lot of calories for her," Lincoln remarks under his breath, shooting me a smile.

I'm not sure how to interpret that. I'm still stuck on the fact that I almost ordered that but didn't for risk of not seeming cool enough. Was copying his order a try-hard look?

"So you wanted to go over your lines?" I ask him.

"What?" Then a look of realization dawns across his face. "Right." Lincoln wrestles his script from his bag and unfolds it. "Mind reading through act two, scene four with me? You can be Viola."

"Sure." I pull out my script and open to the same page, and we start reading.

"'What kind of woman is't?'" Lincoln recites.

"'Of your complexion,'" I read, blushing.

The whole time I'm following along, I can barely pay attention as he looks at me, spouting his lines. He only misses a few, and when I point them out, he gives a serious nod and starts over. We don't put down the scripts until our food arrives.

I reach for my Coke, which I wish were a Sprite. "Can I have a straw, please?" I ask Julien.

Julien gestures to the pile of straws in front of me on the table. Cool, cool.

I unsheathe a straw and pop it into my drink, locking eyes with Lincoln. "I still don't get what you're doing in the play."

A touch of red flashes on his cheeks. "I've always loved theater."

I nod. I can't discount the idea that he joined the play to win over Tim . . . or maybe even win back Travis.

"Plus, I needed an extracurricular to write about for my supplemental essay."

I go to take a sip of Coke, but my mouth can't seem to locate my straw.

"You good?" he asks with a hint of amusement in his voice.

"Yeah. Def." I take a sip. "I didn't know your inner theater nerd was still in there."

"Oh, come on. We only watched *Hairspray* a thousand times during my movie nights."

I can't help but think about how we've continued to dance around the topic of our fallout. Maybe it's just better that way. Pretend like it never happened. Leave the past in the past. That's the way to play it off cool, right? But what about *confident*? Wouldn't New Leo be assertive and ask? And then there's the whole gathering up of Lincoln's feedback. The crown jewel of intel.

He bites into his fork and his teeth scrape the metal. I recoil at the sound. Then I take a deep breath. "Hey . . . what happened between us?" My voice fights a tremble.

Lincoln takes a long sip from his soda. "What do you mean?"

I laugh. "Well, we were friends . . ." I trail off and eventually decide not to mention our kiss. "And then we weren't."

He fixes me with a steady stare. "Oh, I think we were more than friends."

I chuckle into my drink harder than I mean to, spewing bubbles. Did he really just say that? More proof it wasn't all in my head. "You mean our kiss?"

He averts his eyes, gazing at the rain-spattered window. "Ah, our kiss."

My mouth hangs open as my theories swarm my thoughts. Did I have bad breath? Body odor? I force myself to go there. "So what happened?"

He cracks his knuckles. "It doesn't matter. Water under the bridge."

I shrug, pretending like the words don't sting. It *does* matter. To me. "Was it something I did?" I try to sound unbothered even though my heart is pounding hard.

He leans back. "Nah. Just life."

"Oh, okay. Cool." Just life? What does *that* mean?

"I followed you on Instagram, didn't I?" he asks.

"And I *may* have followed you back," I tease.

He grins. "Exactly."

"Did you unblock me on *all* the things yet?" I ask with a nervous laugh.

"Sure did."

I grin, moving my salad around with my fork. "You did?"

"I did. You're going to have to Venmo me for lunch, aren't you?"

I'm not sure if he's joking, so I take a bite of salad. Of course I get a huge leaf. Who ever thought eating was a good idea for a date? No one should ever have to see another person eat salad, specifically me.

After a few seconds of crunching in silence, he looks at me

thoughtfully and says, "You said it was your first kiss."

"I did?" I ask, blotting globs of dressing from the sides of my mouth. It was.

"Yeah. It kind of showed."

I freeze. I want to shout all of a sudden: *Are you kidding me? It was eighth grade!*

I blush. "Oh. Well, I don't know why I said it was my first kiss. And nowadays? Forget it. I could teach a class on . . . stuff." The words linger as I inwardly cringe. Did I really just say that? And am I truly such a bad liar?

"Oh?" He looks intrigued.

"Yeah. So, you ghosted me like a jerk for nothing," I tease, turning pink. I still think it was a cruel punishment for something I technically didn't do wrong . . . but it's something. An answer. "But, you know, water under the bridge."

"I didn't ghost for nothing. I started dating Travis right after then."

"Oh. Yeah," I say. Crap. I didn't want to get the conversation on Travis.

He blinks. "Breakups suck."

"Yeah. I know," I say, thinking about all the pseudo-breakups I've ever had—ours included.

"Well, I'm glad we could clear the air." His mouth quirks into a smile, and I feel his foot nudge mine under the table. "And I'm glad to hear you've gotten in more kissing experience since that night."

"Yeah, well, you know." My throat goes dry. Wait, just how good does he think I am?

Once Julien clears the plates, Lincoln and I continue chatting, this time about what we think of our theater directors and cast-mates. I hope Lincoln doesn't notice how I've nervously torn up my straw wrapper into a million tiny pieces on my lap. At one point, he mentions my ridiculous dance moves, which makes us both crack a smile. I catch Julien glancing over at me on more than one occasion, which makes me positively glow.

"Ice cream?" I ask, surveying the dessert menu. We never went over ice cream while we were—well, whatever we were—and the familiar urge to learn everything about him is too strong to deny.

"I like vanilla," he says.

"It kind of goes. That kind of makes sense for you."

The way he looks at me confirms my words came out all wrong. "What? *Boring?*"

"No, no, no, not at all. No." I laugh nervously. "I meant classic. You're a very classic guy."

"Well, not plain vanilla. The type with vanilla bean flecks. Maybe a chocolate chip."

I nod. "That tracks. I mean, there *is* a *little* something special about you." I give a wink.

He looks nonplussed. There I go again.

I set my menu down. "You know what, I'm feeling too full for dessert."

Then, before I realize it, we're splitting the bill.

"So, shall I Venmo you? You did say you unblocked me, right?" I tease.

Lincoln smirks and rolls his eyes. "Yes. But don't push your luck."

I float through the rest of the school day in a blur, still inside the aura of our perfect lunch date. At rehearsal, my heart skips a beat whenever I glance his way. I never want to stop feeling like this.

By the time I've done my homework and am in bed, however, I'm feeling a heaviness creep in. I drag over my laptop and distract myself from obsessing over Lincoln any further by trying to soak up everything there is to know about the college application process—along with colleges. I've been trying—and failing—to figure out what I want and where I want to apply for too long now.

Do I want to go someplace warm like Miami? Then again, Varsha once told me something about how the University of Miami has an alligator living in its lake. Apparently, students throw french fries into its open mouth when it's out basking, and Varsha thinks it's just a matter of time before Sherman snaps and lunges for a snickering student. But I'm not going to pick which school I want to attend based on the potential wildlife threats or the weather.

There's no way I have the background to even consider applying to Princeton or even somewhere *like* Princeton.

I switch gears and contemplate my college essay. What can I write about that will let schools know who I am and why they should accept me? There's nothing special about me. I didn't invent some life-changing robot or win some spelling bee every year for the past four years, if that's even considered impressive these days. There's the school play . . .

No, that's nothing to write home about. Lots of people are in school plays.

I contemplate FaceTiming Dillon and Varsha. But then I remember their NTB, aka No Text Back.

I set my laptop aside and launch backward, head hitting my pillow.

Miss Tiramisu meows from the foot of the bed.

"My thoughts exactly, girl." Sometimes, it's like she can read my mind, like everyone else. I haven't fooled her with the new me. I've been feeling more sure of myself these days, but right now, I'm more confused inside than ever.

And I'm back on Lincoln.

How can I keep this thing with Lincoln going?

Overwhelmed and unable to turn off my rushing mental faucet, I pull my scrapbook out. I feel good about what I accomplished at the diner—by being more assertive and bringing up the whole fallout thing. Now what do I need to do to keep reeling Lincoln in?

6. KISS LIKE A PRO.

BOYFRIEND MATERIAL CHECKLIST

 1. BE COOL AS A CUCUMBER. ☑

2. GET A GLAM GLOW-UP. ☑

3. HAVE A POWERHOUSE PRESENCE. ☑

4. FAKE BEING RICH. ☑

5. WIN POPULARITY CONTEST. ☐

6. KISS LIKE A PRO. ☐

ALTHOUGH I HAVEN'T HEARD FROM LINCOLN SINCE OUR
hangout—and, yes, it's only been two days—my heart still flutters with excitement every time I see him during rehearsals. But if I'm going to hang out with him again, and if we kiss, I need to be ready.

Which means I'll need a willing participant for kissing practice. Because something tells me practicing on my hand isn't *quite* the way to go.

I eye my stuffed unicorn, who's still mad at me for flinging him into the hamper during my house party. Definitely not. Sorry, Meep.

I rack my brains about possible smooching buddies to ask, even though there's no way anyone would agree to help me. Vincent? No, he'd be too disturbed. Maybe Travis. He was chummy at my party, but being that he's Lincoln's ex-boyfriend, it could go terribly wrong and mess up my chances with Lincoln if he were to ever find out.

Julien may be a possibility, judging from the way he eyed me at the diner. The fact he lives on the other side of town helps. I'm going to keep ignoring the fact I have no idea whether he's into me. That's not desperate, right?

Maybe. But right now, desperate is all I've got.

I send a simple *whats up* on Instagram.

As I wait for a reply, I get ready for bed, taking off my makeup, putting on a face mask, and laying out my outfit for tomorrow: a silky green blouse with a draping neckline and fitted black pants with shiny, pointed shoes. I tuck their receipts into the shopping bags. So far, this buying and returning thing's been working out—for the most part. I wonder what Dillon and Varsha would think of how I want to practice kissing with Julien Ivanov, another unanimously disliked ex-crush.

I consider texting Dillon and Varsha in our group chat again. But I've already texted them a dozen times since the party without any response. It hurts.

Before I can dwell on it for too much longer, Julien replies.

Julien: Nm how bout u
Leo: I was wondering if you could help me with something
Julien: Is this about that self-help thing you're working on?
Leo: Sort of

I decide to just go for it.

Leo: Could you help me practicing kissing

Whelp, there's no way to pass *that* off as some self-help thing.

Ten excruciatingly long minutes later, it shows he's seen my message but hasn't replied.

I take a deep breath, pushing away the embarrassment. Who else could I ask? I reach over to give Miss Tiramisu a kiss on the nose and she darts away. I love you too, Mushy Squishy.

Unfortunately, my roster of boys-who-might-be-willing-to-kiss-me is woefully short. Except one last person comes to mind.

Even though Dillon's straight-ish and only used "them" to describe hypothetical future prospects, he's usually pretty game for the gayest of things, like the time he let me paint rainbows on his nails during Pride month. I guess that's what makes him a good ally, among other things. I wonder if he would draw the line at making out—especially with our friendship on shaky ground. But he's usually into an experiment. At the very least, maybe it'll jolt him into responding to me. I send a private text and hope for the best.

Leo: Hey! I know you're mad at me but . . . I would LOVE your help with my checklist!

Dillon: Which item?

Leo: Can I practice kissing with you? Hehe! 😳

Dillon: You're joking

Leo: I'm not. Please??

Dillon: I'm good

Leo: You're a good kisser?

Dillon: No LOL I mean I'll pass

Leo: So you're not a good kisser?

Dillon: 🤦

Okay so that's not happening. But at least he's responding to me. I feel a small weight lift from my chest.

Leo: I hope you're doing okay 🖤

I skim my social feeds. Maybe there's some random guy at school who'd be willing? Honestly, knowing me, I'd probably end up falling in love with the first guy who says yes.

I start looking up kissing scenes from favorite movies and shows, and take notes—literally, in my notes app. I watch scenes from *The Bachelor* and realize there are so many kissing styles. He puts his hands gently on the lady's ears as he kisses her with full-on tongue. But then for soft, gentle peck kissing, he has his hands around another's waist. He also does a combination of the two. So, if I just copy these moves, then I can be a better kisser in no time.

Just as I'm about to call it a night, I get a message—one that makes my jaw drop.

Julien: Sure, I'll help LOL. Just say when and where

The next night after work, I meet Julien at my front door under a waxing moon. He's in jeans and a cable-knit sweater, his hair freshly showered and gelled. I can still see the neat lines made by the comb. He smells like bergamot. The glossy ChapStick on his lips doesn't go unnoticed.

I put a finger to my lips, indicating we need to be quiet. Mom's asleep, and I really don't want to wake her up with a make-out session. Not that I think we're going to be loud. I just want to feel comfortable without worrying she'll come walking in at a moment's notice.

He points past me into the house, eyebrows rising.

I shake my head, then silently close the front door and tiptoe past him toward the garage. He follows behind me.

I shove the garage door up to my shoulder and then duck inside. It smells like mildew and autumn leaves and motor oil. It's dark until I pull on the cord of the dim overhead bulb.

Julien steps in front of me. We just look at each other. I'm nervous. I've been imagining kissing Julien all day, but I never thought it'd be like this. Me wanting him to practice kissing. Him wanting to help out. It's so contrived and sterile. My old crush feelings for him stir inside. But I'm surprised to find they're not stirring as hard as I thought they would.

I really *do* want to do this for Lincoln.

I push away the sound of Varsha's disapproving voice in my head and focus on Julien.

"So, you were serious?" His eyebrows knit, but there's a slight smirk on his face. "Why couldn't Lincoln Chan help you practice kissing?"

I give a little laugh. "Well, it's complicated. Part of that self-help thing and all."

The sly, roguish smile gets bigger. "I have to admit, I got kind of jealous seeing you two together."

"Yeah?" I ask, fighting the corners of my mouth from raising higher.

He shifts his weight from foot to foot, eyes downcast, and nods.

"I didn't know you thought of me like that," I admit.

"Just recently, I guess. You've changed."

He says it like it's a compliment, and it *is*, but for the first time, I'm finding it hard to swallow for some reason. Maybe it's because it hurts thinking he didn't like Old Leo . . . but then again, *who did*?

Julien jams his hands into his pockets and rocks back and forth on his heels, as if waiting for me to hit him back with something else, but all I can think to say is "Thanks."

"Yep." He blinks at me from behind his wiry glasses. "So, tell me more about this self-help thing . . ."

I wince. "I would, but part of the process is keeping the details a secret. Sorry."

"Right." His eyes dart left and right, then settle on mine. "So, shall we begin?"

I hold up a finger then hastily pull out a stick of gum and pop it in my mouth. It takes a few moments for it to soften up, and for me to quit choking on hard little pieces that break off, and for the mint flavor to permeate everything. Luckily, Julien seems to find it endearing because he doesn't run away screaming.

"Okay." I nod. "Ready." I lean toward him, my eyes starting to close.

"Wait."

I stare at him, frozen.

"You need to take the gum out of your mouth."

I laugh, embarrassed, as I take out the used-up gum and tuck it in the wrapper. "Are you even a good kisser?" I ask.

"Of course I am."

"Yeah, but how do you know?"

He peers at me. "Shouldn't we have discussed this sooner?"

"Sorry. It just occurred to me to ask."

"I've never had any complaints."

I want to ask if he's ever had any *compliments*, but no complaints is good enough.

I nod, indicating I'm set to proceed.

Just then, my phone buzzes, and I nearly jump a foot in the air before wrestling it out of my pocket. "Sorry," I mutter, going to both silence it and check to see if it's Lincoln.

Dillon: Did you find a kissing partner? I could work on a robot for you.

I chuckle, then stash my phone and clear my throat. "Sorry," I repeat again, quieter.

Julien takes a small step, closing the gap between us, and then rests his hands on my hips. I lean in too, maybe a bit too hard, and our teeth clink. I pull back.

"Sorry," I say with a nervous laugh, running my finger across my pained smile.

He sucks his front teeth. "It's okay."

"Now what?"

"Leo," Julien says. "Good kissing is about feeling things in the moment. It's not so prescriptive. Relax. Breathe."

"Okay. Where should my hands go?"

"On my hips is fine," he says. "Now—"

"Wait. Sorry. Should I move my feet farther apart?"

"Sure."

I widen my stance. "Where should I look? Do I close my eyes—"

He leans in and our lips touch.

Thankfully, no clinking teeth this time. His mouth tastes flavorless, which is good. After he kisses my lips a few times, I feel his tongue make its way to mine, and I begin to move mine around, picturing a writhing snake. It's a midsentence kiss—like the ones I've always dreamed of—but it's missing the butterflies. It also feels so . . . rote and mechanical.

He pulls away and ruffles my hair. "Sometimes, you just have to go with the flow."

"Sorry about that. So, how'd I do?"

"Hmm."

I flinch. "That bad?"

"Well, if I'm taking the lead, you should just follow what I do. Kind of like dancing. If I move my tongue in, you should move yours back. Right now it feels like we're tongue-wrestling."

"Isn't that a good thing?" I let out an uneasy giggle.

"Does it *feel* like a good thing?"

I take a breath and we try again. I try not to picture a writhing snake this time. After it seems to be going well for a few seconds, Julien intensifies the kiss, leaning against me. I've always seen movies where the leads bite each other's lips, so I give it a try.

"Oww." He pulls back and gingerly touches his lip.

"Too much?"

He nods. "Yeah." Luckily, I don't spot blood.

I burst into an embarrassed grin.

"It's okay." He places his hands on my hips.

"Where should I put my hands again?" I ask, realizing they've just been dangling at my sides.

"You could put them on my head." He guides them there.

"Roger that."

We kiss some more, this time with my fingers running through his hair at the nape of his neck. To my surprise, it becomes easier—more natural. He shows me how we can pause to look at each other and take a breather before going back in. Even though it's just practice, kissing Julien starts making me tingly all over, and a part of me wonders if he's feeling the same way.

I pull back and give him an expectant look.

He chuckles, straightening his glasses. "Yeah. Much better."

Kiss Like a Pro?

Check.

An hour later, I'm back in bed, spooning Meep and scrolling through TikTok.

After we'd kissed some more, Julien and I hung out and talked for a while in the garage. It almost felt like we connected as friends. Julien even asked how my mom's doing. I wondered if my brother told Julien's brother, Roman, about our parents, but Julien didn't push further.

When I text Dillon back to tell him that no robots are

required at this time, I see something that sets off a flurry of butterflies in my stomach.

Lincoln 🖤🖤🖤 Future Boyfriend: Movie night tomorrow at my place?

Victorious, I bolt up, but stop myself from replying. Let him wait until the morning.

I settle back down, distracting myself with *When Harry Met Sally*. Eventually, my eyes flutter with exhaustion. Who knew kissing could take so much out of a person?

But my heart flutters with excitement at the thought of tomorrow's hangout with Lincoln.

Will it end with a kiss?

SATURDAY, I KNOCK ON THE METAL DOOR OF LINCOLN'S
contemporary-style home and wait.

Being here is both familiar and surreal. I used to come here a
lot in middle school. We would do homework together. Science
experiments, like pouring different liquids onto bean seeds in
pots and seeing how they affected plant growth. We would
watch movies in his den, and Junior would curl up next to me
but growl if I tried to pet him.

I go to knock on the door once more just as it swings inward.

"Um, hi?" Sakura says, looking puzzled. I hear people chatting behind her.

So, my romantic hangout with Lincoln includes his friends?
I can't deny the sting of disappointment.

"Hey. Lincoln invited me over."

"*Oh.*" Her voice is high and surprised. "Come on in, I guess."

I shake off the awkward energy clinging to me—I'm assuming Lincoln didn't tell his friends about my attendance, either—and follow her into the house.

We hang a left into the movie room. It's just as I remember it, with a big-screen TV mounted on the wall and rows of plush chairs. As usual, Lincoln reclines in the single massage chair. Around him, on bean bags, Katie and Eamon nosh on popcorn and snacks while Sakura sinks back down beside them.

Lincoln leans forward. "Hey. There you are."

Typically, I'd make myself as small and as quiet as possible and slither into the group unnoticed, hoping not to be a bother to anyone. But today, in this moment, I stand tall. *Powerhouse Presence*-ing, if you will. And my fresh face of natural-looking makeup is just the armor I need. Despite my fight-or-flight instincts taking over.

"Hey," I say in a voice full of put-on bravado, like I belong here. You know—acting. For the good of the checklist.

People look at each other and nod. At least I've gotten the awkward moment out of the way.

"Let's start the movie, man," Eamon tells Lincoln, who's holding the remote control.

"How's everybody doing?" I take a seat farthest away from Lincoln to show that I'm not trying too hard to attract him, which will hopefully work to attract him. Plus, I definitely don't want to do anything that's going to embarrass him like, oh, I don't know, walking over and sitting on his lap.

We settle in for *Scream VI*, with the Fierce Four chiming in with commentary. Thankfully, I love scary movies, and this is one of my favorites. I practically know it by heart. Fierce Four aside, it's fun to watch it with a group of people who likely haven't seen it before, judging by how they're gasping and shrieking at every jump scare.

I keep getting distracted from the film by getting lost in my buzzing thoughts. Hanging out with the Popular Kids—and outside of school—makes me feel like I'm on a sugar high. I am sitting amongst Eastfield High Royalty. Dare I say I'm one of them? Or at least getting there?

Even though every iota of me wants to get up and shout: *I can't believe I'm hanging out with all of you! What is life?! What is even happening?!*, I try to look as calm, cool, and composed as a cucumber. A cucumber dressed in sunglasses and a driving scarf. Disinterestedly, I ask Eamon to please pass the bowl of buttered popcorn. Though I'm too on edge to eat more than a few, with the fear of kernels catching in my teeth.

Before long, the movie ends, people start to head out, and I'm increasingly nervous at the thought of being alone with Lincoln—and the thought of implementing my new kissing methods. Katie's the last holdout, but she finally says her dad's there to pick her up and slips out the front door, leaving just the two of us. I quietly help Lincoln clean up, tossing out wrappers and stacking bowls in the stainless-steel kitchen sink. It's like he's purposely lingering, brushing elbows—had he been waiting for his friends to leave, too? He places a cup in the sink, and our hands nearly touch. I can't help letting out a nervous little chuckle.

Lincoln wipes his hands on a dish towel. "Do you want me to walk you home?"

I place another bowl in the sink, and the other bowls stacked beneath it slide sideways, sending everything clattering down. It is *just* the distraction I need to gather my composure.

Obviously, I want to scream yes. "No, I'm fine. Thanks, though." I dry off my own hands. "Don't worry, no one's going to leap out of the bushes with a scary Ghostface mask and try to off me," I add.

Lincoln leans back against the kitchen counter and crosses his arms. "I wasn't asking because I thought you were going to get offed. I asked because I thought it might be nice."

My insides tighten at the thought of kissing him. *"Nice?"* I blurt.

"Yeah. *Nice,*" Lincoln says, and Dillon comes to mind.

"You really want to walk me home? And you're not afraid of walking back all on your own?" Suddenly, I'm right back to three years ago when he offered to walk me home at night, which fills me with glee—and also with PTSD for what followed.

"I think I can take care of myself." He winks and flashes a broad smile before tugging on a vintage hoodie.

"You're not afraid of rats?" I ask.

He quirks an eyebrow. "Just because *you're* terrified of rats doesn't mean a horde of them is waiting to crawl up your spine and eat you."

"How sure are you, though?"

"I shall protect you from them."

"How chivalrous."

"For someone who loves Whiskered Warriors . . ." he says.

"Vermin are cuter when they're anthropomorphic," I tease.

"Vermin," he mouths to himself. Maybe I really should stop using that term so loosely.

As I button my jacket, I have to work double time to keep myself from twirling, squealing, and grinning like a circus clown covered in fleas. He remembered my fear of rats and even brought up our favorite book series, like the good old days—but better. I've seen enough romantic movies to know that no one offers to walk anyone home unless they like them.

And may possibly even want to kiss them.

A scrabbling of paws draws my attention as Junior appears, flopping down one step after the other, barking his little head off. His fluffy, triangular ears fly back with each yap.

"Aww! He's so cute!" I reach down to pet Junior, but he lurches to bite, so I bolt up.

"Come here, Puppersizz." Lincoln's nickname for him. That's right. He even used his mushy Dog Voice. Swoon. He intercepts him and drops him on the other side of a kitchen gate.

Outside, we descend the steep driveway we used to sled down and turn onto the street. The dark air is cool and crisp. And romantic.

A bush rustles. I give a startled yelp and run with shuffling feet. Thankfully, Lincoln laughs.

Oops. My personality is showing. But maybe that little glimpse won't hurt.

When he ducks behind the next bush and makes it rustle as a joke, I catch a glimpse of the old him, too. Or maybe the real him that's been hidden under all those rippling muscles and silent, smoldering stares these past few years.

"Hey, thanks for inviting me tonight," I say, kicking aside a clump of wet leaves. "I didn't realize your friends would be there. But they're cool too. You know, for party animals."

He throws a glance my way. "You do know that they're all in the National Honors Society, right?"

"They are?" I laugh, then remember Varsha telling me that Katie is one of her fiercest academic competitors. The thought of Varsha sends a pang of guilt through me. I miss her.

"Well, they're cool," I say as we continue down the rain-slicked road, hugging the curb. "How's your family doing?"

"My mom and dad are good," he says, pulling down the drawstrings of his hoodie to make him look even cuter . . . and more kissable. "How about you? How are your parents doing?"

"Well, my mom and dad actually—" I stop myself.

Normally, I would answer that my mom and dad are good, too. Here's what's going on with her. Here's what's going on with him. Same old, same old. But now, the answer is different. And I can't tell him the truth. That my dad cheated on my mom and walked out on us, and he's still with the Other Woman and she's practically my age, and they seem really happy together, and my mom is really sad, and so am I. And who *knows* what my brother, Silvio, thinks of all this?

So instead, I smile. "They're good," I reply, fighting the impulse to reveal everything.

A part of me doesn't want to tell him the truth because I don't want to seem less than the person I was before, because I used to have two parents and now I only really have one. Even though Mom definitely makes up for two.

And a part of me doesn't want to tell him the truth because I haven't fully accepted it myself.

I'm hoping we can just gloss over it. And we do. We continue walking, casually just talking about rehearsals and some of our favorite moments from them so far. I tell him about working at the teahouse, and I invite him to stop by sometime.

"Seriously. You should come by one day," I reiterate, hoping repeating myself and inviting him to something isn't too try-hard.

"Maybe." He smiles. "Now that you're a ten out of ten."

His compliment makes me glow, but also people who rate people on a scale of one to ten have a special place in Hell. That said, he's cute and he likes me and he's just flirting, right? So I try to swallow the icky feeling and simply embrace the compliment.

"Okay, cool. They have really good caramel apple tartlets."

We hang a left onto Dickens Road and pass a construction site with a half-finished house. It reminds me of that one fateful night once upon a time.

"Rat!" he screams, pointing at something moving by my foot.

I shriek and leap into a bush. Then spring halfway down the street, running with high knees and screaming at the top of my lungs.

He strolls up with a casual air. "I was kidding."

I try to catch my breath but can't compose myself. "What?!" I give him a playful shove. "You jerk!" My heartbeat finally slows. I *hate* pranks.

I also can't believe I just called him the word my friends and I have used to describe him for years to his face.

"Some things never change," he teases, then looks long and hard at me. "But some things do."

Before I can ask him to elaborate, he tears his gaze away and keeps walking.

Outside my little gray house with its faded paint, he opens the gate and we walk up the narrow path to the front door.

"Thanks for walking me."

We're facing each other on the stoop. I'm reminded of Julien standing in the same spot.

"You've changed," he says in a tone that sounds like admiration, and I think of Julien again and how he said I've changed in that same pleased tone.

"I guess I have."

"Well, thanks for coming to movie night." His sight drifts over my shoulder. "Wow, look at that full moon. It's beautiful."

There in the sky is a perfect full moon hovering in a wreath of silver clouds. I turn back to Lincoln and start to speak, when he kisses me.

My lips are cold, and so are his, but within seconds, I can feel the warmth between us growing and growing, his mouth pressed to mine. I barely remember to reach up and run my fingers through his soft black hair. He puts his arms around my waist and pulls me close. I almost have to stand on tiptoe to reach his lips.

This—this feels like the kiss from *Little Women*.

The kiss of my dreams.

It's different than how it was kissing Julien. Kissing Julien was nice, eventually. Kissing Lincoln feels natural. I forget about my planned technique and dissolve into the flow.

I'm making out with Lincoln Chan.

Lincoln Chan is making out with *me*.

After who knows how long, he pulls away, eyes downcast before meeting mine as the ghost of a cunning smile dances on his lips.

"That was nice," I say breathlessly.

"You say it like we're done," he says quietly.

He kisses me again, then he takes my hands in his; they're also cold, but not as cold as mine, and he rubs them together to generate heat. He eyes the door, his eyebrows rising ever so slightly.

My mind races with what to say next because what I want to say all pertains to how exhilarated I am that Lincoln kissed me and likes me, and how I'm shocked about that, and how I want it to happen again and how much my snack locker is bursting with candy bars for him. The wrong line from my lips could deflate the moment. But the right line . . .

The right line could change everything.

"Good night," he says.

And I realize the right line is no line. I flash a coy smile and duck inside my house.

Mom's watching TV in the kitchen. She checks the clock.

"Just on curfew! See? Responsible," I say, grinning. She said I could go out this evening when I told her about Lincoln's exclusive movie-night invitation. She knew how significant it was to me. Plus, I told her how I filled out the basics of some college apps *and* did my day of community service. Hey, it's a start.

"Someone's in a good mood. How was your time with Lincoln?"

"Mom! Tonight was *so* fun."

She sips wine from a glass. "*You* like him, *I* like him."

Minutes later, I fling myself onto my bed with scrapbook in hand, a smile still plastered on my face. I lie in almost complete darkness except for the lamp at the bedside, R&B playing as I fantasize and daydream. Lincoln's section in my scrapbook will soon have another few new additions.

A buzzing sensation consumes me, and my brain feels tingly, like I'm floating on air. Lincoln Chan likes me. It's real. This is *real*. I've actually manifested this, haven't I? With the Boyfriend Material Checklist. I so badly want to text my friends, letting them know everything. E-v-e-r-y-t-h-i-n-g! But the group chat has been dormant for over a week now.

I stare at my phone, willing myself not to type anything and put it down. It wouldn't be right for me to send them a text out of the blue. But they're my friends! I don't need to play it cool with them! Right? So I give in to the impulse of wanting to talk and reconnect with them.

Leo: Hey, I miss you guys! How are you doing??? Big update on the checklist front . . . FaceTime me ASAP!

I wait and wait. I watch TikToks. Seals sneezing. Crumbl Cookies reviews. Varsha's knitting TikTok, and even some soothing scrapbooking TikToks. It hardly calms my nerves. I'm just as amped up as I was when I first got home. Crushing on Lincoln is making me feel restless, like I want the next step already, for Lincoln to ask me out, for us to be boyfriends.

Closing out TikTok, I go on Instagram and post a black-and-white picture I had Emily take backstage at rehearsal a few nights ago, then post it to my story.

For an hour, I check to see if Lincoln liked or viewed it. Nothing. Though Eamon likes the story—now that he and the rest of the Fierce Four follow me. Am I its fifth member now?

I scroll through Lincoln's socials, imagining him posting photos of the two of us, like all those Instagram relationship accounts I follow, of happy couples hugging, kissing, and cuddling in the leafy, brownstone-lined streets of the West Village. Like the ones of him and Travis that he took down. Guess he's over Travis, and not into Tim, either. Or is he? My heart hurts just *thinking* about him even looking in either of their directions. I'm suddenly gripped with jealousy and fear. Last time Lincoln kissed me, it was game over. Is that going to happen now too? Should I text him? There are so many things I want to ask and tell him. Like asking if he still likes Travis. And telling him not to ditch me again.

No. I don't want to risk ruining the perfect, shining moment that was this evening.

Though it's difficult to resist. *Really* difficult.

Should I at least text him asking if he made it home safe? It might be cute if I ask if the rats got him. No. Too try-hard. The rats make me think of his prank. I decide that when Dillon and

Varsha are finally talking to me again, and I fill them in on what happened tonight, I won't tell them *everything*. I'll leave out the prank. Don't want to paint him in a bad light.

I check the group chat for the millionth time. Still nothing.

And I can only watch so many dance challenges on TikTok.

Then I get a separate individual text, and for a second, I hope it's Lincoln, telling me what a nice night it was, and how good of a kisser I am now . . . because, where does the post-kiss leave us? Will there be a repeat? If so, then when?

But it's not Lincoln at all.

Dillon: Hey. Saw your message. You can drop by if you want
Dillon: Don't tell Varsha

I realize I'm about to do something I told myself I wouldn't. Sneak out past curfew.

WHEN I GET TO DILLON'S HOUSE, HE SNEAKS ME IN THROUGH
the kitchen door.

Now, he sits cross-legged on his bed in plaid pajama bottoms
and a white T-shirt. "Wow," he says, blinking at me from where
I sit at the foot of his bed. I just finished telling him all about my
"date" with Lincoln at Mike's Diner and how that resulted in my
trying to be a better kisser and how that led to Julien, which led
back to my "date" with Lincoln tonight.

After sharing everything, my chest feels ten times lighter.

Dillon's room is dim except for the glow of a red lava lamp,
which barely reaches his paintings on the walls and the plants on
his desk. He has a dried smudge of paint on his chin that he hasn't
bothered to remove, and it smells like turpentine in here, which
is typical. There's a half-finished canvas on an easel in the corner.

"Can you believe we *kissed*?" I ask, wide-eyed.

Dillon considers me for a moment again. "I'm still struggling to understand why you're trying to date Abe now even though you *swore* that's something you weren't trying to do."

"I mean . . . same," I say. "But here we are. And we kissed! WE KISSED! Can you believe it?"

"Actually, yes. You've been laser-focused on that boyfriend checklist and nothing else."

"Oh, so it wasn't because he thinks I'm cute?" I tease.

Dillon rolls his eyes. "Clearly he thinks you're cute." He leans toward me. "So, do you need any more help practicing?" He puckers up, the playful sarcasm evident in his expression.

"I think I'm good!" I laugh. "You should have seen it!" I whisper, scooching toward him. "We were standing this close. And he said, 'Wow, look at that full moon. It's beautiful,' and then I looked." I gesture for Dillon to look away. "And then when I looked back." I turn Dillon's face toward mine. "Boom! He moved right in!" I move my lips inches from his, then spin away and flop back onto his bed, a euphoric smile plastered across my face.

Even though I was scared at first to tell Dillon everything, being able to share with him is easy, like always. Anytime I open up to him, I'm left feeling warm and comforted, like I'm wrapped in a tortilla of sunshine. The tension I'd been holding on to starts to melt away.

"Smooth. I'm happy to hear you're having fun." Like how he takes his eggs, Dillon is always sunny-side up. But I can tell he chooses his next words carefully. "Were there any red flags with the OG Ghoster? You know, besides how he ever did that to you?"

I knew telling Dillon about Lincoln might come with its doubts and concerns—which is valid. He's just looking out for me.

I think back to the last few rehearsals. "He used his teeth to open a Mexican Coke bottle and he likes the show *Friends*?" I try.

Dillon laughs. "I mean, *actual* red flags."

"You're really not a fan, are you?" Contemplating his question, I tilt my head back, gazing at the glow-in-the-dark stars still stuck to the ceiling from Dillon's elementary school days. I can't help thinking of the rat prank, and that off remark he said about the girl in the diner and her pancakes, and how I think the only things that should be rated on scales of one to ten are ice cream flavors. But nobody's perfect. Everybody has quirks. "Not really any red flags. I mean, I wasn't thrilled that our second hangout was with his friends, but they were actually really lovely."

Dillon raises an eyebrow. "Are these the same friends who posted about my broken art piece and called it a piece of junk?"

I wince. "I never said they were perfect. And I'm not trying to date *them*!"

"Just Lincoln 'Terrible Human' Chan." He picks some lint off his pajama pants. "Well, my smashed art piece still hasn't miraculously put itself back together again, though I did get an extension to redo it. Do you know how hard it was to make something like that?"

"Dillon," I begin, "I am so, *so* sorry. I messed up. I want to make it right. I totally dropped the ball—or rather, *shattered* the ball?" I let out a sheepish laugh, then read the room. "Is there anything I can do? Use a blowtorch to weld the parts?"

"That's not really how it works."

"Okay, well, if there's anything I *can* do, I'm here. Even if you need me to do your homework for other classes so that you have more time to rebuild your sculpture."

"Well, thanks." He looks a bit more at ease.

"And I promise I'll be a better friend." I clasp my hands together. "Please forgive me."

A smile tugs at the corner of his mouth. "Obviously."

I shimmy in a little happy dance.

He fiddles with the fringe on a pillow. "So, there were really *no* other red flags with him?"

"No, Dillon, I swear, I felt so comfortable around him, I almost told him the truth about my parents—"

The words slip out, and I freeze.

So does he. His eyes meet mine. "What are you talking about?"

I can't believe I'm about to tell Dillon my secret. But it's too late now. "My parents are actually in the process of getting a divorce," I admit. Hearing the words out loud makes it feel more real in a way it hasn't before. A lump forms in the back of my throat.

"They *are*?" Dillon sets down the fringed pillow and gives me his undivided attention. His expression has turned to one of deep concern. "What happened?"

I sigh. "My dad cheated . . . with his secretary . . . who's now his girlfriend."

Before I know what's happening, I launch into the whole story. How Dad kept coming home late from work until Mom found a long, blond hair on his sweater. The nights of fighting, as I listened from the top of the stairs to their vows shatter like the kitchen plates. Doors slamming. Mom's sobs. A shout. And then, the suitcase packed, the locks changed, the end.

Dillon's eyes glint with tears. "Oh, Leo, I am so sorry."

Seeing him tear up is making *me* start to tear up. "Yeah, it's whatever. His girlfriend is practically my age, which is weird." I rub my arms, not sure where to look. "Yeah. It's a lot."

"Why didn't you tell me this before?"

I shrug. "I guess I didn't want anyone to find out. It's really embarrassing."

He nods in understanding. "Thanks for telling me. If you ever want to talk about it, I'm here for you. Your secret is safe." His words make me feel warm and filled with the promise that I have at least one of my best friends back. I wonder why I held on to this secret for so long, when now, releasing it, I feel like I can breathe just a tiny bit easier. Of course Dillon would understand. Of course.

"Thanks. That means a lot, especially in light of ruining your art midterm."

"I'm still mad at you for that." He looks serious. "And *you* need to keep a secret for *me*. Don't tell Varsha I'm talking with you."

I chuckle, but it's a sad chuckle. "Deal. If she ever starts talking to me again." My face falls. "Honestly, I thought kissing

Abe would make me happy for the rest of my life, but I'm worrying about everything. Like, what *are* we now? Boyfriends?"

Dillon looks at me with his serious gaze again. "Leo, what do *you* want in a boyfriend? I mean, your checklist is all about what you want to do to make yourself boyfriend material, in hopes of nabbing a boyfriend. But, like, what are *your* standards for someone else?"

I chew at my lip. "You know me. I literally fall for anyone who shows any interest in me. It's not like I've had much of a choice in the matter."

Dillon laughs. "So, if a rock looked your way?"

"I'd be kissing it like the Blarney Stone."

Dillon lets out an amused sigh. "I was afraid you'd say that. But seriously, though. What is your idea of a good boyfriend?" He forms a tight-mouthed smile and blinks at me, expectant.

Lincoln flashes to mind. "Someone who's cute . . . nice . . . interested . . . I don't know!" I bury my head in the comforter. I feel silly for not having a better answer, but I guess my bar is pretty low.

Dillon peels back the comforter to peek at me. "Does he have to be cool as a cucumber? Or have a powerhouse presence?"

"No. But my standards are different from the rest of the world's," I confess. "I just want someone to love me." I realize how pathetic the words sound leaving my mouth.

"Even if they're not loving the real you?"

I sit up. "I mean . . . the real me?" I laugh, looking away. "The real me is awkward and not cool and *definitely* not hot." I don't bother even mentioning how I wonder if I'll ever be truly happy or find peace. "No one finds me attractive," I add feebly. "The real me, that is. You know that."

"I *don't* know that," Dillon says. "Not everyone broadcasts their feelings."

"So you're telling me a guy has liked the real me but maybe just never told me? What station do I have to tune into to get this news?"

"Pay attention to which guys are giving you attention," Dillon replies.

"New Leo is getting attention. Old Leo is old news. You can't argue that. And all my past crushes could tell I liked them. I wasn't exactly subtle."

"Okay, so once you have this boyfriend," Dillon says, "then what? Will you keep up the charade?"

"Of course! And we'll live happily ever after. Don't you want that, too, Dill Pickle?"

"Me?" Dillon stares at his unfinished painting in the corner. We never speak about his love life, because what's there to speak of? That door is sealed shut until college. "I don't know. What's the point?"

"The point is, someone to make you feel special," I say, playfully pinching his cheek. As much as I appreciate his logical side, I often find myself wishing he would just let loose and live a little.

He blushes. "I don't need someone else to feel special."

How is he so lackadaisical about love?

"No?" I ask, my gaze pointed. "You sure?"

"I'm good," he says with a curt laugh.

The topic is one of the few things we differ on, but I can still tease him about it.

"Oh, please! You are not." It's nice he and I are having a serious, deeper conversation. "Honest question. Do you like Sakura? She's actually sort of nice."

"'*Actually sort of nice.*' Wow, you're really selling it." He shrugs.

"I thought you *liked* nice," I shoot back.

"Well, I just figure, we graduate high school next semester. I know you want a date to semiformal, or a boyfriend on Valentine's Day, or whatever, but what's the point if we're all going our separate ways soon?"

"Well, that's depressing," I remark, pushing aside the thought of potentially leaving behind everyone I hold dear. "We're living in the here and now! Isn't it better to have been loved than never loved at all, or whatever that expression is?"

"I wouldn't know." He smiles, but the wall he's built around himself makes me want to tear it down, shatter it like glass . . . or at least peek over it to see what's really on the other side.

I let my sights wander to his paintings, symbols of how he pours his heart into places other than people. I wonder if he's given any more thought to his sexual orientation since sharing he was "straight but maybe not," so I choose my next words carefully.

"What do you look for in a person?"

He chews it over. "I look for a good heart. Someone who's himself."

I freeze. "*Him*self?"

He shrugs. "Yeah. So?" He scratches behind his ear.

I try not to sound so surprised. It's not a big deal, even if it feels it. "Docs Varsha know?"

"Not yet. I'm just exploring still. But yeah. I'm definitely not looking."

I find myself staring, as if seeing him with new eyes. Dillon is into guys! Maybe that's why he's been so shut off whenever his love life has come up. Maybe his sexual orientation is something he feels he needs time and focus to really explore, and what better place to do that than college, a fresh slate where no one knows a lick about your past or who you were before?

He gives me a look, like he wants to share something more on the topic, and I wait. "So, where does this leave things with Abe?" he asks, and I'm surprised he wants to shift gears.

"Seriously, though! Right?" I say, forcing myself to switch focus with him. "I don't know. I think I've reached a dead end. I was thinking I'd just stay on top of my checklist steps and see what happens. I really want him to ask me out! As in, to be his boyfriend!"

"Why don't you ask *him* out?" Dillon challenges.

"Because I'm not sure he'd say yes."

"*Yet,*" Dillon chimes in.

I laugh. "You're one to talk. You always keep everything inside. Remember that time your burger wasn't cooked and instead of sending it back, you just ate it anyway and got a stomachache later?"

"Well, not everyone is as bold and brave as you are."

"That's right, and I don't have *E. coli* because of it. Now help me figure out what else to do to make Abe my boyfriend!"

"I know you'll figure it out and whatever you decide will work for you."

I give Dillon a flat look, though I appreciate how optimistic and supportive he's been through all of this.

"Just text him and ask him out."

I grab the nearest pillow and try to whack him with it. "Dillon, it's too soon! The checklist. I must follow it! I mustn't stray! I already asked him to visit me at the teahouse. And the true win is for *him* to ask *me* out, right? What if it happens *there*?"

Dillon sighs. "Let's just hope he stops by the teahouse soon."

A CUTOUT OF A COMEDY/TRAGEDY MASK. A SKETCH OF THE skull from *Hamlet*. The phrase TO BE OR NOT TO BE written on an unfurled parchment. A doodle of a spotlight and stage curtains.

A candle illuminates the pages while emitting the soothing scent of sandalwood.

It also lights up the framed photo of Gran on my desk, like she's watching over me. The style of her hair never changed, ever since she was young. In the photo, she's seated across from me at our favorite restaurant, with a molten lava chocolate cake on the table with two spoons, her colorful walking cane leaned up beside her. She's got on her bold-frame glasses, with a vibrant sweater and baubles of necklaces and bracelets, looking her usual best with all the fixings. I can practically still smell her perfume. What I'd give to indulge in one more decadent dessert with her, and take her arm and walk with her out to the car after, raving about how good the cake was and complaining about our stomachs aching.

I pull over her box of craft supplies and dig my hand around in it.

Lincoln's section already has a few new pages, including one for the Halloween party, with pumpkins, ghosts, and ghouls, plus stickers of candy corn. There's also a page for Mike's Diner memories, with the receipt stamped in and sketches of a chef's hat and utensils.

The kiss with Lincoln deserves its own spread. I tape in a movie reel, bucket of popcorn, and puppy paws stickers. A full moon and fireworks. And of course, tons of puckered-lip stickers.

Lastly, I place in a sticker beside his photo.

A big red heart pierced by Cupid's arrow.

AFTER TAKING EXTRA CARE TO LOOK PRESENTABLE FOR
work Sunday, I'm twenty minutes late for my shift and have to
apologize to Judy on the way in. Oops.

It will be well worth it for Lincoln. I texted him that today
would be a good day for him to stop by.

But he doesn't show.

As my shift ends, I realize how hungry I am. Thank god it's
dinnertime. On a whim, I open his socials to see if he's messaged me there—he hasn't—and I end up yet again staring at his
beautiful face.

Is it just a matter of time before he blocks me again?

Vincent gasps from over the top of his phone. "Who is *that*?!"

"Vincent, do you do *any* work?" I ask, eyeing the pile of
dishes that need rinsing.

Ignoring my question, he ogles my screen. "Seriously, who is that?"

"That," I say, smugness rising in my voice, "would be the guy I'm"—*madly in love with since way back when*—"kissing." I play it off coy as I hand over my phone.

Vincent raises an eyebrow. "*You're* kissing *him*?" he says in disbelief.

"Jeez, don't sound so surprised."

"Sorry, hon. But he's hot."

I give him a searing look. "Really?"

He looks away. "I realize I could have expressed that differently."

I mumble in irritation, but the truth is that nothing could burst my bubble. I still can't believe I get to tell people that *this* is who I'm kissing.

"Someone named Dillon messaged you," Vincent says, and I realize he's tapping onto Dillon's profile.

I hold out my hand for my phone back. "Umm, excuse me. You can't just go into someone else's DMs."

"Why? Are you crushing on him too?" Vincent angles the phone toward me so I can see the photo of Dillon he's pulled up. It's a really good black-and-white candid of him backstage at one of his choral concerts, grinning with his cute chipper smile, in a tux and bow tie with his hair neatly combed to one side.

"No," I say flatly.

"Good." He passes my phone back. "You could do better."

I bristle. "What's *that* supposed to mean?"

"Oh, nothing. He's just not that cute. Not like . . . What's his name? Lance?"

"Lincoln," I say, feeling my muscles tense. "And Dillon *is* cute."

"Yeah, yeah. Back to Lincoln." Vincent squints at me. "Wait, so you're just kissing? Not dating? So, he's still on the market?" He hands back my phone, then finds Lincoln on his own Instagram and adds him, which sends an icy stab of jealousy into my gut.

"I mean, not for long," I manage to say. "We're pretty much boyfriends."

Vincent snorts. "That's like being pretty much pregnant."

My face flushes red when I realize he's correct.

A Pretty Much Boyfriend would have showed up today—right?

"So *this* is who your makeover was for. It's all starting to make sense." Vincent glances up, and his eyes shift to my bleached-blond hair. "And you really need to touch up your roots."

No-show aside, by Monday morning, word has spread around the school that Leo Martino and Lincoln Chan are "hanging out." Whatever *that* means. How do I know this? Because in second period, Lu Lockheart turns around in her seat and says: "I heard you and Lincoln Chan are hanging out."

"And I heard you and Lincoln Chan kissed," Candace says.

I immediately turn bright red, wanting to both deny and confirm it at the same time. I know Dillon didn't spill my secret, and if he did, the Robotics Club president isn't a gossip. Did *Lincoln* tell people that we kissed? If he did, could it be that maybe it's a point of pride for him?

The checklist doesn't exactly provide guidance on how I'm supposed to react to being a hot topic at school, so I simply smile at Lu and Candace and give a cheeky little shrug.

Let them eat tea cake! Or whatever that saying is.

After class, Travis skateboards past and puts his head down when he sees me. Oof. Awkward. I take it he's heard the news.

I'm heading to the lockers to retrieve my textbooks when I catch sight of Varsha from down the hall, twisting her combination lock. She sees me wave, but she looks away, and her locker clicks open. *Crap.* I knew this was going to be uncomfortable. I still haven't told Varsha anything about Lincoln or how my checklist is going, and I really didn't want her to find out thirdhand, but I'm too late. Guess word really does spread like wildfire at this school.

I open my locker, and all the little trinkets, key chains, and candy bars I've been wanting to give Lincoln nearly come pouring out. Maybe I should be saving more of my teahouse money, like I was planning to do. Oops.

My stomach flips thinking that someday I might actually be able to give these things to him. You know, when it's more appropriate. Boyfriends give each other gifts all the time, right?

As I check out my outfit in my locker mirror—a cable-knit turtleneck sweater tossed over trendy wide-leg corduroy pants—I hear someone quietly clear their throat.

Varsha is standing beside me, looking annoyed. "MTD," she utters. I can tell she's here as a friend, even if a slightly disgruntled one. "TTM."

Much to discuss.

Talk to me.

Speaking in Friend Vernacular is a good sign.

My face lights up. "I've been good," I say, realizing that perhaps I'm coming off a little too happy for not having talked to her in so long. "I've been good," I say, this time making my voice more flat and much less jolly in a concerted effort to sound more true to myself.

"I heard about you and Abe," she says.

"Oh yeah? Good things, I hope. No really, what have you heard?" I try to act the way I'd act if things were cool between us, perching my hand on her shoulder.

She narrows her eyes. "Just that you two have been hanging out and kissed."

I glance around the hall. "Shh. Not so loud! And yes, that's true. I was going to tell you myself—I mean, you *and* Dillon. But it's just been a little . . . I don't know . . . weird between us, and I just felt funny about texting you out of the blue when we haven't caught up in a while. Plus, you haven't exactly been responsive in the group chat."

"You already talked to Dillon, haven't you?" Her eyes are half-hooded in mock upset.

"No! What? Who? Me?"

She blinks, nostrils flared. "Uh-huh. Well, anyway, it looks like your grand plan is working, and even though we know where I stand with him, I'm all for seeing this checklist through," she says.

"Thanks," I say in relief.

Varsha's mouth twitches. "I just wish there was a line on

your checklist about being a good friend, because—I mean, it feels like you just walked away from us. Like you left us in the dust."

Her words hit me hard, and it feels like being doused in ice-cold water. I know that feeling. That's the feeling that I felt about every crush. The feeling that I felt when Dad walked away. That feeling of rejection and loss.

"Okay. Serious Leo." I blow out a big breath. "I am sorry for getting carried away with the Boyfriend Material Checklist and for how I treated you at the party. I promise I'm going to create a new checklist, How to Be a Better Friend, because I never want to make you feel bad."

Varsha chews it over. "You are forgiven. But you need to tell me everything." She glances into the mess piled up in my locker, waving a finger around. "Starting with explaining how this got to be such a pigsty."

"Bah-bye!" I push Dillon, then Varsha, sending them each flying down the hill on their snow saucers the next day.

It's the first snow day of the season. It's also the first day that things among the three of us are feeling back to normal. Mission: Be a Better Friend is in full swing. I realized how thoughtless I had been, and I never want to act that way again. Starting with my suggestion to gather on the sloping, snow-covered driveway of Eastfield Middle School, our favorite spot for sledding with its stupendous, rolling descent to the bottom. With Dillon and Varsha back in my life, it's a little easier to ignore the fact that Lincoln still hasn't asked me out since our kiss. Even if sledding reminds me of him, and sledding down his driveway.

Dillon screams like a banshee all the way down the hill.

It's my turn. I fold myself up on my snow saucer, tucking my boots in and scooching up a bit. With my mittens clinging to the sides, I go flying down the hill to meet them at the bottom in a joyful spray of snow.

"That was fun!" I cheer. "Let's go again!"

Dillon and Varsha help me up.

The wind whips Varsha's dark hair around her face. "I'm maxed out on my ability to climb this hill."

"Same," Dillon says, his cheeks ruddy with the cold, facing the sun with his eyes closed. Vincent was wrong. He *is* cute. In his own cute way.

"Anyone want to build a snowman?" I stoop and begin to pack snow into a mound.

Dillon and Varsha kneel beside me.

"How about a snow *bear*? Oh my gosh, I just saw the best bear attack on TikTok. It literally charged this guy fly-fishing and nearly took him out! But he yelled and scared it off."

"I wonder if Lincoln is a skier or a snowboarder . . ." I muse.

"So we're calling him by his name now? And how did an attacking bear story make you think of Lincoln?" Varsha's still not enthused that I have Lincoln in my Future Boyfriend crosshairs.

"I'm so glad I have you guys to share my fantasies with so I don't, you know, share them with Lincoln and send him running."

"Lucky us," Dillon mutters in good fun.

Varsha nods. "You know what they say. Don't chase the puppy or it'll run away."

"But I *love* puppies," I say. "If I saw one, and it started to run, I'd definitely chase it."

"But then it would just run faster and faster away," Varsha counters.

"I'm pretty sure I could outrun a puppy," I retort.

"Remember that thing I said about trusting the process?" Dillon asks. "This is part of it."

I glower. "But I *want* the puppy," I mumble, and my friends chuckle.

"The checklist is complete, yeah?" Varsha asks. "You got what you wanted?"

"I mean, he's not my boyfriend yet. We just kissed. And we haven't really spoken since then because—"

"Leo is determined to wait for Lincoln to ask him out," Dillon concludes.

Varsha winces. "That's not a good sign."

My mittened hand flies to my mouth. "OMG, it's not?"

Varsha averts her eyes.

"Dillon?"

"Hey, we're not out of the collecting data phase yet, right? Verdict's still out."

I feel myself paling. "But I'm positive the feelings are mutual. I mean, he told people we kissed!"

"I'm not so sure that's something to be happy about," Dillon says. "Wasn't that moment . . . private?"

"Yeah, but it means he was proud of it!" I shoot back.

"Then why do you sound so uneasy?" Varsha asks.

"Because I want Lincoln to be my first real boyfriend!" I exclaim, then kiss the snowman's cold cheek. "And the holidays are coming up, and I have, like, three hundred *more* Christmas gift ideas for him." Seeing their concerned looks, I add: "Which I'm *not* going to give him."

"Are you finally going to just ask him out yourself?" Dillon says.

It's so close that it's within my clutches, even if I have been nauseated with overthinking. But—maybe I've achieved a level of presence that makes it cool enough to ask him out. And I have to do *something*. Waiting is driving me up the wall.

"Well, after analyzing the checklist, I think it could be time."

"Great!" Dillon says, eyeing my phone in my jacket pocket. "Get to it."

"Not *now*! I want to do it in person. It's more confident."

"The opening night of the play sounds like the best time to ask him out, no?" Varsha suggests. "I mean, once you're not in the play anymore, will you and Lincoln still be hanging out?"

"Yeah, I wouldn't exactly consider Calc class hanging out." I stand up, dusting snow off my jacket. "Hmm. Opening night might be too hectic. Everyone's going to be a bundle of nerves, and there's going to be so much going on backstage. It has to be *before* opening night that I seal the deal. I can't handle being backstage with him during the performances and having this hanging over my head. Then again, if he says no, then won't being backstage with him during the performances be a total and complete nightmare?"

"At this rate, I say just go for it ASAP," Varsha asserts.

Dillon and Varsha stand behind me, and we admire our handiwork. The snowman looks like some sort of blob monster.

I laugh. "Dillon, I expected better from you, Mr. Artiste!"

He regards the snowman. "Snow clearly isn't my medium."

I wrap an arm around each of my friends. "Who's ready for some free hot chocolate at Ye Olde Tea House?"

"Me!" Varsha cheers. "And then we can talk some more about your Getting a Boyfriend Before Opening Night plan."

"The play's right around the corner!" I say, seriously regretting committing to this plan.

"Speaking of getting a boyfriend, I might want one of those plans too," Dillon says.

"A plan to get a boyfriend?" Varsha asks, sounding interested.

He nods. "Yeah. I think I've finally figured it out." Dillon puts his arm around me in return, and we all start walking. The snow crunches under our boots. I can taste the hot chocolate already.

BY THE END OF THE WEEK, THE SNOW HAS HARDENED WITH grime, the roads are slick with black ice, and the cold feeling in the pit of my stomach has dropped to freezing at the prospect of asking Lincoln to be my boyfriend before the opening night of the play.

The next few days pass by in a blur as rehearsals pick up. I've barely heard from Lincoln via text, but at rehearsals, he's consistently sweet and friendly, pulling me into side hugs (as I've told my friends, the difference between a *hug* and an *embrace* is *love*!) and giving me upper-back squeezes when passing by.

But whenever mustering up the nerve to ask him out, I keep *losing* said nerve. It never seems like the right time. And, to add more stress to things, with my efforts in putting on my makeup with the latest TikTok tutorials to look extra nice for Lincoln as his Future Boyfriend and not as a Friend-Zoned Pal, it's made me late for rehearsal. Wednesday is no exception.

"You're late," Dr. Horan says as I race down an aisle in the auditorium. "This is the last time, Leo."

"Sorry!" I fling my backpack onto a chair and peel off my jacket. My body feels like a furnace from racing here under all these layers.

Lincoln—along with the whole cast—watches me from onstage, frozen in place under beaming lights that punctuate the darkened auditorium. They're all in costume. Today's the full-cast run-through of the entire show before opening night tomorrow. I need to get into costume. And fast.

"We'll wait." Dr. Horan looks serenely my way. "After all, if you're late again, we won't have to wait for you anymore . . . because you won't be in the play."

I gulp. I'm wrestling to take off my sweater, and my arm gets caught in my sleeve. I twist in a disoriented circle as it catches under my chin, casting everything in muffled darkness.

Silence falls.

Play it cool, Leo.

I will my heart rate to slow. I leisurely remove the sweater and drape it across a seat.

Then, chest up, I stroll backstage, where I rustle around until I find my costume hanging on the rack: a three-piece suit with pointed hat, a scabbard, and a rubber sword. After the quickest costume change in human history, I emerge onto the stage and find my place.

Lincoln looks over at me, and a small smile tugs at the corner of his mouth.

I start to return the smile, but then realize he's smiling

because my hat is on backward.

I fix it and try to focus. I have to commit to stop being late. Especially when it comes to work after rehearsal tonight. Judy's been less than happy to see me duck in tardy too, especially during busy season, which at Ye Olde Tea House means the season of gingerbread cookies, chocolate peppermint tarts, snowflake sugar cookies, and fancy hot chocolates imported from Switzerland (that are absolutely delicious!).

The stage lights shine bright, and I have to squint to see Dr. Horan below.

"All right," he says, his eyes finally leaving me to address the rest of the cast. "Let's take it from the top of act one."

The dress rehearsal is grueling. By now, everyone's memorized their lines off-book, and we run through the full show before Dr. Horan tells us that we'll receive notes via email in the morning.

Everybody packs up, and I realize I'm going to be perfectly on time to work. Though I would *kill* to spend a few extra minutes touching up my hat hair and melted makeup. I place my costume back up on hangers with tape sporting my last name—when I spot Lincoln. Is this the moment? I start to walk toward him, but my knees start to shake. I can't do it. I give him a little wave and scurry off.

Ugh. I wish I'd have the strength to ask him out already!

Outside, I head to Mom's car. She let me borrow it today since she stayed home from work to prep for another divorce hearing.

A car crunches behind me on the icy gravel.

It's Lincoln, waving with a gloved hand out of his Mercedes-Benz. He looks cute all bundled up in his puffy winter jacket, the strings off the flaps of his wool hat swinging in the wind.

"Hey," I say, my expression brightening as I walk up to the open window.

"Hey." His breath comes out in a frosted plume. "I'm heading to Katie's for a little impromptu pizza party. If you texted me more, you'd be in on all the secrets and surprises."

"Oh. That sounds like fun," I say carefully. So, he *wants* me to text him more?

"Honestly, I appreciate how chill you're being," he adds.

"Huh?" I can't tell if he's kidding, but I smile anyway.

He quirks his mouth. "Yeah. It's cool how relaxed you are about things these days."

I'm reminded of when he told me I'm different now, right before we kissed. Maybe this is part of what he meant. Not blowing up his phone, like I'd normally want to do.

"Sure." Little does he know that I *did* send those texts. Dillon knew how hard it would be for me to resist texting Lincoln a billion times a day, so everything I've wanted to text Lincoln, I've texted Dillon. That's the kind of friend Dillon is.

"I wanted to give you your space." A heavy scarf of anxiety chokes me, but I push myself to say more. "Though I like talking."

Lincoln's expression softens. "I like talking too. I like the idea of cuddling more, though." He winks, then pops open the passenger side door, beckoning me inside.

As much as I want to get in the car, I desperately need to get to work.

Maybe this really *is* my time to ask him out, though. Fate. Destiny.

A few students pass in front of the car. One of them whistles at us, and someone else shouts, "It's kissing time!" as I scooch in. I feel my face burn.

Lincoln raises the window, and we wait for the students to pass, then he pulls me in for a big warm kiss, which feels especially nice after being out in the frigid cold. I'm impressed I'm able to utilize my calm kissing skills in such extreme climates. But I'm paranoid my nose may be dripping.

After a few moments lost in his arms and a Chappell Roan song on his sound system, I pull back, caressing his earring . . . and glance at the time on my phone, wincing. "Ah. Sorry. I really have to get to work."

He kisses me again.

I glance at the time once more.

My heart jackrabbits.

Ask him, Leo. Do it.

But what if he says no?

Lincoln points to my home screen. "Is that . . . *me?*"

"No." I click the screen to black. I can't believe he just caught me. I may have made him my home screen . . . Oh my god. This looks so creepy. I hope he doesn't think I'm super creepy now—

"Listen," he says, "I'm just looking for fun. Nothing serious."

"I mean, we're having fun, right?" I ask, hopeful.

"Yeah." He shakes his head with a little laugh. "But after Travis, I'm not looking to jump into anything heavy. For real."

"Oh. Sure. Yeah, no problem. We can keep it light," I suggest with an understanding smile, when every part of me wants to let him know that *I'm* the answer to his No-Boy Blues. "Anyway, I should get going."

"Right. Don't want anyone to be waiting on their cup of tea for too long. Your job is so dorky," he adds with a flirty smile.

I narrow my eyes at him. "Jerk," I tease.

"So what if you're a little late?" He pulls me close again. "It's not like the place is packed at any given time."

"Oh, and you'd know that because . . . ?" Because he was a no-show.

He grabs the collar of my jacket and kisses me hard. Then his fingers walk up my bicep. "I *could* give you a lift . . ."

"I appreciate it, but my mom let me borrow her car today." I gesture out the window, then give a heavy sigh. I feel the moment slipping away.

"See you tomorrow. Opening night! Woo!" he cheers, giving my arm a little shake.

I peck him on the cheek and hurry into my car, rushing to get the heat going and letting out a chills-driven, teeth-chattering shudder. I'm sorely regretting not seizing the moment to ask him out, but it didn't feel right. Especially after he'd just told me he's not looking for anything serious.

Does that mean he's still not over Travis?

Well, at least Lincoln offered to drive me to work. That means he has to care about me just a little, right? And besides, there's always tomorrow night—opening night of the school play. I'm sure I can find a moment to ask him out then.

Noticing the time on the dashboard, my smile fades.

Oh, crap.

"Leo," Judy says as I burst into the teahouse's oven-hot kitchen, hit over the head with the smell of hot cinnamon tea and freshly baked pecan pie. She looks down at her sensible silver watch on her thin, freckled wrist, then calmly back up at me. "You are fourteen minutes late."

I tense up. "I know. I'm so sorry!" I snatch my apron off its peg. "The traffic was terrible," I add, though I know Judy has a "Kindly, I don't care about the excuse" rule.

In fact, it's written all over her placid expression. Staring at me, her big blue eyes are unblinking through her glasses before she strolls to the far side of the kitchen to check the oven.

I let out a big exhale, relieved that her coming down on me wasn't as bad as it could have been, but also feeling guilty. She's always been so kind and generous to me.

Through the curtains, the dining room buzzes with the hubbub of voices, the clinking of silverware, and the soft bells of a Christmas tune playing from speakers. People sip hot cocoas or ciders, nibble cookies, and share jolly tales. Vincent lent his impeccable handwriting skills to the storefront window to advertise the extended holiday hours, along with COOKIES AND COCOA, which draws in large crowds to enjoy nights that should not be spoiled by latecomer employees.

Vincent clicks his tongue, and I realize I'm standing in his way. I flatten myself against the kitchen island for him to squeeze past. He's in a burgundy sweater with a snowflake brooch pinned to his apron, and dons bedazzled reindeer ears,

LEO MARTINO STEALS BACK HIS HEART

as he carries a tray laden with scones and clotted cream. "Stop coming in late," he hisses. "It's actually forcing me to *do* stuff."

"*Sorry*," I mouth.

He rolls his eyes, and then he's sashaying through the curtain.

I'm distracted the whole rest of the shift. I've checked off nearly all the boxes on my glow-up checklist, but I need to continue refining myself to become true-blue boyfriend material. I'm so close—and I'm not sure if it's been the tireless amount of effort I've been putting into the process, but I am absolutely exhausted. So exhausted that tonight, while cleaning up, I put a jar of fresh jam in the dishwasher before catching myself.

My phone dings.

Silvio: See you next week

My brother and I have barely spoken since he's been away at college in Boston. Sure, there's been the occasional "hey how are you?" text, but we've both just been living our separate lives. That's the way it's always been with us. I look forward to seeing him on Thanksgiving. Even though it's next week, the holiday still feels so far away, because there are three performances and a whole mess of school projects to do between now and then, and I'm focused solely on the play. Well, not solely . . .

Okay, so Lincoln wants something light, and I can give him that. Light and loving. No heavy dramatic thing like what Travis probably served him. He wants chocolate mousse over a decadent chocolate tart? I can give him that. Because things don't need to be heavy and serious to be real, right? They can be light and casual, and who knows where that could lead?

Maybe there's even a new item to tack onto my checklist about making someone want something serious when they show signs they're scared of getting hurt again. He can trust me.

Because when I love someone, I mean it.

This time tomorrow night, I may have my first real boyfriend.

The romance, the checklist, the magic of opening night will be so strong that everything will come together to make it happen.

By the time the teahouse empties out and Vincent and I (okay, just me) are drying off the last dish, Judy seals up a fresh batch of peanut butter blossoms and approaches me.

"About your being late, Leo," she starts. "This can't happen again. I've been nice about it so far, but it's not quite fair to me and the rest of the staff, or the guests, for you to continue to be tardy. Unfortunately, it's just been too many times. It pains me to say this, but please consider this your final warning, young man."

I chew my lip, feeling the hard impact of her words. "I promise I won't be late again."

It wouldn't be the first time I've said it, but hopefully it will be the last.

NEXT THING I KNOW, IT'S OPENING NIGHT—AND LUCKILY,
I'm not even the last cast member to arrive at call time.

The moment I'm onstage behind the heavy red curtain, my insides flutter with nerves. I hear people filling the seats in the auditorium, chatting and creating a jovial din. This three-piece suit is starting to feel a little *too* snug.

I peek past the curtain to find the place is *packed*. My stomach tenses.

But then the sight of Enzi in the front row makes me want to cackle. Remember him? My ex-crush who said I didn't have enough of a presence? And the reason I auditioned for the school play in the first place? Well, Enzi, take a good look at me now! Or rather, shortly.

"It's almost places," Anne whispers to me.

I swivel to give a thumbs-up. I still have till act two before I'm onstage, but I don't want to miss a second of my first-ever high school production, here in the wings watching it all go down.

Lincoln is in the very first scene, so I definitely want to make sure I'm around to see him. I'm still kicking myself that I couldn't strike up the nerve to ask him out before tonight. I'll just need to do it right away. Sometime before the last performance. Maybe even tonight?

"So, are the rumors true?" Anne asks.

"Yeah," Emily says. "Are you and Lincoln the new It Couple?"

I grin coquettishly. Her comment only bolsters the feeling inside compelling me to make it official.

"Did you hear Tim and Janine are going steady?" Anne whispers.

"No, but that's good to know." One less thing for me to worry about. One more sign that Leo + Lincoln is *right*.

The auditorium grows quieter as the lights dim, signaling showtime. Anne and Emily giggle and disappear backstage, and my insides beam with promise and hope at what the night holds in store.

There's Mom in the third row, smiling at me. She took a ride-share over from work so that I could use her car to arrive early. She's still dressed in her tweed suit jacket and dark turtleneck, with her brown hair brushed down nice. Dillon and Varsha are beside her, and when they see me, they light up and give little waves. Honestly, it's more nerve-racking knowing Mom and my besties are in the audience versus if the room were to be full of complete strangers.

The door swings open, and there, drawing all eyes as he struts down the aisle, is Dad.

Ice runs in my veins. *Dad? Here?*

He's in a black leather getup with a do-rag, and when he walks, it sounds like jangling chains.

And he's not even the one who everyone's staring at. He brought his girlfriend. She has long, bleached-blond hair, a form-fitting pencil skirt, a blouse way too low-cut for a high school play, and what look to be seven-inch high heels. She's hanging on his arm, and he stops mid-aisle to search for his seat—they're literally the only people standing by now.

I feel sick to my stomach. What are they *doing* here?

Someone walks in behind them—it's Silvio. I'm touched at the surprise visit and at the fact he's supporting me by coming to the play, but also slightly perturbed that he arrived with the Terrible Duo. My brother and I look nothing alike—with his blue eyes, medium-length dark curly hair, and broad frame—and seeing him now, even from a distance, he feels more like a stranger than ever.

Strong arms grip me from the back, and I'm spun around.

Lincoln plants a big smooch on me.

"Hey! H-how are you feeling about tonight?" The words come out automatically, my stomach still squeezed from seeing Dad, but also pulling in the opposite direction about how Lincoln Chan and I just shared a kiss out in public—even if no one saw it. Though I can't even say I was able to enjoy it.

Lincoln grins, reminding me of a Labrador retriever. "Good."

"Anyone here that you know?" I gesture through the curtain.

Maybe if I can get a conversation started, it can override and distract me from my anxiety spiral. Including the thought that I'm sure Mom's seen Dad by now, and his girlfriend, and I'm not sure how long Mom can handle being in the same room with them.

Lincoln shrugs. "A few friends."

"Are your parents here?" I ask.

He averts his eyes and shifts his body farther away. "Yeah, they might be."

I peek back at the auditorium and see Dad and his plus-one seated in the second row with Silvio. Right in front of Mom, who's reading something on her phone. But I can't tell Lincoln about that whole mess. Not now, or possibly ever. It's too shameful. And I *definitely* can't let this derail me from asking Lincoln to be official-official tonight. Because in just three days, Lincoln and I will no longer be brushing elbows night after night at rehearsals. It *has* to be tonight—or this weekend. But preferably tonight so my nerves can hit the road already.

Despite still feeling nauseated, I force a smile. "You're going to be great."

"I know." He flashes a cheesy smile, the kind I haven't seen since our days when he'd pull out the holographic crustacean card that would end a game of *Dungeness & Lobsters*.

"Maybe you can say hi to my mom after." As soon as the words leave my lips, I'm gripped with fear. This is Old Leo coming out, because New Leo is too shaken up by current events to keep his head in the game! Talk about a try-hard move!

Lincoln shrugs. "Sure."

Phew.

"Places!" Dr. Horan whispers, passing by in a fancier all-black ensemble than normal—this one with a lot of gloss and satin detailing—and a little headset.

Lincoln straightens up, spinning away while smoothing down his snazzy tunic and jacket.

And then, after house announcements, the stage darkens and the play begins.

Lincoln and a group of other actors move into the spotlight and he recites the first lines: "'If music be the food of love, play on. Give me excess of it, that, surfeiting, the appetite may sicken, and so die . . .'"

His striking good looks seem more defined in this moment, more so than seeing him act during rehearsals, or even when it's been just the two of us hanging out, like he's actually embodied the powerful nobleman he's playing. Like a hero in one of my favorite movies. The stage lights certainly help highlight his chiseled cheekbones. He's even more captivating than usual.

After a few minutes, the novelty of watching from the wings wears, so I head backstage, where I find other actors awaiting their scenes by pacing around, reciting lines, referencing the script, or giving each other friendly shoulder rubs while sharing music in their earbuds.

Dr. Horan races around with his clipboard, following the script and making sure anyone hanging out moves to the wings before they're set to go on. Even from backstage, I can hear the actors' lines of dialogue, and notice they're punctuated by someone laughing loudly and obnoxiously. And I'm pretty sure that some of the lines aren't even intended to be funny.

Before I know it, Dr. Horan taps me, meaning I'm on deck. As I follow him back to the wings, my heart races. I'm thinking about Dad when I should be running over my first few lines.

I hear Emily recite her line: "'What is decreed must be, and be this so.'" That's my cue. Dr. Horan ushers me through the curtain, along with Tim, who's playing Antonio, and we enter the bright lights of the bare stage, which feels like a petri dish right now, with all eyes on us.

"'Will you stay no longer? Nor will you not that I go with you?'" Tim asks me.

My mind goes blank. All I can think about is Dad, confused and hating how he's here.

"'Nor will you not that I go with you,'" Tim repeats, his voice now carrying an edge.

The spotlight is too bright. Too hot. I'm no longer New Leo, but Old Leo, shrinking, getting smaller and smaller by the second.

Dr. Horan's voice hisses from the wings. *"'By your patience, no.'"*

I snap out of it. "'By your patience, no. My stars shine darkly over me.'" My knees feel like they're about to buckle with nerves, and I wish I were gripping something sturdy to anchor myself.

"'Antonio, my name is Sebastian, which I called Roderigo,'" I continue. "'My father—'" At "father," I inadvertently make eye contact with Dad. He's a picture of attentiveness, sitting prim and proper, eyes wide, drinking in my disaster. "'My father was that Sebastian of Messaline, whom I know you have heard of.

He left behind him myself and a sister.'"

I stumble over the next few lines, face flushed, body rigid. And I continue to jumble it all up the whole rest of the scene.

My eyes well with frustrated tears, but I push through it. "'I am bound to the Count Orsino's court. Farewell,'" I declare, and exit stage left. The second I'm behind the curtain, I lose control over my trembling bottom lip. A precursor to the tears. I'm so mad at myself for letting Dad's presence rattle me. A few other actors give me sympathetic finger snaps of applause, which they cease when they register that I'm a Crying Hot Mess.

I do the only thing I can think of to make me feel better right now. I dig out my phone from my backpack and text Dillon.

He replies instantly. Of course he does.

Dillon: Guess you saw your dad's here?
Dillon: Screw him.
Dillon: Breathe. Deep breaths. You're doing great.

I know he's just being nice. I smile anyway. The long, steady breaths help.

The breaks between my scenes seem to fly, and I'm back onstage in a flash. Tim and I muddle through our fake brawl, then he tosses a coin purse to me.

"'Haply your eye shall light upon some toy you have desire to purchase—'"

But his line is cut off by the Laugh Offender in the audience.

And then I realize, as another actor says her line, that the Laugh Offender is *Dad*.

I wish I were standing on a faulty stage door.

Finally, Lincoln delivers his last line and we all exit stage right. He grins at me backstage, ecstatic by the end of a good first night. Good for *him*, that is. Fellow actors fist-bump Lincoln and give him validating thumbs-ups.

"I messed up my lines so many times," I find myself whining.

Anne and Emily watch me with wide eyes as if to confirm they saw it all go down in flames.

As I hear myself speak, I realize I've messed up not only my parts of the play, but also the big night for me and Lincoln to become official. I'm in no mood to flirt or set myself up for any more pain, and the voice, urging me to rip the Band-Aid off already and ask him, dissolves.

Dr. Horan guides us back onstage for bows. After this, people are supposed to wait in the audience for the actors to emerge from backstage to say hi. But I don't want to dip my toe into the audience after. I don't want to see Dad, let alone interact with him . . . *or* Margot.

As I bow, I notice Mom's seat is empty. Has she gone to the bathroom? Or did she see Dad and leave? How could she *not* have seen Dad? He's clapping and cheering louder than anyone else, which, while on the outside, may *seem* sweet—like a father supporting his son—it actually makes me *so* uncomfortable, and I wish he would just go away and take that Margot woman with him. Silvio stands beside him, clapping with a vacant smile. I can only imagine what he's thinking.

The cast gestures to the tech crew up at the back of the auditorium controlling the lights, then to Dr. Horan and Ms.

Kennedy, who grin and give royal waves, looking less disgruntled than I've ever seen them, like actual stars themselves. Similar to Lincoln, this is *their* shining moment. I wish it were mine too.

I catch movement out of the corner of my eye and realize, with a lurching stomach, that Dad is dashing up the steps onto the stage. He hands me an enormous bouquet of flowers and poses with me, cheesing as Margot snaps photos from the audience. Silvio looks on with an unreadable expression, then shrugs at me and breaks into a nervous chuckle. Dad laughs and races back offstage, and the wacky moment is finished, thank god.

The curtain drops—and the torture is finally over.

The cast members cheer and applaud each other, hugging and grinning. I try to shake off the bizarre Dad interaction, and the feeling of wanting to plummet through a trapdoor. The adrenaline I'd had during the show starts to fade, replaced by an exhausted weight. The show's over, but there's still the whole drama that happened offstage to contend with. Lucky me.

I realize with a sinking feeling that Operation: Ask Lincoln Out tonight was a total failure. So, when *should* I ask? Not now with all these people around giving him high fives. Since my first jumbled line, my confidence has continued to sink lower and lower by the second. I shudder. I don't think I can muster up enough nerve to ask him now. The thought deflates me. I try to remind myself that there's always tomorrow. I'm just waiting for the perfect time, right?

My night's gone from a Shakespearean comedy to a tragedy.

Most of the actors swap attire, grab their bags, and go out into the auditorium to meet whichever friends or family showed up for them. I text and call Mom but don't hear back. Silvio texts me that he hasn't heard from her either, then sends a follow-up text ordering me to emerge from backstage to say hi.

I contemplate tossing the bouquet that Dad gave me into the trash, but think better of it. I've always wanted to be given flowers—just never from a Terrible Human such as my own father.

Eventually, I quit hiding and search for Dillon and Varsha in the auditorium. I want to be a good friend and thank them for coming.

Unfortunately, Dad is still out here—with Margot. When he sees me, he takes a step toward me, but Dillon shouts my name from off to the side.

"Leo! Over here!"

Saved by the bestie.

I give Dad a slight smile and hold up a finger, indicating for him to wait just a second.

Then I go over to Dillon and Varsha, who are grinning from ear to ear. Varsha's already bundled up in her magenta jacket and knit hat, and Dillon wears a dapper peacoat.

"You were brilliant!" Dillon exclaims, his grin frozen on his face as he presents me with a bouquet of fresh red roses.

"OMG! Dill Pickle! You shouldn't have!" I smell them. "They're beautiful."

He smiles. "Just like you."

"I am so impressed," Varsha adds. "You crushed it, Leo!"

"You guys!" I whine, rolling my eyes back. "I adore you for the praise, but I was awful."

"You did *such* a good job," Dillon insists, and it's sweet of him to say it, knowing why I fumbled. I catch his eyes darting to Dad, then back to me. Varsha looks confused.

"Well, thanks for coming." I jerk a thumb toward the embarrassing elephant in the room. "I have to say hi to the fam."

"We'll talk more later." Dillon gives me a look, as if asking with his eyes if I'll be okay.

I give a subtle nod back, and then he and Varsha head out.

Enzi strolls up to me. "Hey. Stage fright?" he asks with a teasing smile.

I jolt back, bristling. "Well," I say, finding my composure and taking a wide power stance, "I'd say it was just an off night for me." I spot Dad watching us from over Enzi's shoulder. Also, Lincoln is with his friends. I don't see his parents. And thankfully, no Travis, either.

Enzi nods, the side of his mouth quirked. "Well, you looked great up there." Someone across the room catches his eye with a wave, and then Enzi salutes me and swaggers away.

His words lift my spirits—but not by much.

Silvio gives me a stiff pat on the back. "Good job, bro."

"Thanks. You weren't supposed to be back in town for another week!"

"Surprise."

I nod in the direction of Dad and Margot, who are talking to Dr. Horan about who knows what. Probably about Dad's flat-earth theory. "Why did you come with them?" I ask Silvio, my blood boiling.

"What's the big deal?" he asks. Of *course* he wouldn't

know—he hasn't been privy to all the Unfortunate Family Moments while he's been away from home, sheltered from the Parental Divorce Storm.

"He cheated on Mom with that lady," I hiss. "He *left us* for her."

Silvio shrugs. "I asked Dad if he was going to the play. He said yes. So I hitched a ride."

As much as I want to talk to him about what a traitor he is for being so impartial, a small part of me acknowledges that we can't all be in lockstep. But I'm still not happy about it.

Silvio chuckles, eyes flitting from my hair to my makeup. "Nice look, by the way. Mom said you changed things up, but I didn't know it was that big of a change."

I give an eye roll. "Don't you follow me on social media?"

"I unfollowed when you tried being an NPC tavernkeep."

"Fair."

"Hi, son." Dad appears beside me, his smile wide and creepy. "You remember Margot."

Unfortunately.

She flashes bright white teeth. Her lip gloss is hot pink and blinding.

"Hi, honey! Your father has told me so much about you," she says. Then she goes in for a hug, which crushes the bouquets, and she kisses me on the cheek. It makes me want to squirm and overwhelms me with a strong cotton-candy-scented perfume.

I'm pretty sure a thorn from the bouquet is driving its way into my side.

I guess she doesn't remember meeting me at our family bar-becue last year. And I guess Dad doesn't want to acknowledge my new look, which probably reflects his quiet disapproval of it. Actually, when I really think about it, I doubt he realizes I look any different. He's too focused on himself.

Lincoln appears beside me. "Hey. Mind if I catch a ride home?"

Dad, Margot, and Silvio all look at him with curious expressions. Oh, no, no, no. Social interaction overload commencing.

I was not expecting to introduce Lincoln to Dad when I haven't even come out to him. I wonder if he'll put two and two together, but honestly, he's so self-absorbed, he's never going to ask me about it—or anything. Not even a *How you been?*

"Lincoln, you remember my dad," I manage to utter.

Lincoln registers him and Margot, and freezes up. "Oh. Uh . . . hi." He shakes his hand. "Mr. Martino." He turns to Margot and shakes her hand, too. "Mrs. Martino."

I almost cringe at the faux pas and debate whether on chiming in to say: "Oh, that's not my mom." Doesn't he remember my mom from when he used to hang out at our house? Then again, we *do* both have the same bleached-blond hair, which I'm now starting to regret.

As Lincoln and Silvio shake hands, Margot just keeps awkwardly beaming, like she's eager to be accepted by us.

"Awesome play!" Dad says. "You should come watch me when I'm playing drums at the church and you'll see what *real* entertainment is."

Lincoln eyes Dad's boots with an intrigued expression. "Are those real snakes?"

Dad's boots are not just made of snakeskin—they also have

the actual heads of two snakes, one coming off each toe.

Dad beams, chest up. "Sure are!" He goes on to talk about where he got them, which somehow dovetails into the luxury car he drives that is so rare that when he needed to replace a tire, the United States only had one in stock.

He goes on and on about how he's getting additions put on to his lakefront home, bringing up photos on his phone of his tiled garage full of shiny motorcycles and Corvettes. I wonder why he's making his house bigger if it's just him living there—and presumably Margot. Silvio and I don't even have the key to get in. Not that I'm champing at the bit to visit.

I feel awful that Lincoln has to be subjected to Dad. Add this to the growing list of ways that tonight—which was supposed to be full of promise—has totally backfired.

Finally, Dad brings his lecture to a close and winks at Lincoln. "I'm a cool dad. And I look pretty good for my age, don't you think?"

Lincoln's eyes are glazed over. I don't blame him. Here he was coming over to ask for a ride and got roped into Wackyville, USA. And the bouquets are growing heavy in my arms.

"Yeah, for sure." Silvio fills in the silence, shoulders high and hands in his pockets.

Margot scratches the nape of Dad's neck with her long French tips. It gives absolute ick.

"Sorry," Lincoln cuts in, glancing down at his phone. "But I should get going."

I could marry him. I never thought Dad would stop holding court.

"Yeah, let's go," I add, feigning a yawn. "Where did I park . . . ?" I muse.

"Okay. Well, you should come to our church. All three of you. Any time."

We give our hugs goodbye, mumbling in agreement to placate him.

"Nice seeing you, honey," Margot tells me.

I can't help glaring at Silvio as he shrugs and follows behind Dad and Margot.

In the hall, Lincoln regards my bouquets. "Nice flowers. Who gave them to you?"

"My dad. And a friend." I don't want him to misread things with Dillon. I present him with Dad's flowers. "Here. For you. I don't need two bouquets."

He takes the bouquet. "Thanks."

But then I remember my checklist item—*Be Cool as a Cucumber*—and decide that playing hard to get falls squarely within that realm: "You know Dillon. He gave me the roses."

Lincoln tenses up and lowers his bouquet by his side . . . dare I say, *jealously?*

Interesting.

"Come on," he says.

Once Lincoln and I are in the senior lot, I give a sigh of relief. "Thanks for bailing us out back there, by the way. My dad likes to talk."

"I don't recall your mom being so young!"

I deflate slightly. So he *doesn't* remember. But I can't tell him that she wasn't my mom, that it was the Other Woman, and that my family is broken and messed up.

"I'm embarrassed," I admit. "Sorry you had to be subjected to that. My dad's . . . a lot."

"He was fine."

I thought that having someone like Lincoln by my side would make me feel *less* alone, saved from any curveball life threw my way. But his presence isn't magically curing me of my sorrow like I hoped it would. Maybe it's because he doesn't truly love me yet. Why would he? We're not even boyfriends at this particular juncture.

But perhaps there's still a chance for me to shoot my shot.

We hop into Mom's car, and I drive him home, sneezing the whole time. I'm pretty sure I'm allergic to Dad's bouquet.

I pull up to the base of Lincoln's steep driveway, and my mind whirs. Even though tonight wasn't perfect by any stretch, is *now* the time to ask him out? He doesn't seem to care that I messed up my lines. My heart is thumping as I put the car in park.

The night's not over yet. There's still time. Just do it.

He swings his head toward me, hand already on the car door to leave. "Thanks for the ride."

"Uh, bye," I say, disconcerted. All my momentum is suddenly gone.

Lincoln screws up his mouth. "You okay?"

"Sorry. My dad showing up really messed with my head—"

Lincoln leans in and starts making out with me. It feels wrong, like the worst possible time to kiss. But as I find myself going with it, relaxing my jaw, allowing him in, it starts to feel more and more *right*. He runs his fingers through my hair, sending those tingles down my spine.

By the time we pull apart, I'm feeling lighter and more relaxed.

"Hey," I start as he reaches again for the door handle.

He arches an eyebrow.

Ask him. Do it!

I smile. "Really good job today."

He winks, then pops out of the car and climbs the driveway to his house.

I release the breath I'd been holding. I'm hopeless, all right.

I see he left the flowers on the floor of the passenger seat. Oh, well. I could call him about it, but I don't want to tread into try-hard waters, not after an okay end to a rocky evening.

Sure, I chickened out asking Lincoln to go steady. But maybe all is not lost. I still have until closing night of the play to ask him. Maybe that will be even better, because if he says no, we won't have to see each other the next day onstage, and it'll be easy enough to ignore him in Calc. Or at least that's what I'm telling myself.

Minutes later, I'm on the way into my house when I drop Dad's bouquet of carnations into our outdoor recycling bin. I'm sure the raccoons will enjoy it.

Inside, I find a bouquet of roses from Mom in a vase on the kitchen table, with a party balloon saying GREAT JOB, along with a few envelopes with my name on them. Inside, the cards tell me how proud Mom is of the great job I did in the play— even though I'm not sure how much of it she actually ended up seeing. There are also flower sugar cookies from my favorite Italian bakery, a Starbucks gift card, and a slew of other thoughtful gifts. I take after her in the Thoughtful Department, and I appreciate her for it.

I place Dillon's bouquet in another vase beside Mom's flowers.

As if on cue, Dillon texts asking if I'm okay. I reply with a photo of his roses and thank him again. That was so, *so* nice of him.

"Mom?" I call out quietly.

I walk down the hall to her bedroom. The door is shut, and I can hear crying inside. I gently knock.

"Come in," she says in her normal speaking voice.

Inside, Mom's propped up watching TV in her bed, which is littered with used tissues. There's a bottle of wine and a half-filled glass on her nightstand. She lowers the volume on the remote. "Hi, dear."

"Are you okay?"

She sighs, then blows her nose into a tissue. "I'm fine."

I take a seat on an armchair in front of the TV. "I'm guessing you saw Dad and Margot, and that's why you left early."

"No." She shakes her head, fighting a sob. "It was seeing your brother with them."

My stomach drops. "Oh, I thought it was my sad excuse for acting," I say, trying to make light of the matter.

Mom sits up taller, clearing her throat. "Sorry. That was immature of me to leave. I need to do better. In fact, I *am* going to do better. Your early Christmas gift is that I'm going to get my act together." She glances at the wine on her nightstand when she says it.

"It's okay. I get it. I probably would have left, too, if I had the choice. And thanks for the cards and stuff."

She nods, then tilts her head as she scrutinizes me. "Listen, dear . . . I didn't hear you mention hitting your first deadline for college applications."

I wince sheepishly at the accusation. "Yeah. I missed it."

"I'll make a deal. I'll stop getting triggered if you finish applying to colleges."

"Deal," I say, even though I'm still dreading the idea.

"Good. From what I saw of the play, you did a fantastic job." She smiles. "And don't worry. I bought my tickets for tomorrow's and Saturday's shows too."

"You're coming to all three?" I ask, moved.

"Of course I am. You've always wanted to have a speaking role in a school play. We need to celebrate that."

Mom doesn't need to say I love you for me to feel it. She says it in so many other ways.

"Is Silvio seeing it again with you too?"

"He's decided to stay with your father over Thanksgiving break, so I'm not sure what his plans are." Her voice betrays a hint of hurt. "But he'll be here on Thanksgiving Day. At least for a little bit." She shrugs in defeat.

"Well, I'm not going anywhere."

Her eyes well up as she gives a tight smile.

My phone buzzes. "All right, Mom. I gotta take this. It's Dillon."

"Oh! Dillon!" Her face lights up. "Tell him I say hi!" she says as I head upstairs.

Dillon appears on FaceTime. "Hey. How're you doing?"

"I'm okay," I say, slipping into my bathroom and closing the door. "My mom says hi."

"Want to talk about your dad?"

"Meh. Not really."

"That's cool. So, did you ask Lincoln out?"

"Not yet. There was too much going on. But I will." I prop Dillon up behind the faucet and start my nightly skin-care regimen. "Thanks, Dillon. For keeping my secret about my parents," I say while removing my makeup.

Meanwhile, he's meticulously rebuilding his midterm sculpture from all the shattered pieces. He took me up on my offer to help—I spent hours sorting all those fragments for him, and it was worth it. He's been working on it for weeks, and it's starting to look really good.

"I didn't tell Varsha anything, by the way," he assures me.

I drop a makeup wipe into the trash. "I probably should."

Dillon smiles. "Totally your call."

"I hate hiding things from you guys," I admit. "Not that I do."

"Mm-hmm." Dillon glues another tiny piece of sculpture into place.

"So, new plan. I'm going to ask him out closing night. That way, if he laughs and slams the door in my face, I won't have to bear the shame of seeing him day-to-day. I can avoid him in class."

"Rewind. Why would he laugh and slam the door in your face?"

Dillon's right. I've been abiding by my checklist, working on perfecting my persona and my presence, my kissing and my calm-and-cool. But my track record haunts me even still. Every time I've felt love within my grasp, it's slipped through my fingers. Could being boyfriends lead to true love? And if so . . . will having someone mean it's just a matter of time before I won't? Another door slammed, another page turned? Must all good things really come to an end?

Dillon smiles. "I think everything's going to work out the way it's meant to."

Closing night it is.

CLOSING NIGHT ISN'T THE NIGHT.

I was too nervous.

So, I spend the next couple of days recalibrating my life post-play. No more rehearsals means no more easy opportunities to ask out Lincoln. It also means more time in the day to wonder why *he* hasn't asked *me* out so far, and it feels like more time than I know what to do with.

Once I'm finally back in a rhythm, school's closed for Thanksgiving.

Thursday afternoon, I'm standing in front of my bathroom sink at home, patting color corrector on my under eyes as I get ready for Thanksgiving dinner happening in T minus five minutes. On TikTok, Vincent is contouring his nose with black eyeliner and applying makeup with an ice cube, ever the one to be on top of the trends.

"What are you watching?" Dillon asks, coming up behind me. He's in an oatmeal-brown sweater vest, his hair neatly combed to the side, and that crooked grin washes over his face.

"Some makeup hack," I say, dabbing on concealer. "Honestly, I'm not even listening. I'm too anxious about Lincoln. Why hasn't he texted me back?!"

Dillon shrugs. "Maybe he's doing Thanksgiving things."

I spin to him. "Do I look okay? I was going to take photos to send him."

He chuckles. "Yeah. You look great." He says it like I'm silly for asking, with a little head shake as if he can't believe he's entertaining me. It's cute.

"*Great?* Hey, that's a step up from *nice*. Score!"

"I second that" comes Varsha's voice. She holds up a hand on FaceTime on Dillon's phone. She doesn't celebrate Thanksgiving but was more than happy to get ready with me.

I let out a deep breath. "Okay. Thanks, friends." I check Instagram and see Lincoln's posted a photo. It's a selfie of us from closing night, his arm around me backstage once we'd packed up, right after I'd invited him to Thanksgiving in a last-ditch effort to put *something* on the books, and he told me he was already planning on going to Katie's place. Talk about a fail.

But this selfie . . .

"Lincoln posted a selfie of us!" I squeal, then click the post in the story leading to the actual post in his grid.

What does this mean? Is him posting a selfie of us some sort of concrete indicator that he's *that* into me? And here I was, thinking that by not having asked him yet to be my boyfriend, I'd blown any chance, now that we won't be brushing elbows at rehearsals anymore. And that, by *him* not asking *me* out, it was pretty much at a standstill.

"He included the photo in a carousel, so maybe it has less significance than I think," I muse.

"I can't believe he posted a photo of you two," Dillon says. "That's *good.*"

"And we're sure he didn't post it to make Travis jealous?" Varsha asks.

I gasp. "Varsha, Varsha, *Varsha*! You and your conspiracy theories."

"Leo!" Mom calls from downstairs.

"Coming!" I shout. Her roasted turkey and homemade sage dressing smell so good, along with the scent of spicy cinnamon and clove from her pumpkin pie. The *ding* of my cell phone interrupts the grumbling in my stomach and the thoughts reeling in my head.

Lincoln 🖤🖤🖤: Hope you're having a nice time with your fam

"I think the post is a good sign," I conclude. Smiling, I pocket my phone and contour my nose, cheeks, and forehead with bronzer, then dab on more blush and highlighter. In this lighting, it's hard to tell if I look red carpet ready or ready for the circus. "And you're sure I look okay?" I ask, smoothing my tank top.

"For who?" Dillon smirks. "Me and your mom and your brother?"

"For *the photos*!" I say, exasperated.

"Yes," Dillon groans, leaving the bathroom. "But I don't know if your mom is going to like the tank top. Now come on."

"Have fun! I'm grateful for you guys!" Varsha says before hanging up.

"Thanks for coming over," I tell Dillon on the landing. "This is our first Thanksgiving without Dad. But I'm feeling less sad about it with you here."

Dillon nudges my arm in a playful way. "I wouldn't miss it. Besides, being here sounded like way more fun than joining my parents with my grandpa in Alabama."

"Leo!" Mom hollers. "Come down, dear!"

"LEO!" Silvio's voice joins in. "DINNER!"

I spin back to Dillon. "Yikes. Go, go, go!"

We pad down the stairs, passing Miss Tiramisu in a turkey costume that Mom bought her, the smell of cooked turkey and stuffing growing stronger. Even without Lincoln in attendance, I'm excited for our small but tasty and spirited Thanksgiving. Though I feel a little sorry for not making the time to bake my yearly Thanksgiving stuffing bites.

Every year, my family and I usually go to my aunt Jane's house—she invites all my cousins, aunts, uncles, and grand-parents. But one of the odd parts of Mom and Dad's split is that people took sides—and Dad, for whatever reason, won. We haven't heard from Aunt Jane—or anyone from Mom's side of the family—in nearly seven months. Which is sad, because I miss when we'd have them over for pasta every Sunday. Dad told them awful and untrue things about Mom that turned them against her in his smear campaign.

"What are you wearing?" Mom asks me as I step foot into the kitchen.

Silvio eyes my tank top.

"What?" I say, defensive.

"It's not appropriate. Please change."

"Ugh!" I stomp back upstairs and trudge back down in an oversize sweater, just in time for Mom's group photo of us seated around the kitchen table.

Between photos, everyone's eyeing Mom's sumptuous spread. Sourdough rolls. Mashed potatoes, lumpy and salty the way Gran used to make them. And stuffed turkey and all its fixings. Luckily, there's a vat of cranberry sauce—Mom's turkey is famously dry and needs all the help it can get. There's a pumpkin pie cooling on the stovetop, and the air is warm and welcoming . . . and perfectly appropriate for a tank top, IMO.

Once Mom's photoshoot concludes, Dillon offers me the bread basket.

I ignore the empty seat beside me and butter a roll, lost in thought. Silvio's had friends and even a few girlfriends over for dinner, while I've sat alone enviously watching, year after year after year. When is it finally going to be *my* turn?

"How've you been?" Dillon asks Silvio. "How's college?"

Silvio stares at the tablecloth. "Good," he says with a shrug.

"You're in Boston, right?" Dillon asks.

"Boston College."

Dillon nods. "Nice! I love Boston. And that's a great school."

I take out my phone, checking to see if Lincoln's texted me again, then decide it's time to take a few pics to send him. "Wait! Before we dig in!" I hold out a hand, preventing Silvio from reaching for the mashed potatoes. "I want to get some pics." I snap photos of the spread then angle the phone up, capturing my face on-screen—and give my best smolder.

Snap!

"Uh, rude," Silvio remarks. "Are you done? We want to eat."

"The obligatory Thanksgiving pics," I explain airily.

Silvio scoffs, doling mashed potatoes onto his plate.

Dillon talks about chorus rehearsals and the solo he's been practicing for, and Mom looks enchanted. We're halfway through the meal when Mom's attention shifts toward me. I've been mostly chewing in silence and nodding along while eyeballing my phone despite Silvio's pointed looks. I ignore him and fine-tune my selfies. I think selfies are okay now.

"Leo?" Mom asks, setting down her wineglass—that I notice is filled with water.

"Huh? What?" I quickly tuck my phone at my side.

"I *said*, who knew Leo could act?" Silvio says with a laugh.

Dillon flashes a smile. "Leo's a natural."

"Why, thank you." I take a big swig of ice water from my own glass. Then I'm back scrolling on my phone under the table, seeing if anyone's commented on the carousel Lincoln posted.

Silvio shoves my arm. "It's your turn!"

"Huh?"

"Dear," Mom says, "we're going around the table saying what we're thankful for."

"Oh." I wipe my mouth with my napkin.

"Why are you acting so weird?" Silvio asks. "You keep checking your phone every two seconds, bro."

Thank god my makeup hides the red creeping into my cheeks.

"And you've barely touched your food," Silvio adds.

I shove food in my mouth and smile as mashed potatoes ooze through my teeth. "There. Happy?"

"Gross!" he shouts. "Mom!"

Dillon starts talking about the weather, and the bad vibes dissipate. I can't help wondering if Silvio is jealous of the new me. Little does he know I've always been jealous of him, the former popular varsity captain of the golf team. He's always had a girlfriend, and now he's living his best life at college, free to be and do what he pleases. Which isn't new for him, now that I think about it.

A few moments of spirited conversation pass, mostly Silvio telling us about life in the dorms and how he's been hosting a weekly poker night with some friends. His meal plan and the food they serve in the commissary. The clubs he's joined, the people he's met. We're all asking him questions, and a part of me feels a surge of something. Not jealousy, but maybe . . . excitement? At the prospect of heading someplace like that myself. Maybe this is the kick I've needed to sit down and do it. I really should complete my college apps. But first . . .

I excuse myself to the bathroom to post my Thanksgiving photos in secret, then wait to see if Lincoln liked or viewed any of them.

When I return to the table, I can tell my little absence didn't trick anyone.

It's not long before we're scraping our plates clean, fit to burst with both food and laughter. Eventually, I'm seeing Dillon out, still feeling a little badly about how I behaved but not sure how to express it. So I give him plenty of leftovers to take home.

Mom goes to lie down (but not before chiming in with her

usual "That Dillon is such a nice boy!"). Meanwhile, Silvio and I are on cleanup duty, clearing and wiping down the kitchen table, and loading up the dishwasher.

I rinse a plate and hand it off to Silvio. "So, what did you think of Lincoln in the play?"

"Your old best friend who ditched you?"

Ouch.

"He was fine," Silvio says matter-of-factly, fitting the plate into the dishwasher.

"Yeah. Right? That's it? What else?" I press.

Silvio slams the dishwasher shut and practically punches the start button. "I don't know," he mumbles. "Stop asking me." It seems like the dinner conversation took all the zip out of him. "What about you and Dillon?"

I wrap up the brussels sprouts at the counter. "What about us?" I ask, mystified.

"You two have good chemistry."

"Yeah," I say with a laugh, placing the leftovers in the fridge. "We're friends."

Silvio quirks an eyebrow. "Are you sure?"

"Uh, yeah."

He shrugs then wipes the stovetop. "Whatever."

"Well, you're lucky you're away at college and barely spent any time here before that," I confess as I seal the platter of leftover green beans in plastic wrap and shove them into the fridge beside the brussels sprouts. "You haven't heard about all the Dad drama that's been going on here."

"Yep." He laughs his short, staccato laugh. "And I want to keep it that way."

I can't help rolling my eyes. It's not fair he wasn't here on the ground to see how everything's played out. Dad's booming shouts. Doors slamming. Dad leaving. The trials. How it's affected Mom.

I strike a pose. "So, what do you think of my new look?"

"Honestly? I don't like it," he says flatly. "It's not you."

My face flushes. "Yeah, it is. It's the *new* me." I busy myself again, wrapping up what's left of the pumpkin pie, though I gave most of it to Dillon.

He shakes his head. "So does that explain the bad attitude?"

I flinch. "What bad attitude?"

"Showing up late? Being glued to your phone? Ignoring Dillon? Should I go on?"

His words sting. "I did not ignore Dillon," I protest.

"Yeah, you did. You're a tool now."

My whole body goes rigid. "No. I'm just more confident now," I say in defense, but my cracked voice gives me away. He's right. I'm usually so present and never tardy, but lately . . .

"Nah," he says with a wave of his hand. "You've changed." There's that phrase again.

I bristle again. "You're just not used to it."

"Your change isn't as great as you think it is."

"Hey, you've changed too, you know." But he hasn't. Not really. He's still the same old Silvio, who gets mad at me when I'm too slow to order at the bagel shop, or when I modify my sandwich order at the deli, or chew with my mouth open, or sneeze more than three times in a row.

He shrugs and sits at the table, turning on ESPN to watch football replays.

I stand, staring at him, wanting to keep talking even though it's clear he's done. "Well, I'm sorry I was on my phone so much. I agree with you on that point."

He ignores me.

I release a loud, frustrated sigh.

Riiiing!

Silvio pulls out his phone and answers it. "Hey, Dad."

Dad?

Traitor.

"Yeah. Happy Thanksgiving to you too. Thanks for calling."

I can barely make out what Dad's saying. I think he's asking Silvio how he liked the photo he sent of Margot, and answering before Silvio can reply, saying she's gorgeous and Silvio would be lucky to date a girl like her. I'm starting to feel sick to my stomach—and not from stuffing myself silly.

My brother eventually cuts in. "Uh, do you want to talk to Leo?"

I glare, waving my hands and shaking my head to indicate I do *not* want to talk to him.

"Yeah. Hold on." Silvio ignores me and hands me the phone.

I stare even sharper daggers at Silvio and carefully take the phone, as if it could spring up and bite me at a moment's notice like a provoked snake. "Hello?" I ask, tentative.

"Hi, son. It's your father. Remember me?" His voice is light but tinged with venom.

That sinking feeling in my stomach returns. "Hey. Yeah. Happy turkey day, Dad."

"Thanks, man! We just had a wonderful meal. I invited a

whole bunch of people from our church. It was awesome, man. We had the best turkey and all fresh vegetables from Whole Foods. And Margot made a killer pumpkin pie. Better than anything your mother's ever made, I know that."

The mention of Mom makes my hackles rise. Margot probably bought it from the store and claimed she baked it.

"Nice," I utter, letting the word linger. Is he going to ask about me?

"Margot's pretty great, isn't she?" Dad says, followed by a giddy laugh. "Well, I just wanted to say Happy Thanksgiving," he goes on to say. "You know, it's not right that *I* had to call *you*. I'm your father, and I deserve *respect*." His tone goes from jolly to haughty. There it is, right on schedule.

"Okay" is all I manage to squeak out as my heart thuds in my ears.

"Your mother must have brainwashed you against me—"

Oh, not *this* again.

"I have to go, Dad." I hang up and hand over the phone. "Why'd you pick up?" I demand.

"Why wouldn't I?" Silvio sounds puzzled.

"Because he's a monster. He cheated on Mom, and then yelled at her and treated her so awfully before he left. Oh, wait. That's right. You weren't here for that part."

Silvio clamps his hands over his ears. "I said I don't want to hear about it."

"Well, you should know the truth and not side with Dad."

"Whatever. I can do what I want." He turns away again, opening Uber on his phone. "Bye. I'm leaving."

"You're being hypocritical!" I yell. "You're calling out my bad behavior, but not his? His behavior is much worse than whatever you said about mine! He's trying so that he doesn't have to pay for your college and allowance and stuff! And mine too!"

Silvio keeps watching TV, unmoving, while his Uber inches closer to us on the map.

Between the turkey tryptophan and the energy zap from this whole exchange, I'm ready for bed.

I stomp upstairs, thinking about how I was hoping Dad would at least ask me how I've been this time around. He really doesn't care. I'm not sure he ever did. My hope is fading.

In my bathroom, I'm about to take a makeup wipe to my face when I freeze. I barely recognize myself in the mirror. Was what Silvio said right? Have I changed . . . for the worse?

I remove my makeup. What remains is a pale face.

And a lost expression.

Moments later, I'm not sure why exhaustion isn't leading to sleep.

I watch the before/after video on my TikTok profile, which seems like forever ago.

Soon, I find myself wanting to text Lincoln, someone who doesn't know the truth of my life, and I give in to the impulse to share with him like I did with Dillon.

Leo: I hope you had a good thanksgiving

He replies almost instantly, and my tired eyes open wider to read his text.

Lincoln 🖤🖤🖤: Bored out of my mind

I laugh and wonder how I can secure the next hangout, the boyfriend status. I'm too tired to think of anything brilliant, for a plot or for a response, so I just keep my text vague and open-ended.

Leo: Would you wanna hang soon

Five minutes pass of me incessantly checking to see if he's replied, clicking the screen on whenever it fades to black. It feels like a giant fist is squeezing me as I wait with bated breath.

I'm just about to drift off when my phone lights up, way too bright behind my eyelids.

Lincoln 🖤🖤🖤: City on Sunday?

A sleepy, goofy smile spreads across my face in the dark, squished to my pillow. Lincoln and me in New York City? Rockefeller Center. The Rockettes. The Christmas tree. The rink. Dad used to take Silvio and me when we were little, and I've always wanted to go back. Lincoln and I could see the window displays at Macy's, and all the Christmas lights, hot cocoa in hand. I wonder if I could find cheap tickets for *The Nutcracker* . . .

And what better time to ask Lincoln to be my boyfriend?

ON SUNDAY, ONCE THE TRAIN REACHES PENN STATION,
Lincoln and I take the subway to Bryant Park.

It's freezing cold out. We huddle together for warmth as
we wait in a line for hot cocoa, bundled up in our mittens
and gloves, scarves and hats, and thick winter coats. Vendors
line the perimeter of the ice-skating rink, and people crowd
around the gigantic Christmas tree to take photos. Standing
here with him, even in silence as he rocks from foot to foot and
blows into his gloved hands to warm them, feels like a dream
coming true.

"What's your favorite Christmas song?" I ask.

He chews the side of his mouth. "'Blue Christmas.' Hands
down."

"Eww. Why? That's like, the worst one." I can feel myself

thawing into being more myself with him, even if it *is* against protocol.

He feigns outrage.

The vendor calls us up, and we order two hot cocoas with extra tiny marshmallows. Lincoln reaches into his pocket for his wallet, but I intercede, handing the vendor cash.

"My treat."

"Really?" He smiles. "Well, that's nice of you."

"I'm a nice guy," I say, but quickly course-correct, since *nice* isn't *cool*. "Don't mention it."

We enjoy the rest of the afternoon ice-skating on the rink with the sparkling Christmas tree towering over us. I giggle and career out of control on the ice as Lincoln continually skates to my rescue, with his long, even strides, like he spent a past life as an Olympic ice dancer. At one point, he takes my mitten in his glove. While we hold hands skating around and around in dizzying, exhilarating laps, I take a moment to think how lucky I am. It feels like a tiny Rudolph's nose glows bright inside me— after all this time on the hunt for love, have I finally, truly found it? My First Great Love Story?

Then, when we stop and pull over to the side, he kisses me, and I feel like I have my answer.

There are tons of people around—on the rink or looking on from outside it—and I'm thrilled that anyone looking over at us right now may be thinking: *Wow. Look at that nice couple.* I know if it were *me* looking in on us kissing, *I'd* be jealous.

From the rink, we travel out to look at more lights, the smell of roasting chestnuts in the air.

There are about twenty gift-buying opportunities that I force myself to ignore. He mentions in passing that he needs a weight-lifting belt since his current one needs to be replaced; talks my ear off about how much he loves his dog, so I mentally bookmark a website where you can print your pet's photo on a giant fuzzy blanket; and a scarf and gloves because he keeps complaining about wishing he had a thicker, warmer version of each. Naturally, my mind jumps to ordering them online as soon as I get home, or even ordering them on my phone next time I break for a restroom.

I guess now that Christmas is right around the corner, I can maybe get him a *few* presents and ease up on the checklist rule. Gifts for holidays are totally allowed, right?

Lincoln surprises me by taking a selfie of us at nearly every juncture, with all sorts of Christmas tree decor in the background. He's bold enough to snap photos of us, but for the life of me, I can't bring myself to ask to be boyfriends. Not even during the picture-perfect moment on the rink before the sparkling tree. I'm terrified that he'll say no, that asking him will scare him off. I justify waiting, giving it more time—

Until I'm *certain* I'll get a yes.

I haven't mastered my checklist items fully.

And I'm not sure I'm perfect boyfriend material enough yet.

That must be why I'm so hesitant. But will there ever be a "right time" to ask?

When we finish off our roasted chestnuts and the Mapleccinos he was so keen to order from a trendy Canadian pop-up, we decide to head home.

On the train ride back, I rest my head on his shoulder and doze off while he's on his phone, most likely posting photos to his socials—hopefully of us. The last thought I have before falling asleep is that I've always wanted a guy to post adorable photos of us to his socials, that I've always wanted a shoulder like his to rest on . . .

I wake to the sound of the conductor announcing we've arrived at Summit Station, meaning we still have a few more stops to go. Passengers shuffle past us and out of the train car, spurring me to peep my eyes open ever so slightly. Which leads to glancing down at the phone in Lincoln's hand and seeing that someone is trying to FaceTime him.

Someone named Travis.

Travis as in his *ex*, Travis? And my *ex-crush*, Travis?

Lincoln rejects the call. I catch a glimpse of their call log, which shows a bunch of ingoing and outgoing exchanges between them. Lincoln shifts over to TikTok, listening in his earbuds. I resist asking why they've been talking so much recently and close my eyes instead.

I hope he can't feel my heart pulsing loudly in my neck.

Even though it might look like I'm snoozing again, I'm more wide awake than ever.

FOR NEARLY THE NEXT TWO WEEKS, I RUN DOWN MY CHRISTMAS Checklist. It starts with decorating the tree and crowning it with Gran's cloth angel, then goes into putting up festive string lights in my room, making hot cocoa with extra-large marsh-mallows, and singing along to Mariah's first Christmas album.

I've been continuing my Boyfriend Material Checklist too. Which appears to be working. Lincoln posted a candid of me sleeping on the train to his Instagram story—surprising me. It was a sweet gesture, but the angle of me was unflattering, to say the least. I wish he'd asked me first, but oh well. It ended up getting me a bunch of follows.

My mind keeps ruminating on Lincoln and Travis's mysterious but foreboding FaceTime history. As hard as I've tried to swat away the flurry of thoughts, they've been eclipsing the memory of our romantic day in the city. Could Lincoln still like Travis?

All night tonight, I've been trying my best to stay on top of things at the teahouse, but I can feel the stress building. My feet ache, my hands are shaking, and I'm pretty sure I've forgotten to refill the artisanal sugar cube bowl I took out with the last tea service. I debate straight-out asking Lincoln about Travis for the umpteenth time, but I *know* that the checklist would dissuade such unhinged behavior. Besides, there's no opportunity to send a text right now with tonight's work drama.

"Leo, can you go down the street to Mike's and ask him if we could please use his oven for this last batch of scones?"

Judy slams the cold oven shut in defeat. None of us have any idea how to fix it, and we don't have time to try with the holiday rush in full swing.

"I'm on it!" I reply, shrugging into my winter jacket. I can hear the spirited hubbub behind the curtain, along with the carolers we've brought in. Dillon's actually one of them, in a top hat and tails. He catches my eye and waves. He's got that crooked, chipper smile on his face and a twinkle in his eye, and suddenly everything feels a little bit brighter.

To my surprise, Vincent's out on the floor, pouring tea, running drinks, and even cracking jokes with some of the handsome guys around our age. Well, that last part isn't surprising.

He passes me as he heads through the kitchen. "The makeover *definitely* worked."

"Huh? What makes you say that?"

"Because that cute guy out there keeps blushing every time he looks at you."

My heart soars. "Lincoln's here?" I peek out but don't see him.

"No clue who this guy is." Vincent gestures to . . . *Dillon*.

"No, we're just friends."

He tuts and perches on his stool, procuring his phone. "Whatever."

I wave my hand over his screen. "I'm sorry, didn't you tell me he *wasn't* cute from his Insta?"

"That was *him*?" Vincent rotates away, opening TikTok. "Well, he looks better IRL."

I grab a tray of unbaked cardamom-and-clove scones. They're obviously still just raw dough. Then I duck out the back door into the snow-encrusted alley that runs behind the strip of shops. We might actually be able to salvage this shift after all.

Three doors down, I knock, but when no one hears me after a good couple of minutes, I cut through another alley, this one running perpendicular to the first, that leads to the storefront.

I'm passing by Mike's frosted front window with people eating just on the other side when—

There, at a table for two, laughing and leaning in awfully close to one another, are Lincoln and Travis.

For a second, Lincoln's eyes flit to mine, then away, but I'm not certain he saw me. On the verge of tears, I turn to rush back down the alley, but I slip on a patch of ice, and the unbaked scones go flying off my tray. The Boyfriend Material Checklist didn't work. It was all for nothing. And the beauty of our New York City date? Cracked, like a broken snow globe.

Outside the teahouse, I take in a deep, icy breath to collect myself before heading in. I'll have to explain to Judy why I'm down some scones, but I'm too distraught to care.

He may not have fallen for me, but this much I know for certain:

Lincoln Chan stole my heart. Again.

An hour later, the kettle on the stovetop begins to scream, and I shut off the heat and fill the teapot. By the time I'm bringing it out of the kitchen, I can feel my anger for Travis bubbling inside me like I'm a Human Kettle. The choral singers in the teahouse are singing yet another merry song, and every guest's face is lit with joy, but I can't seem to muster up any myself. Not after what just transpired.

Varsha and Dillon were right. The Jaws of the crushes just sank my boat.

As I plop the teapot down with a little more force than intended for a group of women wearing Judy's collection of frilly bonnets, I can't get the image of Lincoln and Travis laughing behind that perfectly frosted glass out of my head, looking more romantic than Lincoln and *I* did in New York City. The OG It Couple, reunited.

Back in the kitchen, I check my phone, and see Varsha's sent me GIFs of people jumping and falling. She has been trying to console me, telling me that I shouldn't *jump* to conclusions before knowing all the facts. But how can I *not*? And that's coming from Varsha, who's always been a Lincoln Skeptic.

Lincoln doesn't *seem* like a sneaky liar, and I haven't felt like a rebound. And besides, we're not even technically together. All I can do is blame Travis for creeping back into the picture like some weasel. Travis knows full well that Lincoln and I have been hanging out—just like the rest of the school.

Between Lincoln and life post-graduation, my future isn't looking all that bright.

Varsha: Just ask him about it! I'm sure Dillon will agree!
Varsha: Right, Dillon?

She's right, but I can't seem to bring myself to do it. Hello! I couldn't even ask him out. Now I'm expected to ask him why he was hanging out with an old flame . . . after I creepily spied on them from a dark sidewalk?! Yeah, no. That would surely seal the deal and send Lincoln running far, far away from me. Though I draft more than a few texts I don't end up sending.

The singers finish their rendition of "O Holy Night," and the guests are cheering and whooping. All cheer and whoops have been leeched from my very soul. I feel like a storm cloud.

I still manage to summon a supportive smile for Dillon.

By the time Dillon and the rest of the chorus leave and the last guest files out, I'm drying the final dish of the night and feel more than ready to head home and crawl back into bed. I'm also eagerly waiting for Dillon to weigh in on all the texts he's missed in the group chat. I really need his two cents on the matter. *Should I* text Lincoln?

I ignore another twinge of jealousy. I don't want to picture Lincoln with anyone else. Not after we've spent time together, smooching and skating across that melty ice. But the jealousy burns in my chest, even though I know I have no reason to feel this way. Lincoln is *not* my boyfriend, after all. Time to forget about him.

I hang up my apron and wave goodbye to Judy. My voice is notably shaky. What am I doing? I've changed so much, which yielded amazing results. But why wasn't it enough? Making Lincoln my boyfriend is starting to seem like a fruitless endeavor. I keep thinking there's one more thing I can do, one more thing that will unlock the puzzle, but maybe there's just . . . not.

Then I remember what Silvio said, about how maybe my changing isn't as great as I've thought. Of course he would say that. He was probably just jealous of my glow-up, like how I'm jealous of Travis.

Leo, quit it. You don't know whether they're actually back together.

I exit through the front door—and stop short in my tracks.

Lincoln, who's leaning against a parking meter, straightens up when he sees me and takes a few steps toward me. He's all bundled up in a scarf and gloves, and his cheeks are ruddy.

"H-hey," he says through chattering teeth and an annoyingly charming smile.

"How long have you been out here?"

Lincoln studies my features. "Are . . . you okay?" So, he can tell.

I wrap my coat snug in the cold, my heart racing with adrenaline. "I'm fine. I just . . ."

"You saw Travis and me." He tilts his head down. "You're upset."

I nod, feeling a bit embarrassed. I don't want to come off as possessive or jealous, but I can't help the way I feel about Lincoln.

And I hope, deep down, he feels the same way about me.

I decide to go off-book. Here's hoping it works out.

"I'm sorry . . . I shouldn't be upset but I am."

Lincoln's mouth quirks upward. "I kind of like hearing that."

"You *do*?"

"Yeah."

He continues, "Well, you have no need to feel jealous." He takes my hands in his gloved ones. "Promise."

My blues start to lift, replaced by a warm and fuzzy feeling. Is everything actually okay? *More* than okay? Then an unsettling thought snakes its way into my mind:

What if Lincoln finds out that I've been fake this whole time?

What if he realizes that I'm not the person who he thinks I am?

I shake it off, feeling my confidence return like a light bulb shining brighter by the second from within. "Well, I've really been liking hanging out with you."

He surprises me with a kiss. "Hey," he starts, "I wanted to ask you something."

This is it.

This is the moment.

My heart gallops.

I wrestle my smile back down. "What is it?" I ask with an air of indifference.

"Do you ever want to . . . do more than just make out?" He winks.

I look left and right, shocked. This is what he wanted to ask me, now?

"Yeah," I say with a smile, although deep down, it's not something I've thought about, and I'm not sure I'm ready to do more than just make out. I've only just learned how to make out without coming across like a fish out of water gulping in air. Or does he mean make it official?

Apparently, it was the right answer, because Lincoln's expression lights up. Then his eyes dart from my lips back to my eyes. "What's that look?" he asks me with a sly smile.

"*What* look?"

He lets out a laugh, his eyebrows rising.

"Nothing," I lie. Because I know the look he's talking about. It's the look of someone who is so head over heels in love.

"I want to do more than make out," I start, "like, maybe, I don't know . . ." *Date?* My heart explodes in my chest, again and again, like a grenade being detonated over and over.

His eyes widen, pupils dilating.

I try my best to look calm. "Do you want to . . . be my boyfriend?"

He smiles, one eyebrow rising. "Maybe."

I chuckle. "Yeah?"

"Yeah," he repeats.

He looks around, making sure it's still only us out here on the freezing-cold sidewalk. Then his arm wraps around my waist, and he pulls me in for a kiss. Deep. Passionate. It makes me worry about the state of my breath.

Is that a yes?

Leo, stop thinking and live in the moment.

We start to make out. Does this mean we're boyfriends? But

he said maybe. I don't know what that means.

The sound of footsteps on crackly sidewalk ice makes me peep open an eye. Lincoln and I pull apart like an ooey gooey chocolate chip cookie.

"Oh! Sorry!" Dillon holds out his hands and slowly backs away. "As you were!"

"I should get back home." Lincoln clears his throat and smooths down his coat. He looks at Dillon with a tight-lipped smile, then ducks his head and stalks off.

"No! It's okay!" I call after Dillon, who's hurrying off in the other direction, leaving me alone on the sidewalk. I want to tell him about what just happened. Because I think Lincoln agreed to be my boyfriend without outright stating it. Right? RIGHT?!

But Dillon's already halfway down the street.

28

WEARING VARSHA'S KNIT FROG HAT, I'M LYING ON MY BED A week later, textbooks and ring binders spread out, while my study buddies Varsha and Dillon keep me company on FaceTime.

But with Lincoln on my mind, I'm too distracted to retain my readings at present. I'm still not sure what to make of our last conversation. I asked him out, but he said *maybe*. I still don't know what that means.

I check my phone and grin. "Lincoln posted photos of us in the city!"

"I'm not surprised." Varsha clacks her knitting needles, with green yarn hanging off one of her fingers. "Everyone at school's saying you're the hot new couple."

"They are?!"

"I thought you said you don't even know if you're official

yet," Dillon says. He explained earlier how he was going to wait for me to finish work and stop by to reply to the Lincoln-Travis sitch IRL when he ran into Lincoln and me smooching on the sidewalk and "wanted to give us privacy." I insisted many times he wasn't interrupting anything. I don't want him to feel like I brushed him off. Truth is, it was just really unfortunate timing.

"I mean, it *feels like* we're official," I reply. "But I'm not sure."

Dillon studies a sheet of music and sings out a few lines, then sighs. "Did that sound okay?"

"Yes! You're going to crush it," Varsha tells him. Tomorrow, we're going to a choral concert at a church, where he's performing a solo.

My phone chimes.

Lincoln 🤎🤎🤎: Now good?

"Hey, guys. I have to go down to dinner," I fib, jerking a thumb over my shoulder. I'm trying not to rub it in their faces every time I choose Lincoln over them. A little white lie.

"Catch you later like a provoked alligator!" Varsha says.

Dillon salutes me. "Don't forget to keep studying after you eat."

"Will do. Bye, y'all!" I hang up and chuck off my frog hat, startling Miss Tiramisu. Then I sit at my desk and call Lincoln, adjusting the ring light and sitting up straight. His brilliant face appears on-screen, and we talk for a good hour about the *Dungeness & Lobsters* MMORPG open beta that we've been playing, from our favorite new gear to the new deep-sea environments and loot. I thank him for posting the picture of us on Instagram, and he says everyone's talking about us.

We've been having so much fun, like old times, and the need to ask him all my clarifying questions screams needy. Plus, would he really have just spent an hour nerding out with me if he wasn't still into me? The Travis thing was a fluke. It meant nothing.

"Dinner!" Mom calls out.

"Hey, I've got to go." I smile at Lincoln. "Text you in a little bit?"

At the dinner table over chicken parmigiana, Mom grills me about college applications, which I *have* been working on, I promise. After, I help with dishes and take out the trash, and soon I'm back in bed, scrolling on TikTok between flipping through my AP Bio textbook. My eyes begin to grow heavy, and I'm thinking of calling it and sleeping.

Lincoln 🤍🤍🤍: Hey. Wanna be my plus-one to Sakura's Christmas party tomorrow?

Did Lincoln Chan just invite me to my first-ever Christmas house party?

Lincoln proceeds to leave me a brief audio note to fill me in on more. It's time for her parents' annual holiday soiree, and as usual, they've told Sakura she can invite some friends. I would *love* to be Lincoln's plus-one.

The only downside is that I'm planning to go to Dillon's winter choral concert tomorrow. He has that solo, and I promised I'd be there to cheer him on. But I can't pass up my first holiday house party with Lincoln, aka My Maybe New Boyfriend. I've always dreamed about spending the holidays with a boyfriend: wearing matching ugly Christmas sweaters and drinking hot chocolate together. Gift giving. I think of the pile of things I've bought for Lincoln.

I reply with a short audio note giving a purposefully non-enthusiastic-sounding yes.

Since Lincoln's going to be away at his aunt's in upstate New York on Christmas and the days leading up to it, this holiday party is a great way for us to celebrate our first Christmas together, which I explain to Dillon in a much longer audio note.

Dillon: I understand
Dillon: I'm really gonna miss you ☹
Dillon: I hope this house party doesn't get raided lol
Leo: Thank you. And me too! You're gonna crush it up there tomorrow.
Leo: Please have Varsha or someone take video. I can't wait to watch it!
Dillon: Thanks

I wash my face and dab on a tingling toner, my insides fluttering with excitement at the prospect of the party tomorrow night.

Though I wonder if Travis is going too. I sure hope not.

I've got Lincoln—kind of.

Now how do I keep him?

BOYFRIEND MATERIAL CHECKLIST

 1. BE COOL AS A CUCUMBER. ☑

2. GET A GLAM GLOW-UP. ☑

3. HAVE A POWERHOUSE PRESENCE. ☑

4. FAKE BEING RICH. ☑

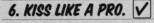 5. WIN POPULARITY CONTEST. ☑

 6. KISS LIKE A PRO. ☑

I GAZE IN MY CLOSET MIRROR AT MY FESTIVE ENSEMBLE:
black corduroy pants and my ugliest Christmas sweater. It's
green with knots of tinsel and a huge reindeer with googly eyes.
While Varsha would exclaim with glee, Vincent would faint at
the sight.

I shrug into my jacket and tug on its lapel, smoothing out the
pockets and striking a pose. I'm so ready for this holiday party,
especially with Mariah Carey's Christmas album stirring up a
jingle-jangle in the air around me. The music, together with the
twinkle lights and tiny fake tree akin to Charlie Brown's tree,
transports me to a Winter Wonderland of my own.

I can just make out the doorbell ringing, and I race downstairs to open it.

It's Lincoln, looking like a present I want to unwrap in his long peacoat with his winter cap on and leather gloves. "You ready?"

"You bet," I say. "Bye, Mom!" I call out. "I'll be back late!"

"Have fun, dear," she says as she carries a large cardboard box down the stairs for her big New Year clean. I notice the box holds Gran's scrapbooks. A pang of nostalgia pulls at my heartstrings, followed by a swell of hope in my chest at the thought of how I'm about to make even more memories.

And then, we're off.

Halfway to Sakura's, we're stuck in a little traffic.

"MOVE!" Lincoln yells at the car in front of us at a stop sign.

His shout makes me tense up, and I'm reminded of how Dad used to drive erratically with Mom arguing with him from the passenger seat, and he'd jerk the wheel left and right while going super fast on the highway to frighten us. I haven't heard someone yell with anger in a while, even if it was just an innocent moment of road rage. My heart tightens painfully.

Lincoln slams the wheel, honking, until the car rolls out of sight. "Finally!" Then he guns the engine, and my stomach lurches at the rapid acceleration. "You okay?" Lincoln asks, shaking me out of my thoughts. He pats my knee. "You got quiet."

"Yeah. Yeah, no, I'm good." I feel myself softening again, coming back to the present.

We arrive at Sakura's estate, and from the car view alone, I can tell tonight's going to be epic. The house itself is the largest house I've ever seen. Each tall window is lit with beautiful wreaths. The Nakamuras clearly spared no expenses, hiring an expert string-lights-installing service, with every trimming of the house perfectly lined with sparkling white lights. I look over at Lincoln behind the wheel, and he smiles at me—and leans in for a kiss.

It's as if the blip with Travis never happened. It's as if this is all meant to be—just like I thought.

Then, I don't know why, but I start to giggle. He stops kissing me and looks annoyed.

"Sorry," I say.

He moves away. "Shall we head in?" He bats back the pom-pom on the top of my winter hat.

We find the front door ajar, and Lincoln gently pushes his way into the monster-size house. Christmas music fills the toasty air, competing with the chatter of Sakura's parents' friends, who line the staircase and the halls, drinks and plates of hors d'oeuvres in hand. Most of them are probably from prestigious law firms or are members of country clubs and golf courses. I notice that none of them have on ugly Christmas sweaters. Maybe it's a Non-Adult Thing.

A lit evergreen garland lines the mantel of a roaring fireplace, where embroidered vintage stockings hang that Varsha would adore. Wreaths with red ribbons line the walls beside gilded oil paintings that Dillon would go gaga over. In the center of the room, a tree that looks to be twenty feet tall and decked out in Swarovski crystals reaches up high toward the twinkling chandelier.

"*Whoa*," I murmur, taking it all in, inhaling the scent of pine and mulling spices.

"Come on." Lincoln collects my coat and hands it to a coat-check person. (There's a *coat check*?!) He eyes my ugly Christmas sweater and his jaw drops, making me incredibly self-conscious—especially when I discover he's in a black blazer with a white button-down shirt. More people enter behind us, followed by a barrage of waiters offering various treats on trays, so we're forced to shuffle deeper into the house. Maybe Lincoln couldn't find an ugly sweater on short notice? He leads me through a wide hall with either side flanked with snow-covered faux trees, and to the back of the house. This place would make Kim K. ever*green* with envy.

We find Sakura and the rest of the Fierce Five milling with drinks in hand in a parlor beneath an ornate Waterford crystal chandelier. The Fierce Five is truly a group of five once more. I wave to Travis, who's almost unrecognizable in an elegant, fitted blazer. Joy to the world. I'm hoping his presence has no relation to being in good standing with Lincoln again.

Travis isn't the only one looking dashing. The other members of the Fierce Five are also wearing sensible outfits, in fact—velvet dresses with lace or suit jackets with green pocket squares—and here I am in my ugliest Christmas sweater.

"If it isn't Eastfield High's newest It Couple." Sakura cackles, raising her flute of champagne. "Nice sweater!" In her shimmering party gown, she hugs me then Lincoln. "Get some drinks! Make yourself at home!"

It's abundantly clear now that I rolled the dice wrong yet again with my ensemble choice. My cheeks probably resemble Santa's, and my stomach wants to shake like a bowl full of tears.

I'd remove the sweater, but I'm only wearing a tiny tank top underneath it, and something tells me that wouldn't fly here. Even *I* know that'd be *inappropriate*, as Mom likes to say.

I catch Lincoln eyeing my sweater, and he chuckles. Maybe he thinks it's cute. After all, we *are* Eastfield High's newest It Couple.

I catch Travis averting his eyes from us and bringing his glass to his lips.

My phone dings with a text.

Varsha: Dillon was amazing!

She includes a video, and when I start it, it shows Dillon in choir robes, singing in front of the whole church at a podium, his tenor voice bright and merry.

Lincoln cuts in, and I pause the video. "I'm gonna get a cup of cheer. Want one?"

"Sure. Sounds good," I say, stepping next to a crackling fire and not sure who to talk to. Everyone in the friend group already seems engaged, telling inside jokes and howling with boozy laughter. I'm not sure they want to talk to me in my ugly Christmas sweater. I shift uncomfortably in the scratchy wool. Vincent would be furious with me. Deservedly so.

I lean, perching my elbow onto the mantel, and stare into the flames like I'm intentionally choosing to do it instead of how I'm too embarrassed to try striking up chitchat with anyone.

Needing to recalibrate, I reach into the vault of my mind like a superhero harnessing their powers and recall everything I've learned so far from my Boyfriend Material Checklist.

I straighten up in an attempt to look more confident and pretend to peruse a painting of what appears to be a candle beside a bowl of fruit, like I'm not trying to get anyone's attention. Upon a closer look, I decide Dillon could paint a better image.

I snap a few photos and post them to my Instagram story, striding from painting to painting, widening my stance, keeping my chest up and arms at my side, working on my presence, taking up space. My expression remains serene, neutral, even though my nerves want to turn up the corners of my mouth in some sort of silly, nerve-racked smile.

Meanwhile, my mind is racing, trying to come up with ways to win over the Fierce Five—and Lincoln, finally.

"Duck confit spring roll?" asks a waiter.

"Thanks." I pluck one from the tray and pop it in my mouth.

Three more waiters bombard me, offering smoked salmon canapés, truffle-infused deviled eggs, and miniature beef Wellington, which I scarf down when no one's looking.

I take my phone back out and click play on Varsha's video again, and it picks up with Dillon's stellar singing. The mic crackles, but Dillon doesn't miss a beat, and I smile at the near malfunction.

Lincoln reappears holding two cups of punch. "For you."

I pause the video and take a sip. It's sweet and tart like cranberry juice. "Thanks." My thumb accidentally hits play on my phone, and Dillon's voice carries through the air again.

Lincoln's eyes flicker toward the screen. He takes a slow sip of his drink. "He's good."

I pause the video again. "He is."

But Lincoln isn't laughing. On the contrary, he looks annoyed.

"Are you *jealous*?" I ask with a laugh.

"What? No!" He musses my hair.

"Mm-hm . . ." I tease. "I can watch the rest later."

He gazes into my eyes. "You're into Dillon, aren't you?"

Does he honestly think I am? I glance at Travis, recalling seeing him looking chummy with Lincoln at Mike's Diner. Maybe I can give Lincoln a little taste of his own medicine.

"Why would you think that? Because of his impeccable singing voice? His knack with oil on canvas and wiring robot gizmos? Or perhaps how he's the best listener a guy could ask for?"

Lincoln's eyebrows climb, the tell that I got to him, even if just a little.

"Well, you have no need to feel jealous." I wink. "Promise." My sights shift to Travis, who's got Eamon in a playful headlock. When he sees me, he looks from Lincoln back to me, then flashes a supportive smile, though I'm not entirely buying it.

Lincoln's eyes flit toward the stairs, and he grins. "Hey, do you want to go upstairs? I hear there are a few empty rooms on the third floor."

My eyes instinctively shoot to his lips, which are stained red from the punch, and my heart begins to race. "Okay."

Light from the hall floods into a dark, empty bedroom. Lincoln flicks on the lamp and closes the door, and we take a seat on the bed. When he looks at me, I stare at his lips while licking my own.

"It's pretty chill that Sakura's parents let her invite us all to the party," he says.

"Oh. Yeah," I say, surprised that he actually wants to have a conversation. "I know. That's super cool of them."

"Yeah, my parents would never allow me to bring my friends to any of their shindigs."

"Oh yeah?" I think about my own parents, and I find myself once more wanting to open up to him, despite every part of me screaming to keep myself mysterious and reserved.

Think of the checklist, Leo! You made a list! You've been checkin' it twice!

"To be honest, my home life has been a little rough lately, and it has nothing to do with the house itself." I take a deep breath, knocking my foot against his foot. "I have to confess something to you," I continue. "I haven't told you the whole truth about my parents."

His eyes widen, encouraging me to go on.

"The lady you met at the play wasn't actually my mom. It was my dad's new girlfriend." My voice is trembling. "He cheated on my mom with her. She was originally a secretary in his office, and she's young. That's who you met at the play."

Lincoln bursts out laughing. "Whoa! For real?"

Not quite the reaction I was hoping for.

His laugh stings. Here I am, bearing something intensely personal, and he's *laughing*? I guess I could see how it might look funny from the outside, but it ruined my life, my family.

"I know. It's not something I go around advertising." I shrug. "But anyway, my dad's always fighting with my mom on the phone, and there was a time he came to the house one night unannounced, poking around for some of his belongings, and my mom had to call the police on him. He's not a great guy."

"I don't remember your dad being so awful." Lincoln cracks a smile. "I mean, what do I know? He was always working when I'd come over."

"We were never really that close. He's always been grumpy, but his anger really got the best of him in the past year. He hates my mom in an obsessed kind of way."

Lincoln shrugs, then shifts uncomfortably. "I'm sorry . . ." He trails off.

"It's okay." Unexpectedly, I feel a huge swell of relief. In fact, telling him the truth makes me feel closer to him, having shared a part of me that I haven't shared with anyone—besides Dillon—and Lincoln not getting up and walking out means everything.

"I like you," he says with his perfect smile. His remark spurs emotional whiplash, and all thoughts of Dad subside, replaced by something like elation.

I can't believe he just admitted *he likes me*. Is it due to him feeling insecure about Dillon? If so, that's ridiculous—but if playing hard to get is working, then so be it. And I guess it *is* working.

Because with that, we start to kiss.

He pulls away, gazing deep into my eyes. "You're a good kisser, Leo."

I bite my lip. "I know."

"Wow, that sweater is almost as ugly as something Emily Sharpe would wear," he adds. "All you'd need is a pet rat on your shoulder."

"Well, I thought it would be fun to wear it," I shoot back. Oh no. Maybe I shouldn't have said that. I don't want him to be mad at me for being so defensive.

"Yeah, if you want to look like one of the two weirdos," he says, on the brink of a laugh. "You should have told me. I would have dressed up as Anne."

What a turnoff. Not to mention uncomfortable. Who talks about people like that?

"I don't think my sweater looks *that* bad," I say, desperate to steer the conversation while also trying to sound self-assured. "I'm glad I wore it. I like standing out. You know, shake things up."

My phone dings with a text.

Dillon: Varsha said she sent you a video of my singing. Don't listen to it. I sound terrible!

I can't help chuckling, then turn it face down and continue kissing Lincoln, who definitely bristled at the momentary interruption. And I'm fairly certain he saw who sent it. Crap.

He holds me at arm's length, staring into my eyes. "Do you want to be my boyfriend?" he asks.

I freeze, stunned. Now? Here? Like this?

My heart is racing. It's not what I imagined, but . . .

Lincoln Chan just asked me to be his boyfriend. It's a Christmas Miracle!

I'm not quite sure how to respond in a calm, cool, and collected way.

I gaze at him breathlessly. "Yes. Yes. I want to be your boyfriend."

He glows. "My totally cute boyfriend . . ." He pulls me in for another kiss. Fireworks are going off around me. I have a boyfriend!

There's a knock at the door, and we hastily pull away from each other. That seems to be our thing nowadays.

Sakura pokes her head in. "There you two are! We're starting our Christmas sing-along. Come on!"

Lincoln doesn't move, not until I'm up and at the door following her out.

Luckily, he can't see the gigantic smile plastered over my face.

Boyfriend, secured!

THE NEXT DAY, I WAKE UP CHRISTMAS MORNING, SMILING TO the smell of chocolate chip pancakes and fresh-brewed coffee.

Last night, after Lincoln and I joined the sing-along at Sakura's family's grand piano, where I couldn't help getting swept up in the holiday spirit and singing out at full volume, he drove me home. I worried I'd deviated too much from my checklist, singing with abandon like that, and blamed the punch. But it seemed to work out—he recorded me keeping the Christmas sing-along going in his car because he thought I was so cute. Then he gave me a present and told me not to open it until this morning. I couldn't help but run into the house and race back out to his car with the presents I got for *him* so he'd have something from me to open this morning. And the best part? I didn't even feel like a try-hard, because it's Christmas, which is all about giving.

So let's recap:

I have a present from my boyfriend.

Side note: I have a *boyfriend*!

Have I mentioned . . . my new boyfriend?!

The checklist worked. Somebody pinch me. Thank you, Santa.

Propping myself up to scroll through my phone, I check the all-time-high view count on my stories. I can hear the clanging of pots and pans and faint holiday music from downstairs. Out the window, icicles hang down from the roof, as if trying to bar my view of our tiny backyard, which is covered in a crisp layer of snow. The turnpike's been salted, and cars line up bumper to bumper. I'm filled with a warm coziness that only comes on a perfect Christmas morning like this one.

I text Lincoln a slew of Christmas GIFs—a good mix of sparkly classic ones and super-silly ones because now that we're boyfriends, I can be more myself, even if just a little more. See: singing in Lincoln's car. We're boyfriends! I want to shout it from the snow-covered rooftops. I. Have. A. Boyfriend. Sure, there's been the self-imposed pressure of the Boyfriend Material Checklist up to this point, but I've been giving thought to what Dillon said in his room that night, and I'm making a deliberate decision to be more myself and really put myself out there—privately, speaking—because I *do* want love. Love for the real me.

But in terms of how I'm putting myself out there publicly, that's still a different story entirely. I post the photo of us in front of a lit-up tree at Sakura's house, which we took shortly before he drove me home, the night ending in one final hot and heavy make-out session before I ducked inside, glowing like the star atop the tree. The photo of us is definitely the Obligatory Christmas Boyfriend Post, with the caption being a single emoji of two guys side by side, letting the whole world know, in a very "cool" way, that we're official-official. A hard launch. Finally. Sure, it's not us kissing under the mistletoe Christmas morning in our matching pajamas or white cardigans and dark jeans, but it'll do. The first of many together, I hope. Just being boyfriends is the best gift ever.

I went to FaceTime my friends late last night, but neither picked up. I texted them an extensive play-by-play of the events leading up to Lincoln asking me to be official, followed by a new development.

Leo: I can retire the checklist! Or sell it for a million dollars to other lonely hearts . . .

I only hear back just now. They aren't exactly enthusiastic—giving just a simple congratulations. They're probably busy with holiday things, and I plan on calling them later today anyway to fill them in and get their thoughts on everything and hear about Dillon's solo.

Speaking of which, Dillon posts an adorable video of him in front of a tree wired to light up on a timer.

Lincoln, on the other hand, posts the video he took of me singing in his car on the ride home in his story. I sound horrendous. Maybe Enzi was right. I thought that video was one

Lincoln took for posterity, not to show his 100,000-plus followers. My face flushes red as I rewatch it, despite the pink heart emoji he's added to the corner of the video.

I click onto his next story slide to find a text conversation we had. In it, it shows the argument I made that purebred dogs need homes too, not just shelter dogs, which is all about my philosophy that *all* dogs need good homes. I know it's a socially frowned-upon view, but I thought Lincoln was a safe space! He added a crying-laughing emoji on top of the screenshot. My name is scratched out in black marker, but still—I feel a weight in my gut.

That conversation isn't a good look for me, and neither is the embarrassing singing video. I text him asking to please take both of them down.

Lincoln 🤍🤍🤍: It's fine
Lincoln 🤍🤍🤍: You're overreacting
Lincoln 🤍🤍🤍: The singing one is funny!
Lincoln 🤍🤍🤍: Fine. I took down the singing one but not the text convo
Lincoln 🤍🤍🤍: No one even knows that's you lol

OK. Maybe it's not that bad. But won't people *assume* it's me? I force myself to drop it and hope not too many people viewed the singing clip before he deleted it. I ask him when he's free to say hello this morning.

Then I wash up and descend the stairs in my red-and-white-striped pajamas, with Miss Tiramisu tickling my ankles as I coo to her in my baby voice, wishing her a merry Christmas. She's just happy I left a can of tuna out for her last night.

"Merry Christmas, dear." Mom is in her fluffy white bathrobe, pouring herself a steaming cup of coffee. "Pancakes?" She indicates a syrup-covered stack on the kitchen table.

"Yes, please!" I say, plunking down beside Silvio. "Merry Christmas."

"Yeah, you too," he grumbles. He's in full sweatshirt and sweatpants, courtesy of his campus bookstore.

"I like your haircut," I say, seeing his fluffy curls have been shorn off into a buzz cut.

"Thanks," he mumbles. "Why are you in such a good mood?"

"Oh, no reason." I reach for the pancakes. "Maybe because it's *Christmas*!" I don't bother mentioning it's our first Christmas without Dad. I'm happy about that too. "Oh, and I have a boyfriend," I continue. "Lincoln Chan."

He blinks, looking almost bored. "Cool?"

"It *is*, actually."

Mom blows into her coffee. "You asked him?"

"Actually," I say in a sly voice, "*he* asked *me*."

She takes a scorching sip. "As long as he loves you for you, dear."

Typical Mom. After breakfast, we make our way into the family room. The tiny fireplace crackles next to a Christmas tree smaller than the one in the foyer. It harbors a little pile of packages. I find my pile, and Silvio finds his, as we sit cross-legged on the rug.

Mom settles into an armchair. "Who's ready to unwrap some gifts?"

I snap a photo of the gifts at the bottom of the tree, the whole time ignoring Silvio's withering gaze. Instead of posting the pics, I decide to do an online image search instead, and end up adding a photo of a grand Christmas tree with lavishly wrapped presents to my socials.

We start by opening our stockings. Mom's packed each one with lotto tickets, chocolate candies, new pairs of socks, and silly little trinkets.

Next, my brother and I take turns unwrapping our gifts. For Silvio, a wireless controller for his game console. A projector for his dorm. And citrusy cologne. I assume whenever Silvio grunts it means he likes the gift. For me, a mini refrigerator so that I have a snack locker here at home. Sparkly phone case. And the latest manga comic.

Mom got us each new clothes too. She went out of her way to find some colorful pieces for me that go with my new style—though I do envy Silvio's new plain black dress shirt and slacks.

Finally, it's Silvio's and my turn to give out our presents. Admittedly, my attention this year has been a bit lacking, with the full force of my focus (and wallet) lasered in on Lincoln and all the gift ideas I had for him. So, I'm not the proudest of the gifts I got—bath bombs and candles for Mom, and a standard golf glove for Silvio—which, in my book, seem more like afterthoughts than anything else, and I pray they don't notice.

Silvio gets me a new *Dungeness & Lobsters* figurine to paint and add to my set and an aromatherapy kit for Mom. She hands each of us a gift "from Miss Tiramisu"—streaming sticks—then unwraps a cat elf costume she got online before fastening Miss Tiramisu into it.

That's one miserable elf.

"Who's that for?" Mom points to the lone wrapped gift under the tree.

"Me." I pick it up. It's light, and rectangular, and wrapped in light blue paper patterned with goats in scarves and Santa hats. "It's from Lincoln. He gave it to me last night and told me not to open it till this morning." There's no handwritten card like I'd included in my gift to him. Oh, well.

I tear off the paper in excitement. My heart skips a beat as I gaze down at the gift—the gift from my *boyfriend*—on Christmas morning. Never would I have thought I'd live to see the day.

It's a gift card to Game World. He knows that's my favorite place to go. My heart feels full. I turn the card over to see how much it has on it. Scrawled in Sharpie is the amount: **$50**.

"Somebody likes their gift," Mom remarks.

I realize I'm beaming. "He got me a nice gift card to Game World," I coo. "He must have seen when Varsha and I were there at the mall and remembered. It's so thoughtful of him."

After narrowing down my list of twenty-five gifts, I gave Lincoln a stainless-steel water bottle for his workouts, a Champion fleece hoodie since it's his favorite brand, and a Spikeball kit for his backyard. Okay, I might've also slipped in a few Three Musketeers bars. And a set of red-and-white-striped pajamas that match the ones I'm wearing now . . . you know, in the spirit of samesie Christmas boyfriends. And that new pair of winter gloves he'd been wanting.

I smile at the thought of Lincoln opening them right now and want to FaceTime him to share in the moment, to see his reaction to my gifts and to thank him for my gift. But he could be doing his own family tradition right now, like how Mom's heading into the kitchen to pop her famous Christmas cinnamon rolls into the oven. Just because we're boyfriends now doesn't mean I suddenly have the freedom to drop the act and become the needy, desperate person I truly am deep down inside. I have to play it cool if I'm going to keep this relationship alive, right? And I haven't heard back from him about when he's free to chat.

But there's that part of me again that just wants to be me, and for him to love me for me.

Should I truly ditch the checklist?

Who should I be? New Leo or Old Leo?

Right now, I feel like I'm straddling the line of being neither.

I'm curled up on the armchair by the fire, flipping leisurely through my new manga comic and biting into a gooey cinnamon roll, when Silvio emerges from the family room, clutching a shopping bag loaded up with his opened gifts.

"Hey. Let's go."

I angle my head up. "Go where?"

"Dad's." Silvio shrugs into his coat by the front door.

My stomach falls ten stories. "What?"

He slips into his boots. "Yeah, dude. Come on."

"I'm not going to Dad's," I assert, sitting up tall.

"He invited us. So we're going. I'll be in the car." He steps outside, the wind kicking up a biting cold into the foyer.

There's no way in a million years I'm going to see Dad on Christmas Day. It will be like the Visit That Stole Christmas. No, thank you. Just because he's my dad doesn't mean I need to have any relationship with him.

My phone buzzes, and my face lights up. It must be Lincoln calling—

But it's only Silvio.

"What?" I ask flatly.

"Come on." He hangs up.

His car idles in the drive. In the kitchen, I can hear Mom singing along to the holiday tunes playing as she prepares the roast chicken for Christmas dinner. I shouldn't see Dad on Christmas. It feels like a betrayal of Mom. Although she's always said she doesn't want to stand in the way of our relationship with him, that we can do whatever we want in regard to him, I know it must hurt her on some level to know we still make space for him. Some of us more than others, apparently.

My phone dings with a text.

Silvio: Now.

I guess this won't be our first Christmas without Dad after all.

Though right now, I wish it were.

31

SILVIO AND I DON'T SPEAK THE ENTIRE RIDE UP TO DAD'S house. We couldn't even if we tried, not with the radio blasting Silvio's favorite rap songs. He's also a precarious driver, speeding and swerving, rapidly accelerating. If his driving style were an animal, it would be an angry bull. Luckily, the roads are pretty much plowed and salted. I hold tight to the grab handle anyway.

After passing through New Rochester, the one-road town where we spent our summers as kids getting pizza and ice cream on the boardwalk, the road begins to wind around the frozen lake. Each turn makes me more and more nauseated.

A pit forms in my stomach while we cross the long bridge that connects the mainland to the island, where Dad's house resides, aka our Former Lake House. I can see it from here. Our quaint summer home is in the process of being transformed into a mega-mansion, with a few additions covered by plastic sheets, a re-landscaped backyard with patios and hedges, and a winding path leading down to the ice-encrusted embankment.

As we close in on the property, my stomach clenches hard. I think about how I've been living a sort of double life. At school, I'm all smiles and laughs with my friends, head in the clouds, daydreaming about boys and true love—and then there's this secret of mine. A dark side to my life I don't think anyone would really ever truly comprehend. It's one of those things you have to live through—and survive—to understand. Except Dillon; he gets it.

The car crunches down Dad's gravel drive, and we hop out and wait at the front door.

I wish Lincoln were here, standing over me like some protective bodyguard.

Silvio and I both eye a statue on the porch. It's a zombie Santa Claus with gray skin, berserk eyes, and hands clawed and outstretched.

"What's *that* about?" I whisper, thoroughly creeped out.

The door opens, and there he is, in a black turtleneck and jeans, huge white smile plastered to his face. It's so weird to think about how he looks so jolly, but can be so venomous and vindictive. The monster inside him could pop out at any moment, like that zombie Santa Claus.

"Come on in! Hello! Merry Christmas!" Dad gives us each a hug and kiss, and I flinch when he hugs me. I notice Margot isn't around. Dad hangs our coats while I take in the family room.

There have been a few new additions since I was here last.

A taxidermized fox. A knife with a bejeweled hilt on display on the coffee table. A lineup of vintage German steins above the doorframe leading into the dining room. He certainly put his own stamp on the place. While the framed photos of Silvio and me as babies are still up on the mantel, any trace of Mom has been wiped. New frames have been added to the grouping, showing him and Margot in various shots.

Silvio shudders. "Is the heat on?"

He's right—it's freezing in here. And it smells like . . . nothing. No savory Christmas cooking scents wafting in from the kitchen. The music that's playing on the surround sound isn't even holiday tunes. It's Dad's favorite oldies.

"Come with me. Have something to drink."

Dad leads us into the kitchen. He pours cider into cups and hands one to me and Silvio. "Merry Christmas."

It's bitter, and I almost cough it out, but Dad's watching with that wide expectant smile, waiting to see how I like it. "Delicious," I manage to say.

Silvio takes a small, pained sip. "Yeah. Not bad."

Dad sips wine from a glass that has what looks to be a bullet worked into its design, sticking out its side. I don't bother asking about it. I don't want to know.

He pulls store-bought chicken nuggets from the oven, and ketchup from the fridge, then tells us to dig in. We load up our plates and make our way into the dining room with its bay window overlooking the lake.

Lake Dalloway is frozen over. It looks so strikingly different from its welcoming jade-green lilt of summer.

"There she is." Dad stands beside us, gazing down into the driveway as a rickety, rusted-out pickup truck parks.

A tense minute later, Margot steps into the kitchen, her bleached-blond hair windswept and her cheeks rosy, in a body-hugging white knit minidress with heels, and bright red earrings that look like bunches of holly berries. "Hello! Sorry I'm late!"

She gives everyone a hug and kiss. When it's my turn, I almost choke on the pungent smell of Bath & Body Works wrapping her like an odor cloak with a sour note beneath it.

We all sit at the kitchen table.

I loaded up my plate lightly, since we'll be having dinner with Mom in only a few hours, and since I want this meal to end as fast as humanly possible.

"How's Boston?" Dad asks Silvio, and I'm taken aback he's showing interest, or at least appearing to. Asking a question is a Big Deal for Dad.

"Good," my brother states.

Dad holds Margot's hand. "Silvio's pretty smart. He's pretty cool. Just like his dad."

The afternoon drones on. Dad doesn't ask me a single question. It might be for the best, because I don't know if I could answer anything honestly right now, especially when it comes to my future, my boyfriend, or how I'm feeling at this exact moment.

I find myself melting back, which is just what being in his presence does to me. Around him, it's best not to be too shiny, or else he attacks like a barracuda drawn to a sparkly trinket.

A century later, all plates are clean. I'm focusing on staying hydrated. There's really not much else in my control here. I feel trapped.

By the time Margot's slugged down her fifth glass of wine, Dad brings out an apple pie that she "baked," even though Silvio and I were telling him we were ready to leave. He didn't seem to care that we'd potentially be late for Mom's Christmas dinner. Shocker.

Dad has it out for Mom. He's been enraged at how much he may have to fork over to her in the divorce settlement, most of which she wants to put toward college for us. That's the consequence of what he did, with many, many more. But he hasn't owned up to what he did—cheating on Mom and abandoning us, and I don't think he ever will. He hasn't acknowledged how it's affected us . . . because he's oblivious and selfish. Not to mention mean. He's everything I don't want to become.

My dad—the person he barely pretended to be—is gone. And I have to accept that.

Nothing is going to make Dad snap out of it and return to the family, like how it used to be. It hurts to think, but I can't put it in a tiny box to ignore and keep down any longer.

I also realize that I have been conditioned to accept crappy love, and I don't want to do it anymore. I'm tired of trying to fit in my dad's mold of being this perfect, sports-loving son who dulls the edges of my true self to make myself more palatable for him, more in line with who *he* wants for a son. And the answer isn't for me to be more myself around him. It's to be more myself *without* him, around people who I feel safe around, like my friends, and Mom, and Silvio.

And soon, Lincoln, hopefully.

As Dad shoots off more distasteful jokes that make even Silvio squirm with discomfort—one of them being about how Mom's side of the family is to blame for Silvio's receding hairline—I can't help thinking that this is the same person who spit the gum at my face. Who kicked Miss Tiramisu down the stairs once in an angry outburst. Who left bruises on Mom's arms that he denied making. And who wasn't there—hasn't ever been there. Not for me. Not really.

I wonder what it is about him I've missed, and come up with nothing.

He eats the last bit of his apple pie and fixes me with an intense, devilish smile. "I got you guys something." He reaches for a black shopping bag.

I can't remember the last time he got me a Christmas gift. This is the same dad who never remembers our birthdays. I wonder what it could be. I'm hoping money or an Amazon gift card. Honestly, anything would be nice—and he can afford just about anything.

"Did you guys like my cup? The one with the bullet in it?"

I look to Silvio to answer, and he shrugs.

"Because . . ." Dad reaches into the black shopping bag. "I got one for each of you." He hands my brother and I glass cups with bullets sticking out their sides. "Merry Christmas."

Remember how I said anything would be nice? I take it back.

IN THE HAZY DAYS BETWEEN CHRISTMAS AND NEW YEAR'S,
I typically lose track of all sense of time.

But this year, my disorientation is even worse, helped along by late nights of long FaceTime calls with Lincoln while he's away at his aunt's. I'm still not recovered from my visit to my dad's, and Lincoln spaced out when I started to bring up the whole ordeal, resulting in a swift topic change, which is probably for the best. Better not to relive it. My besties have been mum, which is just what we do sometimes over the holiday break, knowing there will be plenty of time to catch up soon.

After Mom and I check some of the boxes on my college applications, Lincoln calls to catch up. I change out of my pajama pants I've had on the past few days. Then I hurry to work and career into the lot. The extended FaceTime with Lincoln resulted in me being fifteen minutes late, and I don't think I've breathed the whole way here, with drivers going extra slow to avoid dirty piles of snow and roadkill. I race inside, slipping on black ice, and make it to Ye Old Tea House's side door. Heat from the kitchen blasts me in the face, meaning the oven's back up and working fine.

However, Judy's expression tells me that what isn't working fine is me.

I apologize and bustle past her, hanging up my jacket and wrangling my apron on over a very expensive white cashmere sweater—one I ensured I could get a full refund on for a future return. Vincent comes in with an empty tiered platter and shoots me a warning look. Oh, boy.

All during the shift, not even the ladies wearing all of Judy's zany feathered bonnets and hats can shake my feeling ill at ease. I'm unsettled by how Judy didn't give me her customary greeting, but also still perturbed about my visit with Dad. The visit has lingered with me for the past few days, making me feel discombobulated and thrown, and I hate how deeply it's been affecting me.

Last night, I really wanted to tell Lincoln—my Present Boyfriend—all about my visit with Dad and how it left me feeling sick. I wanted to risk showing more of my true self, having a deeper talk, opening up to him about what happened—from Margot to the janky bullet cup. But I chose to keep it bottled up, even though it's eating me alive inside. Besides, it was late.

I'm so unsettled that I'm carrying Judy's favorite teapot—the shiny red heart-shaped one, full of raspberry tea—when I trip.

It falls and shatters, splashing my white cashmere sweater in a spray of ruby red.

All the diners look my way as I stare, stunned, at the mess at my feet.

A gasp pulls my attention, and there's Judy in the kitchen doorway, eyes shimmering.

Her favorite teapot. Oh no. What have I done?

I go to apologize, but she composes herself and presses past me to get a broom and dustpan and starts to pick up the pieces.

I retreat to the kitchen. Vincent winces at me, and we stand in tense silence, listening to the diners resume their chatter.

I take soap to the red stain on the white sweater and scrub, but it's no use. I won't be able to return it.

There goes four hundred dollars.

Eventually, Judy comes in with a bag of trash, then washes up in silence, and Vincent sashays back out into the dining room while I tend to the dishes. Judy doesn't look at me for the rest of my shift—she's too busy making clotted cream and piping icing onto cookies.

"I'm so sorry," I eventually try again, but she only gives me a sad smile and starts arranging the cookies in a neat row on a tiered tray. I feel horrible. No, *worse* than horrible.

By the time it's closing, I'm shrugging my jacket on over my ruined sweater when she approaches.

"Leo, do you have a moment?" She gestures at a table for two in the dining room, and we sit. "Leo, I've been very nice about it, but you have continued to arrive late."

My stomach knots. "I understand. And I really am truly sorry. About the teapot."

She takes off her glasses and presses the bridge of her nose. "It was my late mother's."

My lip quivers. I suppose there isn't anything I can do to make up for it. "I'm sorry."

"No, *I'm* sorry, Leo." She sighs, then places her glasses back on. "I didn't want to have to do this, but . . . it seems like this isn't a good fit for you anymore. I'm terminating your employment."

I gape, feeling the twist of the knife.

"Thank you for everything. Have a nice night, Leo."

I nod and go. This job was such a glimmer of light in my life, and it felt good earning money to help Mom make ends meet after all the money she's already spent on attorney fees. Plus, buying beauty products and nice clothes adds up. And now it's over.

This little home away from home, full of brownie edges and pie crusts and Judy's warm, supportive smiles. I'll even miss Vincent.

I glance over my shoulder to see him mouth: *"I want my clothes back."*

I let my old self get the better of me and drive over to Lincoln's house now that he's back from his aunt's place. I need to talk.

Especially after I left a five-minute audio note for him, and his reply was "This audio is five minutes long. Can you give me the abridged version?" To which I replied: "Can I come over?"

I'm white-knuckling the steering wheel, feeling like I'm bursting with nerves—and the occasional tear. The whole Dad visit, paired with my blunder at work, compels me to tell Lincoln everything. I'll leave out the part that my best friends are nowhere to be found, and that I miss them. I'm starting to think missing Dillon's choral concert was a more egregious move than I'd thought. Dillon was the first person I'd called, then Varsha, but neither had picked up.

I park at the bottom of Lincoln's driveway and make the steep climb. He greets me at the front door with a hug and a kiss, wearing the pajamas I got him for Christmas, and we thank each other in person for our sweet gifts. After warding off a noisy Junior, Lincoln leads me into his movie room, where we squash down onto the chairs, and I tell him all about my final day working at the teahouse.

I don't realize how long it takes for me to lay it all out, and I can feel the opportunity to share the Dad story fading away, like there isn't time to hit him with both tragic tales. Especially with how Lincoln keeps yawning. I'm so used to Dillon and Varsha jumping in with words of wisdom and have to remind myself that everyone's different.

I bury my face in my hands. "Ugh. I'm mortified!"

Lincoln plays with the remote of his massage chair, which begins to knead his back. "Yeah. That sounds rough, babe."

Babe? I don't know why, but the nickname sounds strange in my ear. Sure, we know each other's least favorite foods (mine is Jell-O, his is pickles), but as far as anything deeper than that, there's still much to be explored. I didn't expect to feel so . . . disappointed about this idea. I wanted to feel *excited* that there's a lot left to explore, not deflated.

"Anyway, how was *your* night?" I ask, eyeing Junior, who's been sleeping in his donut bed, except for when he occasionally cracks an eye open to growl at me and bare his tiny teeth.

Lincoln yawns. "Good. I'm watching this cool new bowling show on Netflix."

"Nice. What's it about?"

He reclines in the massage chair. "Bowling and politics."

"Sounds riveting."

"It's actually pretty good. I'm on episode eight. Let's watch it together. You'll like it." He reaches for the remote control.

"I was going to look at my college apps tonight," I say, recalling the promise I'd made Mom—and myself.

"Each episode is only twenty minutes," he says. "Come on. You need a distraction."

Deciding to lighten up, I smile. "Yeah. You're right."

He tells me more about his newfound interest in bowling as I sit at his feet and cuddle up with his leg, then we start to stream episode eight together. By the end of the episode, he wants to keep watching, and so he convinces me to stay up for one more . . . which leads to one more.

I send Mom a follow-up text, letting her know I'll be home late, though I'm sure she's already asleep.

He pauses the next episode and stretches. "Are you going to do your college apps still?"

I glance at the clock and groan. "How is it already almost one in the morning?"

"I always lose track of time with you," he says. "We have too much fun together."

I smile and feel all melty inside. "We really do." There will be time for my college apps later, I'm sure. While we have a ton of fun, our late-night talks really do take up so much time, and

I know I'm going to be a zombie tomorrow. I really need to start going to bed earlier. It's not his fault. I'm not good at voicing my needs, apparently. I don't want to say anything to ruin things or hurt his feelings. But I feel better about the whole teahouse fiasco—kind of. Even if I don't know how I'm going to pay off my ruined sweater.

"I should head home," I say, feigning a yawn and making my eyes look sleepier than they really are, so that he takes the heavy-handed hint.

"Okay," he says resignedly, and walks me to the front door with Junior padding after us. "Wait," he says, wagging his eyebrows. "Are we going to spend New Year's Eve together still?"

As much as I want to blurt out, *Yes, of course!*, I force myself to pause. Dillon, Varsha, and I have spent the last two years together on New Year's Eve making vision boards, and it's one of my favorite things we do. I'd invite Lincoln, but I don't think he'd mesh well with them, at least not Dillon. At least not yet.

I want my New Year's Eve to be a fun, friend-only kind of night.

"I'm going to spend it with Dillon and Varsha this year," I say. "It's kind of a tradition thing."

"Oh." He looks annoyed. "Dillon. Cool."

I realize I just played hard to get, and it worked, even though I didn't even do it on purpose. But I'm not elated. In fact, there's an iciness settling between us, and I hate the feeling. Playing hard to get is really starting to sour my stomach.

"Yeah! But we can hang out the next day maybe," I offer. "*Babe*," I add with a cheeky smile.

His expression softens.

The checklist would say to act busy, anyway. Not make myself so readily available. That said, many checklist rules seem to have gone out the window, as evidenced by how I'm feeling like I can be more of myself around Lincoln.

I wonder if I can take it a step further by telling him just how deeply the visit with my dad affected me . . . but the night's already over, and that conversation could be a much longer one. Plus, thinking about last time I opened up like that, I don't think I could handle being laughed at again in that way.

"But," I find myself saying, trying harder to salvage the mood, "I was thinking we could go bowling this week. You know, as a fun date-type thing."

His face lights up. "Hell yeah! The New Year is going to be sick. I'm already thinking about what we should wear to semiformal."

The words hit me like a brick. Of *course* we're going to semi-formal together. We're boyfriends.

But . . .

"Right," I say, beaming. "All right, cool. More details on our bowling date tomorrow. For now, I shall let you go."

"Sounds good." He pulls me in for a kiss. "Good night, babe."

"Bye." I give him a playful push. "Babe."

When he closes the door, I fly down the driveway like a dog let off a tight leash.

After blasting "I Know It's Today" from *Shrek the Musical* and "Soon" from *Thumbelina*, and being too tired to sing along, I'm home.

And a few minutes later, I'm in bed with Miss Tiramisu. I

eye the stained sweater hanging off the back of my desk chair, then the clock, and groan. It's so late. I'm going to be exhausted tomorrow—again.

But before cutting the lights, I gaze at the gift card Lincoln gave me resting on my nightstand, then pull over my scrapbook and open to my "Besties" section, where I'd added a photo of Dillon, Varsha, and me after closing night of the school play. I turn to Lincoln's new section, which has been growing from week to week. It's covered with Christmas tree stickers, paper-cut ice skates, and a photo of us holding our Mapleccinos in front of The Rink at Bryant Park. This is what a First Great Love Story is supposed to look like.

My anxiety dissipates, and I'm all aglow once more. Maybe this secret anxiety I've been experiencing with him is normal, and maybe being with *anyone* involves some level of navigating your own Baggage Stuff to get through that. Like being more outspoken and telling him I can't talk or hang out for so long before bed.

But then I fear pushing him away, and we do have so much fun together.

I am clinging on to him, and *us*, and *we*, and *ours* . . .

And it still feels shaky. Why?

I need to figure out how to not feel so much anxiety weighing on me when we hang out. Then it'll only be a matter of time before we're dancing at semiformal and sharing a molten lava cake with a big dollop of vanilla ice cream at a Valentine's Day dinner, red roses and all.

And with that glorious image in mind, I click off the light and sleep.

33

SPENDING NEW YEAR'S EVE AT HOME WITH MY BESTIES THE next day is just what the doctor ordered.

Although with the way Lincoln's been blowing up my phone all night, he might as well be here. He's mostly just sending selfies at Katie's place with a party hat on. I need to stop wondering if Travis is there since he's back in their good graces, but he doesn't seem to be there, based off photo evidence of group shots, which include jocks and pom squad girls. Plus, Lincoln's been continuing to say how much he's into me, but I feel weird saying it back, and I'm not sure why.

"You know gingerbread house decorating kits are my favorite," Dillon says.

I'm sitting with Dillon and Varsha at my kitchen table, using a pastry bag to pipe icing onto the roof of the massive gingerbread house that I didn't end up assembling for Christmas. Bowls of every kind of candy imaginable cover the tabletop. Varsha presses a peppermint to the front door of the house, while Dillon landscapes with lollipops and chocolate bars. *Anaconda* is playing on the big-screen TV, and while neither a gingerbread house nor a movie about a human-eating snake feels very New Year's Eve, our noisemakers and vision board supplies complete the festive vibe.

I get up the nerve to blurt out to Varsha what happened with my parents. She's supportive, like I knew she would be, and she connects the dots as to why I haven't had them over in a while. I don't know why I was so nervous to talk to her about it. And it feels good to just be the real me.

We put on the finishing touches. The candy slides off the roof, and a wall is cracked in half, but there's something charming about it in its imperfections.

Varsha sighs. "It looks . . . not great."

"I think it looks sweet," Dillon counters.

Washing and drying our hands off at the kitchen sink, Dillon touches the corner of my mouth. "You've got a little icing right here."

"Oh really," I say, flickering my tongue out across my lips like an anaconda.

"Yeah," he says. "You keep missing it—I'll get it." He dabs the tip of a wet washcloth on my lip.

"Good?"

Dillon smiles. "Perfect."

We plop down at the coffee table to make our annual vision

boards. My friends concentrate on snipping words and images from the heap of magazines we've got spread out, while I'm hunched over my laptop on the couch, poring over my college applications.

"By heck and high water, I'm submitting these tonight!"

"And we are here to make sure it happens," Varsha says, snipping out the word PEACE.

I plod through the forms, copying and pasting answers I'd drafted up from a Word document earlier this week. Eventually, my friends finish their vision boards and help me, group project style, to button up and submit my college applications that Mom and I had already gotten a jump on. It's truly all-hands-on-deck.

Finally, I click submit and let out a huge sigh.

"Hooray!" Varsha cheers.

"I am so proud of you!" Dillon says.

"Thank you." I picked a whole bunch of schools in big cities, which include UCLA, where I know Lincoln's applying. I try to imagine us attending the same school, but I just can't picture it.

"What's Lincoln been texting you?" Varsha asks.

I shrug. "Stuff. I'll get back to him later."

"You're still working the checklist? Leave him hanging?" Dillon asks.

I peek at my phone. Lincoln misses me. But I don't really miss Lincoln all that much tonight. I miss the idea of spending the night with my boyfriend but . . . I'm feeling a mental block. I felt it this morning when I stopped by the CVS for new makeup wipes and saw they're already selling the chocolate heart boxes for Valentine's Day.

"As a reward for submitting my college apps, it's time I do a little retail therapy with someone else's money." I go online to Game World's website and hold up Lincoln's gift card.

"I hate to admit it, but I think it was nice of Lincoln to get you that gift," Varsha says.

"It's perfect," I agree, scrolling through the site.

"Really?" Dillon asks. "It seems kind of generic. Everyone who knows Leo knows what to get Leo. A plushie with googly eyes, with three to four teeth."

"You're not wrong." I find a Totoro plushie and put it in my cart.

Dillon's face falls. "Ugh. I forgot to bring your Christmas gift!"

I have one for him and Varsha tucked in my closet upstairs. "It's okay. We can exchange next time I see y'all." I put in the gift card numbers and pause as I study the computer screen. "My balance is thirty-six dollars and nineteen cents?"

"But doesn't your gift card have fifty bucks on it?" Varsha asks.

She and Dillon shoot me a look.

I peer at the screen, astounded. "I guess it only had around thirteen dollars on it."

"Did Lincoln regift?!" Varsha hisses.

Dillon grimaces. "It sounds like it."

"No . . . That would be wild," I say, though I don't know how else to explain it.

My friends look uneasy, then get back to fussing with their vision boards.

"I can ask him when I see him next. I'm sure there was just a mix-up."

My friends nod, but their head bobs are halfhearted. Varsha awkwardly changes the subject and flashes her vision board. "Ta-da!" It's lots of hopeful words and images of peaceful oceanside scenes. Right now, I can't relate.

"What's with the ocean?" Dillon asks.

"I like the ocean," Varsha says. "I would just never go in it. Obvi."

"Here's mine." Dillon shows off his vision board, with music notes and a rainbow doodled in, and images of nutritious dishes like salads and avocado eggrolls.

"I like it!" I say, trying to muster some positive energy. I wonder if the rainbow is symbolic of a future boyfriend.

"All right, you need to get started on yours now," Varsha says, pushing the colorful construction paper toward me.

"You're going to put our vision boards to shame," Dillon tells me. "Mr. Shrine-Book Creator." The shrine-book. His endearing term for my scrapbook.

I pick up an uncapped glue stick and swipe it at him. "You know me all too well."

As I get to work, picking over the magazines, Varsha and Dillon cozy up on the couch as Jennifer Lopez fights off the enormous anaconda.

"So, have you guys used the L word yet?" Varsha asks.

"Leocoln?" I ask.

"What?!" Varsha asks. "Wait. Are you trying to combine your two names to make a ship name? *No.*"

"Do you like Lincleo better?" I ask. "That was my second choice!"

Varsha grits her teeth. "*Love*, Leo. The L word is *love*."

"What? No way I have said that to him!" I guffaw.

"But do you? Love him?" Dillon asks. He seems awfully curious.

"Yeah. I mean, I think so."

They're both staring at me. I shove salty-sweet popcorn in my mouth.

"Do you think it's mutual?" Varsha asks.

"I mean . . ." I shove even more popcorn into my mouth. "Totally. Definitely."

"You sound less sure," Varsha retorts.

Yeah, Lincoln loves Fake Leo, I think.

I reach for a large piece of poster paper and change the subject. "So, whatever we tape on it will hypothetically come true in the New Year, right?"

"Allegedly," Dillon says. "Did any of ours come true from last year?"

"Mine said I'd have a boyfriend," I say with a toothy smile.

Dillon laughs. "It says that every year."

I glue on a picture of a disco ball and think of semiformal. I imagine what I hope my time with Lincoln will be like: the two of us, waltzing around an elegant ballroom . . . or more likely, slow swaying on a dance floor littered with glow sticks. But I'm feeling a little queasy about the whole thing. I finished the Boyfriend Material Checklist. Lincoln is my boyfriend, and we're going to semiformal together. So then why can't I shake the feeling that something's off?

I text Lincoln back, replying to his dancing emoji with heart eyes and disco balls.

Varsha glares. "Leo? Are you even listening to what I just said?"

I slide my phone slowly into my pocket, feeling both their eyes on me.

"Uh—yeah! I was telling you about how another killer whale ate an abusive trainer at Sea World and you're texting Lincoln. Dude! Can't you just be present with us for, like, two seconds?"

Dillon just looks at me.

"We get it. We're not as interesting as you are now," Varsha adds.

"Oh, come on, guys. It's not like that. We're just excited for semiformal."

"Leo, he used some of the gift card he gave you for Christmas," Dillon says, annoyed.

"What does that have to do with semiformal?" I say. "What do you have against him?"

Dillon shrugs. "No comment."

"It's not that I don't like him. I mean, I don't, but that's irrelevant. It's just—" Varsha says. "Do you even love him?"

"Of course. We're totally into each other. What are you talking about? We just haven't said it yet."

"You seem sadder than usual," Dillon points out. "Does that have to do with him?"

"I don't think so . . ."

I cut myself off, too embarrassed to tell my friends that they're right and that I'm not happy. That I've been struggling to get deep with Lincoln, show him the real me.

"But he doesn't even know the real you," Varsha says, as if reading my mind.

"He will. And when he does, he'll accept me for me," I say.

"I hope so," Dillon says.

I do, too.

"Doesn't showing the real you also mean confessing how you feel to him?" Varsha asks.

I sigh. "Yes. Yes, it does."

But the thought of telling Lincoln "I love you" is making me ill.

I flip through more magazines and create my vision board, which includes pictures of students with backpacks on college campuses and people holding hands. I contemplate adding a photo of Lincoln to the board, but I leave it be.

By the time my friends leave, just after midnight, I go around turning off the lights in the house. I stop in front of the light switch at the bottom of the stairs. Sitting there is one of the bins filled to the brim with Gran's family scrapbook albums—Mom must be doing more organizing. It's quiet, and there's something eerie about the box, as if it's beckoning me.

I reach in and lift out a photo album with a crinkly laminated case and crack it open. It's dusty and smells like cheese. There's Gran with Grandpa Al, in old black-and-white photos that are yellow with age. They both look so young and dashing and in love.

I keep flipping and find photos of Mom as a little girl, surrounded by all her brothers and sisters—the aunts and uncles who removed themselves from our lives. They were just children once, all of them living under one roof. It's a strange thought, knowing where they ended up.

And then there's a photo of Mom and Dad at their wedding, Dad shoving a wad of vanilla buttercream in Mom's face. And photos of her holding a baby Silvio, and then a baby me, in hospital cots, her smile radiant despite the sweaty forehead and disheveled hair. She always says those were the two happiest days of her life.

The last page shows a Christmas photo of all four of us, with me as a newborn swaddled in a white blanket. Dad looks so youthful, smiling wide. Mom doesn't look quite herself, standing with a hand on his shoulder and an apron on. Her expression is meek. Those were the days she tried hard to make things work, to make herself small for him.

The sight of it turns my insides to ice.

I place the scrapbook back into the bin and trudge upstairs in the dark, leaving Dad and everything with it locked up.

Moments later, I get another text from Lincoln saying he misses me.

I miss him too. But something about the relationship still doesn't feel right. Will it ever?

And then it hits me: I've been hiding behind the checklist. He doesn't know the real me.

And if he doesn't, then does any of this count?

Maybe I'm not finished with my Boyfriend Material Checklist.

I add one last item:

7. BE THE REAL ME.

BOYFRIEND MATERIAL CHECKLIST

1. ~~BE COOL AS A CUCUMBER.~~ ☑

2. ~~GET A GLAM GLOW-UP.~~ ☑

3. ~~HAVE A POWERHOUSE PRESENCE.~~ ☑

4. ~~FAKE BEING RICH.~~ ☑

5. ~~WIN POPULARITY CONTEST.~~ ☑

6. ~~KISS LIKE A PRO.~~ ☑

 7. BE THE REAL ME. ☐

THE NEXT TWO WEEKS BACK AT SCHOOL PASS QUICKLY, AND
the novelty of saying "Happy New Year" to classmates fades as
everyone falls back into the on-the-ground groove of things.
The clean-slate, fresh-start New Year energy feels long gone,
and it's a waiting game until semiformal.

Not to mention I've been procrastinating these past two
weeks on my last checklist item—*Be the Real Me*—aka showing
my true self to Lincoln. For two weeks, we hang at lunch, hailed
by every student at Eastfield High as the It Couple. Travis and
Sergio skitter out of our path in the hall like cockroaches as we
hold hands while Lincoln's lavender bomber jacket keeps me
warm. Iced coffee laps with Dillon and Varsha are replaced by
make-out sessions in Lincoln's Mercedes-Benz in the senior lot.

The third week of January, midterms sound like a series of

frustrated sighs and cracking knuckles—at least for me. Even with finishing and submitting my college applications, by the end of the week, I just want to burrow under a giant pile of blankets and hibernate.

And I miss hanging with my friends.

Two days before semiformal, Lincoln stops by in the hall to say hi.

"Excited for our bowling date tonight."

"Me too—" As I open the door to my locker to get my jacket, a bunch of random knickknacks spill out onto the ground. Small trinkets, key chains, and other things I have been holding on to for months, in hopes I can give them to Lincoln sometime.

Lincoln raises an eyebrow. "What is all this?"

I feel my face turn red as I scramble to pick up the items. "Uh, nothing," I mutter, trying to shove them back into my locker.

"Leo, your locker is disgusting," Lincoln says.

I feel my cheeks flame with embarrassment. "These aren't gross. These are things I got because you said you'd liked them and I kind of have a thing for gift giving . . ." I trail off, at a loss.

At the same time—this is me.

I'm not a stalker, I just *look* like one.

But the expression on Lincoln's face tells me I shouldn't try to explain that.

He jerks a thumb toward the gymnasium. "Umm, yeah. Okay, well. I'll catch you tonight."

As I crouch down, surrounded by the clutter of gifts that spilled out of my locker, I can't help but worry that I might have put a serious dent in things by showing my true colors. Oops.

Regardless of my blunder, Lincoln still agrees to meet at the bowling alley later that day. It's packed, the air is filled with the sound of rolling balls and crashing pins, and it smells like pizza and nachos. Lincoln insisted we go to this one in the next town over because of its retro vibes.

"I knew we should have kept the bumpers on!" I shout as my ball rolls into the gutter. Again.

"Some of us don't need bumpers." Lincoln takes a shiny blue bowling ball from the lineup and lets it rip. It goes gliding down the center of the lane before knocking down every pin. "Strike!" he roars, pumping his fist. He looks so handsome in jeans and a graphic T-shirt.

I point a finger at him. "Curse you," I tease.

He laughs, and we plunk down to have some more nachos and spinach-and-cheese dip.

But the fact he likes bowling doesn't really tell me about who he is as a person, and I'm on a mission to dig a little deeper today and share more of myself. I want to find a real, true connection. I want *I love you* to feel right when I finally say it, and when I finally hear it back.

He doesn't love the real you . . .

"Hey . . ." I begin, dunking a piece of garlic pita bread into the creamy cheese sauce. "I've told you about my parents and family. How about yours? Just as dysfunctional as mine?"

Lincoln crunches a chip. "Not really. We're pretty normal."

"Normal?" I cringe, and my stomach sinks. "Well, that's good.

Glad to know I'm the only one with an *ab*normal one."

"Well, I guess my mom complains that my dad snores," he tosses in.

I mumble, irked that that's the best he could come up with. I rack my brains for another question. Something I don't know about him yet. I stare down at my rental shoes, which actually look really cute with my well-fitted chinos. "What's one of your greatest fears?"

He narrows his eyes at me. "Interrogations."

I bite back a giggle. "Okay. Well, you know what they say about facing your fears."

Lincoln looks deadpan.

"It's just . . ." I wipe my hand off on a napkin. "I don't know much about you."

He scoffs. "What do you mean? We're together." His tone sounds annoyed.

"Yeah, but I want to know you even more." I reach up and trace his silver earring and stroke the black hair perfectly curling onto his forehead.

"Okay. What do you want to know?"

I run my fingers over the curl again. "What happened between you and Travis?"

"He wanted to get serious, and I didn't."

I lean back into the hard plastic chair. "What do you mean?"

"I'm not really into the whole relationships thing right now."

"But *we're* in a relationship . . ." I say.

He lets out an easy laugh, then looks down at the almost-empty basket of chips. "More chips?"

I grow quiet. "Yeah. Sure."

He gets up and heads to the concession stand, and I swipe through TikTok. I'm not happy with his answers. They leave me feeling unsettled and uneasy—and more distant. Does he even *want* to be in a relationship with me? Did he truly give me a used gift card?

When Lincoln returns, I steer clear of any potentially sensitive questions and keep things light, asking about his favorite places he's traveled, and favorite shows and movies he's enjoyed lately, most of which I already know. Another part of me, however, has shut down. The part yearning for something *real*. Something *ours*. It still isn't within grasp—not really.

As he blots cheese grease from the side of his chin, he catches me staring at him. "What?" he asks through a mouthful.

"Nothing."

"What's up?" he asks again.

My heart begins to race, and I take his hand. "When you asked to be boyfriends, did you really mean it? Or were you just asking me because of the whole Dillon thing?"

He chews over the question. "I mean, I wasn't looking to get into a relationship," he says matter-of-factly.

It feels like someone just dropped a bowling ball on my stomach. That someone being him.

My eyes start to well up. He takes notice but looks away, obviously not wanting to acknowledge my extreme reaction.

I don't understand. Is he happy about being in a relationship even if he wasn't looking for one? Or is he somehow upset about it, like I forced him into one? Is he not interested in being serious with me?

"What do your friends think of us?" I ask.

"I think they like you more than Travis . . . for me," he says quickly. "They said he wasn't good for me. They just weren't thrilled about the idea of you hanging around all the time."

"What?" I ask, paling.

"I think they just see you as . . . different," he says. "Unusual, maybe?"

"You mean not cool enough?" Oh no. I feel my facade slipping, my heart racing.

"Well . . ." Lincoln fidgets with his shirt. "That's not where I was going—" Is Lincoln breaking up with me?

I shake my head, unable to process it. "I'm sorry. I have to go." And with that, I race out of the bowling alley before I let my tears fall.

"Hey!" yells the irate owner from the door. "You need to return the rental shoes!"

I can't process it. I can't process anything.

A DAY LATER, I STILL HAVEN'T HEARD FROM LINCOLN, SO I
decide to meet Dillon at his place to do a fashion show for semiformal tomorrow. I'm seated on his bed, dressed in my suit,
which feels way too tight.

"What do you think?" Dillon steps out in a simple black tux
that fits like a glove.

I grin. "You look so good!"

"Why, thank you." He executes a low bow. "Feeling better
about the whole Lincoln thing?"

I sigh, shaking my head. "Not really. I doubt he still wants to
go to semiformal with me."

"Would you even still want him to be your date? Why are
you even still hanging out with him, anyway?"

"Hanging out? We're boyfriends," I insist, but my voice
comes out scratchy and whiny.

"He's done so many things that are bothersome."

"Like what?"

Dillon sits on the bed beside me, crossing his legs. "Let's see . . . He loves pranking you . . . He posts your private text conversations and singing videos on social media . . . and doesn't seem to care that it rattles you. He regifted your Christmas gift . . . Said he doesn't want anything serious with you and his friends don't like you—"

"He didn't say it like that—" I cut in.

"Dare I go on?"

I chew the corner of my mouth. I can't argue with him. But that also isn't the full picture.

"Yeah, but he has so many great qualities too," I protest, obsessively checking my messages.

"Oh? Like when he made fun of that girl for ordering pancakes on your date?"

No messages. I sigh. "I mean, we all say cringeworthy things. Remember when I told you and Varsha that I wasn't a huge Beyoncé fan? And you two said never to share that with anyone or I'd be canceled?"

"I think that's a little different," Dillon says.

"Listen, I know. But I really want to get through the dance. Remember the checklist?"

"Yeah. The checklist for finding true love," Dillon amends. "I wouldn't say that this is that."

"True, love," I say, and laugh, but Dillon isn't amused.

This is what I wanted. It worked. It *has* to be the right thing. But if that's the case, then why is it starting to feel like the *wrong* thing?

"Dillon, my boyfriend is taking me to a school dance. I never thought I would ever be able to utter those words."

"Yeah, but he doesn't even really know you. I know you a million times better than your actual boyfriend."

"Well, you're a special case. A real rare bird." And it's true.

His smile fades, and suddenly he looks sick.

I lean toward him, worried. "Are you okay?"

"I feel like I let you down," he says. "Like I let *myself* down."

I peer at him. "What are you talking about?"

"You might have had a boyfriend or a date to the dance or a Valentine if I hadn't been so . . ."

I stare at him. For the first time in our friendship, I have absolutely no idea what he's about to say.

"I don't know? Scared? Shy? Stuck in my ways?"

I gaze into his earthy-green eyes. "What are you—"

"You wear your heart on your sleeve. It's what people love about you."

"Really?" I laugh in disbelief.

"Yes!" Dillon lets out an easy laugh. "It's a superpower!"

"Well, it also makes me a supervillain, and must I remind you that no one liked me until I hid said heart and started acting like someone else?"

"Exactly. Lincoln doesn't like you. How could he? He doesn't *know* you." Dillon looks at me unblinking. "I like you, Leo. Like, *like* like you. The real you."

Dillon . . . *like* likes me? Why haven't I seen this coming? Here I am thinking I'm this self-aware person, but I couldn't even see that this whole time, my best friend . . .

My thoughts are racing. Is he actually admitting to having a crush on me? Dillon?

I shake my head slowly. It feels like everything is crashing down, like a line's been crossed or a door opened, and depending on what happens next, I could lose Dillon as a friend. And if we were ever to be more, then if things ended badly, I couldn't stand the thought of a rift, of bad blood, of losing him. Everything could either go positively or the absolute worst way.

"You really didn't know? Well, why would you? I kind of . . . hid it well, I guess. Not everyone can show their emotions as well as you can."

I would think he's pranking me, except Dillon would never do that to me. But the nerve-racked expression Dillon's wearing makes me stop cold.

"Dillon, I like you too."

"Exactly. As a *friend*." It looks like his face is fighting not to crumble. He stands up, nearly stumbling, and begins walking toward the door, hanging his head. "See? This is why I never said anything," he mumbles.

I stand. "Wait? Where are you going?"

He freezes in the doorway, back facing me. "I don't know." He turns around and looks at me, his mouth twitching. "Leo, you wouldn't know true love if it smacked you on the head."

I recoil. Ouch. I feel my breath catch in my throat, and my face burns.

"True love is someone loving you for *you*," he continues. "The real you." His eyes swim with tears, and his mouth quirks to one side as he gives a little halfhearted shrug.

"Dillon—I don't want to say anything that might hurt you . . . I'm just processing all this, okay? It's a lot for me to take in."

I take a deep breath, thinking about how true love is about stomach butterflies and longing and dare I say obsession? Not a friend. A best friend. The best friend I'll ever have.

All I've ever wanted is somebody who's just . . . nice. Like Dillon.

"Did me completing the checklist make you fall for me or something?" I ask, reaching for some sort of explanation for his confession.

Dillon laughs. "Screw the checklist. I always said you were perfect just as you were."

He *has* always said that. Am I really so oblivious? Or has a part of me always known, always felt that way about Dillon myself, but never wanted to risk crossing a line for fear of losing him? And now that he's gone and said it, that line has been blown away like sand in the wind.

"You're saying this now?" My lip trembles. "Now? When I finally have what I want?"

He wipes his face. "Do you?"

I chew my lip, holding in so many jumbled words.

"Let's just forget this happened." And with that, he turns and vanishes into the hall.

Back at home, I step through the front door, and Mom pauses to watch me as she's coming down the stairs.

"Leo. Are you okay, dear?"

My body lets out a little tremble, and next thing I know, I'm sobbing again. My mind races to catch up: Is this why Lincoln's been jealous of me whenever Dillon texted me? Why Mom and practically everyone else thought we'd be a cute couple? They saw something I couldn't see . . . until now.

Mom comes over and wraps me in a hug. "What's wrong? What is it?"

"Lincoln . . . He doesn't love me . . . Not even the new me . . ." My words come out broken. I can't even admit to her what Dillon told me, and how I ruined everything there, too.

"Oh. Well, I'm sorry to hear that, dear. There, there." She gives me a few little pats on the back. "It's Lincoln's loss."

I sniffle. "I'm having a hard time seeing it that way."

"Come on. Let's get you situated." She lifts my backpack from the floor and guides me upstairs. She sets out comfy pajamas for me and steps out into the hall as I change.

"What do you want for dinner?" she asks from behind the door.

"I'm not hungry."

"Sushi? I'll order sushi, okay?"

I step into the hall. "What's wrong with me?"

At that, Mom's lip does a little quiver. She swallows hard. "Nothing is wrong with you. Some people can't see us for who we are. Sometimes, people want different things in life. You want someone who wants you the same way you want them. And if that isn't the case, it's the universe's way of telling you to let them go." She smiles. "I know you don't want to hear a pep talk right now, but you are a wonderful person, and anyone would be lucky to have you as their boyfriend. And I'm not just saying that because I'm your mother."

In the den, I sit in front of the TV, and Mom wraps me in a blanket before turning on *Spirited Away* (subbed, not dubbed) and curling up beside me. I try to focus on the movie, but my breathing is fast and shallow, and my heart aches. Twenty minutes into the movie, however, my mind is able to immerse itself in the action.

Before I know it, Mom hops up to get the door. She returns carrying a brown paper bag and begins setting up various sushi rolls on the coffee table. She prepares a plate for me, including the egg she fried that she slides over my favorite dynamite roll. "Here you go, dear." We eat in silence, but I notice she's drinking water again, not her usual wine.

"No wine tonight, Mom?" I say lightly, realizing it's been a while since she's had any.

She shakes her head. "I thought it was time to take a break. I want my head clear." She smiles at me, and I smile back. I don't need to say anything. It's my turn to be proud of her.

After we eat, she kisses me on the top of the head and excuses herself for bed.

I find myself yawning. Bedtime for me too. In minutes, I've gone from Morose Couch Dweller to Forlorn Bed Burrower. Miss Tiramisu hops up and curls against my leg.

Lincoln 🖤🖤🖤: Still up for the dance tomorrow?

Maybe my love life with Lincoln isn't a lost cause after all.

I scratch Miss Tiramisu under the chin, and I tell her about what I've kept pent up all evening. Now I finally let myself think about what Dillon said, but I still don't know what to make of it. And now that Lincoln's reached out, I'm more confused than ever.

I stare at Miss Tiramisu, thinking of my best friend.

"Did Dill Pickle just confess his love for me?"

"HAPPY LAST SEMIFORMAL, FRIENDS," DILLON SAYS AS WE
get ready at my house the next night.

We haven't spoken since our conversation, but things have
felt as normal between us as they could be. We're doing a good
job acting like nothing ever happened. Nothing meaning Dillon
confessing his love for me, and me fumbling in a blunder of
confusion. There's been a lot to think about. With Lincoln,
everything's been coming along—I found what I've wanted—
but not really. He did send an apology text, however, which was
enough for me to realize that we *weren't* over, that he *hadn't*
broken up with me, that everything is okay again . . .

Except everything is far from okay. Deep in my heart.

Varsha steps out of my bathroom and gives us a twirl in her
flowy pink sequin dress with pockets that she made for the

event, paired with some matching pink-and-white kicks and raspberry-pink clip-ins standing out nicely against her medium-length, thick black hair.

"Yes, girl! Work it!" I exclaim from where I'm seated in a sea of plushies on my bed.

She bats her eyelashes, showing off her glittery purple eye shadow.

"You look great!" Dillon takes footage of her striking pose after pose for his TikTok.

Dillon and I purposely wore sweatpants and sweatshirts to take a TikTok transition video of the two of us, spinning away from each other in our scrubs and then spinning back toward each other in our matching tuxedos. It'll probably make Lincoln upset, but that's his problem. And Dillon looks handsome, which is my problem.

"And posted," Dillon says, showing his phone to me.

Lincoln hearts it instantly, and I beam—I'm glad he's playing nice. I'm ready for whatever the night may bring, though I really hope it's just as magical as what I've been building up in my head ever since freshman year. He'll be here any minute.

I take a second to admire the two waltzing princes taped into Lincoln's scrapbook page when I notice Dillon's eyes fall on it.

"That's such a cute spread," Dillon chimes in.

"Right?" I say, my voice higher than I intend. Maybe acting like nothing happened is harder than it first seemed. I close my scrapbook and tuck it into my desk.

Varsha unplugs her straightening iron. "Ready, y'all."

We take the obligatory group photo on the stairs as Mom directs us to pose and smile, even though it feels very awkward, especially with my arm around Dillon's waist. It's seven o'clock, meaning the semiformal has already begun, and we're all itching to get there. I let a genuine smile shine through.

The doorbell rings, and Mom answers.

Lincoln appears, breathless as if he's been running. "Hi. Sorry I'm late!" he shouts, bounding up the stairs two at a time for the photo.

"You look so snazzy," I say, admiring his classic black tuxedo.

"Thanks," he says, squaring off for the photo.

"Hi, Lincoln." Mom snaps a few photos of us all together. "We're glad you could come."

"Traffic was so bad!" Lincoln announces. "There was this lady who didn't know how to drive!"

"It's okay," I say with a little laugh.

He gives a cursory wave to Dillon and Varsha, then turns back to me. "You look great." He pulls me in for a big hug as my friends look on. He smells amazing, like fresh orange slices.

"Thanks." I blush.

Dillon just stares at his shoes, hands in his pockets. I feared Lincoln's presence would make him tense up, and I was right. *Especially* after he told me how he felt about me. But seeing it play out in front of me is worse than anything I could have imagined, and I feel sick.

"Ugh." Lincoln fiddles with the back of his shirt collar. "This tag is driving me nuts. Do you have any scissors?"

"Oh. Yeah. Upstairs in my bedroom desk drawer."

While Lincoln dashes upstairs, I duck into the kitchen to retrieve his boutonniere out of the fridge, thinking the white flower will look nice with his tux.

Then I freeze in my tracks, and a wave of ice floods through me.

I told him the scissors were in my bedroom desk drawer, and I can see them perfectly in my mind . . . *sitting beside my scrapbook*.

I drop the boutonniere and race up the stairs to find Lincoln standing next to my desk. He's got the scissors in one hand and is flipping through *my scrapbook* with the other.

When he hears me, he spins around. His face is red. He drops the scrapbook on the desk.

My heart pounds in my ears. "Oh. You found the scissors."

He holds them up. "Yep! Found the scissors!" He turns around. "Can you cut out the tag for me?"

"Yep!" Maybe if I act like everything is normal, it will be?

But I pray he didn't see too many pages of my scrapbook, to the point of thinking I'm some sort of freak.

I feel numb. Why isn't he saying anything about it?

WHY ISN'T HE SAYING ANYTHING ABOUT IT?!

I snip the tag and place the scissors on the desk next to my scrapbook, which is still sitting in plain sight. I grab his hand and pull him out of my room. "Let's go!" I say.

A flash of a car ride later and the four of us are in the school gymnasium with the rest of the school dancing. The darkness is pierced by round, color-changing lights projected on the walls that swirl around the room like a flurry of confetti. It was on the car ride over when I realized I'd left the boutonniere on the kitchen floor. But that's the least of my worries. I still can't believe he saw my scrapbook. Why hasn't he said anything yet? I'm starting to spiral. Bad.

Passing in front of the DJ booth, we find our table, where Varsha leaves her shimmery piranha purse, and I leave my jacket on a chair because it's already so boiling hot in here. The Fierce Five are standing idly on the dance floor while other students dance around them. Too cool to dance, obviously.

"I can't believe there are underclassmen here," Katie says with an eye roll over the roar of students singing along to Sabrina Carpenter.

I shrug, wondering why that even matters to Katie, and Lincoln drags me into their ring with little foot kicks and shoulder shrugs. His friends weren't thrilled that he wasn't part of their limo ride here. Varsha and Dillon stand apart, mainly just dancing with each other. They're not as comfortable around the group as I'm pretending to be, even when I wave them over. It doesn't help that no one in the Fierce Five does more than acknowledge them with a halfhearted smile.

The semi is slow to start, but then soon enough people are up out of their seats to make the dance floor look like a roiling ocean. Not to mention certain students have started making out right here on the dance floor.

We join the throng of students who've made a clearing on the dance floor as people take to the center for their solo dance moves. Anne and Emily wave me over, and I dance with my theater friends. Lincoln sees me with them and makes a mocking face, which I ignore.

Enzi's here, and when he does the worm, people lose it. Everyone's phones are out. Everyone's chanting. Somebody hands out glow sticks. Lincoln and I exchange an amused glance with each other. I can tell neither of us wants to take a turn in the dance circle.

Varsha hands me a pair of sunglasses to put on and pose with, with the word SEMI and the year, then passes them to Dillon for him to do the same, and then it's her turn. The three of us are hand in hand and hopping up and down, singing our lungs out. Now *this* is fun. No holding back. It feels like I can let go of all the tension I've been holding inside for months. Years?

But every time I catch Dillon's glances, I'm hit with guilt.

Guilt that I want to spend the whole night dancing with *him* . . . instead of Lincoln.

"May I?" Lincoln asks me, taking me by the hand and dancing face-to-face. Next thing I know, we're kissing on the dance floor.

People are wolf whistling and cheering. Some of them even have their phones out to capture the It Couple at work. I can only imagine what Dillon must be thinking. I cut the kiss with Lincoln short and try to gaze past him to see if Dillon's okay.

Lincoln moves his face closer to mine, blocking my line of sight. "Having fun?"

"Yeah. Totally."

Steam rolls across the dance floor from a smoke machine as a slow song comes on, and Lincoln and I start rocking back and forth in each other's arms.

It's everything I've ever dreamed of.

I should be feeling like I'm on top of the world—except I don't. Here I am with my boyfriend at a school dance. But just like at any high school event, I want to go crawl in a hole. Even with a boyfriend on my arm.

He spins me in an elegant arch. I catch Sergio and Travis glancing our way, and Enzi, bathed in purple light, watches me as I'm pulled into a conga line, and again as I strut out into a new clearing of solo dancers being rooted on by the crowd to gyrate and shake their booties.

The rest of the night consists of a fancy meal and lots of breaks from dancing for ice-cold water at our table that there never seems to be enough of. Lincoln and I barely talk during the dinner. He and I do the obligatory step-and-repeat photos before I take them separately with Dillon and Varsha. It's hard to balance my friends and him at the same time, especially when he's more in tune with the rest of the Fierce Five, guffawing and laughing at all their inside jokes.

I can hear Dillon's voice.

This isn't you . . .

He's right.

I start to feel dizzy.

After a few hours, the dance floor smells like a pungent locker room. I turn and I'm shocked to see Lincoln and Travis dancing together. They look happy. I feel a twinge of jealousy: Why would he dance with his ex when I'm his date? Does he truly have no regard for how it could make me feel?

Maybe he got jealous about us coming here with Dillon?

I'm so over playing games.

I never thought I'd think this, but . . . I'm seeing things clearly for the first time, and I need to break things off with Lincoln Chan.

My first real boyfriend.

And probably my *last* real boyfriend.

Once he and Travis step apart, I wait until Travis is a safe distance away. Then, palms sweating, I walk up to Lincoln and tap him on the shoulder. "Hey, you want to go outside and get some fresh air?" I shout over the blaring music.

His face is red and sweaty from dancing. "Be there in a minute!" he hollers, as Katie yanks him away into a mosh pit.

I leave the gymnasium alone.

It's dark and quiet outside, and the cold feels blissful. I've lost my voice and my ears are ringing, but I don't care. It's nice being alone, giving me time to think.

I text Dillon, asking if he's having a nice time.

I'm waiting for him to respond as Lincoln appears.

"Howdy!" he says in good spirits.

I freeze up. I want to tell him that I don't think we should keep dating, but for some reason, I can't go through with it. It seemed right in theory, but now that we're here, the words aren't coming . . .

I don't want to hurt him.

But also, is the fact that I don't want to say it to him a sign that I'm with the wrong person after all? I gulp. I have to trust what I know in my heart.

I sit down on a bench. "I feel like something is off," I start to explain.

"Okay." He doesn't sit down next to me. "Is this about Travis?"

"No." I shake my head. "Lincoln . . . I . . . I don't think I see a future for us."

He clenches his jaw. "What? Because I danced with Travis? Come on! Your locker and scrapbook were much worse!" Ouch.

"No!" I shake my head. "But, seriously, you're going to bring up my locker and scrapbook?"

Lincoln shrugs and puts his hands in his pants pockets. "Hey, I didn't mention your phone's home screen."

"I . . . I just think . . ." But I just can't bring myself to say anything more to hurt him.

Lincoln's expression hardens. "Okay. No. I get it. Fine."

"But I'd like to be friends, if you're open to it," I say, in an attempt to prevent animosity.

"Wow." He laughs, stepping back. "Have a good life. I hope you find what you're looking for." His words are colder than the freezing night air. They hit me like a brick.

"Okay," I say weakly, but I can't mask my hurt.

He walks away. Walks away . . . as if I never meant a thing.

Just like every one of my crushes ever did.

After all that work I put into the checklist, this is what it's come to? Did I really just break up with my first real boyfriend? Have I made a mistake?

I want to leave, but even more than that, I don't want to ghost Dillon and Varsha. I should go find them and tell them I'm heading out. But then I might run into Lincoln. I sit for a long time, putting it off until my toes are numb from the cold, and I have to admit I can't stay out here forever. Of course Dillon and Varsha haven't responded to any of my texts. I just have to hope I can avoid Lincoln.

Back inside, I stand up against the wall where it's dark, trying to spot Dillon and Varsha. They're nowhere to be seen, so I text them yet again in the group chat. Still no response. So unwillingly, I'll have to start walking around looking for them.

As I search for them, I notice a few people laughing and pointing at me. I look down, thinking maybe I have something on my shirt or pants, but there's nothing there. I remind myself they're probably not whispering and laughing about me, and I do my best to shake it off and keep looking for Dillon and Varsha.

But I keep feeling like people *are* whispering and laughing at me. Sergio snickers with his friends, and then I see Travis, who chortles at me from across the ballroom.

Enzi saunters over. "Hey, hey, Leo. My friends and I did a little digging. It turns out you don't have a mansion. That shack on Halloween *was* your house. Yikes, man." He bursts into laughter, and his friends cluster behind him, smirking.

"You're such a poseur," Sergio says, and his friend Zubin roars with laughter in agreement. He drains his punch cup and throws it onto the closest table.

"I . . . I . . ." I'm not quite sure what to say.

Enzi is terrible. So is Sergio.

Terrible Humans. All of them.

Dillon was right. I should have trusted him.

"Oh. And we heard about your scrapbook," Travis says. His friends burst into laughter, drumming their fists on the table.

The ballroom tilts. Suddenly, all I can hear is the blood pounding in my ears. "Scrapbook?" I whisper.

They're grinning at me like a pack of hyenas.

Travis reaches out and grabs my shoulder. "Look out, ghost boy! You look like you're going to faint."

I wrench my arm away. "What do you mean, *scrapbook?*" I say, trying to keep my voice from shaking. I look from face to face, the sinking feeling pulling me under.

"Yeah, loser!" Enzi says. "Your *scrapbook?* We saw the photos."

Wait. What photos?

"I thought you were a try-hard, but this is *beyond*. You're even creepier than we thought." Sergio turns his phone toward me, and there's a photo of one of my scrapbook pages.

Travis holds up his own phone, showing yet a different scrapbook page. "Luckily, my man Lincoln came through with some receipts."

My world is over.

I turn and power walk away, holding back tears. Forget about Dillon and Varsha. Forget about telling them I'm leaving. I can't be here a second longer. As I push my way through the doors and into the night air, one thought keeps crashing into me over and over again.

I hate Lincoln Chan.

I find myself in my car in the senior lot. Did Lincoln really take secret photos of my scrapbook? When did he do that? I suddenly remember the moment I found him in my bedroom before the semiformal. He's had the photos this whole time? I'm too sick to my stomach to even put the car in drive. I just stare at the dashboard, eyes swimming with tears.

Varsha called it too. And Dillon . . .

I messed up. Everything's crashing down around me all at once, and I only have me to blame. Count me among the Terrible Humans. I've become a monster.

Maybe my problem *is* me. Maybe it's been me all along.

I need to make things right.

Dillon knocks on the window, making me jump, and I unlock the door for him to climb inside.

"How did you know I was out here?"

"Saw you run across the parking lot," he says. "You okay?"

"I've been better. Since I last saw you thirty minutes ago, I broke up with my first real boyfriend, had him betray me, and I have to drop out of school and never show my face again."

Dillon blinks. "Wow. You broke up with Lincoln? And wait, *what* else? Remind me never to leave you alone at a school dance again."

I sniffle. "He texted photos of my scrapbook to literally everyone."

Dillon winces. "Oh."

We sit together in silence for a few moments.

I can tell he's struggling to find something comforting to say but, honestly, having him here is comforting me more than he realizes.

"What a jerk," he finally says. "If it's any consolation, I

think you made the right call."

"Thanks. Me too." I blow my nose on my shirt cuff. "I honestly just thought he liked me. Was it all a scam?"

"I'm sure it wasn't a scam."

"Not to mention that now everyone thinks I'm a creep—"

"Does it matter what they think?" Dillon says softly. "*You* know you're not a creep. *I* know you're not a creep."

I smile. "Thank you." I'm suddenly reminded of what Dillon admitted to me. I can see it perfectly in this moment. He cares about me as more than just a friend. It's sweet, somehow. But it's also too much for me to deal with in this moment.

"Lincoln's changed. He isn't the person I knew four years ago. I mean, neither am I. But I haven't turned into a jerk."

"I mean, you've kind of been a little bit of a jerk," Dillon points out.

I grimace, embarrassed.

"But not anymore," he adds. "I mean, you learned a lot this year."

"Not enough." I sigh. "I've been thinking about what you told me, and I just want to say thank you for being honest with me. It means a lot."

His face lights up.

"But I need to spend some time getting back to myself."

Dillon looks confused but nods. "I understand."

"Of course you understand. Because you're the best."

He reaches over and squeezes my hand.

Not like a boyfriend. Like a best friend.

IN MY SCRAPBOOK, I TURN TO LINCOLN'S SECTION AND TAPE in the words THE END. Then I close the chapter on Lincoln Chan, this time for good.

I open a brand-new, hot-pink scrapbook titled BEST FRIENDS and tape in the photo of Dillon, Varsha, and me from semiformal. It's the first page of doing the scrapbook thing right. Celebrating the people in my life who make me feel truly happy and loved. I stick in the torn-out pages from my "Best Friends" section of my old scrapbook too.

Then I pull out a clean sheet of paper and start on a new checklist. There's work to be done. Dillon is right—I do wear my heart on my sleeve, and it *is* a superpower. But I need to protect it. It has to be made whole again, and only I can do that. Maybe one day, when it is, I'll be able to give it to the right person. Someone who won't break it.

And through it all, I'll be okay. Complete, just as I am.

MAKE THINGS RIGHT CHECKLIST

1. WORK ON SELF-LOVE

2. APOLOGIZE TO JUDY

3. CHERISH FAMILY TIME

4. BE A BETTER FRIEND

5. DILLON?

"JUDY, PLEASE HEAR ME OUT." I'M STANDING IN THE KITCHEN
doorway at Ye Olde Tea House while Judy is in the middle
of piping vanilla buttercream onto a heart-shaped strawberry
cake. A painful reminder that another lonely Valentine's Day is
just around the corner.

She blinks. "Yes? I'm all ears."

I hold out the heart-shaped teapot that I'd shattered. I used
what I'd learned watching Dillon rebuild his DNA sculpture
to glue it all back together again. I'm not a ceramics expert or
anything—but perhaps she could still display it with pride.

It's not the only thing Dillon relayed that's been on my mind.

The past two weeks, I've been mulling it all over. I need
more time before I figure out what to tell Dillon about how I
feel for him.

I set the teapot down on the counter. "I know I let you down when you needed me, and I'm sorry. I was hoping that you'd consider taking me back on. I'm trying to save for college." Then I pull out the stack of menus from my bag. "And I made new menus to replace the old ones that I spilled tea on so many times."

She takes the teapot and inspects it, then looks at the menus: at the doilies and construction paper scrapbooked to the pages beneath the lamination. "Thank you. These are gorgeous."

"Thanks. I'm glad you like them."

"Leo, you have an eye for design. You should always let your uniqueness shine bright. Like my tea sets." She signals around at the lavish teapots and colorful cups, then traces the cracks in the fixed teapot. "It's what makes life beautiful."

I nod. "Even if you don't take me back, I wanted you to know that I loved working here. And I'm mad for messing that up. I don't only need the money—I need this place. But even if you don't take me back, please keep the menus."

Her expression softens, and she looks at the mended teapot again. "Okay."

"Okay? I can have my job back?" Tears prick at my eyes.

"Yes. Because," she continues, "I haven't been able to fill the position. It's only out of necessity that I'm saying yes, and please remember that."

I choke up. "Thank you so much!"

"No, thank you. I'm starting to think Vincent might need more help than I expected."

At that, Vincent saunters in from the bathroom. "Leo! Thank

god you're here! Why is jam so hard to scrub off a plate? And why does doing the dishes make my skin so dry and wrinkly?" He shudders. "Oh. Hi, Judy. Didn't see you there."

She flashes me one little smile before gesturing to the sink of dishes. "Take over, Leo. You're the only one who does it properly."

Make things right with Judy?

Check.

Before I put on the dishwashing gloves, I grab a broken cookie from the scrap pile and pop it in my mouth. Just as delicious as I remembered. "I have something for you in the trunk of my car," I tell Vincent. "All the clothes you lent me. Thank you for your help."

"So, no more dressing fashionable?"

"I'm going in a new direction," I say, then I start scrubbing the first cake pan.

He studies my hair. "Okay, but we should still do something about touching up those roots."

I smile. "I've decided I'm going to let it grow out." I watch Vincent blink at me in disgust.

But doing me despite what others may think? It feels so good.

Spending my Valentine's Day alone eating chocolates in bed? Doesn't feel so good.

Sure, it's not how I expected it to go, but I'm taking the day in hand to give myself some much-needed self-care.

Earlier at school, students came in to World History to pass out candy-grams. I felt sick to my stomach, so I decided to cut school the rest of the day. I spent the afternoon meandering my way home, and when I got here, I cleaned out the garage while *Hello, Dolly!* (The New Broadway Cast Recording Starring Bette Midler) played on my phone.

I texted Dillon and Varsha with some Valentine's Day GIFs.

Then I made all the returns at the mall and dropped off Lincoln's lavender bomber jacket. (I left it with his mom. Thankfully, he wasn't home.) Next, I came home to take a bath, light a candle, and use a nourishing, brightening face mask.

I suppose my Lonely Hearts Day isn't as blue as I'd feared. It can't be worse than Mom's day—she's back in court over the settlement stuff. Dad still doesn't want to pay child support, *pendente lite*, or college tuitions, but she's fighting back tooth and claw for my future and Silvio's too.

And then there's Lincoln. A part of me is sad, wishing we were back together, and that I could text him. Then there's another part of me that's angry. Lincoln never really liked me. He just liked the *idea* of me.

And I just liked the idea of him.

Then there's *another* part of me that's at peace we're apart.

I know Dillon would tell me to work through the feels, to take time for myself and refrain from reaching out to Lincoln.

And I know Gran would say when one door closes, another door opens.

All my life, I've been trying to find true love and have always gotten shot down. It always hurts.

But I'm going to keep an open heart and be my authentic self—and treasure the value in myself.

And in falling in love with myself, I'll open the door for others to see, love, and accept me exactly as I am.

Take Dillon, for example. He sees me for me. He always has. He doesn't check all the boxes, but . . . I've realized . . .

Wow.

I love him.

And I've always loved him.

He's someone who I can be myself with, whether we're taking turns biting into an Impossible Whopper from Burger King while singing along to Whitney Houston's "Impossible" between bites, or trying to figure out the best way to split an ice cream sandwich (do not attempt cutting down the middle with a knife when the ice cream gets too soft!), or sharing our deepest secrets. Being around him is easy and warm, and the fact that I know he likes the real me . . . it unlocks a part of me that lets me view him as more than just a friend. I'm realizing I must have always been attracted to him, but I must have turned it off, like a switch, to keep him in the Friendship Bucket.

My phone buzzes.

"Hey," Silvio says when I pick up.

"Hi." I start to tell him everything that's gone down in the past year—including the Boyfriend Material Checklist.

"Dude, you're going on and on. I'm at the hospital right now, so I can't really be on for too long."

"*What?* You *are*? Why?"

"Golf ball hit me on the head, but I'm fine."

"Why didn't you tell me?"

"Dude, that's not why I'm calling. I wanted to tell you Dad

proposed to Margot, and she said yes."

I feel ill. "What?!"

"Yep. Just wanted to let you know. Doctor's here. Gotta go, man."

"Okay. Thanks for letting me know. And I'm glad the golf ball didn't injure you worse."

"Yep. Bye."

I burrow under my covers, groaning. Miss Tiramisu looks up at me. "Happy Valentine's Day," I mutter to her. "At least I've got you to keep me company, Mushy Squishy."

She starts purring.

It feels like I've lost everyone, including myself.

But I'm working to get myself back. I'm done being judged on appearance. I'm done being somebody else—*especially* when it doesn't work.

I'm not Old Leo anymore. And I'm not New Leo, either.

I'm just Leo.

It's a start.

I snuggle up with the googly-eyed dog plushie that Dillon got me for Christmas—he was right, it is the perfect gift. Next up on my Make Things Right Checklist: confess my love to Dillon.

Dillon. Someone who actually deserves me.

And a piece of my big old heart. But just a piece, which is plenty.

I need the rest for me.

THE REST OF FEBRUARY PASSES, FOLLOWED BY THE HIGH
school musical and St. Patrick's Day.

Come the last Friday in March, I'm seated in the audience
of the theater, watching Dillon singing in his Spring District
Choral Concert.

He doesn't know I'm here, but I wouldn't miss it.

When Dillon breaks off into his various solos, he nails every
note. Each one is clear and pure and true.

After the show, I approach him with a bouquet of lilacs—his
absolute favorite.

"You were amazing."

He looks surprised to see me. "Thanks. I thought you said
weren't coming."

I shrug, smiling. "I think I've had enough time to myself."

I notice there are other people waiting to talk to him. Dillon practically has a fan club. As he should. So I give a little wave goodbye. "Great job again. You were incredible up there." I hand him a card.

He glances up at me. "What's this?"

"Just a little something. Open it later. Anyway, are you free tomorrow?" I ask.

He nods. "Yeah. Why?"

"Good. Let's hang out tomorrow. I have something in mind."

He smiles. "I'd like that."

"Me too. I'll text you."

And then I walk off, feeling better—and more myself—than I have in a very long time.

"Where are you taking me?" Dillon asks as the train jostles along the next day.

I thought I'd surprise him with a trip to the MoMA to see the traveling exhibit featuring his favorite artist, Graffix.

"Nowhere," I say with a smug smile.

Before long, we pop out of the subway into warm, balmy air, and Dillon follows me to the museum. His eyes spot the enormous banners advertising Graffix's latest exhibit.

He spins to me. "No *way*! How did you get tickets?"

"This lottery website thing," I say. "Don't worry about it."

"But didn't tickets sell out the first day when it opened weeks ago?" he asks.

"Yeah. I made sure to buy our tickets then."

Dillon looks astonished. "And you've been holding on to them this whole time?"

"It was either this or taking you to this cool robotics lab they have set up at Princeton. I couldn't figure out how to get tickets to that, though. Seemed like a students-only thing." I lead him up the steps and into the museum.

We check out blown-glass sculptures of butterflies and canvases mottled with paint. Dillon ogles every piece of art, and I'm getting a kick out of watching him get lost in them, reading the little plaques and sharing various tidbits.

As the sun starts to set, we've finally made our way to every art piece and file out of the museum.

Dillon turns to me on the steps. "That was incredible."

"It was pretty cool, huh?"

"I like how bold his choices are," Dillon says. "I wish *I* could be that bold."

"What about trusting the process?" I tease.

"Well, as much as I didn't like the idea of you making that boyfriend checklist—"

"You didn't?! I hadn't the slightest!"

"—I've learned from you that sometimes you need to jump in feet first to make things happen." He regards me for a long enough amount of time that I'm starting to feel awkward, like he's waiting for me to say something.

"What is it?"

He looks at the museum, then back at me. "That was just really nice of you."

"I'm glad my gift was appreciated, and you don't think I'm some creep!"

"Anyone who thinks you're a creep should be thrown in jail. And I appreciated the handwritten card you wrote. It was very thoughtful." He takes a step closer toward me, resting a hand on my shoulder. "Leo . . . I think—"

Just then, my phone blares to life, and I go to answer it. "Sorry. It's Varsha!"

Her face fills the screen. "Guess who just got accepted into Princeton?!"

Dillon and I scream at the same time, smiling from ear to ear.

"Congrats! I am *so* happy for you! We need to celebrate!" I shout. I turn the phone so she can see Dillon cheering for her.

"Yay! Okay, I have to go. Half my family's calling to congratulate me," Varsha says. "More soon." She hangs up, and then it's just Dillon and me again. We exchange a little smile.

"Sorry. You were saying?" I prompt him.

"I was saying, I think—"

"Wait," I interrupt. "Sorry. One more thing to say. I know I messed up and got way too self-absorbed and over-involved in that whole boyfriend checklist thing." I gesture down at my pastel garb. "I'm feeling back to myself again, in case you haven't noticed."

"I noticed," Dillon says with a gentle smile.

"You were right," I tell him. "I think that all my ex-crushes wanted different things in a person, and I only want to be with someone who wants to be with me the way I want to be with them. And I don't want to have to change myself for anyone else."

"Yes! That's what I've been saying! Finally!"

This time, Dillon's the one who wraps me in a hug. No. Not a hug. An *embrace*. He stands back. "Come with me. It's *my* turn to take *you* somewhere."

We walk a few blocks until we end up at an entrance to Central Park.

"Central Park?" I ask.

"I know you're always talking about how romantic it is."

"It's only the location from one of my all-time favorite romantic comedies, *When Harry Met Sally*," I say.

"That's why I took you here." Dillon leads me to a wrought-iron bench, and we sit side by side in the coming twilight as people walk by. "Okay. So, you know how I'm always telling you to trust the process? Well . . . I've seen you force the process, and I'm trying to be bold like you . . . if it means scoring the love of *my* life." He takes a big exhale. "Will you be my boyfriend?"

I study him. The way his smile kind of trembles, and his eyes search mine for an answer.

"Are you asking me out?" I tease.

"Yes." Dillon bites his lip. "Or not. If you don't want. You were perfect just the way you were," Dillon tells me. "The way you *are*. Before the checklist." He smiles at me, and I feel . . . peace. Like everything is right in the world.

Is *this* what love feels like?

What I say next comes out easily.

"I love you." I begin to tear up. His eyes start to well up too, and we're holding each other, half sobbing, half laughing. And we can't stop. We don't want to.

Next thing I know, we're embracing, then kissing.

It's different than kissing Lincoln, who was hot and heavy. Kissing Dillon is sweet, and we bump our heads and laugh. It's easy. And . . . fun. And effortless.

We stand. I pull him into an embrace and feel his heartbeat, stronger than ever, against mine.

This is starting to feel too real, too easy. Shouldn't love be hard? Painful, even? No careful months of plotting and planning?

"So . . . is that a yes?" Dillon asks.

I wrinkle my nose, nodding. "I'd love to go out with you."

His face lights up.

"But what about your rule—no dating before college?" I ask.

"I think romantic checklists are a thing of the past, don't you?"

"My heart," I coo, hand to my chest.

"That's right," he says. "Your big, beautiful heart. And mine too. I give it to you."

"And to what do I owe the honor?" I ask in a posh tone.

"You won my heart by being yourself."

"Well, isn't that nice of you."

"That's me. Nice." And it's true. He's a Nice Guy. Always has been.

And I realize that's exactly what I've always wanted in a boyfriend: the Nice Guy.

Because the Nice Guy is Dillon.

EPILOGUE

BEFORE I KNOW IT, IT'S ALREADY TIME FOR GRADUATION.
The ceremony has a fiery energy as everyone grins in cap and gown on the sunny lawn of Tatlock Field on a perfect June day.

We toss our hats in the hot, humid air and cheer. I've decided that I took a little bit of each checklist item and made it my own, integrating it into my very being. Self-care, for example, really is important. But I've also discarded the parts that didn't serve me, which is why I'm beaming a big old cheesy smile right now without a care in the world.

Dad shows up with Margot, unannounced once again, and I

feel sick at the sight of them, once again. Especially at the sight of the big rock on her finger. He's not the right dad in this equation, but I accept him for where he's at. Maybe this is the real him, and maybe his whole life has been a checklist up until now.

When Mom sees him, her smile doesn't waver. She's the strongest person I've ever met. And she's been sober for a few months now. I'm so proud of her. She's standing with Silvio. She claps and roars my name, and it brings tears to my eyes. I know the importance of accepting people where they're at. It doesn't mean I have to accept them into my life, though. Like Lincoln—he's not a bad guy. Even if he did block me again on everything, it's okay. He's just not the kind of guy for me.

After graduation, Dillon and Varsha and I pile into Mom's car, and she drives us down the shore, to a cozy cottage we rented in Point Pleasant. I hold Dillon's hand in the back seat, and Varsha keeps insisting that she's always known we've liked each other as more than friends (no she didn't). I've realized that it took being myself—and loving myself—to draw romance into my life. The right guy came along and saw me for me.

We spend the day in the sun and the sand, and at night, we start a giant bonfire on the beach, talking about plans for our summer birthdays.

I give Dillon a big hug. He was there with me every step of way . . .

. . . and helped me write my own First Great Love Story.

Dillon spends the night pointing out all the wonderful traits I had before even making that silly checklist.

Through Dillon, I've also learned the difference between

a mere crush and real love. I've figured out how to feel complete and trust in myself again. I realize I shouldn't stop being a loving, gift-giving, caring person, because that's who I *am*. It's all about finding the relationships with people who appreciate you for who you are.

As the evening stars twinkle overhead, I look at my friends sitting in their lawn chairs planted in the sand. The firelight flickers on their faces. There's just one thing left to do. I pull the scrapbook of crushes from my bag—the one with the infamous checklist. The one with the diamond rhinestones glinting with firelight on the cover.

I *am* a diamond in the rough. I know that now.

"Thank you for your service." I throw the scrapbook into the bonfire.

"To a new beginning!" my best friends cheer, with the biggest, most genuine smiles.

A DRIED, PRESSED FLOWER FROM THE BOUQUET DILLON GAVE me after the school play on top of a script page from *Twelfth Night*. A photo that Varsha took of Dillon and me after the school play, arms around each other's shoulders. Who knew in a few short months we'd be slow-dancing with our hands once again on each other's shoulders.

I glance at the two of us in one of the Thanksgiving photos that Mom took, remembering with embarrassment how I acted. Despite it, Dillon remained my friend, and look at where we are today.

I'm sitting at the desk in the living room of our cozy rental cottage down the shore, the remains of last night's bonfire on the beach outside the window. My new scrapbook is open in front of me, and all my supplies are in their box next to me ready to go. I look at all of the things laid out in front of me. All from moments of joy over the past year. I can't believe high school's already over.

The last few months flew by in a vibrant blur, full of so many happy memories that I've included in these pages. "Gran," I say out loud, "you'd be so proud of me. I turned out to be such a good scrapbooker." Speaking of which, there she is, the woman who started it all: a photo of Gran and me when I was five years old, and Gran in one of her vibrant sweaters with rows of necklaces. I painted a burst of bright watercolors around it.

I turn the page. There's Mom's recipe for Easter bread, with glitter confetti stickers around it that remind me of the sprinkles she puts on top of her vanilla glaze. Speaking of Mom, the divorce is finally official. Mom got everything, and I'm so happy for her. She deserves it. As for Dad, he's out of the picture, and that's A-okay with me.

Next to the Easter bread recipe, I've glued in my college acceptance letter. I can't believe I got into my top school. And Dillon's excited about Boston University. He'll only be a short metro ride away.

I admire how I've placed the program from the Academic Awards Assembly with Varsha's name circled in sparkly glitter pen. In a photo of the three of us, we're holding a sign Dillon painted that reads HAPPY LAST LAST DAY OF SCHOOL, and we're sticking our tongues out. Next to it is a ribbon stamped with my graduation year from the bouquet Mom gave me after the ceremony and a photo of Silvio standing shoulder to shoulder with me at graduation. In it, I'm beaming, and Silvio is giving his usual pained smile. We may not always get along, but we'll always be brothers.

I flip to a Miss Tiramisu layout, with fish-themed washi tape around all of the cutest photos of her. Truth be told, she deserves her own scrapbook, but this is a good start.

There's a photo of Judy laughing ruefully over a tray of broken, scrapped cookies. Someone's scraps are someone else's favorite snack.

I run my fingers over a photo of the cookie cake that Judy frosted for me that spells out the question: PROM? When I presented it to Dillon, he was over the moon, although he did joke he would dock points for no fried egg on top. Needless to say, Dillon was the best prom date ever. My gaze shifts to a photo of Dillon, Varsha, and me in matching mint-green suit jackets on the dance floor, busting our best dance moves. I can't help smiling at how happy Dillon looks in the photo. Being with him is easy and feels as cozy as cuddling up with hot chocolate on a chilly night. He's always been there for me, even when I haven't been the best of friends to him.

Under the photo, I've drawn a banner and scrawled the words: MY FIRST GREAT LOVE STORY. #DillLeo.

I turn to the next page and pause. This page is special. There's just one picture in the center. It's the same picture I used for my makeover checklist item. I had one copy of the photo left, and I pasted it here. But instead of putting a butterfly sticker over my face, I placed butterflies all around the picture and filled up the page. I've learned to love how I look.

Time to start a new page. I tape in a photo that Dillon and I took just yesterday. We're on the beach, having the time of our lives. As I carefully draw seashells around the edges with a gold jelly pen, I hear Dillon come in through the sliding-glass door from the porch.

"Are you scrapbooking? Can I see?"

"Of course."

He admires the page. "Nice seashell drawings. It looks great."

I look at him. "And you really don't think scrapbooking about all the tiny details of our relationship is creepy?"

He runs his fingers through my hair. "Of course not. It's cute."

I smile at him. "That's why you're the right one."

I close my scrapbook. Because as Gran used to say, when one scrapbook closes, another scrapbook opens.

Then I stand up and grab Dillon's hand. "Come on. Let's go enjoy the summer."

ACKNOWLEDGMENTS

A boundless thank-you to all those who poured so much love into this book:

To Brent Taylor, my brilliant agent and steadfast champion.

To Alexa Wejko, my genius editor, for bringing life to the beating heart of this novel.

To Megan Ilnitzki, my fantastic friend, for getting this book to the finish line with grace.

To the incredible team at HarperCollins: David DeWitt, Audrey Diestelkamp, Jenna Stempel-Lobell, Jenny Lu, Nicole Moulaison, Mimi Rankin, Patty Rosati, Heather Tamarkin, and Karina Williams.